Could I do it?

"So are you going to kill me or what?"

Twist smiled and held out both hands. "No gun."

I didn't buy that. "Then what? You kill me with your sharp wit?"

He laughed. The moment his chin lifted, my hand closed around the cold steel of Mom's favorite pistol. I rose to one knee and pointed the gun at Twist.

He didn't act nearly as startled as I'd hoped he would.

Oh. . . shit. Safety off.

Still no reaction.

His hands slowly moved away from his sides. All emotion left his face. He didn't mock me. There was no you-don't-have-the-balls-to-pull-the-trigger bullshit. He was smart enough to realize that antagonizing the guy with the gun pointed at your heart was dumb.

With a pistol in my shaking hands, there was only one question: was I the kind of guy who could pull the trigger and kill someone?

"Why didn't you just come after me?" I shouted, trying to work myself up. "Why everyone else?"

He smiled.

I had to pull the trigger.

I *had* to do it.

My finger wouldn't move.

This bastard needed to die. If I didn't kill him here and now, he'd find a way back and more people I cared about would die.

I gritted my teeth and willed my finger to twitch.

Do it.

Do it!

Also in the Tango Triptych:
Tango with a Twist
Stretches (Step 1.5)
No Tengo Tango

Coming soon from John Robert Mack:
Third Testament: The Book of John
Tales of Mystery and Woe: a comedy
A Consequence of Folly
Danny Decker and the Horribly Unlikely Adventure

WHISKEY TANGO FOXTROT

JOHN ROBERT MACK

Whiskey Tango Foxtrot
This book is an original publication of Zen Monster Press.
ISBN-13: 978-0692217962
Copyright© 2014 John Robert Mack.
Edited by Lauran Strait.
www.linkedin.com/in/lauranstrait

visit the author at
http://johnrobertmack.com/
http://www.dancemonkeyonline.com/
email: mailto:john@johnrobertmack.com
https://www.facebook.com/johnrobertmack

Contact the author for information regarding volume discounts for classes, studios and other organizations. Bring the author to your live event, in person or online.

This book is a work of fiction. Names, characters, places and incidents are products of the author's somewhat deranged imagination. Any resemblance to actual events, locales or persons, living or dead or otherwise is therefore purely coincidental.

Jacket design by John Robert Mack.
Cover model: Austin Tedder.
Back cover model: Chris Tijerina
Both photos by the author.

For Mom.

Part One

Dream a Little Dream of Me.

Chapter One

Twist traveled in the nightmare world. He'd learned how to stay conscious while asleep so he could direct his dreams. Or something.

The ride was incredible! In this one, he wore black rags and a straw hat like a scarecrow he'd seen at some old campground when he was still a deputy. God damn eerie, right? Eventually, he hoped to hijack Ethan Fox's nightmares so he could totally Freddy Krueger his ass.

He stood in a moonswept, grassy field. A wooden fence ran along one side. He called up an image of Fox's dad, eviscerated him and strapped him to the fence. He created Juicy, sliced her into ribbons and strapped her to the fence. K-pop, he emasculated and strapped to the fence. Corey, he completely disemboweled before strapping to the fence.

Christ, if only he could have so much fun in his waking life!

Ever since he'd hooked up with Mary, he'd learned so much freaking witchcraft. And had a lot of freaking sex. Sex with a powerful witch, with a *hot* powerful witch, was *amazing*.

Movement at the edge of the field caught his attention. Some blond guy crouched there. Ethan Fox? In his damn underwear, of course. What was he doing there? Twist hadn't wanted an image of *him* yet.

I raced through the woods in my Captain America boxer briefs. A full moon lit the path an eerie blue-white, and green-glowing eyes watched me through the bushes and from behind the trees as I streaked past. My breath puffed out behind me in drab clouds as I pushed my body to its limits, running and running, arms pumping, ignoring the slashes from the rocks and twigs that littered the path.

Was I running from or to? I didn't know, but my heart pounded so hard it hurt and panic filled my veins with fire.

A fallen tree! I leapt over it and landed in a crouch on the other side.

The path opened onto a silver field of gently swaying grass high as my waist. A tattered scarecrow standing in the center of the field raised his arms and cackled. He wore black threadbare clothes and a straw cowboy hat. One arm beckoned me.

"No one knows the death of your soul the way I do." It was one of the texts Twist had sent Tango. His voice cracked and slid like ice, the voice of a grackle. The birds swarmed out of the sky and landed on his shoulders, on the grass, on the fence behind.

He crooked a ragged finger at me and a hook sliced through the flesh of my chest, forcing me forward, drawing me to him. No blood flowed, no hook was visible, but I staggered forward, unable to resist the pain. The hook released me, and I dropped to my knees at his feet.

"Please, don't kill me."

He laughed a cruel, humorless laugh. "Why would I kill you when I can torment you instead?" His arms rose, drawing my attention to the fence beyond. Corpses hung lashed to it: Dad, K-pop, Boyfriend, Juicy spread-eagled and bloody, heads lolling in death. Other corpses hung with them, too bloody and disfigured to recognize.

"I've learned a few things since we last played together." He danced over to Juicy's corpse and lifted her head. "Hi there, douchebag." He raised the pitch of his voice and moved her head back and forth like a puppet. "Twist did me up the ass before slitting my throat."

He set one foot against the fence and yanked so hard her head popped off in a shower of blood. He tossed the gory thing at me, and I caught it reflexively.

Her eyes popped open. "I bet she gives good head!"

I cried out and dropped it.

Laughing, she hit the ground in slow motion and shattered like a rotten watermelon, soaking me in blood and brains. I stared up at Twist, unable to move. The bodies of everyone I held most dear hung there, ruined and rotting.

No. Not everyone.

Not Tango. At least Tango was safe.

"Who will be next, Fox?" The scarecrow cocked his head to one side. "You decide." He pulled me close, his putrid, rotting nose inches from mine. "You will be the one to decide who I fucking tear apart and desecrate!"

He licked my face.

"Fuck!" I jerked awake, twisted in my blanket and fighting like a demon to free myself, which pretty much landed me on my ass on the floor. Shit!

"Ethan?" Dad's silhouette hovered over me in a tattered bathrobe. "Bad dream?"

I scooted to sit up against the bed, waiting for my heart to slow down. "I'm fine." Wait a minute. "What the hell is a cruel, humorless laugh?"

Dad extended a hand. "One of *those* nightmares again?" He pulled me to my feet. "You need to talk to Dr. Mike?"

I blinked a few times without speaking, hoping my disdain was obvious, also hoping he'd let me redirect him.

"Still traumatized?"

I searched for clean clothes. "I walked in on the two of you in the shower."

"We weren't *doing* anything except washing."

I spun on him. "And I overheard *what* exactly?"

He sighed. "Me telling him I actually *do* like every song Barbara Streisand ever recorded."

I yanked on a t-shirt. "Yeah. You said that." Jeans came next. "I can never unhear it." Shoes. "And the fact that he admitted to owning every Judy Garland movie ever produced?" I shivered. "I thought we were beyond the stereotypes."

He hovered in the doorway uncertainly. "Well, we *are* gay, son."

I rushed up to him, my face an inch from his. "Are you, Dad? Are you... *really?*"

"What does that even mean?" He lost the grimace and broke into a smile, then grabbed me in a hug. "So you're going to keep pretending the nightmares are no big deal?"

"Yes."

"You realize the bizarre, cryptic misdirection will only work for so long." He kissed my forehead. "Sooner or later you'll have to deal with this."

I hugged him back. "One of the biggest reasons I think you're the best dad in the world is that you let me make my own mistakes."

He held me at arm's length. "However you want to play this, I get it." He gave me his I'm-really-sincere face. "But it's not going away on its own."

What *were* these dreams? They'd plagued me for two weeks. They weren't normal. I remembered more, saw more, hell, *smelled* more. Who the hell smelled stuff in his dreams? I never had... before two weeks ago. They weren't entirely... natural.

And Dad just stood there as if he'd wait all day for me to talk. Shit, he deserved better than a shallow blowing off.

"Do you know why I'm avoiding the whole thing?" I asked.

He squeezed my shoulders. "I really don't. That's the only reason I'm... a little worried."

Dad-speak for totally freaked out.

Deep breath. "Promise you won't commit me?"

"I will believe anything you tell me, son."

If I said it out loud, it meant *I* really believed it. Could I admit that? Even to myself.

His eyes reminded me who he was. He was my dad. He always, fucking *always*, had my back.

"I think Twist is sending these dreams into my head."

There I'd said it. Would he freak out?

Nothing in his face changed. He nodded. "Then Dr. Mike won't be much help." Wow. "Let me process that, okay? Then we'll start googling to find someone who *can* help."

"Just like that? I tell you the lame-ass junior cop who shot me three months ago has somehow become a low-grade *Supernatural* episode, and you act like I. . . I. . . you know what? I don't even have an analogy."

He smiled and hugged me. "You aren't prone to histrionics, unless it has to do with your hair. I know how. . . preoccupied you were when they found the witchcraft books and stuff in Twist's car." Dad-speak for utterly obsessed. "It's not a stretch."

Except, yeah, it was. The more logical conclusion was that my obsession had triggered a spate of ridonkulously intense dreams. But Dad didn't go there.

"So when we google," he asked, "beer or ice cream?"

Wow. Everyone on the planet should hate me because I have the best. dad. *ever.*

Twist sat up in the real world, breathing heavy.

"Oh, well, that was fun."

"You enjoyed the dream?" Mary asked, naked in his bed. Her long, blonde hair hung in waves past her shoulder. Her eyes glittered in the dim light.

Twist turned to her. "Not nearly as much as I'm going to enjoy you." He drew her close and rolled on top. "Please tell me you won't kill me if I fuck you right now."

"Oh, David, if I didn't want you inside me, you'd already be dead, you silly thing."

Sex with a powerful witch was in-de-scribable.

Chapter Two

"5-6-7-8!" I shouted at the top of my lungs. The lights flared white hot as I leapt into action, literally, from my perch on a five-foot scaffold in the gym at the Snowball dance. Ha. Why'd they call it a Snowball dance in Dumass, Texas? It was eighty degrees outside.

Drums split the air with a sick beat, but the screams of the audience completely drowned out the music for a few nervous seconds. I hit the floor and sprang into a forward roll, finding my feet in the exact center of the dance crew. *Please let them keep it together and count it out.*

As much as the crew had improved in the last three months, completely losing the music under the screams of an audience could still throw them off.

Deep breath.

K-pop, Juicy and I started the routine with some ticking and popping while the rest of the crew stalked the stage. Big smiles all around as we matched our rhythms. By the time everyone joined the choreo for the first chorus, the crowd had calmed down enough for me to hear the music, and we were still on beat. Yay!

We circled the stage, popping shapes and tripping complicated figures, perfectly in sync.

Well, pretty damn well in sync.

Well, heck, the crowd was off the chart, and we looked good.

Tango, Cosita and Juicy took center stage to strut their sexy stuff and the rest of us faded back and rearranged. The guys in the audience whistled and hooted, as usual. Our girls were freakin' hot, if I do say so myself. Especially Tango, not that I was playing favorites, except that I was. The fact that most of the audience knew Juicy and Cosita were an item added fuel to the fire. 'Cause guys are like that.

K-pop, Boyfriend and I ran across and dropped into a knee slide. Right in front of the girls, we jumped to our feet and grabbed partners for the second verse. Tango's smiles were all for the audience but there was something special for me as well. Between spins and whirls, she and I connected for brief moments of pure passion. There was nothing hotter than knowing that as much as she might shake her moneymaker for the audience, when it came down to it, I was the only one allowed to make change.

The second chorus highlighted Ephraim, Mono, Woody, Schilling and Retro, who broke out his mad old school shit. As always, the crowd screamed loud enough to rattle the gym rafters and actually chanted his name as Tango strode up and pulled him off to one side.

The entire team hit formation for the bridge in a stylin' hip hop sequence from Juicy. We broke into groups and slid into a waterfall, and that section *was* perfectly in sync. We'd run it a million times and nailed it butt-perfect.

Freeze!

. . .and *go!*

The dudes danced to one side of the stage, the girls to the other. Then we all turned and ran at top speed toward each other as the music screamed to a climax. The girls exploded from the floor and grabbed as much air as they could. . . which was a lot.

Massive screeching chord.

Lights out with the girls in mid-flight.

Let-me-catch-her-let-me-catch-her-let-me-catch-her!

Tango's weight hit my arms while I was completely blind.

Solid.

The crowd managed to make more noise.

The lights reignited and four guys held a girl.

Schilling held Ephraim. . . who was five-foot-five and thin. Schilling was a Russian exchange student, and, at the risk of stereotyping, she was built like it.

Sweet. That was the first time we'd managed the ending without someone getting dropped.

I carried Tango offstage, and, as soon as we were in the wings, our lips met in a mutual admiration society of tongues. I eased her to her feet, and she stayed pressed against me while our friends went crazy around us. She slid her mouth to my ear and whispered, "So is that from the kiss or the adrenaline?" She moved her hips against mine, as if I couldn't tell what she'd meant.

"Both?" The truth was always the best bet, but not always the safest.

She bit my ear and grabbed my ass. Bonus!

When we came up for air, I made sure I stayed glued to her side so my buddies would go for a fist bump instead of a manly hug. There were certain boundaries (and swords) I had no intention of ever crossing and certain information no one but my girlfriend needed to know.

But hells yeah, we did a lot of shouting and backslapping, and within a few minutes I unVelcroed myself so our adoring fans could tell me how great I was. After one last hand squeeze, Tango and I let the crowd separate us. Years of traveling around the world competing had taught me to be patient and gracious. That and a dad who whooped my ass if he ever caught me being rude to someone who wanted to congratulate me or tell me how darn cute I was.

Oh, and I don't mean he spanked me. Dad had never spanked me. He brought me into the ring and made me spar with him. You know, because spanking was bad.

K-pop's familiar arm dropped around my shoulders. "Dude, tell me you're not *actually* going home to study." He looked down at me from on high. I swear he grew taller every day. "Because that would be a tragedy." Our performance had closed the dance, but the crew was meeting up at the studio for an after-party.

I grabbed him back and bumped his shoulder with my forehead. "Dude, I am so freaking far behind in Texas History." My online school hadn't been Texas specific, so I'd kinda found ways around it. I had massive catching up to do. "Dad will pull me out of practice if I don't ace this test Monday."

"Lame." He palmed my face and pushed me away. "You want I should come over and help you study tomorrow?"

"Dude, that would rock."

"Sweet." Fist bump. Pull back and finger wiggle.

"Hi to Kiki," I called after him.

"Hai." He winked, kissed two fingers and held them up. It was his new thing. No idea where he got it.

Kiki was his girlfriend. Yeah, K-pop with a girlfriend. It was über sweet. She was the cute anime-loving girl he'd met at homecoming, the one I'd shoved him into and then told about his Naruto underwear. Yep. Three months and counting. And, no, she hadn't seen his Naruto underwear yet. First time dating for both of them.

To be honest, I kind of envied him. I mean, he was having all those great firsts: first time holding hands, first time kissing. Seriously, seventeen years old and never been kissed? All that had kinda happened at once for me when Monika'd mounted me in the middle of the night out of the blue.

"Bro!"

I braced for impact.

Boyfriend grabbed me from behind and lifted me completely off the ground. "That shit was off the ho-o-ok!" He shook me a couple of times to emphasize the extra Os.

Once I had my feet on good old terra firma, I turned to face the goofball with his main squeeze, Theresa Sanchez, who had my undying gratitude. Since Boyfriend had managed to hook up with the smartest girl in school (and they seemed to "hook up" almost every night) things between him and Tango weren't awkward at all, which was stellar. That way I got to keep my best friend and he got to be happy.

And Theresa kept him very happy.

Very, *very* happy.

Yeah, I probably heard more of those details than I needed because Boyfriend had no filter whatsoever. For the first time in my life

I was actually struggling to find enough time for all my friends. What an awesome problem to have.

I caught Tango's eye through the crowd. She smiled.

Wow.

Just wow.

"Who's the rock star talking to Tango?"

Record scratch.

While Boyfriend's words had been perfectly innocent, the subtle implication in his tone caught my attention.

The guy did look like a rock star: black hair all messy in that way you can tell takes an hour to perfect, expensively ripped jeans, motorcycle boots and jacket. Dark eyes. Pretty sure he wore guyliner. Most importantly, though, was the way he stood there with his hips forward and his shoulders back. Dancers notice shit like that.

I patted Boyfriend's shoulder. "I'm going to go find out."

"You meeting us at the studio?"

"History test, dude. Sorry."

He nodded knowingly and gave me a thumbs up. "I could come over tomorrow and help you study."

"Nah, I'm hooked up. I know you like to putter on Bessie Sundays."

He waved. "Let me know if you change your mind!"

"Will do." I glanced at Theresa to say goodbye, and her lips were pressed into a thin line for a moment before she recovered her smile. Huh.

"Don't keep him up too late, Theresa!" No matter how nice I was to her, she just didn't seem to like me and I could not figure out why.

She smiled, but it was a fake. "He has all those cows to milk in the morning."

See that? Was that comment offhand? Was she mocking Boyfriend? Was she mocking me? That girl intimidated me because she was twice as smart as any of us. I did not get her and Boyfriend together. Oh, and try as he might, Boyfriend hadn't found a nickname that stuck. She would always be Theresa.

I slipped in beside Tango and wrapped an arm around her waist. "Hey, sexy." I kissed the top of her head. "Who's your new friend?"

Okay, I put every effort imaginable into not sounding territorial. Did I pull it off?

"Hey, Caveman, this is Whiskey."

So then: no.

She wrapped an arm around me with a squeeze and a meaningful raise of an eyebrow before turning her attention back to the rock star. "Sorry, the caveman's actually called—"

"Foxtrot." His perfectly manicured hand extended toward me. "Ethan Fox, right? Nice to meet you. I'm Whiskey Mendoza." Black nail polish.

His grip was strong and oddly professional for someone who couldn't be more than a couple of years older than me.

He nodded at the stage behind us. "Your technique is frickin' clean. I'm impressed."

Well, flattery always scored points.

"Whiskey was just telling me about his band." Tango smiled at me in a way that said this was a professional conversation, and I better not screw it up because of my testosterone.

Professional mode it was. "Front man, right?"

He seemed a bit startled, but nodded.

"A front man is always on stage," I explained. "You do it well." I squeezed Tango. "Drummers are never on stage."

He laughed. It was sincere and honest. Okay, I could like that.

"You must know Darla," he said. "Always in her own world."

Nailed it. And chick drummer? Hot.

"They're about to sign a contract with Sony," Tango pointed out.

Sony? Holy shit. "Seriously? Congrats."

Whiskey held up his hands. "There's nothing in stone, yet. We're still waiting."

"What brings you out here?" I decided the small talk portion of the conversation must be over.

He waved at the stage. "I wanted to see y'all for myself." He made an approving face. "I'm impressed." He shoved the tips of his fingers into his pockets. "We were looking at dance teams around the state and saw some of your videos." Man, his jeans were tight. "We're putting together a few music videos as part of the whole package for Sony, and I'm hoping to talk y'all into performing in them."

Holy shit.

Tango squeezed me so hard she managed to tease out a twinge from my formerly bruised ribs.

"It's kind of a retro thing," Whiskey said. "And we're going out to this wicked abandoned Boy Scout camp to shoot for a few days."

"Boy Scout camp?" My skin shivered. Out in the woods?

He grinned. "Well, not literally, but that kind of thing. Lots of trees, abandoned cabins, an old boathouse, big grassy field for a bonfire. We're doing a send up of slasher flicks and ghost stories. Hitchcock, too. We're hoping to talk y'all into going out there with us to shoot material that we'd use for a few videos." He held out a card. "We have a crew lined up, with full make up and costumes. I really want to turn you all into bloody corpses."

Tango laughed.

I grabbed the card, still reclaiming my cool after finding out about the camp in the woods. The comment about bloody corpses hadn't helped.

Dance Monkey was the name of the band. Hadn't heard of them. Didn't mean much. Up-and-comers in Austin could easily have slid under my radar in the last nine months. Could be fun to shoot with them. "Interesting name."

He chuckled. "My last name, Mendoza? It's also a musical instrument called a monkey stick. I wanted to call the band Monkey Stick, but my nana slapped me when I made a crude joke about calling the first album *Spank It!*"

Ha. Damn it. I wanted to like this guy.

Tango still hadn't spoken. Oh yeah, shooting a video for a real band was a huge thing for her, I guess.

Okay, that sounded dismissive and douchey. Bear in mind, I'd performed in professional videos and been on the world stage. I mean, it was cool. Sony, right? Stellar, but I'd walked away from all that. . .

Fine. I'm an asshat and will stop trying to justify my condescending tone.

"So. . . abandoned Scout camp?" I said. "Y'all have a song called,

'Kill, kill, kill. Die, die, die'?" I gave the words a Jason sort of feel.

He laughed. "We don't, but I like that. It'd make a good chorus." He clapped me on the shoulder. "Check out the website. If you like the music, drop me a line."

"Absolutely." I could get over my male jealousy issues to like the guy. Even if he was sex on a monkey stick.

The final smile he gave Tango showed me he knew he'd made a huge impression on her. I didn't like that. Not at all.

He winked at me.

Okay, I took it all back; he was a douche.

When he was gone Tango sucked in a huge breath. "Holy shit, Foxtrot." She jumped me in a huge embrace, which was nice. But just as I was starting to really enjoy her enthusiasm, she pulled away and grabbed the card out of my hand.

"Ohmigod, ohmigod, ohmigod!" She stared at the card as if it were a holy relic. "Can you *believe* that guy?"

That enthusiasm I enjoyed rather less. But a week at an abandoned campground with her? Ample opportunities for making out. Maybe even "making out."

For the record, we hadn't done the deed, yet. Hadn't even been—quite—naked yet. We were somewhere between my two favorite couples. More on the reasons for that later because the coincidence of my nightmare on top of Whiskey's outdoorsy proposal with horror movie overtones gave me the willies, and Tango seemed to notice.

"What?" Her face told me she was upset. "You seem less than enthusiastic."

I shook off the spooks. "Sorry. I just. . ." Time to lie. "You know me. My idea of roughing it is a hotel without room service." So, no, she didn't know about the nightmares. Only Dad did. Why freak her out over something I didn't understand?

She rolled her eyes. "I think you can survive a couple of days for something like this." She gazed down at the card, beaming. "This could mean the start of something really, *really* big."

Which was exactly what I *didn't* want for my life, anymore. "We'll have to see what kind of music they play and start working on new material." Yay! Fake enthusiasm!

She reached up to kiss me. The fact that she didn't immediately see through my subterfuge proved her excitement. We kissed our goodbyes, and I drove home while she and the rest of the crew after-partied at the studio.

I loved my dad, but WTF? Why was I not celebrating with the crew?

What would everyone else think about the possible shoot?

Yeah. I'd hear the screams all the way to Auntie Mac's house.

I stumbled up the porch steps with three duffle bags working hard to trip me. The door opened abruptly by a storming Dr. Mike, who slammed it quite firmly and muttered a couple of choice obscenities before noticing me.

Holy shit! Dr. Mike was the calmest, most low-key guy I knew.

His face seemed to say: *crap, I don't need this, too.* I think he realized what his face had muttered, because it instantly relaxed. "Sorry, Ethan. It's always nice to see you."

"What'd he do this time?" I dropped the duffle bags to tell Dr. Mike I wasn't in a hurry.

He chuckled.

"Hey, I've had tons of arguments with him, and he's always wrong." I shrugged. "So what boneheaded thing did he do tonight?"

Dr. Mike took a deep breath. "I love that you asked, Ethan. I really do." He breathed again. "But I should let your dad field this one."

I shrugged. "Your call, but I'm available for Dad-bashing should the need arise."

He nodded as if it were a bow. "I'm sure I'll take you up on that one day."

"So it's not final or anything?" I stepped aside.

"No, no," he said quickly enough I knew it was true. Whew. "I just. . . I just need some time."

"I get it."

He started across the porch, and I picked up my bags, then set them back down. "Dr. Mike?"

He turned to me.

"What do you know about dreams?"

"Did Dad say anything to you?"

He led me to the wicker chairs. "He mentioned nightmares. They seemed normal after what you went through." He hesitated. "Then, today, he told me to forget about it, which, bless his heart, means something changed."

He was such a standup guy. Could I open up to him?

"Do you believe in the paranormal?"

He startled. "Ethan." A very long silence drew itself out. "I'm going to say 'yes.'"

I nodded. I wiped my hands over my face. "There's some weird shit happening, and I don't want to mess things up with you for Dad. He's dated before. This is different. With you, it's more real."

He almost grabbed my hand. "Ethan." He rubbed his palms together, then he did take my hand. "I love your dad." Wow. "I do. But if you think I can help you? That comes first. That's who I am. It's what I do."

Holy shit. "Okay, you just hit high score on Okay-to-date-my-dad." I squeezed his hand and released it. "Give me some time to think. Dad. . ." Dad what? "He wants you to be part of this. I know he does."

"Are you in a place to tell me what 'this' is?"

"Not right now. I need to talk to Dad some more first, but I don't want him to feel like he has to keep it from you."

He smiled. "So. . . you aren't against the idea that I might be around for a while?"

"You make him happy." I shrugged. "He says you could suck the chrome off a trailer hitch."

He laughed so hard he coughed.

"Yeah. He's *that* dad. You better get used to it." Speaking of which. . . "Oh! Don't ever send him selfies you think I shouldn't see. He *will* show them to me."

He laughed.

When I didn't, he sort of trailed off nervously.

Wait for it.

Wait for it.

"I will remember never to do that," he said quietly.

And with that awkward agreement never to speak of it again, I turned and made my way into the house. Yeah. It'd happened. Nothing gross, just embarrassing and cute. However, it was only a matter of time if I didn't set the boundary now.

Grabbing the open bottle of whiskey from the kitchen table, I made my way to the backyard. Dad glanced up as I approached the patio bar, and I could see he hadn't known who it would be. When he saw it was me, relief flooded his face, like he was so glad he was looking at me and not someone else. It was nice to see his face do that.

He held the glass for me to fill. "I heard Mike laugh," he said. "I thought he might be coming back in."

"Nope. He left. What'd he do this time?" See what I did there?

Dad rolled his eyes and took a sip. "He—" He stopped rather abruptly, and I saw him throwing it around in his head. "Okay, there's no way to say this that doesn't sound ridiculous."

I set the bottle down on the bar and waited.

He sipped again. "He's been looking at jobs in Austin."

That had my attention. Most of my friends wanted to get out of Dumass as soon as we graduated and nearly all of them were talking Austin.

"There's a couple of good possibilities." He sipped again. "Really *good* possibilities." His tone of voice meant big money possibilities. "He says he could sell his place here and get a house in Austin so I could move down there next fall, you know, a place he and I could live in while you go to school."

I gave a low whistle because I could see from the look on his face he already felt like an asshat. "That's pretty low," I mocked. "I see why you're pissed."

He gave me his annoyed face and took a slug of whiskey. "You don't understand, Ethan. It's more complicated than that. I can't just—"

"Let someone take care of you?"

"What? No. That's not it."

"Dad, you've taken care of *me* my whole life. You've always helped everyone around you." Since we were having one of those new man-to-man conversations, I thought I'd push my luck and picked up the whiskey bottle. "You are the poster child for overdeveloped sense of responsibility. Mike does this? You'll feel like you owe him. You let him put a roof over your head and food on your plate, how do you keep your independence?"

I started to take a drink, but Dad grabbed the bottle out of my hand. "What the hell do you think you're doing?" He poured into his own glass. . . which he handed back to me. "Don't drink out of the bottle like a frickin' redneck."

I sipped. And coughed.

He laughed.

I took another drink and let the fire trickle down my throat. I'd had the hard stuff before, but not so much.

"The thing is," I said at last. "We only moved here because we had no place else to go. You hate this town."

"You have friends, now."

"Almost all of whom are racing to Austin as soon as we graduate. With all your managing experience, I bet you could get something lined up before you even moved there."

He took the glass from me and drank. "Nothing close to what Mike'll be making." Funny that he was fine sharing the glass but didn't want me to drink from the bottle. Whatever.

"That's why you're pissed."

He set bottle and glass on the bar, pushing them pointedly away from me. "You think I should say, 'yes?'"

"First of all, I don't think you need to say, 'no.'" Since the bottle had been put away, I wandered closer to the pool as the warm fog drifted in. "I'd love to have you in Austin, Dad. You know that. And I can tell you miss it, in spite of everything that happened there." Okay, time to say something I'd been thinking for a while. "But if you're serious about staying away from boxing, you're starting over. You can't afford Austin on your own."

Hell, I wasn't sure how *I* was going to afford it. Hopefully, I'd get some coaching jobs. "With Mike you'd get to move back to Austin, and you'd get some time to decide what comes next. What you really *want* to do next. You've made me your number one priority for seventeen years, Dad. It's time you figured out what you want to be when you grow up."

Ah shit. His eyes went all misty and he grabbed me. "You will *always* be my number one priority, Ethan. No matter what I do in this lifetime, you will always be the best thing, the thing that makes me proudest."

"That's just the whiskey talking."

He kissed the top of my head and shoved me away. "So while we're being so grown up, you don't think even *talking* about moving to Austin with Mike is way too soon?"

I shrugged. "You said he could suck the chrome off a trailer hitch." Yeah, I was scarred for life by that one. It's one of those things that just can't be unheard.

He laughed.

I wandered over to the bar. "Since we're being all grown up. . ." I led with an eye pointedly on the bottle.

"Oh, I think we've had enough grown up for one night." He ruffled my hair. "I should call Mike."

"Nah. Let him stew a little. You don't want to seem easy."

He laughed.

I glanced up at the moon as if somehow that would let me know what time it was. "I told him about the nightmares."

"Oh?"

"Just that I'm having them." I watched the moonlight dance in the water. "I figure maybe we should see if he can help. In case I'm just crazy."

He sighed. "You want to hit Google?"

Ugh. Not right then. "I'd rather swim."

"What about all that history homework?"

"No way I can concentrate, anyway. K-pop's gonna help me study tomorrow."

I told him about the music video offer.

He whistled. "So. . . a camp out in the woods?"

I nodded.

"It's just a coincidence." He threw an arm around me and led me into the house. "Don't start reading symbolic significance into every little thing. You'll go crazy."

Chapter Three

Calliope music filled the air. Red, white and yellow lights flashed all around me on Ferris wheels, octopus rides and carnival games. Mobs of men, women and children rioted along the causeway, bumping me, pushing me, driving me toward the carnival barker who stood on a box waving a cane in one hand, shouting the night's attractions.

He was tall, that man, and muscular, with tattoos covering every inch of his bare torso. As I approached, buffeted by the crowds, I would have sworn that the images moved and shifted across his skin as if alive. I stopped only a few feet from him, mesmerized by the pictures of great, fat women, boys as hairy as hounds, and women with green scales for flesh. They crawled across his body, interlocking and desperate.

"You're staring at a man's bare chest, Fox," the barker shouted. "You might make me start to wonder."

"Twist?" My eyes darted up to meet his. They were black, empty holes. "Is that you?"

He spun and twirled his cane. "You like the new me?" So different than I remembered.

"How? It's only been a few months."

"For you, maybe." He planted the cane between his feet and popped his knees. *"I have a new friend who knows how to play with time. It's been over two years for me."*

"That doesn't even make sense."

He waggled his eyebrows. *"Nevertheless."*

He exuded confidence. That change was even harder to fathom. . . until it wasn't.

"Ha! You finally got laid, you pathetic shit."

His eyes blazed red and flames spouted around him. He drew the cane up and clutched it in two fists. *"Pathetic? Me? I've taken more than twenty women since you've seen me, planted half a dozen brats and defiled those women in ways you couldn't even imagine."*

I recoiled. *"Bragging about the fact you're a disgusting rapist just makes you all the more pathetic."*

He stepped forward.

"Just sayin'."

He gripped the cane across his hips and his grimace of rage transformed into a manic grin, his impossibly huge lips drew back, his teeth blackened and sharpened into points. *"Which sideshow d'you want to see, Fox? The Elastic Woman?"*

The cane shot out to one side, pointing at Juicy. She lay in a spotlight on a raised platform, made up like a porcelain doll, her naked body twisted into an impossible pretzel. Her eyes stared vacantly at the full moon. A single red tear of blood hung from the corner of one eye.

"Or. . ." The cane flashed to the other side. *"The Ape Man."*

Boyfriend stood on a second platform, but he was deformed, his entire body covered in thin, reedy hair, his arms long enough for his knuckles to drag the ground, his legs short and bowed, his face a Neanderthal parody of his real features. And he stood motionless, his eyes vacant, like a stuffed exhibit in a museum.

"Take your pick, Fox," Twist demanded. *"But if you don't choose soon, you'll lose. . . them. . . both."*

I threw the sheets to one side and pushed to my feet. Panting, I paced the room in the dark.

Wait. Darkness sucked. I flicked on the overhead light.

But I didn't want to wake up my dad, so I padded into the bathroom to close his door. I watched him a moment in the dim light. He was safe. All my friends were safe. I closed the door, turned on the bathroom light and chugged a glass of water.

The dreams felt so real. I'd smelled popcorn and the exhaust of diesel engines.

My whole body shivered.

Shower. I stripped off my shorts and threw them into my room.

Mmmmm. Warm water. Better.

When Twist's car had been searched, they'd found a bunch of voodoo witchcraft stuff. Spooky, right? Spell books and herbs. So when the dreams had started a couple of weeks ago, I'd started thinking, well, why not? I knew it sounded crazy, but those dreams. . . they were like nothing I'd ever experienced.

Something rattled nearby and my skin went cold.

"Dad?"

No response, and he always announced himself. My adventures with Twist, Warren and the entire starting lineup hadn't been so long ago.

Silence.

I must've been hearing—

A doorknob clicked. Shit. "Dad? That you?"

Still no response. No sound of water filling the toilet.

What the hell?

I reached for the curtain, but before my hand touched the plastic, it whipped open.

"Skreet! Skreet! Skreet!" just like the Psycho theme echoed against the tile and a tall guy stood there stabbing at me!

Holy shit!

I managed to pop him twice in the mouth before I slipped. I grabbed the shower curtain for support, and it slowed me down, but I slid to the tub floor, dragging the curtain with me. The plastic ripped free of the rings one by one by one. Pop. Pop. Pop.

I twisted as I fell to see who'd attacked me, but all that accomplished was rolling myself in the shower curtain.

Hands grabbed me.

I tried to fight back, but the damn curtain pinned my arms.

The sound effect changed: "Ba-dum. Ba-dum."

"Dad!"

"Foxtrot, dude," a familiar voice said with a chuckle. "Relax."

The curtain lifted, and I recognized my attacker. "K-pop?"

He stood over me, a towel in one hand and the plastic curtain in the other. He shook with laughter. "Dude, I am *so* sorry."

He so was *not* sorry. Dick.

"What the hell?" I shoved away the hand held in my direction and rose to my feet, pressed against the tile. My heart pounded so hard I swear I could see it beating through my rib cage.

"I heard we're spoofing old slasher movies, bro. Just getting in the spirit."

Dick.

"Ethan?" Dad stood in the doorway to his room in boxers and a wife-beater. From the way his face vacillated between a frown and a smile, I assumed he thought K-pop's prank was funny. Also a dick.

K-pop lost his smile when he saw Dad. "Mr. Fox, I am *so* sorry." He turned away from Dad.

"Oh sure, *that* apology you mean."

Apparently, seeing my dad in his boxers was embarrassing, but mocking me when I was bare-assed was just another day ending in Y.

I nabbed the towel and wrapped it around my waist, climbed out of the tub and pushed past K-pop into my room. "You owe us for a new shower curtain, douchebag."

"Dude, I'm sorry." He looked from me to my dad, obviously confused by my intense reaction. "I just. . ."

"Not your fault, K-pop." Dad stood in the doorway in his bathrobe.

"What? Seriously?"

"It's K-pop, Ethan. How often does he prank someone?" He held my shoulders in both hands and stared me down. "He doesn't know what's going on."

K-pop's face shifted into worry. "Something's going on?"

Dad raised an eyebrow. When I didn't speak, he shook me ever so gently.

"Okay, okay," I lifted my hands, and he released me. "I've been having these creepy nightmares about Twist."

K-pop sucked in a breath. "Oh, wow. I suck."

Yes, he did.

Dad raised an eyebrow.

"No. Dad's right." I crossed my arms. "You didn't know. Not your fault."

Dad leaned in the bathroom doorway. "And the face you made was pretty hysterical. I'm amazed you didn't piss yourself."

"Okay, that's not funny," I insisted.

Dad halfway smiled. "Yeah, it kinda is."

Seriously? "You have no problem with the fact that he broke into our house at Oh-my-God o'clock in the morning and Psychoed me?"

K-pop held up his keys. "You gave me a key."

Well, not so he could do shit like that.

The keys jingling near his ear drew my attention to the black eye darkening K-pop's face. Oh crap, that's right. I'd slugged him. Twice. Well, how was I supposed to know it was him?

Dad followed my gaze to K-pop's eye and whistled. "You're going to have quite a shiner." He moved to K-pop's side and turned his bruise into the light.

"Totally worth it." K-pop looked up at the ceiling while Dad made sure nothing was damaged for real. "To-ta-ly."

Okay, I'd almost started feeling sorry for him. Dick.

Dad released him and ruffled his hair.

K-pop turned his attention to me, and he lost the smile. "I really didn't expect to get you, bro. Seriously." He shrugged. "When you heard the door, I assumed the jig was up, hai?" He looked me up and down. "You didn't hurt anything, did you?"

Just my pride. "No." At least I knew I didn't have to ask if he'd videoed it. After Katy's drama with Twist, there was absolutely no way he'd do something that dumb.

"Tell me you didn't record me naked." You can never be too careful.

His hands rose up between us. "Dude, I would never."

"Okay, I know that." Deep breath.

"Dude, I'm sorry."

I managed a smile. "You are so not sorry."

He grinned. "I so am not."

His eye was going to be really bruised tomorrow. "Sorry I popped you."

He chuckled. "You so are not."

I just shook my head and smiled.

Dad chucked K-pop's shoulder. "Let me know if you ever want some lessons to block moves like that."

K-pop leaned away from Dad's soft blow. "Yeah? That'd be awesome."

I could tell he was being polite and had zero expectation that the lessons would ever happen. "You can work out with Boyfriend and me," I suggested. With all his dance background, he'd probably pick it up fast.

So there was this really awkward pause while K-pop stared at me with his big anime eyes. "Yeah. I mean. . . Dude, I have no money."

Oh shit. What was I thinking? "Neither do I, dude. We only take Boyfriend's money because he's loaded. This is just for fun. I mean, if you want to."

He glanced from me to Dad and back again. "Dude. Yeah. But is it fair to Boyfriend if we're both, you know, there and only he's paying?"

Okay, from the anxiety in his face, money wasn't the issue, but I was damned if I could figure out the real problem.

Apparently, Dad worked it out. "Wouldn't you rather learn tae kwon do or something, anyway? With the anime you watch and with all the dancing, wouldn't that be more up your alley?" He leaned against the closet. "Corey's too big for that, so we'd have to set something up without him."

What? Size didn't have anything to do with—oh! But why would K-pop not want to work out with Boyfriend? We all danced together almost every day.

"I can give you the basics," Dad explained. "Nothing to compete with, but I know enough for dance routines and some sparring with Ethan if you like."

K-pop's face lit up. "Really? I didn't know you did that stuff."

Dad held up a hand. "Just a bit. I was always more focused on boxing, really, and Ethan always points his toes and looks like a ballerina, so I haven't taught him very much." He winked at me to let me know he was trying to put K-pop at ease. All his years as a coach gave him experience in decoding a guy's hesitation.

The excitement in K-pop's face made it obvious he was interested, but something held him back.

"Come here," Dad said.

I moved away to let Dad work his magic.

He shifted K-pop to the middle of the room before he could think about it. He crouched down into a ready stance. "Lose the shoes." Don't forget Dad was wearing his ratty bathrobe because that makes the image tons funnier. "Like this."

K-pop copied Dad's stance pretty well.

"Hold that." Dad rose and adjusted K-pop's stance with a tug here and a push there. As always, he was very hands on. It made sense with K-pop, especially. He'd been pretty much adopted into our makeshift family, and it'd taken him a while to get used to Dad's touchy-feely side. The first time K-pop stayed over, Dad made him give him a hug goodnight. I was mortified, but K-pop didn't seem to mind, even if it was a bit weird for him. Apparently, there wasn't a lot of affection *a la casa* K-pop.

Dad had K-pop's right leg tucked up like a flamingo's. He helped him counterbalance while he extended his first kick. "Dancers," he teased when K-pop pointed his toe. "Like this." He grabbed K-pop's foot and bent it, holding it at the correct angle. "Sickle foot."

While they worked on the kick, I wondered why K-pop didn't want to work out with Boyfriend and how my dad had figured that out before I did. By the time K-pop had the kick, he was grinning.

"You game, dude?" I asked. "Just you and me? I can use the work on my tae kwon do. You can keep my toes from pointing and embarrassing my dad."

His enthusiasm made my night. "Yeah. That'd be great." He gave Dad a little bow. "Thanks, Mr. Fox. I'll practice."

Dad returned the bow. "Okay, but if I'm going to work with you, you need to be honest about why you want to learn. Is it just for dancing and playing ninja, to compete, or to hold your own against the assholes who bully you at school?"

What? Bullies?

K-pop turned beet red. "I. . ."

Dad patted his shoulders. "So a little bit of each?"

K-pop ducked his head and didn't meet my eyes. "Hai." He looked up quickly. "Except for the competing part. Will I have to, you know, fight other guys?"

"Never." Dad squeezed his shoulder. "You do exactly what you want to do. We can even stick with hitting a bag and pads, if you want." He crossed his arms. "Ethan doesn't even need to be there." By the way Dad was not looking at me, I could tell he'd realized I hadn't known about the bullying.

Why hadn't K-pop told me about that? He finally looked at me. "I don't mind Ethan being there." He smiled a little. "I mean, it'd be cool to work out with you." Which was nice to hear after realizing my dad seemed to know my friend better than I did.

"You staying over?" Dad ruffled K-pop's hair.

"What? No." He glanced at the clock by my bed. "Holy crap. I didn't realize—" He turned to me. "I need to show Foxtrot something."

"At two in the morning?" Dad asked.

"I promise to help him ace the test on Monday." It was almost a question, and his face scrunched up as if he were afraid he'd pushed his adoption status too far.

Dad chuckled. "Well, in that case." He hugged me and passed into his room, closing the door behind.

K-pop and I stared at each other.

If I hadn't known about the bullying, what else didn't I know? "Dude—"

As if reading my mind, he held up a hand. "We don't have time to talk about it." He brought his phone out and dragged me over to sit on the bed beside him. "Your phone's off, bro, and I bet you have a thousand texts."

"What?"

He messed with the phone. "The crew is at the studio freaking out."

I grabbed his arm. "What the fuck happened?" My heart raced.

Surprise covered his face. "Whoa, bro. Nothing like that."

"Like that" meant things like assault, kidnapping and stalkers. You know, the usual in this town.

"Now I feel like a drama queen," he said. "Wait, you said nightmares?"

"Not right now."

He watched my eyes a second, then nodded. "Okay, so, everyone's fine, but—" Tap, tap, tap on the cell. "We watched Dance Monkey's YouTube channel." He held the phone between us.

I winced. "Uh-oh. They suck?"

"No, they're actually pretty freakin' sick."

"Then what's—"

The video played.

Oh.

Oh wow, that was too funny.

Ha!

They were a swing band. Old-fashioned 1940s-style swing band.

And they *were* pretty freakin' good.

I took the cell and tapped the next video.

And the next.

Yep. All swing, all the time.

I laughed. "Dude, that is so hysterical. Why the heck does a swing band want anything to do with us?"

K-pop's face told me his world had ended.

I shrugged. "Dude, either they like what we do or they don't. Nothing we can do about it."

He closed his eyes and took a deep breath.

What? It might've been fun, but what was the big deal?

K-pop nodded and opened his eyes as if making a major decision. He rose up beside me, turned to me and took my face in his hands. He towered over me and even hoisted one foot up onto my bed so he could practically bend me over backward as he brought our foreheads together. If I hadn't immediately realized he was channeling Vash the Stampede, I'd have been a bit creeped out.

"I'm being a freak," he said very quietly, "so you know how much

I mean it when I say you are the very best friend I have ever had in my life, and I love you more than my brother, no lie, but is there any chance that for five fucking minutes you could actually try to think this through from a perspective other than your own?" He released me and put some space between us. "Seriously."

I would've been pissed off, but I'd just that night learned he needed martial arts to stop bullies from pounding on him, and I'd somehow missed that completely.

"Okay, that's fair. But I need to wiz." And yes, I needed to wiz, but I also needed a minute to think.

K-pop had the decorum to pretend to look out the window so I wouldn't feel rude closing the bathroom door. See, I always called Boyfriend my best friend, but in so many ways, K-pop got me better. Boyfriend would have kept talking the whole time.

I did my business and rewrapped the towel, then stared at myself in the mirror.

Okay. K-pop's point of view. He wanted to get the fuck out of Dumass and he wanted a life filled with dance and animation. This video shoot might give him an opportunity to show off his mad video skills, too. I'd had a life in the spotlight and had given it all up for my friends, my dad and my new life here. He'd never had his shot.

And if we didn't find a way to impress a swing band, he might never get a shot like that again. How many people found a second chance? How many had a first?

Deep breath.

My hair was a freaking mess. I needed a baseball cap.

No. Not a baseball cap.

I watched a smile play at the corner of my lips in the mirror. Huh. Was it kind of weird and vain to stand there staring at myself?

Back in my room, K-pop sat in the comfy chair, his ankles crossed in front of him.

So. If I was going to play this game, I wasn't playing half-way. I opened the closet. My forties-style flat cap hung from the door. I put it on first. The mirror on the door showed me K-pop's bemused smile as he steepled his fingers and raised an eyebrow.

I threw the towel in a corner and assembled my costume: dance dress slacks, white t-shirt and dress shirt, suspenders and tie, black and white swing shoes.

I stood a few feet from K-pop and hooked my thumbs in my suspenders.

He rose and smiled down at me.

"Okay," I said, "one free punch. Shoulder."

He grinned and tapped me.

I gave him a what-the-hell face. "No, really, punch me."

He laughed. "So what do you think we should do?"

"How far'd you get with Kiki?"

I swear he did a complete double take at my non sequitur.

Score. "Dude." I hooked an arm through his and led him out of the room. "That joke with Psycho? And your Vash the Stampede impersonation."

He stopped on the stairs. "You got that?"

I urged him to keep moving. "If I hadn't sussed it, it would've been wa-ay creepy." We made our way out to his car. "Total man-who-just-explored-a-new-frontier excitement. So how far you get?"

He didn't use a baseball analogy because neither of us would have understood it, anyway. So it was both of them with shirts off. Kissing, touching and nibbling were had by all.

"I got to kiss boobage." He grinned at me over the roof of his car. "I know, I know, I'm a little kid."

"Dude, we already had that conversation." I adjusted my hat, because wearing a cap meant I had to mess with it as part of my gesturing. "Little kids get more action than you."

He rolled his eyes. "Okay, I deserve that for the Psycho joke." We climbed into the car. "And I promise to pixelize your junk in the YouTube video."

"You realize you still have one eye that isn't black? I can change that."

Chapter Four

The studio was strangely quiet, considering the cars of the usual suspects waited in the parking lot. As I reached for the door handle, K-pop grabbed my arm. "Something's wrong. It's too quiet. When I left there was shouting and all sorts of freaking out going on."

No music filtered through the door, but I easily spotted the crew in the middle of the floor. Katy was teaching a swing basic. Looked like Ephraim knew it already, but the other three guys were struggling, especially Boyfriend.

"East coast swing," I said. "From about ten years ago."

K-pop tsked. "Say that to Tango, and I will be forced to purchase flowers for your funeral."

No shit. My instinct was to run in and show them what they needed to do to make this situation work out. I'd been there before. But K-pop and I had made a few plans on the drive over. I was still rattled by the bully reveal, so I settled in to watch my friends for a minute.

K-pop practiced the kick from Dad.

You have to understand, back when I was a big deal, the ex and I regularly performed for floor shows at major competitions. Sometimes, the folks who ran the comp would want all the big shots to perform together for a finale, and we rarely had more than one afternoon practice before putting a routine on the floor in front of a thousand people.

What did that teach me? When you're in a hurry, forget the basics and throw them flash and trash, fancy shit that makes the average person ooh and aah even though it's surprisingly easy. As much as Tango was a better teacher than me, this particular situation landed me in my element.

Juicy snapped at Woody.

Schilling looked like she was about to throw Ephraim over her arm and spank him.

Although, he might actually like that. What did I know? He was one of four crew members I knew by name and nothing else. After three months. Shouldn't I have known them better by then?

"K-pop, buddy?"

"Mmhm?" His kick was already more controlled.

"I need a favor."

"Mmhm?" He had really good extension.

I threw an arm around his chest to stabilize him and helped him lean away from the kick. "When I'm throwing out suggestions, I need you to use your face to tell me if I'm being an insensitive dick." I held his calf and stretched the leg higher.

"Oh, I can already tell you that you will." His foot rose two feet higher than it had been. "Sweet!"

"Dick." I released him.

Wait a minute. Dad worked K-pop through his stress by getting him to move. Maybe the same idea would work here. 'Cause Tango seemed. . . more than a little stressed.

Okay, from her point of view: this was her best shot at the big time. This was just like her mom's thing with that tango review all those years ago, and, as much as I hated to think it of my girlfriend, she was terrified that her less than stellar dance crew might ruin her chance at stardom.

She had every reason to worry, too.

Sorry. Truth.

"Let's lead with your idea about the way they'll record it," I said, "and I'll jump in."

"Hai."

Deep breath.

I opened the door and followed K-pop inside. Tango was counting rather loudly and impatiently: "Tri-ple *step*, tri-ple *step*, rock *step*." Over and over.

Okay, play to her insecurity. "Thank God, you know east coast, Tango. My jive would be completely wrong."

The lesson broke down as everyone used our entrance as an excuse to escape from her clutches.

"What's jive?" Woody asked.

Juicy surprised me a bit by answering. "It's like what Tango's teaching us, but with a stick shoved so far up your ass you choke on it."

Ha ha. Yeah, go ahead and make fun of Ballroom Man. Thanks.

"I had this idea," K-pop threw out before anyone could give me further shit. "This is from the video nerd on the team, hai?"

Tango closed her mouth. I really wanted to go in for the big hello kiss, but when she was stressed like this, she stayed all business. "Go ahead."

"Okay, when they're shooting a video, it's five seconds here and five seconds there." When talking in his element, the normally shy K-pop could really take control. "We don't need a five minute routine. We need some kick ass tricks and a short sequence, like five moves."

We'd come up with this on the way over, but I'd asked him take it because it'd step on Tango's toes less coming from the tech guru.

"Each guy starts on a different move and rotates through so you can't tell it's choreo because we're always doing different moves. We change partners and costumes and suddenly five minutes seems like nothing."

See, Tango thought like a dance teacher. Which was awesome, but they always taught from the ground up. We just needed to learn choreography. Didn't matter if anyone could actually dance a basic afterward.

"You can teach the sequence," I suggested, "and I'll handle the tricks."

"Tricks are hard." That was Retro.

"We already know some," I said, grabbing Boyfriend's hand.

In case you were wondering, he'd kinda kept in the background since he was no longer the captain's boyfriend. I was just happy he'd stayed with the team. One day I'd need to ask him why.

"Roll me in to a death drop," I said.

Boyfriend nodded.

"Set up for a back tuck," I told K-pop, who nodded and took his place.

Boyfriend rolled me in. I stepped across and dropped back first to the floor, trusting that Boyfriend would stop me about an inch from a concussion. He yanked me up and sent me flying.

I landed, dropped into a forward roll, and when I popped up, I did a spinning kick at K-pop who grabbed my foot and tossed me into a back tuck, which I stuck perfectly, thank you very much.

"Catch me," I called to Boyfriend, before dropping backward toward him holding my body stiff as a board. He caught me, lowered me to the floor while I kicked as high as I could, then popped me to my feet. I didn't wait for applause. "Tango, Juicy, you both can pull a back tuck, right?"

The tense glance that passed between them reminded me that all had not healed in Estrogenia. Whatever. Keep them moving. "Juicy, you're with Boyfriend."

To be honest, Juicy should've been with me. Tango needed more help in the tuck, and Boyfriend was stronger than me, but, yeah, that would've been deadly to admit.

I took Tango's hand. "Opposite side from what I did with Boyfriend."

She nodded.

"Get ready to tuck Tango as soon as you send Juicy to me."

Boyfriend nodded.

"5-6-7-8," I called.

I rolled Tango. Boyfriend rolled Juicy. We ran the exact sequence I'd done with Boyfriend, but, with the two couples dancing in mirror image, it was utterly badass.

This time I allowed for the applause when the girls stuck their landings.

Woody stuffed his hands in his pockets. "Please tell me the rest of us aren't going to do some lame step-tap shit in the background while y'all make with the fancy tricks." He leaned against the bar. "Again."

Seriously? What kind of time did he think we had?

"I want to learn a back tuck," Mono said. Wow. That may have been the first time I'd heard her speak.

K-pop coughed, drawing my attention. One eyebrow was raised and his mouth smiled a non-smile.

Oh. That's right. Insensitive dick alert.

Woody's point of view. Okay. Did we really shove him and the others in the background all the time? Meh. Sorta. I guess.

Fine.

"If we're doing this for real and we're *all* going balls out, I need to think like a coach and stop worrying about feelings. Y'all can handle that?"

Everyone nodded a lot and looked around to see what everyone else was doing.

Tango gave me the floor.

"This is going to be harder than anything than you've ever done," I said, "and you will need to eat, breathe and bleed this material."

That got me nods and smiles. No one seemed afraid of hard work if the reward was a real music video.

"First two tricks." I paired everyone up. "Weakest links with strongest." The strong dancers could help the weak ones, and if the weak ones didn't like how obvious it was they were being helped? Well, too bad.

K-pop hit my side closer than a conjoined twin with his back to the others. "Don't make Ephraim follow the trick," he whispered. "Juicy can carry her own weight."

Oh. Well. Duh, I guess.

"You need to lead this one, Ephraim," I called out. "No way to know if Sony will let us play alternative gender games."

He saluted, literally, and his grin told me I'd said just the right thing.

I patted K-pop's shoulder.

So I taught the lean first, channeling Tango and my dad. She was still a better teacher than me, but I'd been paying attention for three months, and I was a quick study. Once I got them into the lean, I ran around shifting poses and putting bodies into the proper alignment.

"See the way Tango and Juicy hold their shoulders away from their partner?" I said to Schilling. "That makes them lighter."

I moved to Woody, whose hips where all out of whack. "Dude," I whispered, "you're more flexible than most guys. Keep a straight line from hips to shoulders." I grabbed his hips and moved them into place.

He smiled. "Thanks."

"More stable?" I asked Schilling.

"Da," she said.

"Why do we call you Schilling if you're from Russia?" I asked. Okay, the thing with K-pop had probably freaked me out more than necessary. Fine. Deal.

She and Woody exchanged a smile. "This one," she said, indicating Woody. "He didn't know I was from Russia. When he met me he said, 'Any king's schilling, eh lass?'"

Wow. I had no idea what any of those words meant.

Woody rose out of the lunge and set Schilling on her feet. "I freakin' love Elvis Costello, and he has this song called 'Any King's Schilling.'" He turned a little red. "I thought she was British, so she'd know who he was." Shrug. "I'm an idiot. What do I know about accents?"

"Elvis Costello?" I chucked his shoulder. "My dad's all-time favorite song is 'Veronica.'"

He did a double take. "Fuckin' A? That whole album is pure genius."

Wow. Would never have guessed the underwear model was a classic music fan. I mean, seriously, the dude could model for Boss. His abs made me jealous.

I held out a hand. Fist bump.

"How long are you here?" I asked Schilling.

"The school year."

That made sense. That's what 'exchange student' pretty much meant. Duh.

Ephraim handled the trick better than I'd expected. I think he saw my surprise. "Years of jui-jitsu," he said calmly.

"Really?"

"Of course not," he said equally deadpan. "Do I look like the kind of guy who'd want to roll around in my underwear with some dude's junk in my face?"

"Um, no?"

Juicy giggled.

"So it's because I'm Jewish, then."

Oh Christ. Now what'd I done?

"You think I can't be a fighter because I'm Jewish? Is that it?" His tone gave me no indication of whether he was serious or sending me up. "Ever hear of Krav Maga?"

"Well, of course—"

"Know where it comes from?"

"Yes—"

"Israel. It comes from Israel." There was absolutely no hint of bullshit in his voice. "My people invented Krav-fucking-Maga."

He glanced at Juicy, who was smirking.

"Am I holding the right position in the death drop?" he asked me.

"What? Yeah. Great." Actually, his hips were out of alignment, but I wanted to get the hell away.

"Seriously?" he adjusted his glasses and looked me up and down. "Even I can tell my hips aren't right." His disdain at my ability was obvious.

Deep breath. I had to get control. Somehow.

"Okay, no, your hips are pulled back." Before he could open his mouth, I moved Juicy to his side. "Let me see it so I can fix it."

When she hit her line parallel to the floor, I knew she could hold it as long as I needed so I moved closer to Ephraim and placed one hand at the base of his spine and the other just under his rib cage. "Give her your hips and keep your shoulders back or you'll—"

He lost balance and skipped forward a step to avoid dropping Juicy.

I shifted my hands to stabilize Juicy, just in case.

"That was my junk you just touched," he muttered.

"Er. Sorry. I was kinda hoping we could pretend that didn't happen."

He sighed. "Just like the Holocaust."

What. the. hell?

He shook his head. "Yeah, just pretend you've never even heard of it." He wandered off. "I have to wiz."

Juicy held it in about three seconds before busting a gut. "Oh my God, the look on your face."

"So that was a joke? Please tell me he was fucking with me."

"No shit, Schuester. You think you'd be on the team if he had the least suspicion you were anti-Semitic? It's just his way of saying hello." She glanced after him. "He gets a lot of shit in this town, so he likes to see how far he can push. Tells him if he needs to worry about you."

"I've been here three months. Why now?"

She made one of her many sounds of disbelief. "Have you so much as touched him before?"

"Of course." Wait. Had I? Maybe not. "What does that have to do with it?"

"It's what Woody said. They've been stuck in the background the whole time." She waved at the dancers around us. "I'm willing to bet you don't know anything about them beyond their names."

Okay, but I'd already figured that out.

"I was back there with them until the big reveal," she added.

Oh. Damn it. I was *not* a bad person. I *wasn't*.

She nudged me. "Looks like you're trying to change all that. It's cool. Just expect a few bumps along the way."

"What's his real name?"

"Ephraim Miller."

"Wait. He doesn't have a nickname?"

She chuckled. "Yeah. Even Katy was afraid to go there. Only Jewish kid in school and *that* sense of humor? He'd find a way to make *any* nickname anti-Semitic."

Aha. Challenge accepted.

"I can work with him," she offered, "if you want to check on the other folks."

Yeah. I needed to make a point of working with everyone. It was going to make practices harder, but my life was slowing down. Apart from a few bad dreams, life was good. I no longer had excuses.

Deep breath.

We had a lot of work ahead of us. And it *wouldn't* be fair to ask the "second string" to sit on the sidelines. This would be the perfect memory for Schilling to bring home to Russia and, as hot as Woody was, he just might be able to land some kind of modeling gig out of this if he had some face time in the video. Just because I no longer cared about fame, didn't mean my friends didn't deserve every shot at it.

Retro was the one to point out the obvious problem I hadn't even considered. "You realize my folks are not going to let me go out there for several days without some kind of adult chaperone."

"What? Seriously?" I regretted the words even before K-pop coughed into his hand.

"I'm fifteen."

"Sixteen here," Ephraim added, "and in the same boat. You know how Jewish mothers are."

"Who else is under eighteen?" I asked.

Pretty much everyone except Tango, Juicy and Boyfriend. I was still seventeen, but I'd been traveling on my own for years. Not so much the younger members of the dance team.

"All the guys in the band are at least twenty," Tango said, and her knowledge was more than a little upsetting to me. "*They* can be chaperones."

Cue a huge round of laughter.

"Don't worry, Mom," Mono said, brushing her long, blond hair over one shoulder. "We'll have a busload of college seniors in leather pants to protect our virtue."

More laughter.

"My dad'll do it," I offered. He wasn't working so much, anyway.

The third round of laughter was even louder than the others.

K-pop punched my shoulder. "Dude, all our parents know your dad'll be the one to buy us condoms and booze."

Well, he did have a point there. The day after I'd mentioned my second month anniversary with Tango a box of condoms had appeared on my bed. Yeah. He was a subtle one, my father.

"My mom would feel better having Conan the Dadbarian with us." Tango's voice was quiet, and her point was obvious. I moved closer and put an arm around her waist. If we were heading out into the middle of nowhere, safety was a concern. Like me, she still woke up from nightmares.

"My mom'll go," Boyfriend said. "She's the best shot in the county."

"And all our parents know her from church," Retro added. "She'll fly."

Murmurs of agreement settled it.

I leaned in close to Tango. "But you snuck past her into Boyfriend's room for six months."

She rolled her eyes. "Which is why the crew thinks she's the perfect choice."

Ah.

Twist and Mary sat together in bed, her straddling his lap, her hips moving slowly. Their bodies were joined, but they leaned back slightly, locking their arms in a circle, leaving enough room between his chest and her pert breasts for a glowing orb.

"So. . ." How exactly should he ask it?

"Our sex powers the orb," she said, saving him the trouble.

"Cool."

"Move with me," she commanded. "Close your eyes."

He obeyed. Even with his eyes closed, he could see the spell that hovered between them.

"Relax. Send everything you have into it."

He took a deep breath and focused on sending. . . Well, he still didn't understand exactly what it was he was doing, but if he just sort of thought "Go into the light, Carol Ann" it accomplished whatever she wanted. Sending his whatever-it-was that made magic.

"That's better," she whispered.

From his point of view, it was pretty fucking incredible.

"We need to practice this every day for a couple of hours," she told him.

"If we have to," he joked. Could they try different positions, though?

Twist took a break from the daily practice sessions and drove to a nearby farm. He needed to get online and see what was happening out in the world, but he couldn't get a signal on his tablet because of the time dilation thingamajig.

Mary said it was necessary to speed up his progress. Something about that guy that was after her, whatever, whatever, whatever.

An attractive redhead answered the door.

"I need to use your computer," Twist said, with a wave of one hand.

"Of course, it's right this way. Laptop okay?"

"It'll do."

While she made him lunch, he explored. He checked in on Katy more out of habit than anything. Her Facebook page was littered with photos of her and Fox. Hugging, kissing, touching.

Damn it! He thought he was over her. Well, maybe he was, but the thought that Fox had her still made his blood boil. It'd been two years, now. They had to be fucking. Knowing that big oaf had nailed her was bad enough, but just thinking about Fox touching her, her touching him. . .

Son of a bitch!

The damn redhead held a plate of sandwiches in his face.

"Fuck off!" He knocked it out of her hands. Twist turned to the computer screen, to a photo of Fox. "Now see what you made me do?!"

The redhead quietly bent down to clean the mess.

God, he just *hated* that guy. He'd ruined Twist's life. If Fox hadn't been there, he could've just waited for Katy to get tired of the quarterback. He'd still have a normal job, a normal life. Cameras in every private place women gathered.

Wait. How long had it been for Fox? Shit, Mary was a great lay and the magic she knew was incredible, but she sure made the whole time thing complicated.

He read more of Katy's posts. Wait a minute. They were going to be in a video shoot. At a Boy Scout camp. Huh. Twist knew the region pretty well from his days as a deputy. He should be able to figure out where they were going. Could it be that old camp where those stupid frat boys died? Ha. That'd been funny. Stupid frat boys.

He googled the band shooting the video. Dance Monkey. They were making a pretty big deal about the video, as well. Son of a bitch. Life went on as normal for all of them. They were getting a big break.

And what about Twist? Chased out of his apartment, living on the run, nowhere to call home, while Fox had Katy and all his friends on the dance team.

He hated even looking at Fox's Facebook page. All those damn happy selfies with his boyfriends, with his dad, with Katy.

"And there's the bitch who shot me." The photo of Lisa Van Zeeland and her shotgun made his back itch. She was the worst.

Back then, he might've been a nobody, no friends, no one in his life but his mom, who he hated anyway, but the little he'd had, the Van Zeeland bitch had taken from him. Left him homeless. Friendless.

There had to be a way to make her pay!

Well, as soon as he finished letting the redhead blow him, had his daily magic sex practice with his amazingly hot partner in crime on the farm they'd taken over down the road. . . after all that, he'd figure out how to punish them for taking everything important away from him.

After Mary magicked dinner. She hadn't taught him how to magic food, yet. A girl had to keep her secrets. In some ways, she was so old-fashioned.

The redhead stood blankly a few feet away.

"Where's my lunch?"

She left to make him another sandwich.

Chapter Five

Sand. Lots of sand. Sand dunes, sand rippled across the sand valleys, sand in the air, sand in my shorts, itchy and hot. I wore Arabian robes with a hood, which rocked because it was hot, seriously fucking oh-my-God-how-is-it-this-hot-and-my-Arabian-robes-are-not-on-fire hot.

A desert? Seriously? How the fuck did I even know what a desert looked like?

Or smelled like. The odor of rotting meat filled the air, that smell you get when your dad asks you to pull the hamburger out of the freezer and put it in the fridge, but you're on the phone fighting with your girlfriend so it ends up in a closet where it takes a really long time to find. Like that but ten times worse. How was anything rotting in a desert?

I walked along the ridge of a dune staring out across an ocean of sand with waves a mile high and valleys really fucking deep. I crested another dune and a hot wind blew the smell of rotting meat into my face. I almost blew chunks, then I looked down into the valley. . . and threw up convulsively.

At the bottom of the valley, ten wooden Xs stood in a cluster, a rotting, bloody body hanging from every one. Vultures hopped from corpse to naked corpse, plucking eyeballs, fingers, toes. Two fought over some poor dude's junk, squawking and flapping and ripping.

"Ethan?" Dad's voice was weak and broken. There, on the end, he hung like a sacrifice.

"Dad!" I raced into the valley, slipping and sliding and eventually completely losing my footing and face-planting in the sand. I rolled ass over teakettle all the way down that sand dune, until I slammed to a stop against the cross where Dad hung, the skin of both legs ripped away and hanging in shreds from his feet.

"Hyah! Hyah!" I chased the vultures away. They hopped and flew to another cross. I hurried to his side, wanting to touch him, to hold him, but every inch of his body had been slashed. Anything I touched would've caused unendurable pain. "Dad. I'm here."

He turned to me with eyeless sockets, blood pouring down his face. "Why Ethan? Why'd you do this to me?" His voice cracked. "Why?"

"No!" I raced to the bathroom and managed to make it to the toilet before I blew out last night's dinner. Not much left to it, so I ended up dry heaving a couple of minutes, too. That wasn't fun. Who actually smelled stuff in dreams? I had never *ever* smelled things before, but that stench was the most disgusting, foul rot I'd ever encountered.

I flushed and dashed into Dad's room. Empty. Shit.

He was out looking for work, you know, on a Sunday morning.

I raced to my room and grabbed my cell. Hit Dad's icon. "Come on, come on."

"Please enjoy this ringtone while we try to reach your party."

"Dancing Queen" by Abba played into my ear.

Come on, come on, come on.

Against all sanity, I sang along. Give me a break. It's a catchy tune.

"What's up, little Fox?"

"Dad!" Okay, now that I'd heard his voice and knew he wasn't dying on a cross in the desert, my panicked phone call seemed a bit melodramatic.

"What's wrong?"

"Nothing." Think, think, think. "I just couldn't remember the passcode for the tablet."

My entire body cringed at how lame that sounded. Would he buy it?

"What was it this time?"

Shit. Busted. "I'm sorry, Dad." I dropped onto the floor and leaned against my bed. "It was just so very fucking real."

"What was it?"

I wiped one hand over my face and hair. "Can I not tell you? I'd rather not. . . I'd just rather not."

"So I was thinking of ordering pizza for you and K-pop while you study for the history test from hell."

Ha. "Food's not at the top of my list right now." But God bless him for knowing how to distract me.

"You'll change your mind by the time I get home. Do you know if K-pop hates anything other than anchovies?"

Huh? "How do you know K-pop hates anchovies?"

He chuckled. "Because everyone hates anchovies," he said. "They're actually a myth. No one eats pizza with fish."

"Well, no, unless you mean 'fish' in a sexist, euphemistic way, in which case, I'm all for eating pizza with fish."

He chuckled. "You okay?"

Deep breath. "Yes. Just a dream. No bearing on the real world in any way, shape or form."

"So once you get through this test, we'll spend a night eating ice cream and googling black magic, okay?"

"You rock, gay dad."

"You roll, straight son."

I disconnected. Fine. I was fine. Twist hadn't even appeared in that dream. No reason to suspect dark, evil powers at work. I lived through a series of traumatic events, and nightmares were a normal coping mechanism. I could read *Psychology Today*.

Fuck it. Back to normal life. Stat.

What time was it? 10 a.m. Five hours of sleep. Meh.

Auntie Mac was in Austin for the week at an expo for restaurant equipment and the people who loved it. Auntie Mac out of town meant one important thing: wake-me-up skinny dipping.

Skrillex blasted out of the speakers on the back bar, the sun was unseasonably warm even for Texas and the pool was heated just enough to keep the chill off. Yeah, I knew how lucky I was to have a heated pool. Dad and I were drop dead poor, but Auntie Mac had done pretty well for herself.

I didn't do laps or anything, mostly just splashed around and dove off the diving board and other juvenile stuff. The water helped me wake up while the coffee brewed. K-pop would text me when he woke up and before he headed my way. To study. Wheee.

I broke the surface in the deep end and gulped air.

"Hey there, hippie."

I spun in the water and shaded my eyes.

Tango's hair shone in the morning sun and her skin glowed.

"I'm naked." I grinned up at her and treaded water.

She smiled. "I sort of figured."

"Auntie Mac's out of town and Dad's not going to be home any time soon." I waggled my eyebrows. "Care to join me for a morning swim?" I slid to a spot where I could stand.

"I was sort of hoping, but wasn't sure if it was a boys-only naked pool."

I snorted. "You know it sounds really gay when you say it like that."

Her eyes sparkled. "Well, you know I'm understanding about your bromances." She glanced at the fence. "Turn around."

Really? "You're looking at me naked right now."

"I can't actually see anything," she said with her hands on her hips. "If you were a normal person with tan lines, I'd be fooled into thinking you were wearing shorts, but your legs are white-boy brown all the way up."

I turned around. "It's the advantage to having a privacy fence." Missing the strip show was a small price to pay for finally getting naked with her.

"Hippie." The volume of the music lowered. "So no one sneaks up on us the way I snuck up on you."

Sneaked, I thought but did not say out loud.

The splash behind me warned me a split second before her arms wrapped around my chest and her warm, warm body pressed against me. Nice. She rubbed my chest and stomach and immediately I no longer had to worry about shrinkage. The water was heated, but not warm enough to do that job on its own. Tango's warm body helped enormously.

Her right hand pressed just below my navel, but went no farther. "Good morning," she said. "I'm surprised you're up so early."

"I wasn't until a few seconds ago," I countered.

She pinched my ass, so I filed that joke away to use again. I turned, wrapped my arms around her and we kissed. Ordinarily, I probably would've tried to keep my junk a bit away until it'd been, you know, formally introduced, but balance was harder in the water, as it were. Gravity carried our bodies together, pretty much from lips to toes. Wow. Her skin was soft all over and she tasted like mint. She had several different toothpastes depending on her mood. Mint meant "frisky." Stellar.

I kissed her neck and she shivered. Also stellar.

She shivered again.

Oh. "As much as I'd like to take credit for your shivers," I said, "I suspect you're actually chilly."

"A little," she admitted.

"We could adjourn to the sun and a blanket," I suggested, "as long as you promise not to make assumptions when I leave the chilly water."

Yipe! Her hand circled my potential embarrassment. "Will that help?"

"Enormously."

She groaned and shut me up by locking her lips on mine and searching my mouth with her tongue.

Just how far was that going to go? Did I want it to go all the way? Well, yeah, eventually, but right now? "I don't have any condoms," I lied.

"Your dad?" she asked.

"Ew."

"Really?"

"No discussion of my dad when your hand is doing what it's doing right now."

"You don't like what I'm doing right now?"

"Hell, yeah. I love it."

"Well, then, there's plenty of fun we can have without needing condoms." The water did cool things to her boobs.

So did I.

We finally made it to a blanket on the grass, and I'm not going into a lot of detail here, but one point stuck out for me. Heh. Heh.

Tango pressed me flat on my back while she continued to do what she'd been doing in the pool. I tried to sit up, but she held me down. "I want to look at you," she said. "Let me do this for you this time so I can get to know your body."

Nothing like that had happened before. It was a little embarrassing, even, being so exposed and vulnerable to her, especially when, you know, the world went white hot for a minute. I'd never been naked like that with a girl. Monika had never liked seeing me naked or me seeing her naked. We did the deed, and, yeah, we were naked, saw each other naked, but we'd never been skinny dipping. And she sure as hell had never done for me what Tango did while I just lay back and enjoyed it.

She smiled down at me. I waited for a clever or snarky joke, but she leaned over and kissed me softly. Apparently, she could tell how vulnerable I felt in that moment.

Well, vulnerable and super-massively *awesome*!

So, of course, I had to return the favor, but this isn't *Fifty Shades*. Go read the slash fiction if you're looking for porn.

About a half an hour later, we lay side by side in the sun, Tango on her stomach and me on my back. It felt perfectly natural to lay there naked with her, now. Mmmm.

Hm. She was awfully quiet considering everything going on. I mean, take your pick, there were about ten different possible topics of conversation more than slightly relevant. "What's up?" I asked.

"Hm? Nothing. Just enjoying the sun."

"Mmhm. That's not true."

"Hm?"

"If you were just enjoying the sun, we'd be gossiping or talking about the latest videos you found or maybe, I don't know, discussing the upcoming video shoot." I nudged her. "You're only quiet like this when something's wrong."

She looked at me out of the corner of her eye. Wow sexy. "I don't suppose there's any chance I can distract you by grabbing your junk again?"

I nudged her foot with mine. "What's wrong?"

She dropped her forehead onto her arms. "I might as well be a lesbian." She rolled onto her side facing me. Gravity did kinda weird things to her boobs. I tried not to stare at them.

"Do you think the whole team is going to be able to pull this off?"

I'd sorta figured. "Depends on how you look at it." I slipped my hands under my head. "I think we could all have wicked fun together."

"You know what I mean."

I did, but I didn't want to. I wanted this entire project to be about oh-my-God fun with my friends.

"If we upgrade what they all do," she added, "we'll end up spending a lot of time coaching them instead of really perfecting our own material."

I'd been worried about this possibility. "'We' meaning you, me, K-pop and Juicy?"

Tango nodded. "K-pop has come so far in the past few months. He's worked damn hard."

"They all have."

She sighed. "I'm an utter bitch, I know, but is it really so wrong of me to want to have the best shot at this I can manage?" When I didn't reply immediately, she looked directly into my eyes. "Do any of the others even have a shot with this? Really?"

"Actually, from a certain perspective, Woody and Cosita might have the best shot of any of us."

Her entire body radiated her what-the-fuck cluelessness. "What?"

"Think about it from typical entertainment industry standards," I said. "They're the hottest of any of us. Even a marginal dancer can look good ten seconds at a time, but hot is hot."

"Cosita's hotter than me?" she asked.

Since we were, somehow, in professional mode there at the side of the pool, I didn't bat an eye. "Woody is ten times hotter than me, and he's not a bad dancer, good enough for ten seconds at a time, anyway." I shrugged. "And Retro's the star of the meme. Give him some Charleston to play with, which he can practice over and over on his own, and for all we know *he'll* be the one to steal the show."

"Damn it." She rolled onto her stomach.

And *that* was the real concern. It wasn't that the others weren't good enough. It was: what if they were? What if someone else stole the show? She looked at me. I think she realized her fear was pretty unflattering in the bright sunlight because she rolled to her feet and dove into the pool.

See, this is one of the big reasons I gave up all that fame and shit. It's damn hard to have friends when you're ultra committed to winning. Friends get in the way. They trip you up. Me? At that point, you couldn't have pried my new friends out of my cold dead fingers with a crowbar, but Tango? Well, if she had something like a deal or a show with Sony, her mom would never try to keep her in Dumass.

I joined Tango in the pool. And wizzed. Hey, she'd never know.

"You think I'm a bitch," she said the moment I surfaced.

"Not at all," I said. "I think you're fucking brilliant." And I took her in my arms.

Both seemed to surprise her.

"If you weren't looking at it that way, you'd be naïve." I released her, swam to the steps and sat on them. She joined me. Hanging out naked with her was über cool. To me, that was the important part of it: hanging with my girlfriend. My priorities had shifted so much in three months.

"Look," I said. "Dance Monkey wants the whole crew. You can build just as much cred letting them see your coaching and choreo skills. To be honest, dancers are a dime a dozen out there. Teachers and choreographers? They make the real money."

She scoffed. "Tell that to Beyoncé."

Deep breath. "I'm not talking superstars, but a well-known coach pulls in a hundred to a hundred-fifty an hour, and that's nothing to scoff at."

She shook her head and stared at her hands, so I could tell the conversation was over for now. How weird was it that K-pop and

Boyfriend both talked to me about their feelings more than my girlfriend did? Oh wait, *that's* why she'd said she might as well be a lesbian. I was a girl.

I moved in close and kissed her shoulder. "You have to remember that you have several advantages."

She turned to me, and the little girl innocence in her face flooded me with the need to hold her and protect her.

"You're pretty and hot and you're a phenomenal dancer." I kissed her boob. "Also, your partner. . ." I indicated myself. "Will be working hard to show *you* off rather than trying to get the attention for myself. Can you imagine Schilling trying to draw the camera away from Woody?" I kissed her forehead. "You'll have me working to make *you* look ten times hotter and sexier than you already are."

And we were in each other's arms, kissing and exploring again.

Until "It's Raining Men" exploded on the sound system.

"Crap!" After one more quick kiss, I slid out of Tango's arms and out of the water. "Someone's at the front door."

"That's your doorbell?" Tango asked, hurrying out of the pool.

I threw on a pair of jams and headed for the gate. "Blame Dad for the musical choice. If we don't answer the front door right away, people tend to just walk back here, so he rigged up a warning." Of course, Auntie Mac had said numerous times that if we ever wore swimming suits, the alarm wouldn't be necessary. Whatever.

"Foxtrot!" The urgency in her voice stopped me. She pointed.

I looked down. My shorts were also pointing. Crap. *Dead-babies-dead-babies.* That'd kill it. "Thanks." I tried to angle it less conspicuously. Damn loose shorts.

"Lucky?" That was Dr. Mike's voice. Well, it could've been worse.

I hurried through the gate and shut it solidly behind me. "Hey, Dr. Mike." I leaned back against it to give it that extra very-closed-gate ambiance.

Dr. Mike looked me up and down. "Hey, Ethan. I take it your Dad's not home." I saw the math in his eyes as he glanced: wet hair and skin plus dry shorts equals. . . "That's not K-pop's car in the driveway, is it."

"Not sure where Dad is, Dr. Mike." I tried my innocent smile.

Please let me not have hair gel by *There's Something about Mary*. "Y'all have a date?"

He checked his cell. "Shit. Didn't notice the text. He's stuck in a meeting." He shrugged in a way I think was meant as nonchalant. Epic fail. "I am going to leave now and come back in an hour and pretend it's the first time I saw you today."

He turned away.

And there I was trying to see it from his point of view. Damn you, K-pop. "Dr. Mike. Wait." I led him away from the gate and kept my voice down. "You don't have to hide this from Dad. Katy's here. She surprised me, but I know Dad will be fine with it. I don't want to be something you have to lie to him about. That's not cool." I lowered my voice so far he had to lean in close to hear. "Besides which, he dropped a box of condoms on my bed last month."

His eyes opened into two huge spot lights.

"We didn't—I mean, we weren't having *sex* just now. We fooled around." I began to think the whole other person's perspective thing was overrated. "This is so freaky." Deep breath. He was an adult. I was trying to get there. "I lied and told her I didn't have any condoms so we wouldn't have sex, yet. Why would I do that?"

He glanced at the fence behind which my girlfriend waited, most likely worried that we were in big trouble. He nodded his head to lead me farther away. "Ethan, you tell me time and again to take off my psychologist hat with you, but that sounded like a request for Dr. Lopez, not Dr. Mike."

I started. "Oh, sorry." I didn't want him to feel obligated to analyze me. "I just. . . I'm just trying to be more. . ."

"No, no problem. . ." He dropped a hand on my shoulder. It was the first time he'd touched me apart from a hand shake at our first official introduction. "I just want to make sure we're perfectly clear about when I'm Dr. Lopez, PhD and when I'm your friend Dr. Mike."

How cool. "Dude, if my dad doesn't marry you, he's an idiot." Oh fuck. So not my place to spout off. "That. . ." Let me die. Please. "I can't take that back."

His hands found his pockets. "Why would you?"

Deep breath. "I don't know. I'm just weirding out right now and want to start all over." I glanced back at the gate. How freaked out was Tango by now?

Dr. Mike actually chucked my shoulder. "I'm going away. I'll be back in an hour. Go to your girlfriend. And you know what? Maybe you should try to figure out why you asked me that question. As far as I'm concerned, she's a very lucky girl. And it's not just because of the washboard abs."

I glanced down at said abs. "You are too much like my Dad."

I watched him think for a second. Uh oh. "Ethan? For the record? Your Dad and I haven't done the deed either. Not the actual deal."

"What?"

He shook his head.

"Why not? It's been three months. That's almost a decade in gay time."

He raised both eyebrows.

"Sorry. Dad talks like that. His fault."

He chuckled. "We've waited twenty years to find each other, Ethan. Why rush things now?"

Which made all the sense in the world. Wow. Maybe Dad really *did* need to marry this guy. As he turned to leave, I called his name.

He looked back.

"While I'm certain to tell *Dad* Tango was here, so you can feel free to add whatever hideously embarrassing narrative you'd like. . ."

He grinned. "Your aunt would birth a bovine if she knew you and Tango were groping each other's naked bodies in the pool."

I closed my eyes and felt my face burn.

"You can blame your father for that one, too."

"Touché."

"Ethan?"

I opened my eyes.

"I did some research. Let me know when you want to talk."

A cold chill ran down my spine. "Thanks. I have a ridonkulously evil test tomorrow, but Dad wants to worship the Almighty Google after that. You can hang with us? There'll be ice cream."

He smiled. "As long as you have Rocky Road, I'm in." He held a fist up. "Am I way too creepy old for fist bumps?"

I bumped his fist and gave him a sly grin. "I'll give you a pass this time."

I hurried back to Tango.

She was pacing awkwardly near the bar. "Are we in trouble?"

"No." I slipped into my shirt and headed over to her. "Dr. Mike is almost as cool as my dad."

She cocked her head. "And it's perfectly fine that he might end up being your. . . What would he even be?"

I shrugged. "Stepdad, I guess."

We stood about two feet apart staring at each other. Would all that amazing comfortableness abruptly morph into awkwardness now that we were dressed?

She chuckled, tried to stifle a laugh. Failed.

I laughed, too, and closed the space between us. "It was nice just, you know, hanging out naked." As always, she felt perfect nestled in my arms.

"That was the high point?" She kissed my chin. "Not the mind-blowing money shot, but the casual conversation while letting it all hang out?" She hugged me. "You are such a lesbian."

She smelled like cinnamon. Must have spritzed while I chatted with Dr. Mike.

"Ethan?" She held me at arms' length and bored into me with her eyes. "What's the real reason you didn't borrow your dad's condoms? I know you both. That *can't* be a boundary issue."

So much for my secret with Dr. Mike. "I'm going to sound like a total prude." How could I say it without sounding like one? "Just because we've both had sex, I don't want to jump into it too fast. I mean. . ." Fine. Might as well have it out in the open. "I talk to K-pop. You know? And he and Kiki. . . everything is so new. . . and exciting for them. He unbuttons her blouse and he's over here on his skateboard with a progress report." That really happened. "I. . . I never had that. I kind of went from zero to sixty in one night. I mean, I *want* to have sex with you. Oh my God, that first tango we danced, that one kiss we had was better than anything I ever had before. I just. . . I just want to. . . Crap. I am such a girl."

She shook her head and hugged me. "No, I am. And a darn lucky one. Remind me to thank K-pop."

"I will."

"So how much *do* you tell each other?" she asked into my shoulder.

"Uh-uh. You can't nail me on that one. Gay dad. I know girls tell each other *far* more than guys ever do, so as long as I have to be embarrassed around Juicy, you need to turn red every time K-pop sees you."

"And Boyfriend."

"No. Not so much." Because *that* wouldn't be hideously awkward.

She led me over to the gate. "For the record? Juicy not so much either."

That surprised me. "I know things are still tense, but I figured. . . best friends and all that."

She squeezed my hand. "She and Cosita spend all their time together now." The look on her face about broke my heart. I needed to remember that. She'd need me to talk to more than usual.

"I'm sorry," I said.

"I still have the dance floor, right?" She shrugged. "And you."

Chapter Six

The bathroom tiles were green and black, cracked and broken. Inside the stalls, all I found were holes in the floor. Their purpose was obvious but hideously unattractive. The urinal was a trough set along one wall, filled with ice. The whole bathroom was either porn video disgusting or utterly nouveau chic.

A group of girls entered the room, spotted me and stopped, giggling and murmuring amongst themselves. They stared, as if waiting for me to take care of business while they watched.

"I don't think you should be in here," I told them.

They giggled more and huddled together, but showed no sign of leaving.

"Fine." I exited through an open doorway that led to another room. A murky pool filled the space. It was lit from below, scattering green spider webs across the walls and floor. Water dripped somewhere, echoing in the dim light. I couldn't even see all the way to the far wall.

Sure enough, the gaggle of girls followed me and hovered in the doorway, as if waiting for me to take a bath in front of them. Okay, fine, I wasn't going to let them intimidate me. I stripped down to my shorts and dove in without giving them a second glance.

The water felt tepid, like the warm spot in a kiddie pool. Ugh.

Something grabbed my foot. I whipped around in the water. A naked girl. A second naked girl grabbed my other foot. Okay, wow. Maybe this scenario had promise after all.

I curled my body to draw closer to them. They smiled. . . then a third girl grabbed me around the neck and all three of them dragged me down.

I struggled against them, fighting my way up.

They dragged me down.

That's when I saw him. Submerged in the water a few feet away, Twist floated calmly as if his presence were the most logical thing in the world. His hair streamed out in a fan. "This one I like," he said. "The naked chicks are hot."

Down, down and down they dragged me.

Water streamed past as my lungs burned.

I choked water. What the hell? Someone had hands on my chest.

I lashed out to free myself.

"Ethan, shit, it's K-pop. Wake up, dude."

K-pop? I let my body go limp. Didn't want to punch him again.

Light. Water. Heat. My lungs hurt so freaking bad. My throat, too.

I opened my eyes.

K-pop was on his hands and knees above me, dripping wet and fully dressed.

I lay on my back at the side of the pool. Electronica played in the background.

I sat up. "What the fuck?"

K-pop helped me. "I don't know, dude. You were asleep on the floatie thing when I got here. I went inside to grab sodas, and when I came out again? You were halfway to the bottom in the deep end, thrashing around like you were fighting something. It was fucking unreal." He sat back on his haunches. "I dove in and pulled you out. You weren't breathing, dude. Thank God I know CPR."

My whole body ran cold. I grabbed a blanket from the grass and jumped to my feet. I stared into his eyes. "I wasn't breathing?"

"You choked out half the pool, bro." His face was white. More white than usual.

These dreams. They weren't normal. They weren't dreams.

It was Twist. He was trying to kill me.

"Ethan."

Would he think I was a freak?

No. This was K-pop. His face was concerned. He was afraid for me. He wanted to help, but had no idea what to do. And. . . he'd literally saved my life.

I pulled the blanket tighter around me. It was the blanket where Tango and I had just shared our first orgasms together a couple of hours earlier. I shook my head in micro-shakes. "You literally had to breathe me back to life?"

He nodded. "I'm glad you brush the teeth."

"My Dad's ordering pizza for the study session," I said. "You get to have any fucking toppings you want."

He choked out a laugh, then his whole face switched to scared. He shook his head, shook out his whole body. "Sorry. Really. It was just. . ." He closed the space between us and held me close. "Jesus, Foxtrot, I thought you were dead."

I held him best I could wrapped in a blanket. I dropped my head against his shoulder. "Twist is trying to kill me in my dreams."

His body fell still.

Shit. It was too much. Duh.

He pushed me out to arm's length and stared into my eyes. "I know a nun who can help."

What. the. fuck? "You don't think I'm crazy?"

He shook his head with his own what-the-fuck expression. "I saw that happen. It's not a stretch."

I grabbed him again. A single sob broke through. "I thought." I held him tighter. "You really don't think I'm insane?"

"No. You're not insane. I saw it. I don't know what it was, but whatever *you* think it was is *not* a freaking stretch."

Ah, shit, I pulled a total Boyfriend, utterly broke down and sobbed on his shoulder. I mean, Dad was supportive and Dr. Mike had to make me think he believed me, but I knew how it all sounded.

I was the one trapped in those dreams. I was the one who'd almost just died because I lost myself in them.

K-pop had brought me back. He'd saved my life, and, more importantly, he really *believed* me. I could see it in his eyes. He didn't just support me. He believed me.

A harsh slap woke Twist, yanking him from the nightmare world.

"What the shit?" He rubbed his cheek and slid out of bed, staring back at Mary. Wow, she looked freaking pissed.

"I didn't teach you to walk the nightmare world so you could create dreams with naked women to fuck."

Oh. Well, if *that* was her problem. . .

"I'm trying to get into that asshole's head, Mary." He tried to adjust the boner tenting his Fruit of the Looms without drawing attention. "He spends all his time. . ."

She raised a hand and Twist was smart enough to shut up. She rose from bed, naked, hot and indescribably fuckable. Mist circled her bare feet. It rose and gave off a faint glow as it circled her.

"What is it about this *boy*," she demanded. "Why are you so obsessed with him?"

Twist sighed. "Mary, darling?" Discussing an obsession with Fox was enough to eliminate all possibility of tenting. "You ever have a. . . kernel of popcorn stuck in your teeth? You try and try to remove it, but nothing works. Maybe it seems irrational, but after a while, you'd kill someone, just to get that popcorn kernel out of your tooth."

He shrugged. "Fox is my popcorn kernel." He clutched both hands into fists. "I really, really *really*, want to make that God damned motherfucker's life eternally painful." He smiled. "I'm sure you understand."

She sighed deeply. After a moment, she padded to Twist's side and shoved her hand into his underwear. "Yes. I suppose I do."

We were hard at the books when dad arrived with pizzas. "Anything interesting happen today?"

K-pop and I exchanged a glance.

"Well, Tango stopped by for a while," I misdirected.

Dad paused in the act of laying the pizzas on the kitchen table. "Unsupervised girlfriend time. That *is* interesting."

I made room for the pizzas. "Don't let your imagination run too wild, but I did have to find my shorts poolside when Dr. Mike stopped by."

"Holy crap!" That was K-pop. "And you didn't share that little tidbit why?"

I glared at him.

"Oh. Yeah."

"Okay, that look you just gave him." Dad opened a pizza box. "What did that mean?"

Deep breath.

"Sorry." K-pop withdrew into himself.

I waved it off. "No worries. I was bound to spill eventually." Deep breath. "I fell asleep on the floatie in the pool and had a nightmare."

Dad sat in a chair and scooted it close to me.

"Long story short, I fell off the floatie and almost drowned." How much would he freak? "But K-pop was right there and took care of me."

"Define 'took care of?'" Shit, he knew me well.

"Pulled me out of the water and gave me mouth to mouth so I'd start breathing again."

All the color drained out of Dad's face. "What?" He glanced back and forth between us. "Why the hell didn't you call?"

"Dad, I'm fine. Yeah, it was scary. But I'm fine."

He shook his head with his we-will-deal-with-you-later-young-man expression. "K-pop? Your side?"

"He fell into the water, and it looked like he was fighting someone or something." His eyes held mine, and I made sure he could tell I wanted him to be honest. "By the time I got him out, he wasn't breathing and. . . and his heart stopped, but it was just a few seconds until I got him breathing again."

"You realize you are now officially a member of this family," Dad said. "I'll get bunk beds if you want to move in."

K-pop laughed. "The air mattress is fine." But I could tell Dad's declaration meant a lot to him.

Dad looked back and forth again, then settled on my face. "You're really fine? You swear?"

"I swear."

He moved forward and grabbed me in a hug. "Okay, I can't be that cool." He kissed the top of my head. "I can't believe I almost lost you and didn't even know it." And then he finally said it. "Is this connected to your theory about the nightmares? Are we talking Freddie Krueger here?"

"Mr. Fox?" K-pop leaned forward. "I saw him in the water. It *really* looked like he was fighting someone. Really."

Dad nodded. He kissed me one last time, then rose. "Okay, boys. Eat pizza. Nail this test. Ethan, you're sleeping in my room tonight. I'm going to start googling. Tomorrow night we try to figure this shit out."

So in movies, people always went weeks or months with no one believing them and making them feel like freaks. Thank God this was real life.

Boyfriend showed up a couple of hours later. "Za!!" He grabbed a cold slice and munched on it over my shoulder.

"Aren't you hanging with Theresa?" I asked. "And by hanging I mean having wild monkey sex."

He nudged me. "We already made it twice on the tractor." Munch, munch. "She thinks my tractor's sexy."

"I worship you, bro." K-pop raised a fist that Boyfriend air-bumped from across the table.

"It was her idea for me to come over and help. I totally aced Texas history."

Her idea? Something about that bothered me, but I couldn't quite name it.

He pointed over my shoulder at my practice test. "You have the Mexican-American war mixed up with the Texas War for Independence, yo."

Wait. He actually knew this stuff?

He scooted a chair up close to me. "Dude, it's just like football stats. My brain likes numbers." He grabbed another slice. "You mind if I jump in, K-pop? I don't wanna step on toes."

"It's a three-way."

Boyfriend and I stared at him in frozen discomfort.

He grimaced. "Can we just pretend that was something actually witty and clever?"

"Let's pretend you said 'trio.'" I grabbed more pizza.

He did his new kissing two fingers and raising them thing. "Spot on."

After another hour I screamed in a manly, deep-voiced way and needed a break, so we retreated to the garage.

"*West Side Story* has some cool dude dances that we could steal for the retro swing thing," I suggested.

"I worship Gene Kelly," K-pop threw out.

"Okay, yeah." Boyfriend hesitated.

We waited.

"Okay." He waved us over while he called up YouTube on his tablet. "There's these Russian brothers who do this cool-as-shit balancing stuff."

"I've seen that," I said as the video played. It was an amazing cross between tumbling and acro.

"Yeah?"

"Holy shit," K-pop said about this move where one guy did a one-handed handstand on the other guy's head.

"Right?" Boyfriend called up another video. "You just know the girls are going to throw together some sexy, Andrews sisters/Shakira shit. We need to find something for the guys, right?"

Yes, I had to work to avoid my shock that he knew the Andrews sisters.

"And we need to get the other guys in on this," K-pop suggested. "Retro and Ephraim are small enough we could really toss them around, hai?"

He and Boyfriend turned to me, waiting for the seal of approval. I nabbed the tablet. "Okay, you two will help me figure out the moves, and we'll teach it to the other guys." I tapped over to Gene Kelly. "I'm not showing anything to Ephraim until we have our shit down. He scares me."

An hour later, Dad poked his head into the garage and forced us back to Texas history.

Meh.

Boyfriend's cell rang. He opened the text, grabbed his bag and bolted for the door.

What the hell? "Booty call?"

"You know it," he called without slowing down.

I turned to K-pop.

He shrugged. "I guess twice in one day *isn't* enough."

Chapter Seven

Why the hell wasn't it working? Twist stormed out of the house shortly after sunrise. He stomped across the porch barefoot, which might not have been the best idea since he really wanted to stomp for all it was worth, but he rarely wore more than a pair of jeans these days, and taking the time for a pair of boots—

Argh! He was doing everything Mary had taught him.

Everything.

He did the whole peaceful centering bullshit thing, and he cast the stupid spell correctly. Once in the nightmare world, he spent time just kind of exploring, getting his bearings sorted.

He called up a suitable world, drew in an image of Fox. . . and that's as far as he could get.

He wanted the *real* Fox, the smug, smarmy douchebag so he could play him like a puppet.

Son of a bitch! He padded out to the hen house and stormed into the chicken wire enclosure, greeted by a flurry of cackling, feathery bodies. He nabbed one fat hen by the head. It squawked once before he broke its neck and stuck it to the wall with a bowie knife. There were several blades hanging from the belt he'd strapped into on his way out the door.

"What the hell am I doing wrong?"

Mary's nightgown was so sheer, she might as well have been naked, but even that didn't distract him from his frustration. "I have to admit it's a quandary." She closed her fingers through the chicken wire. "You're certain it's *not* really him?"

"You said he'd fight me, right? That I'd feel his struggle, right?"

She nodded.

"I don't feel shit. He's just there, like a hologram or something." He snatched another hen from the ground, wrung its neck and stuck it to the wall of the hen house. "How long until I get into his fucking mind?"

"Patience, David." Her voice was soothing, but that only pissed him off more. She sounded like a mother with an angry child.

The third chicken dead and pinned to the wall didn't help, either.

"You realize that's a waste of food, David?"

That was it. Her whole patient-and-understanding-woman thing drove him mad sometimes.

"Waste?" He opened his palms low at his sides. "It's a waste to make myself feel better?"

He lifted his hands, palms up and every chicken in the yard shot six feet into the air, squawking. He bunched his hands into tight, closed fists and the squawking was cut short with only a single soft "urk." When he snapped his hands open, fingers spread wide, every chicken in the yard exploded in a bloody, pulpy feathery mess.

It was like a sorority pillow fight in a slasher film. With blood and gore sprayed warm and friendly across his bare skin.

Yeah. Maybe the dream thing didn't make him a total failure. Exploding chickens was cool.

"Who cares about a few birds anyway?" He lowered his hands. "You magic all our food out of thin air for us."

"Is that what you think?" She slid her fingers away from the chicken wire. "No one can 'magic' food from thin air, David." With a plucking gesture, she pulled a chicken from the wall of the coop. It hovered a few feet from Twist. Although she stood ten feet away, she held the hen in one hand and with a single sweep, yanked all the feathers from it, depositing them in a neat pile on a bench.

Every gesture mirrored what happened to the chicken. She plucked its head and feet, and removed the guts, all of which made neat piles on the bench. At a wave from her other hand, a swirl of herbs and bits of other stuff flew into the hen yard and covered the bare skin.

The brief flash of fire around the bird startled Twist, but when the flames vanished, the chicken hovered in the air before him perfectly cooked and smelling delicious. Hm. He hadn't had breakfast, so he yanked a leg from the bird. Perfect. He held it up and nodded approval as he chewed.

"Why do you suppose we live on a farm?" she asked.

"It's out in the middle of nowhere."

She shook her head. "A lot of places are in the middle of nowhere, David. A farm has food that allows us to stay away from the towns."

"So you can't just magic stuff from thin air?" He nabbed the other leg.

"No one can, to the best of my knowledge."

That sucked. He'd been looking forward to learning that spell.

"Can't we just steal stuff from a distance," he asked.

"In theory." She settled against a nearby fence. "But this is safer, and I haven't lived as long as I have by taking unnecessary risks." Her smile was sexy. "Don't forget I grew up in a time before we had mini marts and big box department stores."

He pulled a wing from the bird with a wry smile. Department stores. Nobody used that word any more. Sometimes, he forgot that she'd lived over three hundred years.

Question 4,357: How many sperm were swimming in Stephen F. Austin's sack on April 21, 1836? And what were their names?

Okay, maybe that was hyperbole again, but Jesus H. Christ, that test was freaking hard. Especially because Boyfriend's usual desk beside me sat empty. No explanation. All texts and calls unanswered.

Mr. Gonzalez, the history teacher who wore too much cheap

cologne and seemed to think he was a clever character in a Nickelodeon series, walked the aisles and looked down at me over his glasses. "You should worry less about Corey's absence and more about the test. You don't ace this test and *you'll* be history."

Groan.

Boyfriend's disappearance the night before *hadn't* been a booty call.

I'd bumped into Theresa before class and found out she hadn't heard from him at all. "What, he bolted without saying goodbye, and you assumed he was too horny to be polite to his best friend?"

"Fine, Theresa, I'm an asshole. Any ideas?"

None. We couldn't reach his parents, either.

The bell rang and everybody jumped up to escape history. Except for me. I was still scribbling my last best guess. As I rose, I noticed the tail end of the stragglers making room for someone on his way in.

An adult. Dr. Mike.

He hurried to Gonzalez's side, and they huddled together in an adults-not-wanting-students-to-hear manner. They looked up at me, and Dr. Mike seemed tired and looked shitty and holy fuck, my heart stopped. I couldn't breathe.

Don't-let-Boyfriend-be-dead-don't-let-Boyfriend-be-dead.

They went back to their conversation, and Mr. Gonzalez nodded and left, his face sad, hurrying the last few students out the door and closing it behind them all.

Don't-let-Boyfriend-be-dead-don't-let-Boyfriend-be-dead.

Dr. Mike must've noticed my dread. "No one's dead, Ethan. Don't panic."

Thank God. I breathed again.

He gripped my shoulder and there was something strange about his whole demeanor. Was this Dr. Lopez rather than Dr. Mike?

Deep breath. "What's up, Dr. Mike?"

"One of Corey's closest friends tried to commit suicide last night, and I think he'd really like to see you right now."

"Let's go." Oh shit. I'd been too caught up in Texas history and assumed booty call. Stupid Texas history! "Where is he?" I grabbed my books.

"Dumass Memorial." The moment I moved, his other hand came

up and pressed into the center of my chest, holding me fast. "Wait a minute, Ethan. This is more complicated." I'd watched Dad with his boxers enough to know that he was working me. Something was going to piss me off. "We're talking about Gunner."

"He tried to kill himself?"

"Yes."

"Did he live?"

"So far."

"That's too bad."

Dr. Mike's hands dropped away. "My God, Ethan, I wish I lived in a world as simple as yours." He pinched his nose between his thumb and fingers. "Gunner might *not* live. No one knows yet." He crossed his arms and regarded me.

Apparently, my utter lack of emotional response did not impress him.

"First of all, I'm here as Dr. Lopez, not Dr. Mike. And I'm here for Corey, not for Gunner. I don't care if you go home tonight and light a candle to pray for Gunner's death. I wouldn't blame you. But there's some stuff you need to know because it affects Corey, the guy you call your best friend, one of them, anyway. He's the one who needs you. You care about Corey, right?"

I stared at him and tried to care what happened to Gunner. Fail.

"That wasn't rhetorical, I want an answer."

"Yes, I care about *Corey*." I shook my head. "Of *course*, I do."

"Okay." He did the pinching his nose thing again and moved over to the windows. "I'm still wrapping my head around all this myself." Seemed like he hadn't slept at all.

So, in order to keep practicing the looking-at-life-from-other-people's-perspectives thing, I forced myself past the fact that we were talking about the guy who'd led the party to beat me unconscious.

"Are you okay, Dr. Mike?"

"I can't be Dr. Mike right now, Ethan. This is that messed up." He sighed. "Corey blames himself for everything. For the attack on you, for Gunner's suicide attempt. There's a lot of stuff I can't tell you. About his parents. Corey never saw it. Never suspected. They've known each other since they could talk." He turned away from the window and found my eyes. "I'm not asking you to care about Gunner, but Corey hates himself and he needs you."

"Fuck." I joined him at the window.

We stared out at the schoolyard, where hundreds of students were laughing and messing around, completely unaware and ignorant. Wished it was me.

"Gunner's a sociopath," Dr. Lopez said, "and you have no reason to pity him. But pity Corey. Anyone with hindsight can figure out that Gunner was abused, but Corey's convinced he should've seen it years ago. He should've helped, should've had Gunner move in. He'd have stopped getting hurt, you wouldn't have been beat up and Gunner would've never tried to kill himself."

That's exactly the way Boyfriend would see it. He'd blame it all on himself. Jesus.

"I'm hoping you might at least convince Corey that your attack wasn't his fault." He looked at me. "You don't blame—?"

"No," I interrupted. "I told him that the next day." I wiped my face with my hands and ran them through my hair. Why did he have to take everything onto those huge shoulders? It was so like him. Monika, Gunner. . . everything was his burden to hold.

Like Atlas. Damn lit class.

"For Corey," I said. "I'll go for Corey. Of course, I will."

"That's all I'm asking." He seemed relieved. "I already cleared you for the rest of the day."

Shit, couldn't he have cleared me *before* the history test?

Dumass Memorial held no fond memories for me. Ironically, the last time I'd been there was because of the sociopath I now visited. Dr. Lopez led me to the ICU and seemed to have permission to do pretty much as he liked.

The antiseptic and sick-people-smell turned my stomach. I shivered. A nurse rattled by with a cart, and I jumped. That place held nothing but bad memories.

"Hey, Dr. Lopez," I said, trying to keep the mood light, "this is where we first met." Which was true. He'd been recording blackmail material against Officer Friendly for me and Dad. "Of course, you were just Mike back then."

He patted my shoulder and showed me Gunner's room.

Boyfriend was in there, hunched over and holding Gunner's hand. I couldn't see his face, but I didn't need to see it to know it was red and puffy from crying. He'd been there all night. Wouldn't leave Gunner's side.

Gunner looked dead. He didn't look like the same guy. He seemed fragile and weak. Maybe if I kept telling myself that, that he wasn't the guy who'd almost sterilized me, then maybe I could get through it.

"Boyfriend?"

He looked up. "Foxtrot?" He stared at me as if he thought he must be hallucinating. "What're you doing here?"

"I'm the one who doesn't laugh when you cry, remember?" What else could I say?

He didn't stop crying for an hour, maybe more. The nurses moved us to an empty room. Between his sobs, he told me the stuff Dr. Lopez hadn't.

"It's his fucking parents. The verdict comes in on the trial tomorrow, but it's pretty obvious he's going away for a long time. I mean, he fucking did it."

His face filled with guilt over that, too. I saw why Dr. Mike had asked me to be there.

"So his parents decided they had one last chance to 'fix him' themselves. This time though, they sliced open an artery by accident and had to take him to the hospital. First chance he got, he stole a lot of drugs and took them all." He stared at his hands. "They have a shed out back. I've seen pictures of it. It's covered in piss, shit and puke. There's this harness of wires that plugs into a bare socket. There's a cupboard full of stuff that almost made *me* puke just to look at it. A power hose."

Okay, his parents were sick. Poor Gunner.

"I never figured out that at least once a week his parents tortured him for some lousy made-up sin. If I'd seen what was going on, I could've stopped it. I mean, why the hell were all the sleepovers and parties at my place? Never at Gunner's. Fucking duh, and I never *once* thought to ask why."

He wiped at his face. "Neither did Dr. Cherkasky, and he's been trained to look for shit like that when he gives a guy a physical, you know? That's how good his parents were. They researched. Did you know there are websites out there to teach you how to hurt someone without leaving a bruise? What the hell is that?"

"That's how he knew." A pit opened up in my stomach. Jesus. "That's how he could hurt me so badly without killing me."

Boyfriend nodded. "Even the jokes Gunner makes. 'My dad's gonna fry my nuts for this one.'" He looked up at me. "The old man ran so much juice through Gunner's balls, he might never have kids."

I did not point out that that was probably good, all things considered.

The nurses wanted to sedate Corey, but Dr. Mike intervened and convinced them the best thing for him was to cry it out.

Which meant I got to sit there with him while he cried.

No. That sucked. I was glad I could be there for him. He was one of those guys nothing bad should happen to. Ever. We didn't spend so much time together, maybe, since he'd found Theresa, but I'd always have his back.

After the hundredth, "I'm so sorry about what he did to you," I took his face in my hands. "What Gunner did to me was not your fault. Okay? You feel bad for what happened to him, and I get that. But none of it was your fault."

Eventually the sobs turned to murmurs and Boyfriend started nodding off from exhaustion. I bundled him into the room's empty bed, but I couldn't leave him, so we ended up lying there together with Boyfriend curled against me, his head on my chest, whimpering until he fell asleep. He'd been awake since he'd milked the cows at five the previous morning.

"Hey, Fox." A faint, distant voice. "I'm going to fucking drive you insane."

I jerked awake with Boyfriend snoring softly in my arms.

Dr. Lopez sat in a chair nearby. He started when I spazzed awake, then his face went all soft, and he gave me a total lolcat face, like, how cute were we. Ugh. He sidled up to the bed. "You've been here eight hours, Ethan. You should get some rest, yourself."

Holy shit. Eight hours? How much of that had I slept? Boyfriend drool soaked my chest. Not the first time.

Dr. Lopez helped me slip out from under him, leaving the big goon curled up against a fake Ethan made out of pillows. When I picked at my soggy t-shirt, he found me a scrub top.

"I'm sorry I said your world was simple," he told me. "Not many people would have done so much for him."

What had I done, really, that anyone with a pair of arms and ears couldn't do? "Can I just please get the hell out of here? I'll feel proud of myself tomorrow."

"Go ahead."

He'd arranged for Dad to pick me up. Apparently, Dr. Lopez was still needed at the hospital.

As Dad hurried toward me, I called back. "Dr. Mike? You have my cell. He needs anything. Any thing at all, a coffee better than the swill they serve here. Call me."

"Swill?" But he grinned.

"Blame Dad."

More than anything, I wanted to hold Tango and bury my face in her breasts and not for any of the obvious reasons. I just needed something pure and good and loving to wash out all the sociopathic bullshit and tragedy.

Chapter Eight

Dad needed some convincing before he'd drop me off at the studio, but Tango's car was there. I told him I'd slept and that what I really needed was to jump up and down for a while. He grumbled but acceded to my request. Yay. Hopefully she was alone. My cell battery had died hours before, so I hadn't been able to tell her what was happening.

Not sure I would have anyway.

So now there were two things I hadn't told her.

Swing music played through the door.

His swing music. Whiskey's.

Yay.

Laughter.

Double yay. Hopefully, Tango would notice the scrubs and send Juicy packing.

It wasn't Juicy.

Whiskey was there. In person.

Wait. Really? Or was I asleep at the hospital?

He and Tango danced swing to one of Dance Monkey's songs. They were laughing and smiling a lot.

Please God, let it be a nightmare.

"Foxtrot!" She ran up and kissed me. Mint. Frisky? Damn it.

She released me. "Wow, you look like shit." She picked at the shirt. "Nice fashion choice. Very *Grey's Anatomy*."

My brain gave me nothing to say.

Rock Star wandered over. In his stocking feet. His boots and jacket were on a table. He seemed to follow my eyes. "I drove my bike down from Austin."

"Bike?" I'd have noticed that parked outside, right?

"It's in the alley." He flexed his toes. "Fortunately, Tango's such a great dancer I feel perfectly safe. Didn't know we'd start dancing right away."

Crap, the boots and jacket weren't an affectation, after all.

They stared at me for a moment. Oh, was it my turn to say something?

"You okay?" Tango asked.

"Yeah, great." Please make him go away.

She didn't read my mind. "Okay, cool." She dashed back to the floor and dragged me along. "Whiskey has this great new version of jitterbug you need to learn."

The music was depressingly cheerful.

Wait. Whiskey was a singer. The bastard could dance, too?

I wore chucks, which aren't great for dancing. The rubber on the soles is sticky.

Tango took my hands and moved me through a few steps. They were familiar but seemed wrong because they didn't feel like something I didn't know.

Tango'd said this was new, right? She twirled.

"Wait." I recognized the dance. "This is hustle, right? Like, old-time hustle?"

Whiskey nodded. "I hang out at this place called GoDance. It's one version of what they teach for jitterbug there."

Yeah, fine. "I used to dance there. If that's what they're teaching, it must be right." I'd been working on International Ballroom, so I hadn't paid a lot of attention to jitterbug, but once I recognized what Tango was trying to show me, it clicked, and I took over.

Whiskey leaned back against a table. "Cool."

Tango and I danced. Okay, that was nicer. We had a chance to play around a bit. Then she looked over at Whiskey. "Is this right?"

"Yep."

Seriously?

"I just want to make sure it's the same as what the band wants for the video," she said, as if noticing my simmer. "There's so many different versions, you know."

Oh, right, because I wasn't the one who'd shown them to her on YouTube.

She pulled away. "Okay, dance with Whiskey. You can lead. He follows." When I didn't speak or move, she settled into one hip, but even that didn't help, considering my mood. "I want to see what it looks like from the outside. The moves are the same as what I know, but the technique is throwing me off."

"It's all forward and together instead of side to side." He stepped closer to me. Oh my God, he was so sure of himself and smug. What a douchebag.

"Dance with him," Tango directed. "Hello?"

I was moving through molasses. The day in the hospital with Boyfriend had taken more out of me than I'd have guessed. I offered a hand to Whiskey and Tango smiled.

We danced. He followed really well and had good control of his weight. Damn it.

Just to throw off the walking Alpha Male, I pulled him in closer than I normally would, and threw a few back bends at him, stuff guys usually don't like to do with another guy.

He followed them all with a wry grin, like he knew I was testing him.

Awfully comfy dancing with a dude.

Just sayin'.

Okay, that was totally hypocritical considering me and my buddies. It'd been a long day, all right?

"I danced a lot in the swing scenes." He started throwing in hitch kicks. "I first got into playing swing by dancing it." He pulled a foot up and tapped the back of my leg. "My little brother's gay, and he was my first teacher."

Oh, sweet Jesus. Seriously?

"The west coast and Lindy folks especially expect a guy to be able to follow, so I made a point of following all the dances I do."

"What dances *do* you do?" Tango's interest was only logical, but she was doing that wide-eyed thing girls do to make guys think they have her undivided attention.

"East coast, west coast, Lindy, Charleston, shag, salsa and. . . tango." He grinned when I almost tripped. "Just 'cause."

What an unmitigated douchebag!

He missed a turn. "Sorry. That was strong. Threw me off balance."

Tango giggled. "He's used to choreo more than lead/follow."

He smiled at me. "Makes sense."

I threw a triple spin.

He stumbled out of it.

"Sorry, used to folks who can spin."

He shrugged. "I'm just a guy, I guess."

Tango's smirk told me I should know better than to lead stuff my follower can't, er, follow. Aw hell, my day had sucked. Why did I have to play nice with Rock Star?

"Okay, I think I have it." Tango pulled me out so she could dance with Whiskey. She was stellar as always, and made everything he led look genius. Since he knew the song, he could lead to hit all the musical breaks, which made it seem choreographed. Damn it.

Fuck, they looked good together.

Mind you, his footwork sucked. Wait, he didn't *have* any footwork, just danced everything flat footed, which Lindy dancers hated. He led all his turns with two fingers. Lame. He dipped her all the way to the floor, as if that was cool or something.

Tango's breathy little shriek implied *she* thought it was.

She adjusted her ponytail when she stood on her feet again. "We need to choreograph the duet for me and Whiskey." She kissed my cheek. "You should help."

Record scratch.

"Duet. With you and Whiskey?" Deep breath. "And I should 'help'?"

Tango looked at me as if she were explaining why stuff fell down instead of up. "Well, he's the front man for the band, Foxtrot. I'm the crew captain. Of course, we'd dance a duet." She shrugged. "I mean, I didn't really think of it that way until Whiskey pointed it out, but it only makes sense, right? I mean, I'll dance with you, too, in other scenes."

Whiskey hunched over a little and sort of bounced from foot to foot with his "dukes up." He punched my arm a couple of times. "You're the ballroom guy, right? Don't want to sully your amazing technique with something like Lindy." Jab. Jab.

Sully? Who talked like that?

"That wasn't Lindy." *Don't-deck-him-don't-deck-him.* "But, yeah, I can help. I've watched a few of your gig videos. Nothing too hard." All swing dances use the same moves, so now that I knew which version he wanted, I had at least five sequences I could throw together off the top of my head.

Tango moved close to me and took my hand. "Some of the jive moves you did for World's would be perfect." Cinnamon. "And the tricks."

Her back to Whiskey, her voice was exactly that of a girl trying to placate her jealous boyfriend, but her eyes were all business. *Please don't mess this up for me*, they said.

It was a challenge. What I *wanted* to say was that if Rock Star wanted to dance with the best dancer on the team, he'd be better off with Juicy or me, but, yeah. . . saying that out loud would have driven her directly into his arms.

Her eyes were dark and beautiful. Her hand holding mine made my skin tingle. Wow. Was it just the day before that we'd lain in the sun basking in our first time naked together? Just yesterday?

How best to keep this friendly? I faced Tango. "The fastest way to make it work would be for you and me to figure out the choreo and then for you to teach it to him."

She smiled. "Perfect." She turned to Whiskey with her fake surprise face. "Holy cow, is it really that late? My mom is going to kill me."

"That's right." Whiskey's smile couldn't have been more feral. "You have school tomorrow, don't you?"

"Don't you?" I asked.

"Not tomorrow." He shrugged. "I don't take classes that start before noon, anyway."

Tango's surprise at *that* was genuine. "Oh my God, that would be heaven for a dancer!"

He shrugged and headed for his boots. "That's my life, darlin', just a little slice of heaven."

She started shutting things down. I helped. Anything to get him out of there faster.

"Where are you staying?" she asked. "You can't drive back this late." She glanced over her shoulder at him with a curiosity I did not enjoy. "And we could maybe get a little more work done tomorrow?"

The rock star slipped into his boots. "It's warm out. I like to sleep under the stars."

"No." The edge in her voice drew both of our attentions. She seemed to notice how abrupt she'd been. "Sorry. It's just. . ."

It was just that only a few months ago a homicidal maniac and an overzealous cop had proven to all of us that a small town wasn't necessarily safer than the big city.

"Why the big silence?" Whiskey asked. "Aren't small towns supposed to be safer than the big city? I've slept outside in Austin a bunch of times."

"Really?" She was way too impressed with this poser! "It's just that you're a celebrity guest here." What was this? Scooby Doo? "You could stay at Foxtrot's place."

Another record scratch.

"What?"

She slid up to me. "K-pop and your boyfriend stay over all the time."

"Boyfriend?" Whiskey's face implied all the wrong questions.

"Long story." I hoped Tango would just let him sleep out in a cow field where he could roll over into a pile of shit.

"He could always stay at my place," she suggested nonchalantly.

Damn. I was beaten. "Nah," I said, but decided I might win at least one point back. "Your mom gets annoyed when we close the blinds at the studio." Huh. In my head that'd been kinda sexy, but not really, I guess. I turned to my new arch enemy. "Dude. No sweat. *Mi casa es su casa.*"

Kill me. Kill me now.

So the queerest moment there, in all definitions of the word, was that I wished I were back in the hospital with Boyfriend drooling on my chest. With him everything was simple. Does that make me evil?

I really wanted a few minutes alone with Tango, but there was no way to do that since Rock Star didn't know where I lived. After she locked the door, I took her in my arms and kissed her. It was nice, but she held back. It was her normal on-the-clock thing, but was that all it was? She'd been a bit hesitant with Boyfriend when I first came to town, too.

"Can we get some time tomorrow?" I asked.

She kissed me. "Of course."

She shook Whiskey's hand. "Call me tomorrow?" The hand shake was strictly professional, but was it maybe just a little bit *too* strictly professional?

He nodded.

She ran off.

"You can follow me." I had no car. "Shit. I have no car here."

"You can ride with me."

Joy. I followed him into the alley. Wait. He had a motorcycle, that meant. . .

"You can ride bitch." He grinned. "Just a biker word. No offense meant."

Offense was taken. I guarantee it. But I wasn't going to say a thing.

My friends might be able to ride this douchebag's coattails to fame. I would *not* do anything to ruin that. Bitch it was. At least it wasn't a crotch rocket.

He steadied the bike, and I hopped on behind. "What do I hold onto?"

He glanced over his shoulder at me, annoyed confusion on his face. "Hold onto me." He turned forward and grabbed his helmet. "For a dancer, you're kind of a homophobe, dude."

In another universe, that would've been funny.

I grabbed a blanket and pillows from a closet. "You'll need to sleep on the couch." No way was he getting the air mattress on the floor of my room the way my friends did.

"Nice place. Homey." He pulled off his boots. "So Ethan, I think we need to have a conversation."

His tone told me exactly what he was about to say. "About?"

He laughed. "Really? You're going to play the game? You're obviously uncomfortable with me and Tango working together." He stripped off his socks and balled them up.

I spread the blanket on the sofa.

He undid his belt. "I want you to know I would never, ever, in this or any other lifetime, try to steal a guy's girl, especially when we're all working together."

Did I have any reason to believe him? "Really? 'Cause while we're being all cozy, you did seem to be putting the moves on Tango."

"Pfft. No. Not at all." He pulled off his pants and rolled them up. "I'm really sorry if it looked that way." He stripped off his t-shirt. "Of course, if she makes any kind of move on me, that's entirely different."

Wait. What?

He smiled. "She's an adult. She makes her own decisions. She wants to fuck a rock star, who am I to deprive her of all this?" He gestured at his body in a manner that immediately made me think of Boyfriend. Except when Boyfriend had done it, it'd been endearing.

Whiskey climbed under the blanket. "You're a total rock star for letting me crash here, brother." He lay down with his back to me.

I couldn't move. I thought about Boyfriend and Gunner. About Tango and my dad. And this pretentious dick on my couch in his Dolce Gabbana briefs that he obviously padded.

Shitstix. Sleep.

I walked up to my room, closed the door very firmly behind me and was likely asleep before I hit the bed.

For the first time in a couple of weeks, I didn't dream at all.

Chapter Nine

Twist crouched out near the barn with the morning sun on his back. "How long do you think this warm spell's going to last, Mr. Bunny?"

Mr. Bunny twitched the nose of the saleswoman who'd tried to sell Twist disaster insurance. Twist smiled. He liked the ghost rabbit more than most people he'd known. He'd never had a pet before.

Well, he'd had a cat named Doc for a while. Then one day he'd wondered what things looked like on the inside. That was how he'd learned that when you took the insides outside, the animal died. When his mother had found him in the backyard with Doc splayed out like an enormous, soggy butterfly, she'd pretty much insisted he wasn't allowed pets.

"She's not going to live long like this." Mary's voice startled him. She gazed down at the saleswoman critically. "Not enough blood."

Twist rose to his feet, his bloody hands held away so he wouldn't mess up his jeans. He'd managed to peel most of her skin back and nail it into the hard packed dirt, but Mary was right. She'd be dead by the time he removed the first layer of muscle.

Her pale blue eyes flicked from Mary to Twist and her nose twitched.

Ha! He just loved the way Mr. Bunny held her so still, but just couldn't keep from twitching her nose. It was so cute.

"May I offer a suggestion?"

Twist sighed. He really preferred to have this kind of time to himself.

"I can show you how to keep her alive at least another hour or two."

Oh, well that would be fun. He waved one hand over his project to invite her assistance.

"*Ad erant veritus interesset mel.*" She knelt beside the saleswoman and yanked out a hank of her mousy brown hair. "*No sint augue maiorum eum.*" She lifted a twig from the ground and tied the hair around it, making it seem easier than it was. Hair was hard to tie.

While Mary intoned the words of her spell, Twist wondered again that someone so powerful still needed the incantations for nearly everything she did. Twist had found out shortly after meeting her that he'd been born with the magic inside him. It had just taken the desert witch's book to tap into his power.

Mary, on the other hand, had needed to find the magic, whatever that meant. One thing it meant was that once he figured the shit out, it was easier for him.

She shoved the hair-covered twig into the woman's stomach, where it disappeared without leaving a scratch. Mary brushed off her hands. "There you go, sweetie. She'll stay alive at least a few hours now, no matter what you do."

"Wow."

"That's how you make a zombie." She rose. "It's called a gris-gris."

"We can make zombies?" Twist had to suppress the urge to jump up and down.

Mary crossed her arms and smirked. "Boys and their toys."

Wait a minute. "I thought zombies were made by some kind of virus or something."

"I hate movies. They always get it wrong." She shook her head. "Magic has been the fundamental source of zombies for thousands of years. Eating brains and biting each other is a myth."

"No zombie apocalypse?"

She laughed. "As far as I know, it's not a possibility. Sorry to disappoint."

Bummer. He'd always thought a zombie apocalypse would be fun.

"I'll leave you to your game." She turned to go, but stopped. "You know, with the gris-gris in her, you don't need Mr. Bunny to hold her down."

"No?" He crossed his arms, remembered they were covered in blood. Oh well.

"You're missing the best part." Away she walked.

The way she rolled her hips in that skintight skirt was hot. Unfortunately, now that they were close to whatever her goal was with the sex magic, the only time they fucked was during the ritual. Too bad. He'd have to find time for the redhead on the next farm to blow him.

"Ghost rabbit," she reminded him from the porch.

Oh yeah.

"Okay, Mr. Bunny. Hopsky outsky."

The moment a flash of silver raced around Twist's feet, the saleswoman's eyes opened wide and she let out a scream that would've been heard for miles if they hadn't sealed the farm against that sort of thing. She'd only found it in the first place because Twist had seen her on the road and dropped the barriers so she'd visit. He hadn't had much luck in the nightmare world for a couple of days and had needed a distraction. For some reason, he couldn't call Fox's image into his dreams.

The saleswoman screamed and screamed.

"Nice set of lungs on this one." Twist crouched beside Mr. Bunny and picked up his hatchet. "I think I'd like to see them."

"Ethan?"

My first reaction was to pull the blanket higher. Wait. That was Dad's voice. Oh, thank God. Wait. Why was he still up?

"Hey, Dad." The clock said seven o'clock. What? It felt like I'd been asleep maybe five minutes.

"Why is there a douchebag sleeping on our couch?"

Ha. I struggled completely awake, realized I wasn't even under the blankets. "Sorry. He's the guy from the Austin band. Long story." There were lots of long stories. "How'd you know he's a douchebag and not my new BFF?"

He sat on the bed beside me. "He's on the couch, your door was closed and you fell asleep fully dressed." He pulled me in and kissed my head. "Ergo. Douchebag."

"When was the last time I told you I loved you?"

"Do I need to make breakfast?"

"For him? No." How was I going to get rid of him?

"Well, he's dressed now, and, I think, just waiting to say good-bye."

Thank. God.

I felt grimy and gross. Was there any chance I could get rid of the rock star and still sneak in a shower before school?

Fine. Professional mode. I hurried downstairs. "Hey, Whiskey. Sleep okay?"

"Better than you, I bet." He winked. Fully dressed. Good. "You look better, brother."

I pointed at Dad. "This is my dad. Mr. Fox."

"We've met." He shook Dad's hand. "Sorry if I caused any problems."

"Any friend of Ethan's is a friend of mine." He bumped me. "By the way, K-pop is starting those tae kwon do lessons, and I can use your help tonight." Off he went.

Most likely a total lie, but it had the desired effect.

"Tae kwon do?" Whiskey asked.

"Oh, my dad coaches boxing and stuff." I opened the door. "Gotta get to school."

"Yeah. Yeah."

Heh.

"Thanks again." He sauntered down the walk.

"See you soon."

He waved.

Boyfriend's Challenger pulled up to the curb. Whiskey kicked his bike to life as Boyfriend passed him. They nodded a greeting.

As soon as Boyfriend's face was past the rock star, it gave me a neon sign of what-the-heck? What an awesome friend.

Whiskey drove off.

"I was forced—against my will—to see his Dolce Gabbanas."

"Bro, you have. . ."

Not the point. "How's Gunner?"

He shrugged. "He'll live."

"Good. That's good."

He crooked a smile. "You don't have to lie, Foxtrot."

I held his arms. "No. No lie, dude. You care about him. I can get over myself at least enough to know that bad things happen to your friends and you feel bad. So, I'm glad he's going to live."

Hug. Duh.

He held me tight. "Thanks for visiting. That had to suck."

After a moment, we moved apart.

"So. Douchebag's in town?" he asked.

I laughed. "Learning a routine to dance with Tango."

Eyebrow raise.

I shook my head. "I know. I know."

"Why doesn't he dance with Juicy?"

"Because passing Katy over to dance with Juicy would make it all kinds of better, right?"

"Wow."

"Yeah. Wow."

He fidgeted. "Did this video shoot suddenly turn into a very bad idea?"

"I don't know. It could be fun." I knew Boyfriend wasn't as tied into it, either. "I mean, lots of fun. If we let it be fun. I just don't know." Deep breath. "You here to work out with Dad?"

He gave me a what-the-hell face. "I came to say thanks and see if you needed a ride to school."

I held up a hand. "Sorry. Brain dead." I glanced around. "Look. I'm disgusting. You mind being late for first period to hang out and gab while I shower? You can tell me how Gunner's doing while I scrub, and I bet I can guilt Dad into pancakes."

"Any chance Auntie Mac has kolaches?" Big smile. "And you can tell me what's up with the rock star. You listened to me all day, yesterday."

How much shit was he dealing with? And he could still smile like that? Man.

"Dude, there are *always* kolaches in this house."

School sucked.

After school, I made a beeline for Starbucks. Without serious caffeine, I would likely kill someone at practice, especially if Rock Star was there. I popped half a pain reliever leftover from my beating. The muscle relaxant would be just enough to smooth out the edges without making me groggy.

Woody held a fist out over the Starbucks counter. "*Hola.*"

Bump. "How'd you get here so fast after school?"

"Last period off," he said. "Lets me get in a couple of hours before practice."

"Word."

Fortunately, the line was short and within minutes I had a hot cup of steaming, caffeinated goodness in my hands. I turned around—

Gunner smiled at me from inches away.

The café slipped away into oblivion.

I lay on the concrete and every inch of my body hurt.

His fist hammered into my kidney. His breath smelled like popcorn. "I won't let you take Corey away from me," he whispered. His smile opened into a grin. . .

"Foxtrot?"

The real world rushed back screaming.

Woody stood beside me somehow instead of behind the counter.

Faint laughter echoed in my midbrain.

No. It wasn't real. It was a dream. Had to be.

"What the hell did you do?" The big dude in a uniform jerked Gunner away from me.

My lungs pumped for oxygen. Where'd my coffee go? It was in a puddle at my feet, and the counter was pressed into my back. I could barely catch my breath. My hands shook.

I'd remembered. That one moment had come back.

Gunner was still smiling. He sported a grey jumpsuit and handcuffs. Verdict must've come through.

The image of his blood-spattered face was burned into my brain, now. The blood had been mine.

I had to get out. I shoved money into Woody's hands. "S-sorry about the mess."

"*Se sente bien?*"

I pushed past some couple on their way in. The guy swore, but I was out the door before he could do more than that.

"That's it," Gunner's guard said. "I should've known better than to make a stop for you."

The door closed behind me, and I ran to the middle of the parking lot, as if I could somehow hide there while I caught my breath. It was the only waking memory I'd had, and now I couldn't shake it. The way shock had forced me to forget the assault made so much freaking sense all of a sudden.

"I didn't do anything." Gunner's voice reached me from across the parking lot. "I swear to God. I even smiled at him, for Christ's sake."

"You're a freaking saint, kid," the guard said. "No more stops."

Good. The asshole shouldn't have been allowed to stop at all on the way to wherever they were taking him. Some kind of juvy hall. Or prison.

I risked a look. They reached a van and the guard fumbled with his keys.

Gunner stared at his cuffs. Boyfriend had cried over those hands. The hands that had beat me senseless. Hands his parents cuffed so they could string him up in the middle of the winter and blast him with a power hose.

He just wanted a cup of coffee.

The coffee in the hospital was disgusting.

Coffee at the juvy prison was probably worse.

Did they even have coffee?

Shitstix.

Before I could think about it, I jogged over to the van. "Excuse me, sir."

The guard looked up and his hand went to his gun. Everyone knew about Gunner's football buddies, I guess.

I stopped and raised both hands. "He didn't do anything. In the Starbucks. He didn't do anything."

The guard's hand moved away from his gun, but he stared at me as if I was spouting Alien.

"He should get a decent cup of coffee," I said, "before you take him to wherever the hell it is he's going."

Gunner grinned a cocky grin. "Aww, are you suddenly sweet on me?"

I stared him down. "I fucking hate your guts you sociopathic bottom feeder, but I care about Corey and he cares about you. He'd want you to get a cup of coffee."

Gunner lost the smile. Seems that Boyfriend's name meant something to him. From the shit I'd suddenly remembered him whispering in my ear that night, I'd guess Boyfriend's name might mean a lot more to him than anyone would guess and more than he'd ever admit.

"Aren't you the kid he nearly killed?" the guard asked.

"One of them, anyway." I couldn't take my eyes off Gunner. "Can I talk to him a minute? Alone?"

"Kid, if you think I'm leaving you alone with him, you're insane." He crossed his arms. "I'm not sure who'd be more likely to kill who."

Whom.

I held Gunner's eyes. He was curious. Quiet.

"Can you just move a little bit away? He has a friend who wants me to relay a message."

"He does, does he?"

I finally turned to face the guard. "Look. I know he's a dick, but you don't need to be one, too, okay? I'll pay for coffee for both of you if you just give me five minutes." I recognized the guard from the hospital. "The guy who sat at this asshole's side the entire time is a friend of mine. Corey. I need to tell Gunner something for him. Please?"

Fortunately, this cop seemed cut from a different cloth than the deputies who used to run the town. He regarded me seriously, as if trying to judge my motives. He raised a hand. "Five minutes. And I don't want either of you to move."

"Thanks."

We were alone. What exactly did I need to say?

Gunner shifted. "Well, you got my attention." The half smile made a comeback.

Deep breath. "I just want you to know that Corey sat there, next to your bed, the entire time you were unconscious. He sat there holding your hand."

He lost the smile, then it was replaced with a different one, a sincere smile that kinda confirmed my suspicions about Gunner's feelings for Boyfriend.

"He even got permission to bring in his Xbox," I added, "and he played the old Three Stooges videos you like."

"Ha!"

"You are such a dick." I immediately regretted saying anything.

He held up a hand while he got control of his laughter. "I'm not making fun of him, asshole." He wiped his face. "No, fuck, it's just funny. I fucking *hate* the Three Stooges." He shook his head. "Leave it to Corey."

He met my gaze, which must not have been friendly because he lost the smile. "Look. He watches all these gay eighties TV shows, right? And he used to make me watch with him, and I made a joke about him growing a vagina if he watched one more episode of *Three's* fucking *Company*."

Okay, that was almost funny, except for the word choices.

That sincere smile returned. "He was so fucking hurt, I lied and told him I liked the Three Stooges so we'd have *something*... So from then on it was Three Stooges t-shirts for my birthday and DVD's and fucking *boxer shorts*. What dude buys another *dude* underwear?"

"Corey."

He tried to cross his arms but couldn't because of the cuffs, which reminded us both that this wasn't just two guys having a chat. He barked out another laugh. "Ah Jesus, what kind?"

I couldn't stop myself from smiling. "Twilight Zone."

He laughed. "See? That is so Corey." He tried to cross his arms again, gave a frustrated tug on the cuffs, then glanced up at the guard who had already moved forward a step. He lowered his hands. "Why the fuck are you being nice to me?"

"I'm not," I said quickly. "I'm being nice to Corey. If he'd done for me what he did for you? If he'd balled his eyes out in that hospital for twenty four fucking hours because he wasn't there to save me from myself? I'd want to know it so I could make damn sure I thanked him."

Gunner made that macho sensitive-guys-are-pussies face and opened his mouth to speak.

"Don't you fucking dare make fun of him," I snapped. "You care about him. I *know* you do."

His eyes grew extra guarded, as if worried about what I suspected.

To make absolutely sure no one could overhear me, I chanced the guard's wrath by moving closer. "Skip the macho bullshit, Gunner. I can tell you're compensating for something you don't want anyone to know."

His eyes narrowed, but he stopped breathing, too, so I could tell it was shock he was feeling.

"Get your fucking coffee and get the fuck out of town. And when you get wherever you're going, call Corey and give him a proper fucking thank you."

I started to move away but a hand snatched my wrist. An instant cold sweat broke out across my entire body, but the alarm drained away just as quickly. Fear clouded his eyes, and desperation. He opened his mouth, but no words came out. He closed his mouth and gritted his teeth. "I don't have phone. . . privileges."

"All right you two, make some space." The guard was on his way back in a hurry.

Gunner's whole face begged me, but he couldn't say the words.

"I'll tell him thanks." When I realized what fears he might have, I added, "*Just* thanks."

He gave one short nod.

"I said make some space," the guard bellowed.

Gunner threw my hand away. "I'm done with this faggot, anyway."

The guard stood between us. "Don't waste your time, Fox. You can't save this one."

"Just paying a debt, sir." I pulled out my wallet and grabbed a ten spot. "Get him his coffee and get him the hell out of town." I shoved it into the guard's hand and walked away. "And thank you, sir." Always be nice to the man with the gun if he does you a solid.

As I walked away, I finally noticed the sweat drenching my body and the hardcore shakes in my hands. Spots of light flashed in the air. I gulped to try and slow down my racing heart.

But it'd been for Boyfriend. So it was worth it.

I stopped at the corner, one hand on the brick wall to steady myself. For a split second, the world fell silent. Man, I had to be exhausted.

A flash of movement caught my attention.

There at the corner, half in shadow.

Twist.

He stared at me, motionless. The breath choked in my throat and bile coughed up into my mouth. I swallowed it. I spat. I looked up at the corner.

He was gone.

But he'd been there.

I swear to God.

Twist jerked awake and rolled off the couch. Son of a bitch. What was *that*? He'd been enjoying a nap after his afternoon workout. He sat up and pushed the hair out of his face.

It was like a dream, but not really. He'd seen Fox, standing on a street corner back in Dumass, somewhere near the Starbucks. For a second, he'd been there, standing across the street from his enemy, clear as day, like it was real.

Then, he'd been sucked out and thrown back into his body.

Son of a bitch.

Chapter Ten

I walked around for half an hour to get rid of the adrenaline. What the hell? Had I really seen him? I mean, had he really been standing there? Was it a hallucination?

By the time I reached the studio, I felt nothing but tired from the post-adrenal crash. No bike at the studio. Bonus. I even checked in the alley, where he'd hidden it last time.

If the cars parked in the lot were any indication, all the usual suspects were there already. Good. Immersing myself in a dance practice was exactly what I—

Holy crap, what the hell was that?

Two very distinct and recognizable voices screamed at each other in the studio. Tango and Juicy.

If I thought the fight I'd caused a few months back was bad, I was so-o-o wrong. I rushed inside.

They argued in speed Spanish. I had no idea what they were saying.

Boyfriend stood near the door. As soon as I hurried forward, he grabbed my arm. He shook his head. "Juicy just found out about the big duet with Whiskey. She says it should be her since she's the better dancer."

The two girls were nose to nose in the middle of the floor, yelling and gesturing. Every other member of the crew hid in the shadows. No one wanted a piece of that action. Everyone turned to me expectantly.

Surreal much? I was new guy, right? Why me?

Because I'd dealt with this kind of shit all the time on the circuit.

Yeah, it's also exactly why I left the damn circuit.

Why today?

K-pop slouched just the other side of Boyfriend, drinking a Monster. He finished his sip and held the can out to me. "You need this more than I do."

He had no idea. I hurried to his side and took the offered slice of heaven, chugged it. I grabbed him in a fast, tight hug and kissed his cheek. "I fucking love you, bro." Didn't care who might mock me for it later. It needed to be done. I handed him the empty can.

Deep breath.

I walked directly but casually over to the sound system, turned the volume all the way up, grabbed the mic, clicked it on and held it up to the speaker.

A deafening feedback shriek shut them the hell up.

Every eye stared at me as I reduced the volume and moved away from the speaker.

"Now that I have your attention. Juicy, please come outside and talk to me." No drama. No histrionics. I put down the mic and walked outside without a backward glance. When the door jingled, I turned to face her. "Okay. Here's the deal."

"Do you have any—"

I clapped once really loudly. "Shut the fuck up, you pathetic amateur."

She took a literal step back in stunned silence.

It was something one of my coaches did when Monika or I turned into drama queens. One thing I'd learned since moving to Dumass: haul out the stuff good coaches did that worked.

I could have done a whole peace, love and harmony spiel, but after my confrontation with Gunner, I didn't have any of that available. "Remember when I first found out you can dance and you said you didn't think you had anything to learn from me? Well, here's one thing:

the band hired us. The band will fire us and go on to a crew that's better than us and easier to handle." I let her think about that for a second.

"Whiskey picked Katy for the feature because he wants to have sex with her. If you think I like that at all, you're completely insane, but the band hired us and the band tells us what they want us to do. We have two options: do what they tell us or let them hire a different crew. So if you want to dance in a music video for Sony records, you will go back into that studio and say, 'I'm very sorry, Katy, for being a drama queen. Of course, I'm thrilled with whatever part I have in this project.'"

I didn't even try to read her reaction. I wouldn't have been able to do it if I'd tried. That's how fried I was.

"You want to do this for real? Well, here's your chance. I had a fucking world championship title, but when someone hired *me* to dance in a video, I was just as replaceable as Fruit of the Loom underwear. You have to get over yourself. Right now, you probably hate me more than you think you hate Tango, but when you land job after job because you're not a drama queen like my bitch of an ex, who cost us at least ten major contracts, you'll text me a thank you."

I didn't even wait for a response.

What could she say?

I walked back into the studio where everyone watched the door.

K-pop stood nearby, holding out another Monster. "You don't need to kiss me again, unless you really want to."

"Maybe later." I had to ride the adrenaline if any of my friends had a chance at landing this gig. Whiskey was bound to show up at some point, and if he found the dancers in a screaming match. . . well, he'd find someone else he wanted to fuck.

Just sayin'.

Juicy was about ten seconds behind me. She walked directly to Tango. "I'm very sorry, Katy, for being a drama queen. Of course, I'm thrilled with whatever part I have in this project."

Wow. Word for word. Impressive. A trifle lacking in sincerity, but whatever.

"Okay." Tango glanced at me, and I could tell she really wanted to know the secret behind my magic trick.

"Can I offer one suggestion?"

Everyone in the room sucked in a frightened breath.

Tango knew enough to recognize an olive branch. "Sure."

Juicy offered a hand. "If you and Whiskey do this trick on the opposite side of the crew it makes you stand out more, and when you roll in. . ." She rolled Tango into her side and paused. "Go for fan kicks. The first one is on your strong leg, and Whiskey can stabilize for the left, like this." Tango kicked and Juicy slid a hand onto Tango's ass to help raise the leg a few extra inches. "To the camera it just looks like he's grabbing your ass, so no one knows he's helping you." She released Tango and stalked past me to the waters. "Then the death drop."

Tango met my eyes. She shrugged. It was a good suggestion. And now Whiskey would be grabbing Tango's ass every practice. Stellar.

"I see what you just did there," I whispered to Juicy.

"Mmhm," she muttered. "Pray that's all I do. Like you said, when I'm working full time at Sony, *then* I'll thank you."

That wasn't exactly what I'd said, but she didn't seem *too* pissed. Good enough.

Boyfriend sat off in a corner. He kept checking his cell. Waiting for an update on Gunner? Maybe he didn't know the sociopath had been released from the hospital. I needed to relay my promised message.

Everyone sort of milled around, not sure what to do.

Guess who got to take charge? I clapped a few times. "Okay, folks, time to get some work done. You have sequences to learn, and we need to keep working the tricks." I gave Tango a one-armed hug and kissed the top of her head. "Can you get them started on the tricks? I need to do something."

I could tell she had a million questions, but after the miracle I'd worked with Juicy, I guess I had a few freebies in the trust department. She nodded and kissed me. Mmm. I wanted more of *that*.

"Okay *chicos*," Tango called out. "*Tenemos que sacar al trabajo. Ahora!*"

Woody ran up before I left the floor. "You okay?"

Oh yeah, Starbucks. "Yeah, fine." I grabbed his arm. "I'm really sorry about the mess."

He waved it off. "Yo, the number of *pendejos* who spill shit and *don't* tip me to clean it up?" He held out the ten-spot I'd given him. "Not necessary, but appreciated."

I ignored it. "Completely necessary. Thanks."

He nodded and dashed off to take his place on the floor.

I nabbed Boyfriend and led him outside.

"What's up?" he asked.

"I bumped into Gunner at Starbucks."

His eyes nearly exploded from his face. "What? He's out of the hospital?"

"His guard. . . ian bought him some coffee before they drove out to Gunner's. . . new residence." Didn't think I needed to mention the cuffs and the jumpsuit.

Boyfriend grinned and grabbed my arms. "So he's okay?"

No, he was a sociopathic nut job. "Seems to be. He wanted me to thank you for staying with him."

He pulled me into a bear hug. I was actually surprised he'd waited so long. An evil thought jumped to mind. "He was stoked that you brought the Stooges."

He jerked me out to arms' length, his face a perfect copy of the Comedy mask. "Really? He could tell?"

Didn't want to push my luck. "I sorta mentioned it to him, but he was pretty touched." Well, at least "touched" was the truth. Just a different definition. "Oh!" I pretended to just remember something. "I think he really misses his Three Stooges boxers."

He laughed. "Okay, I can totally send him some more."

Score. I know, petty.

Boyfriend frowned. "But I don't know where he is, where he'll go, now."

"Dr. Mike knows."

The smile relit his face and he grabbed me again. "Thank you so much for letting me know he's out of the hospital. If they're sending him home, he must be okay."

He wasn't going home and who knew if that boy would ever be anything close to okay, but Boyfriend was so happy I wasn't about to go into it. And, while the idea of Gunner opening a care package of Stooges underwear warmed my heart, I needed to keep this real for Boyfriend.

I held him out. "I don't know Gunner that well, but I think I can assume he's not the most sentimental guy you know."

Boyfriend chuckled. "You don't need to be psychic to get that."

"It was really, *really* important to him that I thank you."

His eyes teared up. He nodded. "Why'd you even talk to him?"

I released his arms. "I won't lie to you, Boyfriend. I don't like the guy, but. . ." But what? "But he's been your best friend your whole life."

He wiped his face. "I don't think he's my best friend, anymore." He wiped again. "I mean. . . I don't know."

Music started up in the studio, distracting me.

Boyfriend nudged me toward the door. "We should get back in there." He grabbed the door handle. "But is there any chance you have some time we can talk about all this Gunner stuff?"

That would not be at the top of my bucket list. I patted his shoulder as I passed into the studio. "Of course, man, that's what friends are for, right?"

"Fuckin' A."

Indeed.

A couple of hours later, we had some material solid enough for a run through. We'd been one dude extra since I'd joined, so I sat out to watch. They took their places, and I hit play.

Ephraim danced with Juicy, since she had the best control and could help him the most. He was sweating buckets and working hard. Tango danced with Retro, who was actually getting the moves pretty well. He'd also found some Charleston on his own, and she helped him with that as well.

K-pop was with Mono. She was so quiet, I barely knew anything about her and kept forgetting to ask how she'd come by her nickname. I knew that in Spanish, Mono meant 'monkey' but she was about as Hispanic as me.

Boyfriend was with Schilling since he was the only guy who could hold her weight. Not fat at all, but very muscular and tall.

That left Woody with Cosita. For everyone else's sake, I'd pretty much decided I needed to keep those two apart for the actual shoot. Their dancing wasn't great, but they *were* freaking hot and very expressive. The cameras were going to fall in love with both of them, and no one else would get any screen time.

To be honest, Tango and I shouldn't dance together, nor me and Juicy. But if the real reason for all this was to have fun with my friends, shouldn't I be allowed to dance with my girlfriend? I mean, isn't that the *definition* of fun? And shouldn't Juicy have a chance to really show off her mad skills?

The pairings all balanced pretty well, but was it fair to force the better dancers to help the folks who struggled? Damn it, trying to see things from someone else's perspective sucked when there were ten different perspectives on deck. And who could I talk to about all this? No one, really, since all my friends were involved.

Since I had the least to gain from the shoot, I really needed to be the one to sort out the couples, but wouldn't I end up making enemies no matter what I did?

The song ended. They struck poses.

Applause broke out behind me.

What the hell?

Oh. Whiskey. Joy.

"Looking good, y'all." He toed off his boots. "I see I picked the right folks for the job."

His folksy charm was utterly fake and worked perfectly. Everyone beamed and crowded around him while Tango made introductions. He did the whole say-someone's-name-back-to-them-so-you-remember-it thing. He shook hands with both of his.

Yuck. I felt dirty just watching him.

"We have everything lined up for winter break," he said. "We have a bus scheduled to arrive here first thing Saturday morning and it'll bring you back Monday night or Tuesday morning." He glanced at Ephraim. "Chanukah will be over. Christmas is still a few days off." He grinned. "And the roadies who celebrate Solstice are fine with being away from town since they'll get to celebrate out in the woods."

Schilling raised a hand. "Solstice?"

"It's the pagan holiday that celebrates midwinter." He glanced around in alarm. "I assumed no one here would be affected."

Tango laughed. "No pagans out here. Just Christians, Jews and atheists."

Ha, ha, ha.

Shitstix.

We ran the material a few times and explained how we planned to piece things together. I gave K-pop the floor to field the tech questions. He'd been correct about only needing a few phrases at a time. This opportunity *had* to work for him.

"One song's going to be mostly green screen," Whiskey told us. "We're going to shoot y'all one couple at a time and then layer everything into an actual airplane hangar with period planes to make it look like a huge space full of ghost dancers."

Everyone murmured in excitement. K-pop asked a number of questions and Whiskey seemed impressed with his knowledge.

"Tell you what," the singer said at last. "Let me get you in touch with Sarah, the director. She'll know more than me." He grinned. "We're thinking of doing some behind the scenes stuff, too. If you have a camera you could start filming practices."

K-pop glowed.

"No promises, but I can try to get you a credit."

K-pop broke for cool. "I'd appreciate that. Thanks."

"How many folks total?" Whiskey asked, looking around.

"Eleven dancers and two chaperones," Tango said.

"Chaperones? For what?" For the first time, the smarmy front man smile dropped off his face. It didn't bounce.

Tango stammered. "A few of us aren't eighteen. Without the chaperones, they can't go." She gestured at Boyfriend and me. "It's Boyfriend's mom and Foxtrot's dad."

Whiskey glanced from face to face, decidedly unhappy with the development. What was that about? I mean, of course it meant a couple more mouths to feed and heads to bed down, but he seemed more upset than that would merit.

K-pop and I exchanged a look. He seemed just as curious as me.

The rest of the crew fidgeted. Would the minors be forced to stay behind?

Then Whiskey's slick smile made a comeback. "No worries. We hadn't factored that in, but it makes sense." He seemed to notice the worry on the younger dancers' faces. "Not a problem."

Murmurs of relief washed over the crew. I filed his reaction away to discuss with K-pop. No one else seemed to notice.

The crew resumed practice.

"Are these couples set in stone?" Whiskey asked while we watched.

Oh, hey. There was my way to avoid pairing off my friends. "Nope. Any guy can dance with any girl. We want to make sure the video crew had as many options as possible."

He nodded. "You've done video before, right?"

"Yep."

Another nod. "Thanks again for letting me crash." He crossed his arms while we watched the crew dance. "As much as I like sleeping under the stars, your couch is a lot more comfortable."

"No worries."

"Hope I didn't shock your dad too much."

I gave him room to elaborate.

"He seemed surprised to find me making coffee when he came into the kitchen." He shrugged. "I forgot to put on pants. We don't worry much about them in our apartment."

I laughed. "That would not be a problem."

His face filled with curiosity.

"When my aunt's out of town, the house is a total man cave. Pants not needed."

He laughed.

Before he could keep chumming me up, I moved to the dance floor. "Okay, folks. You're done."

No one had to be told twice.

All I wanted to do was go home or, even better, take Tango home with me, but there would be time for that later. If Whiskey had his heart set on dancing, he needed to start learning choreo.

And I was definitely going to be there for the entire session.

Meh.

I went to Tango for a hug, which she granted, but her face as we pulled apart told me she thought I was acting jealous.

"It's not that," I whispered. "Just been a crappy couple of days."

Her face showed her concern. "What's going on?"

"Later. No emergencies, just crappy."

She hugged me tight. "He'll be gone tonight, so you can tell me all about it tomorrow. Okay?"

And I felt a million times better just for hearing that.

Although it did bring up a point.

After the hug, I turned to Whiskey. "You need a place to crash tonight?"

"Nah." He stretched his arms. "I really need to drive back. Thanks for the offer. Maybe next time."

I managed to avoid reacting.

Of course, he'd be back to practice more.

Duh. Didn't mean I had to be happy about it.

"Next time. Absolutely." As long as the alternative was him bedding down at Tango's house, he could run around *naked* in my living room for all I cared. It'd be fun to watch Auntie Mac chase him across the front yard with a broom.

So it was time to work on the big duet. "I have a routine from state last year that should work for the two of you."

Tango gave me a quick kiss. Probably her way of letting me know she was grateful for the help. K-pop, Boyfriend and Schilling headed for the door, but the rest of the crew lounged around toweling off and satisfying curiosity.

I lunged onto my left foot and held my left hand across my body to her. "Press line to the right and give me your left hand." That meant she held my hand and extended her hip away from me to create a connection like a rubber band pulled taut. Press line. My right hand went to her hip. "Figure four as you pull away. Right hand around and out when you set for the spin."

She nodded, took my hand and pulled into the press line, bringing her left foot up like a flamingo—that was the "figure four." Her right arm swept an arc and landed on her hip and she jutted it out in that line I had enjoyed since I met her. We wound her up for the spin, she hit four turns, we reconnected and rock step.

"Ta-daa." I turned to Whiskey. "You can make as much of it as you want."

I offered my hand to Tango and she reset with me.

"Casual." We redid the same move, but I relaxed it and played it as if I couldn't be bothered to care. Ephraim and Woody hooted.

"To extra-ballroom."

Another run through, and I went over-the-top stylized. Mono and Cosita clapped for that one.

"I'll stick to the casual." Whiskey moved closer and went into a badly balanced lunge. I adjusted his line so he could shift better.

"I figured, but I'll show you all the options until I get a better read on your style."

Tango took her place. "Okay, bring your weight to your right foot to start," she told Whiskey. "You'll need to shift over to your left foot when we go into the press line."

"Press line?"

"Hold my weight," she said. When he was stable, she leaned away from him. "When I give you my weight like this, it creates a stretchy look. That's called a press line." She turned to me. "Foxtrot."

I took a place directly in front of Whiskey, and Tango took the step forward to dance with me. She eased us into and out of the line so we looked all rubber-bandy. And yes, "rubber-bandy" is a technical dance term.

"Like that."

He picked up fairly quickly. We taught him the first few bars of the duet that way, and my main goal was to get a read on his ability before deciding just how much I'd have to simplify the routine.

No, that's not ego. Remember, I was world champion. Expecting this singer to perform exactly the same routine would be like asking me to play "Freebird" on his guitar.

If he played guitar. Whatever.

Tango and I took a water break. "He picks up fast," she said. "But I think you'll need to take the rest of it down a couple of notches."

I agreed. "K-pop level or Woody?"

She glanced over at Whiskey. "Try for K-pop, but can you have a couple of simplifications for the second half just in case?"

I nodded. And smiled. "You're sexy when you're all professional like that."

She grinned and leaned into me. "We do work pretty well together, don't we?"

I lowered my voice. "We play pretty well together, too."

She nudged me and took her water back to the floor. One sparkle from her eyes and the crap from the day drained away.

Time to teach him the group material, which the crew had seen, so the last of them headed for the door. Whiskey picked up the next part a lot more easily, which was only logical, since it was designed to include even the more dance-challenged guys.

He especially liked the section Juicy had flipped. *Especially*, especially the ass-grabbing part.

"I don't think I quite have the leg assist yet," he said more than once. "Can we run that part again?"

I couldn't tell if Tango's smirk was fake annoyed or real annoyed. It pissed me off to think she might be enjoying the move as much as he obviously did. Bastard.

While they marked run-through after run-through there wasn't much for me to do but sit and watch. Of course, I didn't mind playing chaperone and had no intention of taking my eyes off them.

Him.

Off of him.

How did I get into a dance studio with no door? The room was square and mirrors covered all four walls. The floor was parquet and the ceiling black. I'd never danced there. What the hell?

A long, low chuckle startled me, and I spun. I could see the entire room.

I was alone, but that had sounded like it was right behind me.

I stared into the mirrors.

There. In one reflection.

Twist stood shirtless in white tights as if he knew ballet. But he was darker than I remembered, his hair longer. He actually had muscles.

I glanced around the floor. It stood empty.

He moved closer in his mirror. "It's all a matter of perspective, isn't it?"

He raised one hand.

K-pop appeared, spinning endless pirouettes in a tutu like a doll in a music box.

He waved the other hand.

Whiskey stood in fourth position wearing nothing but a dance belt, one hand extended. Katy, in boy shorts and a sports bra spun chaînés *across the mirrors to him. He dipped her to the floor and climbed on top.*

Juicy and Cosita, both completely naked, made love in another mirror.

"All right, Twist, what the hell's your point?"

He moved toward me, stepped out of the mirror and onto the real wood floor. All his movements said he was a dancer, a real dancer, from a studio in New York.

"I don't need to torture you, do I?" He laughed. "You'll do fine on your own." He gestured. "This is all from your own mind. I have nothing to do with it."

Katy and Whiskey made love in the same scene as Juicy and Cosita. K-pop and Kiki joined them. Then Boyfriend and Theresa. A massive orgy of all my friends.

All my friends but me.

Twist laughed. "You hardly need me to torture you, Fox, you fucked up shit."

"Foxtrot?"

I jumped awake. "I'm not drooling." I wiped my mouth to be sure. My eyes darted around the studio.

Tango settled into her hip. "Go home. You need to sleep." She was fully dressed, and so was Whiskey. No sex at all.

I sat up. "I'm fine, really. Wanna show me how it's going?"

"It's going fine." She grabbed my hand and pulled me to my feet. "We have at least another hour here, and your snoring is distracting." She hugged me and we kissed. "Go home."

Well, not a lot of wiggle room there. If I refused, I'd look like I didn't trust her.

Which I did.

Of course. Completely.

I forced a smile. "Don't have too much fun without me."

She kissed me again and pushed me toward the door.

Whiskey waved and smiled way too innocently for me to trust him at all.

And the door closed behind me.

It was just a dream. At worst, it was Twist torturing me in my dreams. I couldn't let myself start believing they were true. . . or, what? Prophetic?

Where the hell was Auntie Mac's car?

Shit. It was with Auntie Mac. . . in Austin.

And I'd planned on Tango driving me home.

My chin dropped onto my chest. Damn it. Well, it wasn't that long a walk.

"Hey, dude." K-pop's voice startled me. He pushed out of a relaxed lean against his car and walked over.

"Dude, what are you still doing here?"

We met in the middle of the lot. "Not still," he said. "Again. I visited Kiki and was driving past on my way home. I saw that Whiskey was still here and figured you'd need a ride." He grinned. "Don't worry, I wasn't going to wait more than a few minutes."

"Okay, let it be officially recorded that you rock, but one kiss a day is enough."

He laughed. "Hai."

"Thanks."

I followed him to the car. "So any new firsts with Kiki?"

He huffed as if he were offended. "A gentleman never kisses and tells."

"So, no, then."

"Nah. Nothing new tonight. Which is not to say that nothing happened."

The fist bump was so obviously necessary neither of us had to look at the other to make it connect. Pull back. Finger wiggle.

I almost nodded off twice on the short ride to my house.

He pulled up to the curb and turned to me. "So I'm guessing all you want to do is pass out right now, but you know if you need to talk. . ."

"I know, dude. I know." I gathered my shit and grabbed the door handle. "I don't deserve you."

"Indeed you do not." He patted my shoulder as I got out.

"Tomorrow. We'll talk about it tomorrow." I held his gaze solid so he knew I meant it.

He nodded. "Tomorrow."

I made my way into the house. . . something, something, Dad was there. . . he said something. . . something, something. . . walking upstairs. . . something. . . passing out. . . must sleep.

Zzzzz.

Chapter Eleven

A woods at night, but not like the woods in Texas. It was like woods I'd seen in movies, huge pine trees and thick, thick underbrush. The kind of place where you had to stay on the trail or you'd end up a statistic. The trail was lit with a silvery glow, enough to see but not enough for details.

"Kill, kill, kill," a voice sang softly. "Die, die, die."

I spun. No one.

"Kill, kill, kill. Die, die, die."

I spun again. It had come from a completely different direction.

"Kill, kill, kill. Die, die, die."

The brush to my right shivered and shook.

I ran. My heart beat fast and the air bruised my lungs, but I ran as fast as I could.

Footsteps, loud and crashing!

I glanced back. A huge football player, a linebacker in full uniform and helmet. He ran after me with an axe raised in one hand.

Fuck! I ran faster.

The helmet masked his face.

"Kill, kill, kill. Die, die, die."

The woods opened suddenly, and I sprang forward.

The path dropped out from under my feet.

I grabbed a branch, barely able to stop myself from falling down a cliff so high I couldn't see the bottom.

The football player stopped a few feet away and laughed.

I knew that laughter.

Gunner.

Then it changed, the tone of the laughter changed. The linebacker lowered the knife and yanked the helmet from his head. Twist. Of course. He dropped the helmet.

"This one's fun," he said. "But this. . ." He held up the knife. "I have a better idea."

The knife flashed as he sliced his arm down once. When the arm pulled back up, it held a chainsaw instead. He grabbed it with both hands, and it roared to life.

"Now this *is what I'm talking about!"*

Holy shit!

He skirted one edge of the wide path, almost as if giving me room to run. I hovered along the edge of the cliff, then made my way to the other side of the trail.

"Go ahead," he said. "Run, rabbit. Run!" He jabbed the chainsaw at me and it roared louder.

I ran. But the path narrowed. Tree roots snaked across it. Rocks pushed up through the soil. My foot hit something, and I flew five feet before skidding to a stop on the rough path.

"Gotcha!"

His voice sounded so close, I rolled to my back.

He stood directly over me, revving the chainsaw, grinning from ear to ear.

Literally.

Fuck me.

It was a dream. It was only a dream.

He raised the chainsaw over his head.

If I tried to get up, he'd kill me. If I stayed there, he'd kill me.

I lay on my back at his feet. If I could wake myself up, I might escape.

I knocked my head against the ground.

He revved the chainsaw and waved it manically.

I knocked my head against the ground a second time.

"Kill, kill, kill. Die, die, die."

I raised my head one more time and crashed it backwards onto the hard, hard ground.

Lights flashed in my eyes.

"Ethan? Ethan? Ethan!"

I fought my way to consciousness. "I'm not drooling."

Crap, my head hurt. I sat up.

Dad sat beside me on the bed, one hand holding my shoulder. The moment I touched the back of my head, he forced me to lean forward and checked me out. "You were slamming your head on the headboard."

It felt like it. "It was a nightmare. I was trying to wake up."

He pulled my hands away from my head. "Don't mess with it. There's a bump, but you're not bleeding." He stared at me. "You're not supposed to be able to do that."

"Do what?"

"When you dream, the brain releases a chemical to paralyze your body so you don't go through the motions of your dreams."

He must've been googling.

"You said it was okay to talk to Mike," he explained. "He told me that."

Okay, so I shouldn't be able to move in my dreams. What did that mean? "What about sleepwalkers?"

He shrugged and raised his hands in defeat.

And what about my tumble into the pool?

I lay down. What time was it? 10 a.m.? Crap! I jumped up and swung my legs out from under the blankets.

Dad placed a hand on my chest. "Whoa there, speedy. I called you in sick for the morning." He gently forced me to lay down and drew the covers over my chest. Huh. I'd stripped to my skivvies in my sleep. "I can call in the rest of the day if you like." The hand stayed on my chest.

"But I just missed a day."

"And you aced the history test, so I'm not worried about grades." He settled himself more comfortably. "I'm worried about *you*. The way you came in last night? In all your years of coaching and prepping for comps, I have never seen you look so much like the walking dead." He rubbed my chest again. Call me a little kid, but it felt nice. "And this nightmare thing worries me. We never took the time to do the googling."

"It's been a pretty hellacious couple of days." I dug deeper into the covers.

"Hellacious, huh?"

I propped my hands behind my head. "Yeah, the word choice is entirely your fault."

Someone knocked on the door frame. Dr. Mike held up a steaming mug of coffee. "May I come in?"

"If that's for me you can."

He entered the room and held the cup out.

I pushed up to a sitting position and tucked the blanket around my waist. "Oh man, why is everyone being so nice to me?" I held both hands out for the mug. "Not that I'm complaining, but at some point I'm going to have to pay all this back, right?" Oh my God, I worshipped that coffee.

"You did me a huge favor the other day, Ethan. I still owe you."

"I can live with that." Should I push my luck? "Pancakes?"

He was about to move away, but Dad snaked an arm around his waist and held him there. Awww.

"Another time. I have to get to work." Dr. Mike ruffled my hair. Hm. Seems the touching barrier had officially faded. Nice.

Dad rose and Mike offered a quick peck, but Dad drew him closer, and it lasted long enough I decided to be obnoxious by clearing my throat. Yay for Dad and all, but I had to give the old men some shit, right?

Mike chuckled and made his escape to the door. "Take care, boys. I'll see y'all tonight, after work." He met my eyes. "We'll figure things out."

I nodded, and off he ran.

"Was that massive PDA for me or him?" I asked as soon as his steps faded down the stairs.

Dad sat again. "Him. It's still weird for him that you're so okay with it."

Really? "Because he's a dude?" I held out the coffee.

"Don't be stupid." Dad took the mug and set it on the dresser for me. "Because most kids have issues with parents dating. Don't forget, you never had a second parent. For you, it's no big deal. Most kids have the memory of a second parent that anyone new has to contest with."

"Huh. Bonus for you, right?"

"Meh."

Now that I knew I didn't need to go to school, the exhaustion caught up with me. I slid down under the covers. How much could I milk it? "Dad. I've had to be really mature and shit the last couple of days, and I'm afraid this weekend trip is going to be a nightmare." I curled up with my head on his knee like when I was a little kid. "Any chance we can pile up on the couch and watch action movies all day." I looked up to see if my cute son routine was working. "Oh, and eat ice cream. I really want ice cream."

Dad stroked my hair. "You haven't curled up to me like this since you were ten."

"Is it working?"

"Of course." He rose up so quickly I dropped rather abruptly onto the mattress. "And Mac's gone all day, so you don't even need to put on pants."

Stellar. Holy rocking stellar!

"You okay?" Tango had called several times before I checked my messages. Made me feel guilty and warm and tingly at the same time.

"I'm fine. Dad called me in sick and let me sleep late."

"Wait. Your dad called you in sick and you're fine?" Her concern was nice. "What aren't you telling me?"

Sigh. How much did I want to tell her over the phone? "Have you heard about Gunner?"

Silence stretched out a few seconds. "Yes. What the hell does that have to do with you?"

"Boyfriend means a lot to me, and I've been spending a lot of time with drool on my chest."

"And?"

Sigh. "And I fell asleep on the pool floatie and almost drowned."

She laughed at first but stopped abruptly. "Wait. Seriously? How close to almost?"

Might as well admit it. "Although I don't remember it, K-pop has now also kissed me."

"What?"

"I was lucky. He happened to stop by when I fell in, and he had to mouth to mouth me back to life."

"Jesus, Foxtrot. Why do I not know about this?"

"Honestly? It wasn't that big a deal, and you have everything you need to deal with on this video."

Silence stretched out between us.

"Have I really been *that* preoccupied?"

Thank God she was the one to say it.

"I'm fine, Tango." Please buy my redirection. I would never, *ever* find a correct response to her question. "I'm just bonding with Dad today over ice cream and action flicks."

"Should I stop by after school?"

Wow. She was asking, but her tone told me she didn't want to. Just. . . wow.

"Nah, I'm fine. You'd hate it. You can't stand movies with all that macho bullshit, remember?

She chuckled. "It's just that me and the girls were going to meet after school to come up with some choreo."

And Boyfriend had nailed it.

"Yeah? Sweet. Me and the guys are working on some stuff, too."

The silence that followed was both brief and frightening.

"That's cool. When do I get to see it?"

Goosebumps covered my skin. "We're working on some acro stuff you could help with. I'll let you know when we're going to show it to Retro, Woody and Ephraim."

"That is awesome."

The rest of the conversation was lame and superficial. It was obvious she was afraid we'd put together a routine that would steal the glory from the girls. On the one hand, I should make sure the guys' routine was basic enough to avoid upstaging the girls. On the other, I owed it to those guys to show them off as best I could.

I was going to Hell no matter what I did. How awesome was that?

Please recognize my extreme sarcasm.

K-pop stopped by that night to join the dudes' party at the nightmare factory.

Dr. Mike showed up after his normal work day, at seven or so.

We sat around the kitchen table with bowls of ice cream, because ice cream had been promised.

"So." I pushed chocolatey goodness around the bowl. "The ice cream makes the whole Twist-must-be-trying-to-kill-me-in-my-dreams thing seem kinda melodramatic on my part, doesn't it?"

They exchanged awkward glances.

I raised a hand. "Not criticizing."

K-pop was the first to speak up. "You know I believe you."

Stellar. I nodded.

Dr. Mike glanced at all present parties. "We all have an open mind, Ethan. We're all here because we love you."

Yeah, even Dad did a double take.

Dr. Mike gave him an annoyed glare. "What? You're the only one who gets to be Lifetime Channel for Women and Gay Men?"

Everyone laughed at that.

Nice.

So.

We pulled out laptops and tablets. Any idea how many internet sites pertained to our search? Billions. Seriously, billions.

Did you know that there are sites where you can pay someone—with a credit card—to cast spells for you? And they'll read tarot for you and cast astrology charts, too. Wow.

At one point we took a break from the googling while Dr. Mike, in his guest-starring role as Dr. Lopez, asked me to describe every detail I could remember about the dreams.

When I reached the dream from the studio where everyone was boinking on the parquet, K-pop shook his head. "I haven't even had sex with her in real life. I get more action in your head than in the real world. How unfair is that?"

"The dreams are pretty standard, Ethan," Dr. Mike said. "Drowning, exposure, sex." He shrugged. "And some of them are only natural after everything with Twist. Being chased. Seeing your loved ones killed."

"But they're so much more real than my normal dreams."

He swallowed a spoonful of ice cream. "I'm not an expert on dreams, Ethan. I know that intentionally banging your head like that is uncommon, and almost drowning? Extremely rare, but not unknown. It's called REM sleep behavior disorder."

Somehow the fact that it had a medical name made it seem more real and less spooky. "So you don't think Twist is trying to Freddy Krueger me."

"I can't say for certain he's not," he admitted. "But I *can* give you a more scientific explanation for everything you've experienced without resorting to something paranormal." He glanced at Dad, who remained nearly expressionless. "Let me talk to a few colleagues who'll know more about the disorder. I'm old enough that I'm skeptical of what I find online." He pushed his bowl away. "In the meantime, you shouldn't sleep alone."

I raised an eyebrow.

K-pop coughed into his hand. "Tango." He grinned and started gathering his stuff.

Dr. Mike rolled his eyes. "I am not prescribing the gender or identity of your babysitter."

Besides which, she was probably still working with the girls.

I swallowed ice cream. "Um, dude?"

K-pop looked up at me, then shoved his pack to one side. "Hey, Foxtrot? Any chance I can stay over? It's really late."

Stellar. "Thanks."

He waved it off. "No worries."

Of course, I could sleep in Dad's room, but I kinda wanted Dr. Mike there, too. You know, just in case? I wasn't about to sleep in the same room with the two of them due to the fact that there *were* in fact certain boundaries I didn't want to cross, but it didn't seem fair to kick Dr. Mike to the couch.

K-pop and I cleaned up the kitchen, then climbed up to my room. We were already in sweats, so I grabbed the air mattress.

"Um."

I regarded him in the faint light from my bedside lamp.

He hugged himself self-consciously. "If I'm really here to protect you, I should just. . ." He waved at my bed. "I might not wake up if I'm on the floor."

The bed was queen-sized. Built for two, anyway.

I nodded. I would never, *ever* be able to repay him. "So. . . I'm known to strip down in my sleep. Any chance you can pretend that's not creepy if I do?"

"I think I can cope." He climbed into bed. "I'm here to keep an evil bastard from killing you in your dreams. I think I can cope with sleep-stripping."

"Cool." I slipped in beside him, took half a tablet of the muscle relaxant and flicked off the light. One, two, three. . . Deep breath.

"K-pop?"

"Yeah?"

"You know what Dad said before, about you being part of the family, now?"

Long silence. "Yeah?"

"Doesn't even cover it in the slightest."

I felt a tap on my back. "'Night, bro."

"Good-night, brother."

Chapter Twelve

Twist stood in an empty lot in the nightmare world. He'd been practicing, and he had the world building pretty much down. He had his fake Ethan back, which was cool. And that freaky wow in the dance studio with lesbian sex had been. . . double wow! All he needed to do was figure out how to get into Fox's head.

Mary assured him it was possible, which just made him angry because she was so condescending about it. Bitch. Sometimes the whole natural born magic thing was a pain. It made things easier. . . once he figured out how to do it. The figuring out sometimes sucked.

Anyway, he could whine about it later. He already knew what he wanted to do with this world. It'd be classic!

The parking lot stood empty. Twist concentrated and created an old-fashioned motel to one side. He made the neon sign red and blinking. He concentrated harder and a high hill grew out of the grassy field and an enormous old house built itself at the top. A long stone stairway wandered its way down the hill to the back of the motel.

He lit one window of the old house and created a silhouette to break the feeble light. Nice.

He added a staticky crackle to the neon sign. Perfect.

He raised both arms to the sky and clouds boiled into existence. The clouds released with a thunderous crash and a cold, steady rain poured down.

All he needed was. . .

And there he was. Fox. Right on cue.

Okay, how to make this scene perfect? He had it. An enormous knife appeared in one hand. He stalked toward the son of a bitch and raised the knife high over his head. "Mother says I need to kill you."

Fox wiped the rain from his face. "This is a dream! You can't hurt me, you pathetic dick. It's just a dream!"

What? He didn't want Fox to say that. What the hell? Whatever. He started toward Fox again. "I always obey my mother."

Fox glanced around. He looked toward the old-fashioned metal chairs that sat near the office door for ambiance.

He vanished.

What the hell?

He reappeared beside the motel, a chair raised overhead.

"Hey," Twist called, "that's not fair."

"Fair? What the hell is fair about any of this?" Fox stomped toward Twist, chair over his head.

Twist stumbled a couple of steps backward. What the shit? This was not going the way he'd planned it. He wiped an arm across his face and squinted through the rain.

Son of a bitch!

Was it possible?

"Fox? Is that really you?"

"Who else would it be?"

The knife fell to Twist's side. "You mean. . . I'm in your dream? For real?"

"No shit." He brandished the chair as if it might do some good. "Wasn't that the plan?"

If that was really Fox, everything changed.

Twist shook water out of his hair. He looked up into the pouring rain. "This is great for the mood and all. . . but it's cold and wet."

The world shifted. Twist took them into the house at the top of a very long flight of stairs. Best scene in the movie. Well, after the naked shower scene. He shook himself and the water soaking him dried instantly.

"Better."

Fox's clothes dripped on the carpet. "So you've been messing with my dreams and didn't even know it was working?"

How much should he admit? "I thought I was having some vivid and wonderful dreams, your dad eaten by vultures, you drowned by hot naked girls." He rubbed his hands together. "Juicy and Cosita lesbian sex. I totally turned that into a three-way when you vanished."

"But we found that occult stuff in your house," Fox whined. "What was all that?"

He was about to brag about everything he'd learned since the desert witch, but, no. Better to leave him guessing. "Shit didn't work on you at Corey's farm, did it? Why the hell should I believe it was working now?" He raised his hands. "So this is really you?"

Fox stepped back toward the incredibly long staircase behind him.

"Hot damn!" Twist slammed the center of Fox's chest as hard as he could.

The son of a bitch toppled backward into the air and closed his eyes.

He vanished.

"Well, shit." Twist sighed. It had seemed a little too easy, but what the heck. Worth a try.

He looked around. "Cool place though."

And now he knew he could get into Fox's dreams.

Bonus round!

Hands shook me. "Wake up, Ethan,"

I lay at the top of the stairs, tied up in a knot with K-pop, who also held my t-shirt in both hands. Dad and Dr. Mike filled the hallway a few feet away. Huh. Didn't even know Dad owned pajamas.

K-pop moved one hand to hold the back of my head. "You awake?"

I nodded and looked over his shoulder. The reality of the hard wooden stairs I'd almost met with incredible force and velocity penetrated my muddled brain. I shoved myself away from them. "Holy shit."

K-pop followed along. "You're okay, bro. You're fine."

My eyes flashed from him to the stairway that had nearly killed me. "Did I try to kill myself?"

He shook his head. "No. Not really. You were asleep. I don't think you even knew where you were. What were you dreaming?" He grabbed my shoulders. "Ethan. Don't freak out."

My stomach lurched. I pawed my way past him and dashed for the bathroom. Not my finest moment, letting K-pop and Dr. Mike watch me puke. At least I hadn't stripped.

When I came up for air, Dad knelt beside me, rubbing my back. He held out a glass of water. I rinsed and spit. I drank some water.

"Can everyone pretend y'all didn't just watch me blow chunks?"

Dad helped me to my feet.

"Does that happen every time you dream?" Dr. Mike asked.

"Well, every nightmare is pretty puke worthy." I filled the glass.

He touched Dad's shoulder. "May I?"

Dad stepped aside to allow Dr. Mike closer.

"May I touch you?" he asked. His eyes were so intent.

I nodded. What the?

His hands felt cool and gentle on my face. He stared deeply into my eyes and turned my head one way and then the other. He flicked the light off and then on. He checked my pulse. "Please open your mouth."

I did. He studied me.

He took a deep breath. "I need to ask you a couple of extremely personal questions. We might want the others to leave."

I shook my head, settling my gaze on K-pop's face. Dad was a given and my friend had saved my life twice, now. "I have no secrets from either of them."

Dr. Mike nodded. "Okay." He removed his hands from my face. "What are you on?"

"What?" I glanced from him to Dad. "What am I *on*? Like, am I taking drugs?" I searched Dad's face. "Dad. Come on. You know me."

Dad's face perfected the blank expression.

Dr. Mike touched my arm with one hand. "Your eyes are dilated and unresponsive, Ethan. Your pulse is erratic. It's not natural. There's something in your system."

"Wait." I scrambled for the bedside table and brought him the bottle. "It's just pain meds. They have a muscle relaxant. I take them once in a while to relax. It's not like drugs or anything." My heart raced. My breath came in gasps. "It's legal. I just didn't want to waste them."

A warm golden glow enveloped Dr. Mike.

I stumbled away from him and bumped into Dad. He was glowing, too. What the hell? Was I still asleep?

My eyes darted to K-pop. He glowed with a warm golden halo, as well.

Dr. Mike held his hands out. "What do you see Ethan?"

"It's. . . you're glowing."

He nodded. "Calm down. You're fine. No one is mad at you. Your Dad's right there. He always protects you, doesn't he?"

Dad's hands gripped my arms. "What's going on, Mike?"

"Everything is fine." He held up the bottle. "Where'd you get these?"

"Dr. Cherkasky. They were prescribed after the assault. I swear to God. Pain pills."

"I believe you."

"Then why are you talking to me like I'm a fucking junkie?"

"I'm sorry." He opened the bottle and exchanged a glance with my dad that I didn't understand. He examined the whole thing, dipped a pinky into the bottle and licked it. "What happened to the label?"

"Oh. . . that's why I had extra. Remember the night Tango was kidnapped? I jumped in the pool with my clothes on? That bottle was in my pocket. So the label got washed out. After the whole crazy mess, my clothes were still out on the back porch over the bar."

Wait.

Seriously. Wait.

That was the night I'd outed Juicy. The night I'd seen angry lasers of death shoot out of her eyes. The night I'd had a crazy dream about a dance competition. "Holy shit."

"The night you were a supervillain?" he asked.

I could only nod.

"You saw things that night, too, didn't you? Things you can't explain? Auras?"

I nodded again.

Dr. Mike looked over my shoulder at Dad. "There's some kind of powder on these pills, Lucky. We need to get him to a hospital. . . immediately."

The motherfucker poisoned me.

Dr. Cherkasky wasn't even certain what Twist had used. The bottle was on its way someplace fancy along with several samples of my blood. Dad and K-pop sat with me in a room that smelled of bleach and piss at the same time.

"Drink some more water, Ethan." Dad held a bottle in my face.

"I'm going to wash away as it is, Dad."

Dr. Mike entered the room and sat on a stool in front of me. "You're going to be fine, Ethan. I talked the doctors into letting you go home." He must have understood my confused expression. "Small town, buddy. This is exciting for them. They wanted to keep you for study." He glanced around. "I didn't tell anyone about the dreams, and I recommend you keep that info to a tight circle. Keep drinking water to wash out your system and. . ." He glanced at K-pop.

"I'm camping with him until he kicks me out."

Dr. Mike nodded. He touched my knee with one hand. "This stuff should be out of your system in a day or two."

I grabbed his hand. "Dr. Mike. . . Mike. Thank you for keeping it quiet." What kind of nightmare could this ordeal have turned into?

All that time I thought I was being attacked by magic or some stupid thing, and it was just plain, old-fashioned drugs.

"I'm just glad you're going to be okay." He squeezed my hand before releasing it.

We drove home, and K-pop and I piled back into bed.

There was no way to thank him. He'd saved my damn life. . . again.

"Dude?"

He rolled over to face me in the semi-darkness. "I ask one favor."

"Anything."

He smiled. "Don't let Tango kill the dudes' routine, and make sure the other guys get their fair share of screen time."

I held his gaze while I processed that. Compared to what I owed him, it was nothing. "You believed me even though I was totally full of shit. All that magic was just a hallucinogen in my blood." Deep breath. "I can't *ever* repay you." I held up a fist. "But I will do everything in my power to try."

He grabbed my fist and squeezed it, then rolled over to give me his back. "If you strip naked I'm posting the photos on Tumblr."

Ha.

Wait. He was joking, right?

Chapter Thirteen

So with one situation essentially resolved, another had to rear its ugly head without an actual moment of peace for me, right? Well, duh.

"Foxtrot!" Boyfriend's voice woke me far too early the next morning. "You are not going to believe—"

"Hey, Boyfriend." K-pop's voice in the bed beside me explained why Boyfriend had floundered.

I pressed my face into the pillow.

"Hey, guys. Um. I'm going to get some coffee." Subdued is the only word to describe his voice. Off he ran, thump, thump, thump down the stairs, which only the night before had nearly killed me.

"Shit." I rolled onto my back.

K-pop giggled. "You think he actually thinks we, you know. . ."

I threw off the blanket and dropped my feet to the floor. "Hard to say what he thinks." Still fully clothed, so that was a bonus. "Um. Give us a minute before you come down?"

"I need to pee anyway." He jumped out of bed. "How'd you sleep?"

"Good. I slept good." I met his eyes. "Thanks."

His hair looked like a porcupine had raped a hedgehog. I stifled a laugh.

He lifted one side of his mouth and patted his hair with one hand. "I shall also shower, if that's okay."

I glanced around for my cell.

"Seriously?" He crossed his arms. "I save your life. . . *again*, and you want to Instagram my flocculent shame?"

"Without a doubt." I also wanted to google flocculent.

He shucked his shirt and threw it at me.

I dodged it. "All kidding aside. . ."

He raised a hand. "Don't set aside the kidding, brother. Never set aside the kidding." He escaped into the bathroom and ran water into the shower.

I gave him some privacy by heading downstairs to deal with Boyfriend. Who was taking care of business with the coffee pot. When I stumbled into the kitchen, he beamed an incredibly exaggerated smile.

"Morning, bro. Coffee should be ready in a minute."

"You know we're not having sex, right?" Why be subtle?

He stared at me wide-eyed and silent. Would that even bother him?

"I slept in the same bed with you at the hospital," I reminded him.

He deflated. "I know. It's not that." He busied himself with coffee filters and fresh roasted beans. "That wouldn't bother me." He looked up. "I hope you know that."

I did know that. I waited.

He turned to me with that pissed-in-his-master's-shoes expression I hadn't seen in a while. "Something's wrong with you, isn't there? Something you don't want me to know about."

Oh God. He was upset because there was something I was keeping from him, but that K-pop knew about.

Tango was right. We were lesbians.

"Boyfriend. . ." I went right up to him. "Corey." Having friends was super awesome, but could I have just one day that didn't belong on Lifetime? "Yes. I've been going through some shit. The *only* reason you don't know about it is all the Gunner crap you're dealing with. I didn't want to add to your. . . stress. So K-pop's been helping. Please don't think I've been. . ." Been what? "I'm not shutting you out. You really want to know?"

He nodded.

Deep breath. "Pour us a couple of mugs. It's a long story." The toilet upstairs flushed. "And pour a mug for K-pop, too." I moved closer and held his arm with one hand. "Please let us all be friends and don't be jealous. I honestly wouldn't know what to do about that."

He met my gaze and held it for several seconds.

Fine. Was there a short version?

"When Twist was here, he laced my pain meds with poison. I've been taking those meds the last couple of weeks without knowing they were poisoned, and I spent last night in the hospital while they decided whether it was going to kill me or not. K-pop stayed over by doctor's orders to keep me safe."

His eyes opened wide, then his whole face relaxed. "Oh my God." He shook his head. "I'm sorry, bro. Theresa. . ." His face colored. Well, that was an interesting slip. "I had some dumb shit going through my head. You almost died?"

"Coffee, bro. And both of us need to put this crap behind us with a Quentin Tarantino marathon."

He poured coffee. "Who?"

I laughed and punched his shoulder. "Do not let my dad hear you say that."

The three of us piled out of Boyfriend's Charger about an hour later. Boyfriend was all caught up on the poison nightmare scenario, and K-pop had been briefed on the Gunner suicide situation. Strangely, my girlfriend was the only one who didn't know all the weird stuff in my life.

Go figure.

Swing music blasted us as we entered the studio. Female vocalist. All five girls skipped and shook their moneymakers on the floor. The routine rocked. They kicked and did the Charleston, they shimmied and they shook. They'd even done their hair and makeup and wore Andrews Sisters-style dresses. Even Mono, who was usually invisible, shone like a star.

The music ended. They struck a pose, and applause filled the air. Over at the bar, Ephraim, Woody, Retro and, joy of joys, Whiskey clapped and whistled. My compatriots and I joined in the applause as we maneuvered around the tables to the floor.

Tango grinned like a madwoman, still a little breathless from the routine. Man, she was hot. She pounced on me with a bear hug. "Howdy, stranger."

I kissed her. "Amazing routine." Which would be the most important thing to her.

"Yeah?"

"Hell, yeah!" That was Boyfriend. "Y'all look awesome."

The other guys concurred. The girls beamed.

Tango turned to Whiskey. "What'd you think, boss?" Because his opinion mattered the most. Well, okay, it did, but I didn't need to like that fact.

"I think we need to use it." He clapped again. "That was amazing."

The girls cheered and celebrated.

"*Mira*, is there any chance of something like that for the guys?" Woody asked.

I rubbed my hands together. "Actually," I began, "the three of us have been working on something."

Tango's smile faded for one-tenth of a second.

"Okay, I *really* appreciate the enthusiasm," Whiskey started, and I could tell he was about to shoot us down since he didn't want to have sex with any of *us*.

"Give me a chance to tell you about *your* part in it, boss." I threw an arm around him while I improvised.

K-pop watched me with his I-can't-wait-to-hear-this face in place.

"My part?" Yep. It would work.

"Of course. *You're* the front man," I explained. "Why would we choreograph a routine without you in it?"

Tango's expression was just as expectant as K-pop's, but far less friendly.

"We were planning a sort of a *West Side Story* meets *The Road to Morocco* with a dance-off featuring you and Woody against Retro and K-pop, with Boyfriend and me playing backup and acting as base for some stunts with Ephraim." I punched Ephraim in the shoulder. "Want to get thrown in the air?"

"That... would actually... be really cool." One corner of his mouth lifted in the largest expression of spontaneous emotion I'd ever seen on him.

Woody's face exploded because of the size of his grin. "I get a *feature* with the lead singer?"

"Of course." I met Whiskey's eyes. "To keep in the theme of the project, we could go for the whole wolfman versus vampire shtick, you know, the Lon Chaney/Bela Lugosi version, not the shirtless, sparkly skin style."

Whiskey sort of smiled and nodded, radiating his appreciation for my bullshit ability. "Okay, we'll have to give that a try."

The guys did fist pumps and said, "Yes" a lot.

Whiskey moved out of my arm and punched my shoulder. "As long as I get thrown in the air, too."

"You know it, boss." In the air. Off a cliff. Whatever.

The guys formed up around me with a million questions about the presumed routine. While I pulled answers out of my ass, I watched Tango and Whiskey going over details about the girls' routine. I could see in her face she wanted to tell him that, of course, they could work him into their routine, as well, but if she tried that now, she'd just look like a suck-up. When she caught me staring, she smiled and winked, but I could tell she felt threatened.

Crap.

I wished she'd get over that. The delight in the guys' voices made my day.

K-pop leaned in. "We are so even, bro." He glanced at Tango. "You just totally took one for the team."

Yeah, and not in a sexy way.

Two weeks passed like nothing. Well, they also crawled by like an interminable hell. What with school and dance practice, there wasn't much time for anything else. "Anything else" being making out with Tango. I mean, we found a few minutes here and there, but nothing close to a repeat of our time by the pool.

Whiskey seemed to like the guys' routine, so I had to focus on that, especially since the guys needed a lot of work. Tango was less than thrilled by the attention he gave us. The amount of time I had to spend with my hands on the singer without throttling him made me crazy.

Then there was all the time I had to spend helping Tango teach the group sequences. Every time Whiskey saw us, he complimented our progress, but he always had ways to tweak the moves that created more and more work. I don't think I was entirely paranoid in thinking that Whiskey was pushing us hard to keep Tango and me from having any "quality time" together. You know, where "quality" implied being naked.

"You're paranoid," was her final word on the matter. "By the way, he's staying over at my place so we can practice tomorrow."

Uh-huh. Paranoid.

"Well, with the guys' routine," she explained in a matter-of-fact way that implied the entire situation was my fault so I had no room to complain, "you'll need to focus on the boys, and I need to squeeze in what time I can with Whiskey so he looks good. He is the *boss*, after all." She crossed her arms and cocked her hips. "And since we have extra rooms at my house, he won't need to sleep on the *couch*."

And now I regretted not letting the douchenozzle crash in my room. As much as I'd hated the idea of him parading around my place in his Dolce Gabanna's, the fact that he might be doing so in Tango's house nauseated me.

"He's totally cock-blocking you," Boyfriend declared one night while we talked in the parking lot. "I see the way he looks at her."

Since he had football and a non-dancing girlfriend, I saw him pretty much not at all those two weeks except to dance. We did our best to catch up after practices.

"Same way you looked at her when you first moved here."

Well, that made me feel better.

"Ah crap, sorry, dude." He patted my shoulder. "Difference is you're a kickass dancer. He's a musician. Why would she go for a musician?"

"Sony records and movies," I admitted. "I know how important it is to her to get out of this town. Now that I'm not on the circuit, I don't have as much to offer. Not like this guy."

Boyfriend's mouth pressed into a thin line. "I ain't gonna lie and tell you that never crossed my mind."

Of course, it had. He'd warned me right after she dumped him for me.

At least, he was decent enough to avoid "I told you so."

So I found what time I could to be the perfect boyfriend and coach her, too, which would sound like a total ego trip, except that it was Tango. If I proved how much I could teach her, she'd realize I still had a lot to offer. I also pulled in a few of my old contacts to check out our practice videos and offer suggestions.

Yeah. I know. Pathetic.

"See, Tango, see how useful I am? Arf, arf."

<*Wags tail enthusiastically.*>

K-pop practically moved in, which was awesome. In addition to everything else, we were working together on the video journal. Dad called a halt to *that* the morning he discovered us passed out together on my bed, fully dressed, with the laptop between us rendering video.

"You know I'm the last one to complain about finding my son in bed with another guy, but if you're too tired to get under the blankets, Ethan, you're going to make yourself sick. You just spent two weeks eating poison." He handed us both coffee. "I know how important this is to y'all, but you have finals before the field trip, and this is regular school. You can't just reschedule the finals for two weeks later."

"Wait." K-pop took the coffee and thanked Dad. "You could reschedule tests when they interfered with your competition schedule?"

I shrugged. "Rich people have it made."

He whistled. "All the more reason to make sure this video makes it big for us." He pulled his t-shirt away from his chest and sniffed. "I need to stop home for clothes I haven't slept in."

"I can lend you a t-shirt," I offered.

His face scrunched up, but he didn't seem quite able to find the right words.

Dad saved him. "With all the garbage he already gets at school, I doubt he needs to be seen roaming the halls in one of your t-shirts, and, yes, people will notice and, yes, they will give him crap about it."

K-pop grinned. "No offense."

Dad laughed. "None taken."

"Besides. . ." He gave me an "icky" face. "Same skivvies two days in a row? No can do." He lifted his backpack from the floor. "I'll swing by and pick you up after I change, hai?"

"Hai."

After he'd run down the steps with a hearty, "See you later, Auntie Mac," I turned to Dad.

"How'd you know about the bullying? Dr. Mike?"

"Mike would never break confidence." He picked up K-pop's coffee cup. "I just know that look he gets sometimes."

"What look?"

Dad smiled. "That look that says a kid is getting bullied at school." And that was all he'd say about it. "If you want to know more, Ethan, ask K-pop."

"I tried. He didn't want to talk about it."

"Try again. He does."

When I saw Juicy, she wasn't much help in the how-to-handle-Whiskey department, either. "You really don't want my opinion, Foxtrot."

"Yes, I do."

"No, you don't"

Back and forth it went, like a bad scene from a black and white comedy.

"*No mames!*" she exploded. "I'm not going to tell you what I think because you will blab it back to Tango, and she's hard enough to deal with as it is these days, thanks to you."

"What?"

She sighed. "Ever since you so politely suggested I suck it up and play the professional, she's like a kid with a new toy. She had to accept I'm a better dancer, but now she gets to be 'the one the band wants more.' So every time I try to fix something she's messing up, it's 'Well, Whiskey wants it done this way' or 'Whiskey likes it *my* way,' or 'Whiskey says he'd rather have us suck his *verga* for the camera.'"

"What?"

She growled. No, literally, growled. "You're the only one who gets to exaggerate?"

Fine. So, long story short, it was the longest two weeks of my life, it was the shortest two weeks of my life.

Finals happened. I did fine.

He'd finally realized he was inside the son of a bitch's dreams, and then it stopped working. What the shit?

"You seem distracted." The irritation in Mary's voice was obvious. It brought him back to the present where he was fuck-training with her.

"Sorry." He opened his eyes, and, yes, her face was visibly irritated as well.

"How can you think about that little worm when you're inside me?"

"Sorry." He focused and the ball of golden light between them brightened.

"Now, pay attention. We're almost at the level I've been telling you about."

Whatever. Some deep Nirvana bullshit connection he didn't really care about. He just liked the sex. Oh, and she claimed at the end of it, he'd be able to tap into the "vast reservoirs of his true magic potential." That seemed nice, too.

While the orgasms were, indeed, mind-blowing, he was getting a little bored of the same position, sitting facing each other day after God damned day. And now she wouldn't let him mesmerize the local farmer's wives and daughters, either. Something about wasting sexual energy.

Whatever. Needy much? He'd just done it for a little variety.

"It'll be worth it when you reach your untapped potential."

She really liked that phrase, and it was spooky the way she seemed to read his mind sometimes. She swore she couldn't, since she'd taught him how to protect his thoughts, but he sometimes wondered—

"I wouldn't lie to you," she said.

See? Like that.

Fine. He focused.

Deep inside, he saw a shining star. He'd felt it, seen it hovering at the edges of his attention when they practiced. He turned his full attention to it while adjusting his weight back onto his hands so he could thrust harder.

She gasped. "That's it, David. Right there. That light."

He touched it. Ouch! "It's frickin' hot."

"That's how strong you are," she said, "how powerful."

He reached out again, but the light was so damn hot.

She rocked on his hips. Wow. That. . . that was better than ever.

"Take hold of it, David."

He was close. . . so close.

He grabbed the light.

Held it in his mind.

"Yes! Yes!"

Oh yeah, their bodies writhed on the bed while the white, hot energy poured into him, into every cell, every muscle, every hair. He held it, channeled it, felt it rip through him.

It tore him open.

It was like an orgasm the same way a candle was like the sun.

It lasted forever and ever, the most intense, painful, beautiful amazing oh-my-God in the universe.

When he could think again, he opened his eyes. He lay on his back with Mary astride him. He was still inside her while she writhed, and a white line of light stretched from the center of his chest to a spot between her naked breasts.

Her hands ran through her hair in ecstasy. Her body shifted and undulated on him, but he barely noticed.

If he'd been a smoker, he'd have craved a cigarette.

He felt weak.

Wow. It'd been like having sex with God.

But what was with the line that connected them?

Weaker. He felt weaker. Drained.

Weaker still.

Something was wrong.

"Mary?"

Her movements slowed until she sat quietly, gazing down into his eyes.

"I don't feel so good," he said.

She smiled and touched his nose. "Of course not, silly. I'm stealing all of your natural born magic. How do you think I got so powerful?"

"You're what the helling my what?" He felt nauseous.

"I'm bleeding you dry." She squeezed his junk with her loins. He'd always wondered how women did that.

His hands found her sides, and he tried to shove her off, but he was so weak. "Mr. Bunny," he muttered. "Help me, Mr. Bunny."

The line of light connecting them flickered and died.

With a satisfied gasp, Mary finally rose and released his pecker.

Twist lay still. "Please don't kill me."

She strode around the room, glorious and shining. "Why would I do that? You're no threat to me." She bent over him and touched his nose. "Besides, you'll be so much more fun to disembowel if I keep you alive."

"Mr. Bunny. Kill!"

A streak of silver shot across the room and invaded the witch's body. She shivered. "Oops." She shook. "Oh my." One arm quavered, as if shaking off a chill. The hand rattled as if throwing off annoying mucus, and Mr. Bunny's ghostly form appeared in her fist. She seized his neck and squeezed.

The rabbit screamed. Just once. Then he faded away to smoke.

"Mr. Bunny? You *killed* Mr. Bunny?"

"Really, David?" She climbed astride him again; her pert breasts seemed to defy gravity. "You thought a ghost rabbit could hurt me?"

He muttered quietly.

She leaned closer to listen.

Twist brought his knee up hard and nailed her in the crotch.

She grunted.

Not nearly as painful as it would be for a dude, but he followed through with both legs, and she sailed over his head, rolled off the bed and landed in a very undignified heap on the floor.

He rolled onto his stomach, snatched the pistol he kept strapped and magically concealed under the bed. He fired it three times, point blank into her head.

Bam! Bam! Bam!

She slammed against the floor and lay still.

Well, not completely still. Her eyes stared up at the ceiling and her chest still rose and fell with her breathing. Yeah, he hadn't thought an entire *clip* to the head would kill that witch.

"But it sure as hell slowed you down, didn't it?"

He'd always made sure he let a few of his thoughts slip through the barriers she'd taught him. That way she didn't dig too deep and he could keep a few things to himself, like the fact that as much as he loved the way she fucked him, he still had a few spare guns hidden around the house, just in case.

The adrenaline wore off and he dropped onto his back on the bed like a sack. One leg bent under him. Ouch. He rolled onto his stomach and opened the drawer on the bedside table. He let it fall to the floor and reached into the space it had filled. He kept a syringe of adrenaline taped there. A couple of antitoxins as well.

Wait a minute! He snapped his fingers. That was it!

He shot himself with the adrenaline and waited for it to hit.

Those pills he'd magicked for Fox. That must've been what had allowed him into the son of a bitch's dreams. He'd read online that Fox had been treated for poisoning. One reported symptom had been hallucinations. The little prick must've had some of those pills left.

The magic connected them, which was why it had seemed too easy. He'd already done the work. If he could just find a way to dose the son of a bitch again.

Ooh. The adrenaline hit his system, and he dragged himself from the bed.

Mary lay there, bubbling. Her eyes focused on him. Wow. Already healed that much. Scary. He considered screwing her one last time while she was incapacitated. After what she'd done to him, it'd have been justified, but he was afraid her ya-ya would sprout fangs or something. He shivered.

He kicked her in the ribs. "That's for stealing my magic, you bitch." He kicked her again. "And that's for Mr. Bunny."

She stared up at him with blatant hatred in her eyes.

He thought about really killing her, burning her or dismembering her or something, but she'd warned him against that. It'd been on one of their first nights together, while they'd lain comfortably together post-coital, watching some lame chick movie on Netflix.

"You know," she'd purred. "In case you ever think of killing me, I have so many protective spells in place, you'd never figure out how to do it, and even if you *did*, my soul is attached to a catafalque somewhere in India, and I will come back as a vengeful spirit and send *your* soul to the ninth circle of Hell where demons will bugger you for eternity."

He'd chuckled. "Bugger? What are you, British?"

He stared down at her unmoving body. "I could make it harder. I could chop you up and send the little bits all over the world and it would take you years or decades to pull yourself together." He slipped on his clothes. "But you have taught me a lot." He smiled. "Enough that I can make do for a while until I drag my full powers back." He grinned. "Yeah, I *do* know that you can't suck the power out of a natural born witch forever. I can get it back. I read stuff."

He shouldered his duffle bag. "I really could have loved you, Mary, if you hadn't been an insufferably greedy bitch." He kneeled down and kissed her bloody cheek. "I hope the fact that I'm leaving you in one piece proves that if you ever decide to stop stealing my powers, I think we'd be good together."

And hopefully she'd be nice enough not to hunt him down and snuff him out the way she'd snuffed out Mr. Bunny. The loss of his familiar choked him up, and he kicked her again. He immediately regretted it. "I'm sorry. I really loved that rabbit."

He left the room and headed out the door and across the porch.

He waved a hand. "*Lorem ipsum dolor sit amet.*" The spell bags around the house ignited, massive gouts of flame from the basement to the attic. The words didn't really matter, they just helped him focus.

Once he'd sussed what all the sex was about, he'd memorized some spells and made up a few potions and curse bags. After Mary had told him what to look for, it was amazing what he'd found on the internet while the redhead blew him.

The first had been that as long as he was receiving regular blow jobs from the redhead, Mary couldn't completely suck the magic out of him.

God love the internet.

The house exploded.

He climbed onto his cycle and kicked it to life.

A flash of silver caught his eye on the ground below.

"Mr. Bunny!"

The ghost rabbit shook itself and rooted around in the grass. It didn't quite seem to grasp its inability to eat.

Twist watched the roaring flames consume the house.

"Well, I just feel bad now." He glanced down at the rabbit and then gazed up at the house. "I thought you killed my rabbit."

Maybe burning it to the ground around her was a bit over the top.

"What do you say, Mr. Bunny. Want to go for a ride?"

Mr. Bunny wiggled his silvery nose.

Part 2

Into the Woods

"Kamp Lindy-Ho-Ho"

Ethan's Map

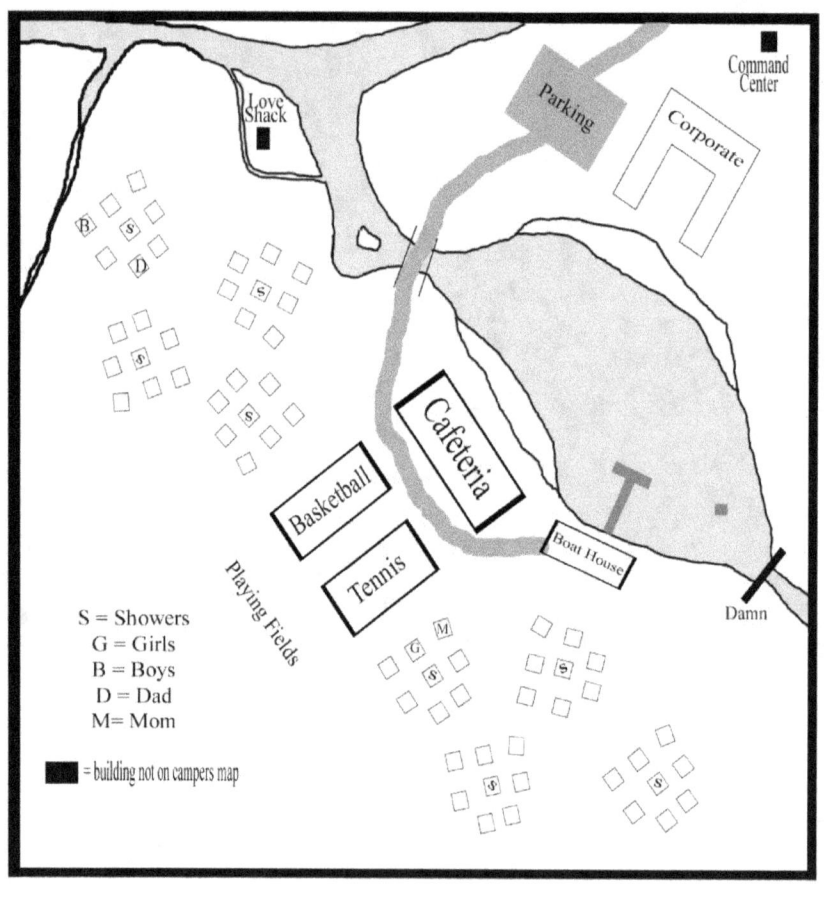

Command
Center

Parking

Corporate

Love
Shack

Cafeteria

Basketball

Tennis

Boat House

Damn

Playing Fields

S = Showers
G = Girls
B = Boys
D = Dad
M= Mom

= building not on campers map

Chapter Fourteen

And so arrived the day of our departure. Tango and I waited outside the studio, making out against her car. In deference to the members of the crew whose significant others would not be joining us, Tango and I, as well as Cosita and Juicy, had promised to keep it professional in public.

So we were getting in a little some-some before anyone arrived. The band's bus was due in five minutes, which meant the dancers would arrive in half an hour according to Dancer Standard time.

"So, with all those empty cabins," I breathed, rubbing her back with both hands, "we're bound to find a quiet little corner of our own."

She smiled while kissing me. "With you, it won't be so quiet after we find it."

I grinned and nipped her lower lip. "I can be quiet if I need to."

"Really?"

"I haven't needed to." Mind you, I hadn't had a *reason* to make noise since our day at the pool. Yeah, that's how busy we'd been, and why. . .

"You'd better put that thing away, co-captain." She pressed her hips against mine. "The troops'll be here any minute."

I pressed back. Wow. "These are dancers. They won't be here for half an hour." Hmm. Kinda lightheaded. "You know, we haven't broken in the storage closet where I first got to see the purple bra. We could get naked."

She chuckled. "These are *my* dancers. I have them trained."

"Get a room!" Juicy arrived right on cue, shouting at us from the window of Cosita's Mini-Coop. "If you and her royal highness mack down in public at the camp, I will end you both. And there better be free time at some point for sex, or I will get twitchy."

"As long as you don't want to sleep, there should be time." Tango pushed me away, which forced me to quickly turn my back to the girls.

"Who needs sleep?" Juicy asked.

I tried to adjust myself without anyone—

"Are you sporting wood right here in front of us?" Juicy called out as she dragged her bags out of the car.

"You two get to sleep in the same cabin, beyotch," I reposted over a shoulder. "I need to get mine while I still can."

"You know," Juicy said in an entirely different tone of voice, "I've been wondering how that flew past the parent patrol."

With my libido under control, I turned to face them. "The funny thing is, Dad and I spent hours hashing through the sleeping arrangements but decided boys in one cabin and girls in another just made the most sense, and, oddly enough, no one said anything." I shrugged. "Honestly, I think y'alls relationship is so new around here that no one thought to question things."

"*A toda madre.*" Cosita locked up the car with a beep-beep. "Tell me Mrs. Van Zeeland isn't in the same cabin with us."

"Who?"

Tango punched my shoulder. "Mrs. Corey's-Mom, doof."

Oh. "Van Zeeland? Boyfriend's last name is Dutch?"

"Have you even *met* his dad?" Cosita asked. "*Ese güero tiene piel clara y pelo rubio.*" Essentially, that meant, "That cracker is blond and pale."

Huh. You know, I *hadn't* met Mr. Van Zeeland. How weird was that?

I glanced at my cell. "Bus is late."

"Well, duh," Juicy said, "Musician Standard time is even worse than Dancer Standard."

"Try Gay Standard or Jewish Central," I joked. "Wow. A gay

Jewish dancer who played in a band would be so late he'd show up a week early."

The girls stared at me with obvious contempt.

"What?"

Juicy scowled and turned away. "You must be a really good kisser, because your sense of humor is lame."

"Oh, come on, that was funny."

Tango chuckled.

Juicy played with the strings on Cosita's hoodie. "So late he'd be early? Google 'lame' and that joke will be right there as an example."

Tango pressed her hands against my chest. "He is a *very* good kisser, though." She gave me a quick peck. "And he has a fabulous ass."

Well, that was true. I did.

The Woody-mobile pulled up and honked. He and Ephraim jumped out and grabbed duffle bags from the trunk.

A car I didn't recognize stopped at the curb. Ah. Retro. He rushed out the passenger side, but not fast enough. His mother hurried to meet him at the trunk.

"Now you have fun, *mijo*," she said, "but not *too* much fun." She squeezed his cheeks and glanced my way. Suspicion parked itself in her eyes and made a home. Yikes.

"Mom, I'm not a little kid." Unfortunately for Retro, there was no way to utter that statement without sounding like a little kid.

Ephraim dropped his duffle bag at my side. "That is why I rode with Sam, er, Woody. Jewish mothers are better than anyone at humiliating their sons. It's their birthright after four thousand years of male oppression." He shook his head. "Poor kid."

I wanted to chuckle, but Ephraim still scared me.

When Schilling arrived, her host parents made a big deal about hugging her, and it was obvious *she* didn't mind in the least. Her host mom smiled her way over to me and Tango with a business card. "I wanted to make sure you had a number for us."

"Thanks, ma'am. And just so you know, we have a complete contact list." I was used to dealing with parents from my years of competition. "Did you get the email we sent out with *our* contact info?"

She smiled. "We did. Y'all seem so organized."

I nodded. "Well, my father and I have traveled the world with groups of dancers and athletes. He kind of has it down to a science."

She looked around pointedly.

"He drove up to Austin last night to finalize everything with the band's manager and to drive up with the bus." He was also finalizing things with his lawyer, Saundra Delacroix, who'd insisted on drafting contracts to make sure we didn't sign away all our rights because we were starry-eyed. In her defense, Dad had kinda messed up with his gym and we *were* pretty starry-eyed. "He'll be here any minute."

She waved. "Oh, we all had a long talk with your father and with Lisa. You kids have fun."

"Lisa is Mrs. Van Zeeland, right?" I muttered after she walked away.

Tango just shook her head.

"So. . . this is a chance for me to get to know everyone," I said.

The crew seemed utterly jazzed, and no one was bitchy or pissed off at anyone. Maybe the trip would end up being a blast, after all.

Three cars arrived at once: Lisa Van Zeeland, whose name I now knew, Boyfriend and Theresa in her Jeep, and Mono in a Hyundai with a guy I assumed was her boyfriend from the way they lingered in the car while he kissed her fingers.

Boyfriend dropped his bags in a rush. "Gotta pee." He ran to the studio, which remained unlocked for just such an emergency. A long drive lay ahead.

Theresa stopped at my side. "Hey, Ethan." Not so much into the nicknames, as has been mentioned.

"Hey, Theresa."

She tucked a small package into Boyfriend's duffle bag. "It's a surprise," she said, then looked around and seemed to notice Mono and her boyfriend kissing their good-byes. "'Tis almost morning. I would have thee gone and yet no further than a wanton's bird."

Well, *Romeo and Juliet* was for suckers, but maybe it'd be a way to bond. "I would I were thy bird," I replied from the play.

She raised an eyebrow. "Sweet, so would I," she quoted. "Yet I should kill thee with much cherishing. Good night, good night!"

I joined in, and we finished the quote together. "Parting is such sweet sorrow that I shall say good night till it be morrow."

She chuckled and smiled at me. First time for that.

"You realize that 'cherish' is talking about petting or stroking," I said, hoping for more points. "So, in effect, they're talking about choking his chicken so much it kills him."

Her eyes opened wide. "You just made that up."

I raised a hand with three fingers pointing up. "Scout's honor! Found it in a college text book."

She laughed. "That is hysterical. I need to tell Corey before he leaves." She looked around for him. "He'll end up with a boner all the way to the camp."

Wow. She was pretty cool. "I guess opposites attract," I said as way of conversation.

She glanced at me, did a subtle sort of take and the smile morphed into a scowl. "What do you mean?"

Uh oh. "Well, Shakespeare? Not quite Corey's thing. You know?"

She shook her head, crossed her arms and moved closer. "Are you implying that he's too stupid to enjoy Shakespeare?"

"What? No!" Oh crap, I screwed the pony. "I don't think he's stupid, but he's not, you know, Mensa material."

"Neither are you." She raised an eyebrow. "I, on the other hand, am."

"I don't. . . Corey's like a brother, Theresa."

"Ethan, stop it. You do think he's stupid. You *do*. It's obvious to anyone paying attention." She took my arm and drew me away from the studio. "You care about him, I know that, even though you think he's dumb. You respect him in *spite* of it."

I was not going to say a word until she had it all out.

She lowered her voice. "And you don't even realize he knows it. He *knows* you think he's stupid, and it kills him. He has so much damned respect for you, Ethan. God alone knows why. Can you even imagine how bad it makes him feel, the way you treat him?"

"I. . . I had no idea."

"No. You don't. And do you want to know what he did last Sunday? You know, when he was puttering around with Bessie? That's what you called it, right? Puttering?" She took a breath. "He pulled the engine out of her, broke it down into nuts and bolts, explained to me how the entire thing works, and then put it back together so we could ride Bessie out into the field for a sunset picnic. He broke down and rebuilt an entire internal combustion engine."

"Wow."

"Yeah. Wow. Can you even change the oil in your car? Do you know what kind of oil to use?"

I had no idea how to respond.

"Do you? It's a simple question."

"No. I don't."

"He may have a hard time in school because of the dyslexia. . ."

"He has dyslexia?"

She closed her eyes for a moment. "You don't even know that." When she opened them she gave me an artificial smile. "So maybe school is hard for him, but he has all the parts to an internal combustion engine memorized." She took a breath. "Just because something isn't important to *you* doesn't mean it doesn't take brains. When was the last time you showed an interest in anything he does?"

"I watch his football games."

"How many points did he score last week?"

No clue. I'd kinda worked on choreo in my head the entire time.

"I thought not. You attend the games, Ethan. You don't pay any attention to them." She took a deep breath. "I suppose it's really stupid of *me* to make an enemy of you, Ethan Fox, but I have to tell you, I don't understand why he's even your friend." She glanced over my shoulder, and her face lit up as she brushed past me. "Over here, sweetie. Just taking some girl time with your bestie."

My brain refused to engage. All the little jokes I'd made, all the eye rolls, they all ran through my head. That horrible slip up the night of the kidnapping was only the most obvious tip of an otherwise profoundly subtle iceberg.

I turned and watched Boyfriend with Theresa. The way he laughed told me she'd just laid the Shakespeare joke on him. He understood it. He kissed her and held her close and tucked a stray strand of long, brown hair behind her ear.

He glanced my way and winked.

I faked a smile and did an upward nod of my head.

No wonder he loved her so much.

Okay. Calling myself a supervillain changed nothing. It wouldn't correct the problem. That would take more work.

I pulled out my cell and sent her a text: *Thank you for pointing that out. I will try to be a better friend.* I checked spelling before hitting send.

She glanced at her phone and sighed a deep sigh. Good. She deserved to know I wouldn't resent her tirade. She deserved that. She looked my way and nodded, then gave Boyfriend her full attention again. You know, when she smiled at him like that, she was amazingly beautiful.

I probably needed to start calling him Corey.

Someone cleared a throat behind me. Yikes!

"Jumpy?" Mrs. Van Zeeland, about an inch away from me, watched her son and his girlfriend. How much had she heard? "She scares me, too, you know."

"What?"

"I may have graduated from Harvard. . ." Had not known that. "But that girl could *teach* there."

I utilized my super power of letting people talk.

"She's protective of him, and I respect that." Her voice was low and kind. "But methinks the girl doth protest too much."

I raised an eyebrow.

She sighed and shook her head. "Some women *like* a man who's not as bright as they are. Life can be simpler that way. It's easier to win all the arguments." She smiled. "They say every boy is doomed to marry his mother and every girl her father."

She patted my arm. "You're good to Corey, and you're good for him. You challenge him. So does Theresa, in her own way." Her lips pressed into a thin line. "One of which is to keep him up way too late way too many nights."

Holy crap, she knew?

She moved away. "I played in the same sandbox as your father, Ethan Fox. Never underestimate my ability to smell the feeble machinations of teenagers." She paused. "And Ethan? She's not wrong about *everything* she said. You *should* take more of an interest in his toys and games. But it's easy for *me* to see why Corey is your friend. You're a good boy, too, just like he is." Corey waved her over and away she went.

She was the only adult to call me a "boy" in years without sounding condescending.

My brain hurt.

"Hi there."

"Yikes!"

"Sorry. Deep thoughts?" Tango took my arm and followed my gaze. "Don't tell me you're crushing on Boyfriend's new gal."

I blew out a quick breath. "Not when the hottest, smartest girl is over here on my arm." I kissed her.

"Good answer."

The bus arrived, driving all other thoughts to oblivion.

It rocked the universe.

Holy shit!

An antique, although I couldn't judge a year. Not so much my thing. Maybe I should ask Boyfriend, er. . . Corey. It was smaller than a modern bus and sky blue with white trim, lots of silver accents. Truly a work of art. Very Deco and Steampunk.

"Wow." Tango said it perfectly.

The crew went insane. They whistled and hooted. I grabbed Tango's hand and dragged her over. The logo plate read, "Bronte."

"She's the cat's meow, ain't she?"

The voice was a blast from my past.

"Jimmy Russo?"

"Ethan Fox." Jimmy wore a white Zoot suit with sky blue shirt and fedora that matched the bus. He grabbed me in a rough, wild hug.

"You're with the band?"

"Black men invented jazz, white boy. Don't be so surprised."

"I didn't know you played." I held him out at arm's length.

"My major is music, bro. Just because I knocked you out half a dozen times don't mean I can't wail a tune, too." He released me and doffed his hat, giving Tango a bow. "And who is the lovely young woman you tricked into walking up on your arm."

"Tango Montez." She offered her hand.

Jimmy Russo kissed it. "For the record, what they say about black men is true."

"They all like fried chicken," I said.

He laughed. "Don't forget the watermelon, mista. We all likes the watermelon."

I threw a couple of fake punches, which he dodged. "Jimmy Russo was one of the UT boxers who worked out at Dad's gym, and he actually did knock me out once. Oh my God, it's good to see you." It was true. He reminded me of simpler times.

"Why haven't you come to Austin?" He instantly realized why I hadn't been to Austin and waved off his own question. "You have to talk the old man into giving lessons up at Camp Lindy-Ho-Ho."

"Wait. Camp Lindy-Ho-Ho?"

He laughed. "It's what we're calling it. You know how all those summer camps have fakey Indian names?" He leaned closer. "And we're calling the ladies the Camp Lindy-Ho-Ho Hos. You know, for the holiday." He winked. "Whiskey's brother even made up a camp song."

Yowsa.

Corey appeared.

"Corey, this is Jimmy Russo," whom I needed to introduce with both names, for some reason.

Corey shook his hand, but gave me a question mark. Oh. Yeah. "Sorry, buddy, Theresa calls you Corey. I figure I should follow the boss's example."

He grinned and nodded a lot. "Awesome." He shook Jimmy Russo's hand some more. "It's great to meet one of Foxtrot's old friends."

"Foxtrot?" Jimmy Russo laughed. "Can't believe no one thought of that before."

Corey tugged on an arm, and I let him draw me aside. "I got an e-mail from Gunner."

"E-mail?"

"He said good luck with the video shoot."

"He has a computer?" He'd said something about not even having *phone* privileges.

Corey laughed. "Dude figured out how to sneak into the

counselor's office." He looked so relieved. "He's going to *run* that place before he's done."

Because, you know, that would be a good thing.

"He's sneaking in there to keep tabs on the video shoot. Doesn't want me to let the groupies go to my head so the band can take advantage of me." He smiled. "Says he still has my back."

The weight of the world seemed to have lifted from Atlas's shoulders. I had to be grateful to the sociopath for that.

"He told me to say hi to you." The hope in his eyes gave him that lolcat look.

"Hi to him, too." I chucked his shoulder. "I'm glad he's staying in touch."

"Foxtrot?" His brow furrowed. "I'm really glad he's doing better, and that he's, you know, reaching out, but I remember why he's in there in the first place." He shrugged. "Having you at my back. . . I trust that more."

"Ethan?" That was Dad waving us to return to the group.

There didn't seem to be more to say to Corey, so I raised a fist.

Bump.

We rejoined the others.

Dad dropped a hand on my shoulder. "Hey, straight son."

"Hey, gay dad."

"Jimmy's trying to talk me into giving lessons in the camp gym."

Double take. "They have a gym?"

Jimmy Russo laughed. "A bag, some free weights and a couple of yoga mats. A jump rope. The band's been there a few days practicing and filming. Some of them wouldn't go an entire week without any kind of work out." He chuckled. "Whiskey was afraid he might lose an ab."

Ha. So I wasn't the only one who thought he liked himself a lot.

Corey tagged Jimmy Russo's arm playfully. "So you're Italian?"

My old friend showed a stony face. "Yeah, why? Do I not look Italian?"

Deer. Headlights. Bam. "Uh. . . I. . ."

Jimmy smacked Corey's arm. "Aww, just giving you shit. Let me help you with the bags."

"Hey, thanks." He held out his duffle.

"Seriously? Do I look like a porter, man? I just drive the bus." And with that, he walked away.

Ephraim nodded sagely. "I like him already."

Dad laughed. "Sorry, Ephraim, he doesn't play for our team."

Stone cold silence.

Ephraim's face lost every trace of color.

Juicy chortled. No, really chortled. "Tough break."

Dad gripped Ephraim's arm. "Wait. Was that a secret? Really? Nobody knows?" His voice told us all he thought that was impossible.

Corey scoffed. "I knew."

Ephraim's eyes grew wide.

Schilling nodded. "Dah, I knew."

K-pop, whom I hadn't noticed until just then, ran past and dropped his duffle bag at my feet. "You have a poster of Adam Levine in your room, hai?" He ran into the studio.

Woody lost it. "*Ese*, I've been telling you for *months* that everyone knows." He grabbed Ephraim in a headlock, which is something I would never do. "You are so the drama queen." He punched Dad in the arm. "And don't you dare apologize, F-bomb. You are the best thing to happen to this repressed Jewish boy."

So, yeah, that happened.

K-pop and Kiki kissed their goodbyes. Hm. Something had changed. She saw me watching and waved with a blush and a smile before heading for her car.

I waved at Kiki, then slid to my friend's side. "So has she met Naruto?"

"Dude." He elbowed me. The grin on his face erased all the awkwardness from my conversation with Theresa. "She totally shook hands with Vash the Stampede." He tugged on the waistband of his briefs, then leaned close. "I almost. . . you know. . . right in my shorts." He glanced around to make sure no one was listening. "I think we're going to get naked when she welcomes me home."

"So she can 'shake hands' without Vash getting in the way?"

He elbowed me again. "That's the plan."

"Bro, we are going to have the best. weekend. ever."

"Hai."

Chapter Fifteen

All cell phones lost reception as we reached the camp. "Middle of nowhere, people," Jimmy Russo explained. "What'd you expect?"

"My mother is going to have cardiac arrest if I don't call her, and it will be your fault." I probably don't need to point out that Ephraim had said that.

Keeping his eyes on the road, Jimmy Russo called out, "Oh phenomenal, you're Jewish, too? *L'chaim.*"

For once Ephraim seemed stunned. "You're Jewish?"

Jimmy's face turned petulant. "What, don't I look Jewish enough for you?"

Ephraim, against all odds, fell silent.

Jimmy Russo sputtered a laugh. "Naw, just messing with you." Which earned him props and hoots. "Don't worry, I'll have Whiskey email everyone first thing. He has a land line in case of emergency."

"As you're *not* Jewish," Ephraim pointed out, his dry, sarcastic tone returning, "you'll not understand that a Jewish mother unable to keep twenty-four tabs on her sixteen-year-old son *is* an emergency of epic proportions."

"And *there's* my little uptight brother," Woody laughed. "I was worried for a minute."

The red gravel road into camp wound through thick woods stripped bare by the season. The cedar and live oak were the only trees that still had their green this late in the year. The clear blue sky kept the place from becoming the land of utterly dismal.

"That's a lot of trees," I said.

Corey, who shared my seat, nudged me. "Not a lot of woods in high-class hotel ballrooms?"

"Not so much." The forest wasn't dismal, maybe, but still utterly spooky.

Tango turned in the seat she shared with Juicy and winked at me. Well, lots of empty woods did mean it would be easier to find naked time together. Woods for the wood, as it were.

And, yeah, couples had already separated.

The sense of isolation returned as we pulled into an empty parking lot. I mean, not one car. "I thought everyone was already here."

K-pop made a lonely whistling sound from some old western.

"Yep." Jimmy Russo pointed at the building on one side of the parking lot. "The gang's all here."

Sure enough, college students swarmed the lawn beside a big, ol' cinder block building. Jimmy popped open a window and swing music completely changed the mood of the place.

Yowsa.

About a dozen folks, tossing Frisbees or lying out. One guy played a guitar.

Dad moved to the front of the bus and leaned over Jimmy's shoulder. "Are you telling me this is the only bus you have?"

"Dude, *look* at this bus. How much money do you think we have?"

As we passed the building, which had obviously seen better days, everyone craned their necks to check out the party.

"Holy naked flesh!" Woody called out. "That chick has no top on!"

"And I'm pretty sure those aren't actually swimming suits they're laying out in," Ephraim added.

The entire crew rushed to my side of the bus to gawk. K-pop squeezed in with me and Corey. And, yes, most of them cavorted in their skivvies rather than actual bathing suits. They smiled and waved at the passing bus, including the topless redhead who beamed unselfconsciously as she did so. The dude with her was a ginger hippie-looking guy in tie-dyed jams, which would explain why he didn't seem to mind the world getting an eyeful of the girl. He rubbed lotion onto her back, completely unconcerned.

Jimmy Russo chuckled at the small-town kids. "So I assume none of you has been to Hippy Hollow?"

No one had. They'd heard about it, though. Lake Travis, just outside of Austin, had a nude beach. I'd never been, since you have to be eighteen and they card, but it was obvious the group outside was used to a much freer lifestyle than most any of my friends had lived.

As the bus continued away from the building, folks settled back into their seats, but the buzz had started.

"Oh my God, it's just like a movie set," Tango said.

"Let's just hope it's *Animal House* and not *The House on the Hill*," Juicy added.

Woody pressed his hands on the rear window. "When do *we* get to get naked?"

"When I'm dead, Woody," Mrs. Van Zeeland said. "Sit down."

"Don't worry, ma'am," Ephraim assured her. "Not all of us want to be porn stars."

"Dude." Woody jabbed him in the arm as he sat.

"Joking. I'm joking. Remember, my people are born comedians."

"Why aren't we stopping?" Woody asked.

"We're staying in cabins across the creek," Mrs. Van Zeeland explained. She rose into the aisle and faced us. "Actually, Jimmy, let's pause here a moment."

Twist rubbed the last of the lotion on his own arms and lay back on his elbows, flinging his hair out of his face. The antique bus slowed to a stop near the bridge. No one had recognized him. Perfect.

The redhead whose name he didn't know reached for her top.

Twist snatched it away playfully. "We've all seen 'em. Why cover up now?"

"That was just to tease the boys and keep them thinking with their dicks and not their heads." The girl took her top from him. "I don't normally parade around with my tits hanging out."

"Don't know why not. You have great tits." He wondered how long the attraction lotion he'd rubbed on her back took to—

She took his hand and cupped her breast with it. So, it didn't take long, then.

"And the boys don't normally play Frisbee in their underwear." She tugged on the strings of Twist's jams. "Mr. Modesty."

"Nothing to do with modesty." He stared at the bus full of Fox's boyfriends while he massaged the girl's boob. "I've just seen enough dudes in their jockeys to last a lifetime. I don't even want to go there."

She giggled and pressed her breast into his hand.

Sure enough, as soon as the bus started up and moved away, several of the guys reached for shorts. Some of them didn't bother. Neither did most of the girls, who seemed too comfortable to care.

Finally, a group where the girls were more prone to nudity than the guys. He'd probably end up liking them. Pity he'd likely end up killing them, as well.

Why the skin show, though? He'd have to ask around.

His shorts grew uncomfortably tight while he played with the redhead's boob, so he glanced around to see if anyone else was making out. Just how decadent were these people?

"Can we fuck right here, or should we find some place more private?"

The girl rose and helped him to his feet. "We should probably find a room if we're going to fuck." She took his arm. "My name's Ginger, by the way."

Whatever.

Jimmy stopped the bus near a bridge.

While Mrs. Van Zeeland and Dad sorted out a folder of papers, I checked the sights. Out the front of the bus and to the left lay a perfect view of the lake and a bathhouse on the other side. The water sparkled in the sunlight. The beach on this side was a bit overgrown, but the sand across the lake leading up to the bathhouse was clean.

"Check the pontoon raft." K-pop leaned forward and pointed. "Midnight. No moon tomorrow. How many stars will be visible on that bad boy?"

Ephraim scoffed. "And how many horny teenagers have been killed on it? Anyone, anyone?"

Jimmy Russo laughed. "That's why we're here. The whole place *screams* slasher film. Wait'll you see the empty wing in Corporate—that's what we're calling the building back there. It was originally for big corporate retreats, but it screams haunted house."

His enthusiasm infected us all.

"We're all shacked up in the rooms in one wing, but the other wing was left a disaster for filming. Broken desks, beds, all kinds of shit. Oh, except for a couple of rooms that we painted entirely green."

"Whoa!" K-pop leaned forward, chin on his hands. "Seriously?"

"You must be K-pop." Jimmy Russo winked at Dad, who was handing papers around. "Your Borderlands dance video is pretty wicked. The director, Sarah, wants you to play with her, too. She wants input from a dancer who also speaks geek."

"Fantastic." K-pop's dream come true.

"Okay folks. Here's how it's going to work." Dad leaned forward with a hand on either side of the aisle with his I-really-mean-it face. "Those folks are all adults and most of them are twenty-one or older. They are legally allowed to have whatever drunken orgies they like, and they know that they will go directly to jail for contributing to the delinquency of a minor if they so much as let you sniff a bottle or touch a boob."

"No boobage?" Woody whined.

"No boobage," Dad confirmed. "Unless you can get Juicy interested."

She made one of her famous noises of dismissal. "As if."

"I know this is exciting," Dad continued, "and we want you kids to have fun, but this gig is huge and there's going to be a hell of a lot of work involved."

As if on cue, Mrs. Van Zeeland took over. "While we're here, call me Mom and you can call Mr. Fox, Dad. We are your parents while we're here, and we report to your real parents as soon as we get home."

The papers showed maps of buildings and the campground, along with a list of rules. I'd seen them.

"I know you want to think of yourselves as worldly and mature," she continued, "but these people are in an entirely new league and puking your guts out because you're not used to anything other than stolen sips out of your parents' liquor cabinet will not impress them." She glanced pointedly at Corey. "The rules are on the last sheet. You will sign that sheet and hand it to me as you get off the bus."

"Wait a minute," Juicy exclaimed. "Really? If we get caught doing any of this stuff we'll be cut to the floor?"

Mom smiled a very tightlipped smile. "That was my idea. I'm bad cop." She gave Dad a look. "We know y'all wanted him along because he's automatic good cop."

Dad didn't disagree. Of course, none of them knew Dad. Sure he gave me condoms and booze, but I was *his* son, and I'd managed to travel the world on my own without killing myself. None of my friends could say the same.

"If you're caught breaking any of the rules," Mom continued, "just once, not only will you be cut from the project and moved to my cabin or Dad's, you will be automatically removed from all existing footage."

"That's ridiculous," Juicy complained.

"Only if you planned on a drunken orgy at the 'wrap party' when getting banned from shooting won't matter anymore."

No one spoke, but the generally uncomfortable silence proved her point.

"Mm-hm."

"Look, folks," Jimmy Russo threw in. "I'm in favor of drunken orgies as much as the next fella, but once we start filming tomorrow, we're gonna run pretty ragged anyway. And don't even ask any of us to help corrupt you. We can't afford to reshoot if one of you delinquents messes up." He looked down the length of the bus using an overhead mirror. "So save the parties for when you get home and your parents can blame themselves for your hedonistic ways."

Grumble. Grumble. Grumble.

Schilling raised a hand. "I am sorry, but what is this 'drunk energy'? I don't understand the term."

Mono spoke to her in perfect Russian, and Schilling's eyes popped open. "Da?"

Mono nodded.

Schilling sank down in her seat, red in the face. "They do this over there with the college people?"

Which broke the tension nicely.

Keep in mind, I'd actually helped Dad draft up the contract. I was used to balancing "fun" with "work." My friends were not. I also knew that if we wanted to let loose a little with a quiet bottle of something or to sneak off into the woods for a discreet shag or skinny dip, no one was going to complain. The massive edifice of boundaries was there to keep us from overindulging, and to keep the more experienced folks on the other side of the creek from taking advantage.

"Okay, let's head out." Dad turned to front again. "So the moral of the story is have fun, but don't forget that I was a world class boxer, and I have killed a man."

"I shot one," Mom added slyly. "Don't know if he died or not."

Corey nudged me, and we exchanged a smile. Our parents were badass. It was good to see Dad joking about something that had almost crippled him with guilt less than a year ago.

We crossed a rickety bridge and Juicy jumped up. "Holy shit!" She pointed to the right of the bridge. "Go back, go back, go back!"

Murmurs of excitement and curiosity filled the bus.

"You saw that?" Woody asked. "I thought I made it up."

Jimmy Russo threw the bus in reverse with a grin that told me he knew exactly what they'd noticed. Gasps and exclamations in English, Spanish and Russian brought Corey and me to the other side of the bus, squished in with K-pop.

"What. the fuck. is *that?*" Woody and Ephraim spoke in perfect unison.

That was a scarecrow, at least that's what my brain told me it looked like. It was built from branches and some kind of black fabric. The base was a pyramid with a branch tied across the top like arms. The cloth wrapped the frame and fluttered in the breeze. A straw cowboy hat crowned it.

"Who the hell built that thing?" I pushed away from the window, my breath shallow, my dream of a Twisted scarecrow vivid in my memory.

Jimmy Russo chuckled. "Freaky, right? Whiskey found them here when he was scouting locations."

"Them?"

"Yeah." His voice sounded uncertain. "There's a few of them scattered in the woods. You okay, man?"

All eyes locked on me. K-pop's face showed his understanding.

Tango moved up the aisle and held my hand.

"You didn't build them for the shoot?" I asked.

"Man, they've probably been here for years."

"Please tell me that is you messing with us again."

"Nope. Seriously. No idea who built them or why, but we've already done shots with the band playing around them."

I shook it off. Coincidence. It had to be.

"Sorry," I said. "Overactive imagination."

Everyone turned back to a perusal of the grim reaper on a rock in the middle of the stream.

"Were these grounds used by some cult?" Dad asked.

Jimmy shrugged and put the bus into gear. "I have no idea. We just figured it added to the witchy hoodoo of the place. Figured some other group of college kids was out here for a frat initiation or something."

Again. Coincidence. Had to be.

Tango squeezed my hand and gave me a sympathetic smile as she took her seat. K-pop and Corey flashed me understanding looks, too.

"Whooo-eeee-ooo." Woody moaned like a ghost.

K-pop smacked his head, but everyone else laughed.

I forced myself to join him and make spooky ghost noises of my own. Pretty soon, the entire bus was moaning and groaning.

Jimmy Russo parked outside the cafeteria, which was on the butt side of the bath house.

"Whoa," Corey said as he left the bus.

"I second the whoa," Tango said.

Jimmy Russo opened the baggage compartment. "Yeah, we had to pay extra to get permission to distress it."

"I thought it was abandoned, anyway?" Tango asked.

"The owner still hopes to sell it as a camp."

Black and red spray paint covered the front of the building. The windows were broken out and boarded over. The words "Keep the fuck out!!!!" with that many exclamation points dominated the wall.

"I'm waiting for a tumble weed to blow past," Ephraim muttered.

Woody repeated K-pop's spooky whistle.

"Wait a minute." K-pop dashed forward, then turned to face us with awe covering his face. "I saw the video of this on your site. You did a bunch of before shots with it all cleaned up, right?"

Jimmy Russo leaned against the bus while Corey and Woody hauled out everyone's bags. "Yeah, we spent an entire day cleaning the damn place just to trash it again the next."

"What for?" Juicy asked.

"We filmed shots of the band in the spit and polish cafeteria," Jimmy Russo explained. "All decked out in tuxes and gowns, right? Roadies and film crew dressed up, too, and did the whole bob and sway thing with goofy fake smiles. Then we trashed it, and we'll film the same scenes with y'all dancing hard core jitterbug and made up like corpse ghosts."

The entire crew stood transfixed. Okay, me, too, but how cool, right?

"Then we'll slide, cross-cut and fade between the two with an app that tracks the camera shots so it'll be seamless."

Woody elbowed K-pop. "Dude, you just shot a load in your shorts, didn't you?"

"And I'm not even embarrassed about it."

"Oh my God, you really do have a hard-on, don't you?" That was from Juicy, who pointed.

K-pop burned beet red and turned away. "I do not."

"So why was the place abandoned, anyway?" Ephraim demanded in his increasingly familiar Wednesday Addams persona. "Some horrible gruesome death?"

"Oh, you know it, buddy," Jimmy Russo said in all sincerity. "Gruesome."

Ephraim perked up. "Really? I was just shitting you. Who died?"

Jimmy Russo nodded sagely. "The economy." He laughed and closed the baggage compartment.

And rimshot riff.

"Okay, folks." Jimmy Russo shook Dad's hand and lifted one foot onto the bus doorway step. "Mom and Dad have maps marking the cabins we cleaned for y'all. Get settled in and the cafeteria is open for practice. You'll meet the band and the crew there. Makeup will want to check on allergies and wardrobe will want a fitting."

Up he climbed and away he drove.

"Here we go," Dad called out. "Guys with me. Girls with Mom."

Everyone grabbed their gear and headed out, chatting and laughing. Tango and I lingered a moment.

She kissed me. "Don't have too much fun with your boyfriends."

"Dad's map has a couple of outbuildings he erased on the general copies so there'd be fewer secluded places to lure the innocent." I gave her the good, old eyebrow waggle.

She smiled and kissed me again. "I suppose we can find a few minutes at some point. Since we're not so innocent, the reasoning doesn't apply."

I held her close.

"Ethan!" Dad called. "You realize you're my favorite for making an example."

Kiss, kiss, buh-bye.

We crossed the caliche road. Basketball and tennis courts lay abandoned without nets but covered with both leaves and grackles. Those birds lived everywhere in Texas. Spooky.

Past the courts was a wide playing field of grass.

There were two villages of cabins, one on either side of the courts and fields. When the place had been full, no doubt guys were housed in one set of cabins, girls in the other. Although there were only a few of each in our group, the parents had set us up in cabins as far from one another as they could. Because, you know, we didn't know how to walk.

In each village, there were several rings of five or six cabins, each ring surrounding a central bath facility. Our man cave was the farthest away from the action. Although he'd deny it, Dad'd figured if we were a bit out of the way, we could have a little rowdy fun without getting in trouble. His squat was two doors down, far enough away to allow us privacy, but close enough to hear if anything got out of control.

K-pop entered our cabin first. "This place is *stellar*."

Which gave me hope until Woody followed him in. "Are you coked?"

"What? The place has been empty for ten years." K-pop opened a window as I made my way up a step and across a small wooden porch. "Would you want to sleep on ten-year-old mattresses? Why do you suppose we brought sleeping bags?"

It was an empty room. Spacious enough, but there weren't beds or dressers or carpet for that matter.

"This is a joke, right?" I said.

Dad leaned in the doorway, pose of which he was quite fond. "Look guys, they cleaned the place a lot." He flicked a wall switch. An overhead light lit. "And they had to fix a line for electricity. It's not like you're going to be doing much more in here than sleep, anyway."

"Dear sweet Jehovah, tell me there's running water and a shower." Ephraim shuddered. "I do not want to live three days with these unwashed animals."

Dad gave him a perplexed scowl. "Yeah, you really know how to keep the whole gay thing under the radar, Ephraim. I see why you thought it was a secret."

For a second, panic flashed across his face, then he relaxed and sort of, actually smiled when everyone joined in the razzing.

"Showers and bathroom are out here." Dad winked at me. Yeah, Ephraim was his new mission. Nice.

We filed out after him.

"Advantage to being a guy," Woody said. "The forest is our bathroom."

"Oh my God," K-pop dashed away, then stopped and pointed.

"We have our own stream." The delight on his face was infectious, so I hopped over to join him.

"Dude, you are hard core into the camping thing, hai?"

"Oh my God, you have no idea."

The stream was pretty and burbled along like a normal stream-type thing. Woody glanced at it over my shoulder.

"Huh." He nodded and moved away. "And now I have to pee."

I laughed and dragged K-pop away, but made a mental note to see if the stream was warm and deep enough for late night stargazing and swimming. I still owed K-pop enormously for everything he'd done.

The bathroom was almost as Spartan as the cabin. A row of urinals faced a row of stalls. A line of sinks stood out from the wall closest to the door. An open space of about a foot separated the wall from the ceiling, so at least the smell wasn't hideous. Fortunately, we were in the middle of a heat wave. Sitting on a frigid toilet was not my idea of a good time.

"Thank God for stalls," Ephraim said. "I was worried."

The first room opened onto a second with a couple of benches in a sitting area, a hip wall and then an open space for showering. Three posts with a few nozzles each were spaced across the tile floor.

"Not a lot of privacy," Retro said quietly.

"Come on, bro," Corey enthused. "We've all had gym together or something at least once."

Retro glanced at me.

Corey snorted a laugh. "Holy crap, Retro have you been to his house? He's a freakin' streakin' nudist."

I had to laugh, because it was true, but it did point out that these guys had years of history together, and I was still the newbie.

"You've all seen the blog, right?" K-pop elbowed me. "What underwear is Ethan Fox wearing today dot com?"

Corey snorted again.

"Captain America boxer briefs," Ephraim and Woody chorused.

Woody laughed at my surprise. "The girls won't stop talking about 'em, ese."

Okay, maybe I wasn't such an outsider after all.

As we filed out, Dad stared back into the bathroom. "No offense to their cleaning crew, but I brought my own mop and bleach. There won't be much to do while y'all rehearse, and I'm used to cleaning a locker room."

"You didn't have a janitor?" Retro asked.

Before Dad could respond, Ephraim chimed in. "Because a middle-aged gay man is going to give up a chance to hang out in a men's locker room so he can pay someone else to do it?"

Dad laughed and gave him a high five. "First game to you, Ephraim."

As we walked back to unpack, K-pop sucked in a big lungful of air. "A few hours of practice and we're gonna sleep like the dead."

"We can only hope," Woody muttered. There was an edge to his voice I didn't understand.

"Bad analogy at Sleepaway Camp," Ephraim protested.

He and Woody lingered a bit behind. I overheard Ephraim say, "What are the chances of anything happening tonight of all nights?"

"*Mijo*," Woody whispered, "think about the triggers and do the math."

I held up a step. "Everything okay?"

"Yeah. Of course." Woody gave me a "duh" face and hurried up the steps into the cabin. "I get a spot right by the door, so I don't wake y'all up sneaking in after banging band groupies."

Ephraim rolled his eyes. "You know I could hate a guy like that if he wasn't so adorable." He glanced at me, then smiled. "Wow, it feels good to be able to say stuff like that in public."

Er, yeah. Misdirection much?

Twist rode the re-head doggy style. He'd really missed doggy style while he and Mary were doing their "training," which had been her way of figuring out how to steal his magic. Bitch.

"Ow."

"Sorry." He eased up. "So, tell me. Why the skin show for the kiddos?"

"Oh, that? Well, we're just trying to keep the small town kids a bit starry eyed. They were involved with some psycho a few months back. Out in some place called Dumb-ass, Texas if you can believe it. Did you hear about it?"

"Let's assume I did."

"So when we decided we wanted to do a whole slasher, backwoods thing, Whiskey thought it'd be great to get a group of dancers who'd just made headlines with their own personal fucked-up, psycho stalker. Ow!"

"Sorry." He eased up.

"Good for publicity."

"Can they dance?"

"Well, sure, but that's just icing on the cake."

Interesting.

"Are you almost done?"

"You bored?"

"Oh, no, it's just I have a rehearsal coming up. Take your time."

Chapter Sixteen

The cafeteria buzzed with activity. The band warmed up onstage, making a racket. Film crew folks wandered the space painting and spraying spider webs. The room itself was, well, a cafeteria, big and square with a full stage on one side. The lighting rig flashing and strobing had obviously been added by the film crew. Three or four people walked around with cameras on their shoulders.

Having been involved in the business before, I managed to hold my cool, but my friends, pretty universally, stared open-mouthed and frozen.

"Hey, gang!" Whiskey trotted over. Black leather pants, black vest open to show off his abs, ridiculous air of superiority: he wore them all. "I hope the trip out was okay."

Tango practically jumped up and down. "This is a-ma-zing."

Whiskey's smile turned feral. "We're pretty happy with how it's turning out."

"Whiskey?" A round Black woman called to him above the hubbub. "Today?" She was decidedly lacking in jolly.

He waved, then turned back to us apologetically. "Look, I know you just got here, but Tammy will kill me if we don't get costumes sorted out. She wants to get your bodies into everything to make sure it fits so she has the night to do last minute alterations."

Mom stepped forward. "You got my note on dressing rooms?" Her tone was friendly, but with a promise to slide back to Bad Cop if he crossed her.

"Yes," he clapped and held his hands together. "Separate dressing rooms." He pointed at segregated curtained areas in the back of the room. "We have those in here, and two rooms at Corporate."

Ironically, Tammy was at the stage commanding three band members, two girls and a guy, to strip off right there and hand over their costumes. She snapped her fingers at a fairly young dude nearby and pointed at Whiskey. The dude trotted over.

"I can't control what my people do," Whiskey said to Mom, "but your folks will be protected from Tammy's complete lack of inhibition."

Mom turned to the crew. "I can't stop them from getting naked in front of you, but if any of you looks like you're enjoying it, I will end you."

The crew fidgeted.

Mom shifted so only I could see her face, and she winked. Yeah, there'd been this girl named Veronica Porter who'd thrown pool parties when Mom and Dad were in high school. Ew. Calling them Mom and Dad, just made the entire image worse.

"Uh, Whiskey?" The younger dude glanced back at Tammy's wrath, and I was amazed he didn't turn into a pillar of salt. "She wants the pants."

Whiskey shrugged at Mom. "Sorry, ma'am. Tammy owns my ass." He unbuckled and kicked off the boots, nodding at the kid. "My brother, Lizard. Lizard, the gang." He handed over his pants and stood unselfconsciously in bike shorts that were decidedly less revealing than his Dolce Gabannas had been. He opened his hands to Mom. "Doing my best to keep it decent for you, ma'am."

"Much appreciated." She moved off toward the girl's dressing area. "But you didn't need to tuck everything away and hide it for my sake."

"I didn't—" He broke off and turned red.

"Pwned!" Lizard called out. Him, I liked.

"Feel free to go it commando," Juicy added, earning a slug from Cosita. "What? Just because I'm on a diet doesn't mean I don't like to look at the menu once in a while."

"I thought you were a vegetarian these days," Woody said.

"Omnivore."

Lizard pointed at the dressing room with a giant male symbol pinned thereon. "I'll be over there to help the guys with their costumes, since, you know, the gay kid is the only guy capable of sewing." He gave his brother a withering glance.

Ephraim scoffed. "My entourage does the exact same thing to me."

Lizard's eyes opened wide.

Woody's turn to scoff. "Dude, you came out to them five minutes ago."

His friend displayed him with one hand. "See what I have to deal with."

Lizard backed away a few steps, smiling, then threw his brother's pants over a shoulder and dashed off to Tammy, who was already shouting his name.

Whiskey leaned closer to Ephraim. "That's actually why I told him to help with the costumes." He winked, and Ephraim blushed, speechless for the second time in one day.

Dad barked a laugh. "Did he *really* think it was a secret?"

I winked at Tango, who blew me a kiss as we were once again segregated boys versus girls. Inside our dressing room, a ten-foot rack filled with clothes dominated one wall. The next hour was an endless parade of costumes: suits, jeans, boots, hats.

Playing Ken doll innumerable times over the years rendered me pretty immune to the whole thing, but the guys were totally stoked at the clothes. Apparently, their experience with costumes was minimal.

Watching Ephraim, Retro and even K-pop, bashfully stripping off, the wisdom of separate changing rooms made sense. While Corey and I wouldn't care and Woody would probably relish parading around in front of the girls, the other three were pretty shy for the first half hour even with just us guys, but by the end of it, the monotony of stripping and dressing and standing there in their underwear while Lizard shoved pins in their pants rendered them all pretty immune to embarrassment. Tammy the Terrible even stormed in at one point, bellowing, "None of you has anything that I haven't already seen and sucked on, so deal with it. I want that chart!"

Everyone just laughed, even the guys down to their jockeys.

Twist peered into the cafeteria through a window.

Wow. It looked like a movie set. He'd thought the whole thing was going to be lame and cut-rate, but this band was the real deal. He had to find a way to sneak eyes and ears behind the scenes. Especially in places where the girls were going to get naked, although, judging by the way the redhead stripped down on stage for the big costume woman, glimpses of naked female flesh would be the rule rather than the exception.

Still. He missed his cameras and mics.

Mr. Bunny stretched up on his hind feet and caught his attention.

Hm. He'd been able to ride along with that big linebacker, but it'd taken potions and shit. What had that desert witch's book said about it?

He closed his eyes and held a hand out to Mr. Bunny. "*Pro no verear utroque.*"

When he opened his eyes, he saw himself, standing about twenty feet tall.

Whoa.

Mr. Bunny dropped onto all fours, and Twist experienced a moment of vertigo while he tried to make sense of his surroundings. Holy Christ, grass smelled amazing.

"Okay, buddy, let's see how this works."

With a twitch of his nose, Mr. Bunny hopped through the wall and headed for the girl's dressing room.

Once the poking and prodding had finished, we met up with the girls in the main room, all of us once again in comfy workout clothes. The band continued to fart around onstage as they'd done during the entire wardrobe session.

Tango tagged Lizard. "Any idea when we can have time to practice?"

"Up to you. Room's never locked." He chuckled. "Heh, who the hell would try to steal our stuff way out here, right?" He was a mini-me version of his brother, except not so full of himself. Partly, I think, because he was younger and still a bit awkward.

"I mean, when is the band going to be done?" Tango asked.

"Huh? Done?" He shrugged. "Those cats will likely noodle until midnight."

Oh. I saw what she meant. She assumed we'd get the room to ourselves at some point. Yeah. That was not likely. "Never mind, Lizard. Just ask Whiskey how we signal the techies if we need the system for a run-through."

He nodded a lot, obviously glad to finally have a request that made sense.

"By the way," I said before he could dash off. "You taught Whiskey his first swing, right?"

More nodding.

"Any chance you'll work with our weak link, here?" I prodded a thumb at Ephraim. "I'd really appreciate it."

Ephraim puffed up. "What do you mean—?" He recovered admirably. "Yes, yes, I am horrible at swing. I could really use your help."

Lizard grinned and saluted. "At your service." He dashed off.

Ephraim refused to look at me, but he glowed. "All right, Foxtrot, that wasn't utterly deficient and contemptible. Thank you."

Tango grabbed my arm. "While *that*—" She waved a finger at Ephraim, "was cute, *that*—" she waved the same finger at the band. "What was that?"

"We're going to need to share," I explained.

"What?" The face she gave me was the same sort of face she'd give me if I asked her to walk across the ceiling instead of the floor. "How can we practice with all the noise?"

"We'll have to get used to it."

The entire crew stared at me.

I shrugged. "One benefit to a small town studio is you get to lock the door whenever you want. Welcome to the rest of the world."

Tango hemmed and hawed, then shook it off. "Okay, we'll—"

Music blared over the PA system drowning out the band.

I recognized the tune instantly: *Every Rose has its Thorn.*

Tango jumped.

What the hell? I turned in a circle.

That was the song spray painted on Tango's car four months before. The band and techies seemed irritated by the volume and the interruption, but no one except the dancers reacted to the song itself.

Dad and Mom ran into the building, Dad brandishing a mop. They spotted us and ran over. Dad waved until he got Whiskey's attention and flagged him. He met us in the middle of the floor.

"Do I need my guns?" Mom asked.

The music dropped in volume. A young male voice spoke over the music. "Teddy here. I have the campground PA working, y'all. Sorry about the loudness." The voice was not Twist's.

Tango curled into my side, and I held her tight.

"Why the hell did he pick that song?" Dad demanded.

"What the hell?" Whiskey sounded as belligerent as Dad. "Why is everyone freaking out?" He pointed at Mom. "She has guns?"

Jimmy Russo and a few others gathered around us.

Then an announcer came on asking us to buy some lame brand of pizza from Houston that would never deliver out to us anyway.

It was a commercial.

Dad startled, then relaxed, breathing heavily.

"What's your deal with that song?" Whiskey demanded. A couple of camera people circled us filming reaction shots.

"Oh shit, man." Jimmy Russo clapped a hand over his mouth. "That's a messed up, frickin' coincidence." Apparently, he'd followed our drama.

"What?"

Dad fielded the explanation. "There was some trouble a few months ago," he explained. "Someone started the whole thing by spray painting lyrics from that song on Tango's car."

The band and crew closed in as Dad outlined the basics.

"Wait, that was y'all?" Lizard asked. "I heard about it, but. . . wow."

"So I apologize for the excitement," Dad concluded. "We're still a little jumpy, I guess."

Woody scoffed. "And y'all never heard anything about it? It was all over the net."

Whiskey waved it off. "Most of us are in college and trying to make it in the biz. Sorry if we missed the CNN report."

"Whatever happened to the guy?" Jimmy Russo asked.

"We don't know," I admitted.

Murmurs filled the room.

"Wait, y'all have your own freaking stalker and you didn't think to mention it to us?" The girl with the attitude was a redhead made up like an Andrews Sister. I recognized her from videos. Female lead.

"Seriously?" Woody moved forward, but Dad stopped him with a hand in the chest.

"Okay. Time for the dancers to take a break." Dad turned to Whiskey. "That okay with you, boss?"

Whiskey seemed a bit confused by the entire episode. "Yeah, sure. Take a couple hours. We'll do lunch back here at 3 p.m. then kick in rehearsals again. Sorry for the scare, folks." He glanced pointedly at Tango, who still clung to my side.

"Not your fault," I called after him.

Lizard lingered. "Uh, Ephraim, you want to work on some swing."

"Yeah. . . that'd be cool."

Yowsa. His first date. How cute was that?

I gave Tango my full attention. "How do you want to play it?"

She blinked as if I'd surprised her. "Sorry. Damn camera was pointing right at me when the stupid song started up. I feel like an idiot."

In that case, I knew exactly how to play it. "Okay folks, free time. Do what you want. Let's get here half an hour early. We might be able to get the floor to ourselves."

As I led her out the door, Tango rested her head on my shoulder. "Thanks. I feel like such a little girl, but I just want to get away."

"Sounds perfect to me." And I knew the perfect place.

So we were naked again on another blanket. We lay on our sides, switched around so I could trail a finger up and down her shin and she wrapped a hand around my calf, kneading it contentedly. I'll let you infer what we'd been doing just a few minutes earlier. I checked another first off the list, but we'd still be saved from slaughter if life was a slasher film.

Something rustled against the wall, and I sat up quickly. Bright beams of light filtered through the widely-spaced planks of the very old shack I knew from Dad's Harry Potter map.

"What is it?" Tango asked.

"Don't know."

More rustling, a little digging and a pointy nose poked its way into the shack, followed by the hard-shelled body of a tiny armadillo.

"Oh, he's adorable!" Tango said.

The little guy jumped, squeaked and tucked back through the hole he'd just dug. I laughed and lay back down. Time for practice was closing in, but I wanted to eke out every naked-with-Tango moment I could.

"Just think," Tango teased, "if you were an armadillo, you'd carry your protection with you wherever you went."

One hand clutched my bare chest. "Oh, that kills me." I trailed a finger along her inner thigh. "Although I didn't hear any complaints a few minutes ago."

"No, no complaints." Her fingers touched down on my stomach and drifted a bit south. "Do you trim?"

"What?"

She sighed. "Juicy and I were talking about guys who manscape."

I chuckled. "You are the queen of non sequitur. One of the many reasons I love you."

Her fingers froze.

So. I'd said that. Awk-ward.

That was the first time either of us had used the "L" word.

She breathed deeply and her fingers moved across my skin again. "If I say, 'you too,' it'll sound like it was just because you said it. I don't want that. I'll find my own time." Her fingers trailed along my hip. "So, trimming?"

A+ for redirection. "No. I'm naturally a pretty sparse landscape, enough for some scenery but not so much you can't see the forest for the trees."

Her fingers drifted across to explore said landscape. "That was the worst metaphor I have ever heard." Her fingers circled the oak tree rising.

"It got you to play with my junk again, so, mission accomplished." She chuckled.

"And you?"

"I trim a little. Do you like it?"

Monika shaved completely, which had always bothered me, but I would never, ever say that out loud while another girl played with my block and tackle. "I think you're perfect exactly as you are."

She sat up slowly.

Damn, naked time must've been over.

Then she leaned over me. "What do you know, all I can see is one tree trunk. Just lay back so I can get a closer look."

Whoa! Stellar.

So. . . telling Tango she was perfect while naked? Definitely a tactic to remember.

Twist hopped Mr. Bunny away from the shack where Tango and that asshole hadn't even had sex. What kind of guy didn't carry condoms with him? He had to remind himself that he'd spent almost two years with Mary while the rest of the world had only passed three months, but even so. . . three months and no sex?

Wuss.

He'd enjoyed watching her face during the show, and was surprised how little pain he'd felt seeing them together. Maybe he was over her, after all.

Fox was still that popcorn kernel stuck in his teeth, though. Just seeing him made Twist want to kill something. He was so fucking smarmy and cutesy and, Jesus, he just *hated* that guy.

When Mr. Bunny looked up and Twist recognized himself standing on the bridge with his hands on the railing as if he was studying the scarecrow, he blinked and settled himself in his own mind again.

The scarecrow had helped him remember the camp. He *had* been there before. A few years back a bunch of frat boys and sorority girls had snuck in and played *Blair Witch*. It was all fun and games until someone accidently cut the air hose to the three guys hiding under the diving pontoon. They'd planned to surprise a group of girls who'd said they liked to skinny dip at night.

In their defense, the plan had worked. Those girls *had* been scared half to death when three bloated corpses surfaced.

Twist stared up at a scarecrow left over from that game. It stood watch over the bridge. He smiled. He and Warren had had some good laughs over those bloated corpses. One had been so saturated, the stomach freaking *exploded* when Warren had poked it with a stick. He'd smelled like rotten frat boy guts for days.

Ha. Good memories.

He'd taken the straw cowboy hat off his own head that day and tossed it at the scarecrow. The hat had sailed true and plopped dead center on the top spike. Still there.

Huh. Had there been a bit of magic even then? The creepy thing had been his inspiration for the scarecrow in that dream he'd sent to Fox.

He held a hand up and muttered a spell. A small ball of fire ignited above his palm. Yep. His power was already returning. He extinguished the flame. Mary had taught him too much for her own good.

People usually took one look at him and assumed he was a lot dumber than he was. Something about the corn-fed face, red hair and freckles most likely. He didn't mind being underestimated. It'd saved his can more than once.

"Pretty creepy, aren't they?"

Twist jumped and turned. The singer, Whiskey, leaned against the other railing with his ankles crossed working hard to look relaxed and sexy at the same time. That guy was definitely a case of someone easily *over*estimated. Douche.

"Know what they are?" Twist asked for the sake of conversation.

The douche shrugged. "They were here when I first saw the place. I was pretty sure I wanted to use it, but once I saw *those* things? Sold." He closed the space between them with a hand out. "I'm Whiskey. Are you with the dancers?"

Duh. The singer knew all the dancers by name. It was a test.

"Nah. I just move shit around for the film crew. Sarah asked me to see if there was any chance we'd have enough light with all the shade from the live oak."

Whiskey nodded and looked around. He seemed to buy it.

Twist had learned that he could move around as he liked as long as he stayed away from the dancers. To the roadies, he was on the film crew. To the film crew he was a roadie.

The singer pushed away from the bridge and headed back to the main building. "I think she's about to do some test shots. You should probably head back"

"Don't tell me what to do you poser."

He stopped and turned. "What did you just say?"

Oops. Twist waved a hand. "These aren't the droids you're looking for."

Whiskey's eyes turned glassy.

He waved again. "You should probably head back."

"You should probably head back," Whiskey repeated.

"You're right," Twist said. "Thanks for the info. I'll be there in just a minute."

Whiskey blinked a few times, shook his head, and walked away. "Don't be too long."

Once he was alone, Twist slipped off the bridge and followed the creek into the woods, past the old half-fallen shack and away from the camp where he could recruit his spies. He couldn't risk being caught setting up cameras, but the beauty was he no longer needed them.

He needed more eyes and ears.

Deep in the woods, he found a clearing and painted a large circle with blood and cast the containment spell. He'd learned quite a bit since his adventure with Mr. Bunny and now knew enough to cast the spell as a dome rather than a tube open at the top. He also cast this one much larger than Mr. Bunny's.

Right on cue, the rabbit appeared and watched Twist work. He wondered what a ghost rabbit did when he was elsewhere. Maybe he found girl ghost rabbits for devil bunny love.

Twist moved into the center of the circle, throwing feed onto the grass. It was a collection meant to draw a variety of animals. He muttered the spell as he tossed the feed around. Since that bitch'd tapped his mojo, he needed the actual spells a lot more. Bitch.

Within moments, the underbrush rattled as animals approached. Rabbits, squirrels, birds. . . a beaver. Even one cute little fawn. As they crossed into the circle, the air shimmered with magic. Twist raised his hands and a trio of grackles alit on one arm. A small hawk on the other. A pair of squirrels climbed up to his shoulder and chattered.

He took a feather or a tuft of hair from each animal, then shook himself and the animals lifted from his body and dropped onto the grass.

Twist felt a gentle tingle as he stepped out of the circle. A grackle tried to follow and was repelled by the wall of the containment spell.

While he waited, he tucked the bits and pieces from each animal into a special web to keep track of each. He'd actually used a cheap dream catcher from a tacky souvenir store as the base, but since he'd drenched it in the blood of a pregnant cat, it would serve its purpose admirably.

After a moment, the animals started moving around the space. Slowly at first, then more frantically. One by one, they dropped onto their sides and convulsed wildly.

Splat! They all exploded at the same time and drenched the entire containment dome with blood and gore. "Oh, yeah." That was cool. A bubble of blood.

One by one, the spirits appeared, silvery and translucent and visible only to Twist.

This time, when their eyes turned to red fire, the entire petting zoo slashed and flashed against the magical dome, crying and hooting and cackling like a silvery menagerie of Tasmanian Devils. Twist lifted a hand. *"In eos assum quodsi delectus."*

The whirlwind slowed. The ghostly apparitions all came to a standstill in formation, eyes red and glowing, but their faces calm.

Twist glanced down at Mr. Bunny. "That spell would have made *our* friendship so much easier."

He dragged a heel through the circle of blood, and the gory dome fell to the ground with the slap of wet flesh. The animals surrounded Twist. The birds fluttered and landed on his upraised arms. The squirrels reclaimed their posts on his shoulders. The fawn nudged his hip. He couldn't feel it, but it was cute as hell. His own little, red-eyed ghostly petting zoo.

"Eat your fucking heart out, Disney Princess."

He lifted his arms, and his menagerie took to the ground, trees and air. Flashes of silver cruised away at speed. All but Mr. Bunny, who stayed at Twist's side. He crouched down near the dream catcher. He touched the feather of a grackle and his vision swam for a moment. . .

The air rushed past his body. The trees sped by below.

Twist jerked his hand away from the feather in surprise "Holy shit." Who needed cameras and mics when he could ride along with any of his malevolent little helpers?

He took a deep breath and reached once again for the shiny black feather.

Chapter Seventeen

Back at the cafeteria some time later, one or two techies puttered away, and a couple of tables overflowed with sandwiches. Tango and I were the last of the dance crew to arrive. Ouch. Bad form.

Juicy glanced at her cell when Tango and I walked in, as if checking the time. "Hm. I just wanna know—"

"Yeah," I said, "and if you weren't licking honey off your chin, I'd take that from you, Juicy."

She raised an eyebrow, but she smiled.

The girls wore practice dresses, and the guys wore swing pants with suspenders. I ran to the changing area and dressed the same way. Since most of the crew wasn't used to suspenders, we needed to make sure the girls didn't snag themselves during the tricks.

For the most part, we had the room to ourselves, but the place would be crawling with loud boisterous musicians within half an hour. The crew had assembled in the open space in front of the stage. The lights were up, and K-pop was playing with the system.

Hm. Just how well did I know these folks? I knew them well enough to be certain they'd be stressed and awkward if we tried to rehearse with an audience of rowdy, loud musicians and roadies who, unlike my friends, had tons of experience working in a noisy environment.

I channeled Dad, trying to pull something out of my ass that would make my friends comfortable.

Oh! Yeah, if I could pull off my badass persona, it just might work.

I clapped loudly. "Let's go, folks. Places. Swing number one." I yanked off my t-shirt and pulled on a tank. "Hit the tablet, K-pop." I gave him my best sidelong glance. "You're already hooked in, I assume?"

He grinned. "Hooked in and on deck."

Sweet. But everyone stood around watching.

I clapped my hands again. "Five!" Everyone scrambled for places. "5-6-7-8!"

A fast as hell jitterbug screamed out of the amps, and the dance crew grabbed floor. K-pop slid over the tech table to join us. Partners nabbed hands, and we danced the bejesus out of it.

I'd learned shortly after I met my friends that forcing them to go balls out without stressing the details brought the best shows. I danced with Tango, even though Asshole-in-leather-pants would dance with her for the real shoot.

I danced as hard as I could. Every spin was a triple, every trick threw her three yards in the air and every ass grab simply *had* to remind her of the insane orgasm she'd just enjoyed in a dusty shack in the woods. A sharp gasp shot out of her lips when I clutched her for the death drop.

"Trust me," I said, and let go.

She fell.

One of the sandwich girls shrieked.

I grabbed Tango's hands and caught her with her skull half an inch from the floor.

'Cause that's how I roll.

The half-dozen people watching applauded and whistled.

I yanked her to her feet.

Her face flushed.

I held her close, kissed her hard and rolled her out for a bow.

Our tiny audience screamed.

My friends hooted and blushed at the attention. The camera crew circled us, taping. If I could keep this working, I might just overcome my friends' lack of experience.

Okay, what next?

I clapped my hands as loud as I could. "Okay, ladies, places for the girl-power dance."

The girls scrambled.

I ran to K-pop's side. "How much control do you have?

He grabbed his tablet and smirked. "What do you want, brother?"

"Hack the camp PA and broadcast this shit."

"I thought you wanted something difficult." He grinned.

The music stretched the airwaves and echoed across the lake.

Tango strode to her spot, front and center. She glanced at Juicy, who grinned. She glanced at Mono, who smiled self-consciously and nodded.

Tango waited a few beats for their cue, then pulled up tall and proud. "5-6-7-8!"

The girls hit it hard and sexy. By the time they were halfway through their routine, the room had filled.

It was Andrews Sisters with a sexy Shakira vibe. The girls strode forward to the cameras and shimmied and shook and managed to make an eight beat twerk work in a big band routine.

K-pop slammed his hand to his chest. "I have a girlfriend. I have a girlfriend."

They pulled out all the stops on a Charleston sequence that had their kicks over their heads. They hit every line perfectly in synch. They'd practiced the *shit* out of this choreo.

The song came to a climax, and I would not have been surprised if at least a few of the guys watching could say the same thing. The girls did cartwheels and landed in splits, arms up, jazz hands waving.

And the crowd went wild.

The girls popped up out of their splits, and their brand new fan club mobbed them.

It was time for the icing on the cake, the *coup de grace* that would ensure that the director played the game our way. I stalked over to K-pop.

"Our turn," I whispered, pulling off my tank top and tugging the suspenders back in place. I plucked at K-pop's shirt. "You know you're hot, dude. Give up the shy routine. Right now."

Ephraim touched him with one finger and pulled it back as if he'd burned it. "It's true."

K-pop hesitated. He was so not used to thinking of himself as hot.

"What? My opinion doesn't count because I'm gay? No, wait, it's because I'm Jewish, isn't it."

K-pop laughed. "All right, already, I'll do it." He grinned and stripped off his shirt.

I spotted the director, the woman who eyeballed the entire room as if she were in charge, because she was. Sarah, right? Had to be her. I could see her rewriting the entire shoot. Score.

The energy in the room blazed.

I sprinted and slid to her side. "Trust me. You'll only need one take for sex on a cracker."

She smiled, then started snapping her fingers at every techie in the room.

I grabbed K-pop around the neck and huddled all the guys. "This is our shot to make sure this routine makes it into the final product." I threw an arm around Corey, who already had his shirt balled up in his hands. "Sell it guys. Sell it!"

I nabbed K-pop's shirt and stalked over to one of the video guys, staring directly into the lens as I tossed the shirt into the camera. Woody and Corey took my lead and threw their shirts at cute girls in the audience as if they were rock stars.

Ephraim and Retro kept on their wife beaters, but Ephraim strode over to Lizard and draped his dress shirt around Lizard's neck.

The crowd hooted and whistled.

Stellar.

I snapped my suspenders. "Woody, you're front and center."

His eyes went wide.

"Whiskey's not here. You wanna take point?"

His entire body shuddered. He nodded, like, a lot.

And slo-mo took control.

I kissed two fingers and jabbed them at K-pop.

He tapped the tablet and spun it, tossing it through the air to Juicy.

And jazz ruled the world.

We snapped our fingers and ran across the floor in a crouch. The

West Side Story sequence was a variation on the fake sparring from the previous dude routine, but smoother and more complex, since we had six guys this time.

The cymbals crashed: seven-eight.

Hit spot. And hold.

Breathe. Breathe. Breathe. Breathe.

We slid into a jazz sequence that was all Gene Kelly. Massively hard, but with the energy solid and all the guys grinning and mugging for the cameras, any flubs looked intentional.

The trick sequence rocked. We paired up with me climbing Corey's shoulders, Ephraim with Woody and Retro with K-pop. The balancing act drew spontaneous applause and gasps.

Corey grabbed my foot and hauled so hard I hit the back flip solid. Ephraim, Retro and I nailed the floor at the same time. All six of us danced a hardcore Charleston sequence as if the planet would explode without us.

Retro took the lead.

For three phrases, we let him play it solo.

He did windmills, moonwalking and moves with names I didn't know. The crowd laughed and laughed.

We all jumped back in, hit the break, knee spin, pull to feet and—

Hold.

Hold.

Trumpet screech!

Drop into bow.

Voices screamed all around us. No, seriously, s-c-r-e-a-m-e-d.

Corey grabbed me in a bear hug.

K-pop lifted me off my feet and spun me around, yelling.

Ephraim pumped my hand so hard he almost took off my arm.

Woody played it cool and bumped a fist.

Retro faded into a swarm of teenage girls.

The adrenaline faded, and I shook off the energy. Sarah had her crew filming the crowd reactions. I caught her eye and raised my hands palms up, sending her my question mark face.

She smiled and winked.

Nice. Mission accomplished.

Where was Tango? Off to one side, she stared at me with her best fake I-don't-hate-you face.

The world slowed to a near standstill.

My buddies grabbed me, ready for our close-up as the cameras surrounded us, but it hardly mattered because the girl who made my world worthwhile stared at me as if I'd just betrayed her.

Damn it.

Whiskey appeared out of nowhere. Normal time resumed when he grabbed me tight, as if I didn't hate him. "Baby doll, I can't wait until you finish teaching me *my* part!"

Tango hovered off in a corner, hating the attention Whiskey gave me.

Corey punched my arm. "Bro, that's what this whole thing is supposed to be."

Tango walked away.

Fuck.

No. . . Seriously. . . *Fuck.*

Corey took my face in his hands and forced me to focus on him.

I took a deep breath.

"What you just did for us was a miracle, bro. A God damned miracle. Okay?" He glanced in the direction Tango had stormed off. "What you did was *right.*"

So why did it feel so wrong?

"Tango." I jogged to catch up.

She didn't slow down. Man, she could walk fast when she wanted.

"Tango!" I broke into a run and cut her off. I didn't touch her, just planted myself in her path. "Would you please ask me why I did that before hating me?"

"You did that because you have more of a hard-on for your 'bros' than you do for the girl who just blew you."

I staggered a step. "You really think that?" Wow.

She crossed her arms. "Feel free to feed me a line of bullshit excuses."

"What?" Anger built in my chest. "You say you want to be a professional dancer, and then you pop off this jealousy crap, when *you're* the one who has Whiskey grabbing your ass?"

Get it under control, Foxtrot.

Deep breath.

"Think about music videos with dancers. How much dancing is there these days and how much time is spent watching the band dick around and play their instruments? They're the stars here, not us." I pointed a straight arm at the building behind her. "Now the director knows the dancers are more interesting than a bass player spinning his axe. She knows that letting us dance through the whole routine rather than doing five second shots is powerful."

Her face changed. Relaxed.

"Y'all can't even *practice* with the band warming up. How well do you think it's gonna go with the director shouting cut literally every. ten. seconds? We will suck. *Suck.*" Deep breath. "And now the boys have already had *their* take the way *they* would want it, rough and informal. It's done."

I didn't point out the bonus that the director likely wouldn't want to waste time reshooting to add Whiskey to the dudes' routine.

"So now the girls have had a run-through to practice, and the director knows the best way to film you is to let y'all get the full makeup and costumes and then dance the routine straight through with everyone yelling and cheering, which is the best way for *you* to perform." I felt lightheaded. "I did this for *you.*"

She seemed conflicted. "Why didn't you tell me ahead of time?"

I flapped my arms in manly exasperation. "Because I just thought of it five minutes ago and pulled it out of my ass as we went along."

"You just came up with all that on the spur of the moment?" Her hands planted themselves on her hips. "You expect me to believe that?"

"I'm a *fucking* world champion, Tango!" Okay, I kinda lost it. "I used to come up with shit like this before breakfast on a weekly basis. I had to choreograph entire routines and memorize them and perfect them over a dinner break before performing them for the entire bloody world." I forced my voice quiet. "I hold back *every* time we dance so I don't show up the rest of the crew, so I don't show you up. I hold back *every* time, but it would be nice if you remembered that I know what the hell I'm doing and if you trusted I was looking out for *everyone's* best interest. Not just sucking up to the lead singer so I can get my own personal fifteen minutes, and my friends be damned."

I stormed past her toward the cafeteria.

"Foxtrot," she called after me.

I turned.

"I'm sorry." She looked wrecked with guilt. "I'm sorry I didn't trust you."

"Yeah, and in fifteen minutes I might care." I finished storming off to the cafeteria.

Fifteen minutes later, I didn't care. Trust me, no one knew it but Tango, but the "professionalism" I maintained for the rest of the day was less a product of my sincere desire to portray a sound business ethic and more about me holding a grudge.

I'd tolerated her flirting with Whiskey, putting her own bright and shining star above everyone on the crew. Those were our friends, people who had just as much right to a spotlight as she did. I'd never once done anything to put myself forward, and I was tired of pretending that the selfish nature she'd revealed didn't bother me.

So I was polite, but I needed space. She was smart enough to give it to me. We ended practice late, and K-pop had been right. We'd all likely sleep the sleep of the dead.

As everyone slogged off in different directions, Tango approached me quietly. "I'm really sorry, Ethan."

I hugged her and kissed her forehead. "I know. Just give me a night to sleep on it."

She kissed me gently. "I love you."

Oh, shit. That should've helped, and I forced myself to stay relaxed. "You, too." I kissed her lightly. "Get some sleep."

She hugged me and headed off to follow the girls.

Is it me or was that declaration of love just a wee bit manipulative?

Maybe I'm overly sensitive because of my ex.

Maybe.

Twist watched the girl through Mr. Bunny's eyes. She lay on a blanket in the light of a sliver of silvery moon, tall, skinny, blonde, with her hair in braids and beads. She wore a thrift store dress and her sandals lay on the grass beside her. Apparently, she'd never heard of that strange invention, the razor.

The ghost rabbit hopped near her head so Twist could better see her cleavage.

Her eyes opened and she sat up abruptly, as if she somehow sensed the ghost rabbit's presence. She looked around, her braids swaying with the movement. She pulled her legs in and crossed them Indian-style.

"Hello?" She reached for her cell. "Is someone out there?"

Twist hopped the rabbit to see whether—

Her head moved and her eyes flashed frantically. So, she could tell something was nearby, but couldn't actually see Mr. Bunny. She held the cell to one side, as if waiting, then brought it up.

Twist wasn't worried, cells couldn't—

"Are you there, Teddy?"

"Teddy here, Daila."

Not a cell, a walkie talkie or something.

"Now, Mr. Bunny, take her!" He stepped out from the brush, where he'd hidden.

The ghost rabbit's eyes flashed red and he leapt into the girl.

"Daila? You there?"

She dropped the radio and fell back with a grunt as Mr. Bunny fought for control. "Help. . . me," she whispered, eyes wide and staring at the sky.

Then her eyes flashed red.

"Daila?"

Twist closed his eyes and shifted into her through Mr. Bunny. Would it work? He made her pick up the radio. "It's. . . me." Talking through the girl's mouth felt odd. His voice sounded wrong in his ears, except they were her ears. "I dropped my walkie talkie."

Laughter over the line. "Walkie talkie, eh? You having fun playing in the sandbox, too?"

What was the loser's name? Teddy? He'd need to pay for mocking Twist.

"What do you want, Daila? Have you had enough 'me time'? Do I get to see you. . ."

"No, Teddy. In fact, I need a lot more. . . me time. I'm. . ." He thought about the way the girl dressed and didn't shave. "I need to go commune with nature. . . and stuff." He winced. Lame.

"Oh shit, Daila, you're not going off on another one of your. . ." Over the line, Teddy sighed deeply. "We're at a shoot, honey. You can't just take off again."

She was prone to taking off? That was lucky. No one would look for her right away.

"I do whatever the goddess tells me to do." That was hippie chick talk, right?

"Goddess? Last week it was Jesus. Daila, seriously—"

"Don't mock my religion!" Twist shrieked, then smashed the radio against a rock because he couldn't find an off switch.

As he stepped into the clearing where the girl sat, he handed control over to Mr. Bunny and opened his own eyes. "Just keep her still, buddy. I can take all the time I want, now."

A single tear fell from one eye.

"Aw, you poor thing." Twist gestured for the rabbit to make her stand. "Scared?" He wiped the tear away with his thumb.

Oh yeah. She'd be fun to play with.

He leaned close and sniffed. Patchouli. What was it with hippies and that stuff?

He closed his eyes and slipped inside her head.

Fear. Panic. *Oh my God, don't let me die.*

He opened his eyes.

Her nose twitched.

Ha! "Oh my God, Mr. Bunny. Don't do that." He laughed some more. "How can I get in the mood to slowly peal her skin from her body if you keep being all cute like that?"

He patted Mr. Bunny's head. "There's a cute little devil bunny, but no twitching her nose while I'm trying to terrify her."

From the look in her eyes, she was plenty terrified.

He stroked her hair.

Another tear leaked out.

"Some guys like the chase," he whispered into her ear, trying to get back in the mood. "Me? I like the helpless despera—"

Nope. The mood was gone.

No sense in even trying to play, now.

He slammed the knife hard into her stomach, and her eyes popped open even wider as she gasped. He twisted the blade and shoved it all the way up into her rib cage.

Blood gurgled from her lips.

He drove the blade farther, until he was certain he'd sliced open her heart.

He yanked his arm back and shoved the girl so she fell off his knife arm and landed in a heap. Warm, dripping blood covered him up to his elbow. He shook his hand twice to spatter it on the blanket.

"Hey, look. Orion."

He thought about something Mary had done.

"Should we make a zombie, Mr. Bunny?"

He crouched down. The girl's body had started to cool. Mr. Bunny sniffed at her hand.

"Oh. I think she needs to be alive for that to work."

Twist lifted the girl's hand and released it.

It fell heavily.

"Maybe next time."

He glanced around. They were too close to the camp for him to just let the corpse rot, and there was no way he was going to dig a hole in that rocky soil. Hm.

"Oh, hey." He rose. "Mr. Bunny, round up the gang and bring me a couple of mountain lions, or bears." He realized what he was saying. "Maybe a tiger if you can find one."

Mr. Bunny regarded him quizzically, head cocked to one side.

"The tiger thing was a joke. Find a sense of humor, too, while you're at it."

Chapter Eighteen

Screams of terror yanked me out of a sound sleep into unfamiliar darkness. Unfamiliar freaking *blackness*. Something held me down. The screams raped the quiet night.

A sudden light showed me that my attacker was my sleeping bag.

That's right. Camp Lindy-Ho-Ho.

Ephraim crouched by Woody, who was still screaming. The little guy just sat there not doing anything. What the hell?

Bam! Woody knocked Ephraim aside as if he weighed nothing.

I scrambled to free myself from my bag.

K-pop dropped into place and grabbed Woody's face. "Wake up, Woody. Hey! *Hey!*" He pushed himself nose to nose. "*Hey!*"

"K-pop, don't," Ephraim insisted, but K-pop shrugged him off.

The screaming stopped. Woody sucked in air and his eyes searched K-pop's face in a way that made me very glad I didn't have *his* dreams. He grabbed K-pop's wrists. "K-pop?"

"That's it. It's K-pop. You're fine, Ed—Woody. You're fine." He glanced at the four guys standing around with their cell phones on for light. "We're *all* fine." Ed was his brother's name.

The door slammed open. Dad rushed in with a lantern. "What happened?"

Woody shied like a frightened colt. K-pop held him fast.

"Nothing." Ephraim pulled K-pop aside and took his place. "Bad dream." He focused on Woody. "You can go back to bed, Mr. Fox."

Dad crouched down near them. "What happened, Woody?"

Woody's wild eyes flicked to my dad. His brow furrowed. Recognition dawned. Even in the dim light, the flush to his face was visible. "*Mierda*." He pulled away from Ephraim. "*Nada*." He glanced around with frantic eyes. "What are y'all staring at?"

We all kind of looked away.

Except Dad. "Woody, I need to know what happened."

Good ol' Dad. The moment he realized we weren't being eviscerated by Jason, he switched gears to make sure Woody wasn't covering for something one of us had done.

Woody pushed to his feet and backed into the wall. "*Nada* happened, okay?" He stared at the floor and hugged himself tightly, pretty vulnerable in nothing but his Old Navy briefs. He was still panting.

"Sam's fine, Mr. Fox," Ephraim said in that cool emotionless voice he usually reserved for his wacky jokes.

"I'm sorry but I need to hear—"

"Fine." Ephraim gestured at the rest of us. "Let's go outside—"

"No." Woody started shaking. "*Estoy bien*." He pushed between Dad and Ephraim. "I just need to take a piss."

Dad caught his arm.

"No!" His voice erupted in panic. "*No me toques!*" Don't touch me.

Dad pulled back.

We all stared.

Woody looked around. Embarrassment colored his face again. "I'm a *huerco chiflado* who has nightmares, okay? I shouldn't have come on this trip with you *pendejos*, anyway." He ran out the door.

Ephraim grabbed Dad's arm before he even moved. "Don't. He just needs to walk it off."

Dad seemed torn, which made no sense. Woody could get hurt out there.

"Really," Ephraim insisted. "We shouldn't've even woken him."

Dad didn't move.

"Screw that." I rushed to the door before Ephraim could stop me. "He could get hurt out there."

"He doesn't want your help," Ephraim insisted.

I glanced at Dad. "Yes, he does."

Dad nodded. He'd stop anyone else from following. Woody needed a friend, not an audience.

I found him a short distance away, crouching against a tree, hugging himself. Thank God the moon was bright. I moved carefully to avoid slicing open my bare feet, glad I'd decided to wear a t-shirt to bed with my Captain Americas. Chilly.

"Woody?" I didn't want him to just notice me standing there, both spooky and creepy.

He jumped to his feet with a gasp. "*Jesus*, can't you give it a rest?" He turned toward the brush.

"Woody, don't. You'll kill yourself out there."

The nearby creek burbled quietly. Who knew what he might stumble into? He stopped.

"You don't need to say anything," I told him. "I don't either. I just don't want you out here by yourself like this, okay?"

"Like what?" His voice was belligerent.

"Like I was at Starbucks."

He took a breath, hugged himself. "*Qué fue eso* anyway?" What was that?

Deep breath. "Flashback to the assault." After what I'd witnessed in the cabin, the words came easily. "It's like I was back on the ground again getting beat down. I wasn't even in Starbucks for a second there."

"That happen a lot?"

"Not a lot."

He seemed to be waiting for more.

"A couple of times at night, maybe." I nodded at the cabin. "Not like that, but I'm glad Dad's always right there with me when I wake up screaming."

"Screaming?" He turned to me, his face crying out with hope.

"Maybe not screaming," I admitted, "but loud enough to wake up my dad." I swallowed. "You heard about the poison?"

He nodded. Small town.

"It gave me nightmares." I hugged myself. "Bad, bad shit. My dad wouldn't let me sleep alone because I almost accidently killed myself."

Woody stared off into the darkness. "You're really lucky with your dad."

"Yeah. Yeah, I am." The stream burbled beside us. "And now I have to wiz."

He chuckled. "You bastard."

We turned our backs to each other while we took care of business. When I turned around again, his eyes were already on me. "I really *don't* want to talk about it right now."

"*Está chido, güey.* You seem fine. I can go."

He smiled at my Spanglish.

"Although you might want to throw on a pair of shorts in case someone's wandering around."

"Pffft." He ran his hands through his unkempt hair. "I jack off online for cash. I could give a shit who sees me in my underwear."

Um.

Another um.

"Is this one of those fucking-with-me things like Ephraim does?" I asked.

"Nope. Although. . ." He grimaced. "Okay, maybe I shouldn't have dropped that."

I raised a hand. "Not judging. I was just surprised because Retro and Ephraim are so shy. Figured it was a small town thing."

"It's a Mexican thing," he said. "*Apacado.*" Which made no sense since Ephraim wasn't Mexican. Then Woody winked. Ah. He and Ephraim *were* friends, after all. "Not many people know about that, *güey.* Just Effy and K-pop. To be honest, it kind of slipped out."

"K-pop?" I thought Woody was closer to Corey.

"Remember the cameras?"

"Oh." So *that* was why he'd needed the cameras during the whole Twist fiasco.

He must have seen me connect the dots. "I need hidden cameras so I can leave them up without my parents finding them." He smiled. "Also makes it look like I don't know they're there. People are sick." He fidgeted. "I never show my face. I don't really want a lot of folks to know about this."

"My lips are sealed."

"*Chido.*" He smirked.

Uh-oh. "That *does* mean 'cool,' doesn't it?"

"It's just funny I need to be careful what I say in Spanish around a *güero* like you." He shivered and hugged himself. "Okay, I'm just cold, now." He looked at me. "Thanks for coming out here. That was solid."

"You coming back in?"

He stared at the cabin. "'Cause that won't be awkward."

"Pffft. We're dudes. None of them even remembers it happened."

He scoffed. "*Ese*, you and your buddies are so *Teen Wolf* bromance I'm surprised no one's calling you Boyfox and K-trot."

"Oh. . . man. That *kills* me." I clasped my chest with both hands. "How many tea parties did it take for you and Ephraim to come up with those nicknames?"

He laughed, but he did head toward the cabin. "Actually, I stole them from Juicy."

As expected, the guys were all bunked in again so Woody could pretend nothing had happened. A dim lantern helped us avoid stepping on anyone.

Dad was gone, but he'd likely stationed himself nearby so he could watch without being observed. He'd hear the report in the morning. Seeking him out now would be rude to Woody, who was bound to notice.

Speaking of noticing, K-pop's sleeping bag lay open and empty.

"Pissing," Corey whispered. "But a while now."

My sleeping bag called to me seductively.

"Ask him again," Dad had said to me a couple of weeks ago.

The bathroom glowed in the dark as I neared it. Steam drizzled through the openings in the gap over the shower walls, and the sound of running water reached me above the sound of the gurgling stream.

K-pop's clothes lay strewn across a bench in the changing area, but he remained invisible at first, although I noticed the running showerhead right away. As I reached the tiled half-wall that separated me from the showers, I spotted him on the floor leaning against the shower pole.

"Oh shit, dude!" I turned away abruptly. Holy masturbation, Batman. "Sorry." And time to make an embarrassed retreat.

"What? Wait, no!"

I stopped, but didn't turn to face him.

"I would not jack off in a freakin' public shower, hai?"

I turned to him.

He'd risen to his feet, and was rinsing off. "Bro. How well do you know me and you think I'm that uninhibited?" He shut off the shower. "I just like water."

A snarky comment died on my lips as he wrung out his hair. There was more to it than liking water. "I don't actually know you so well, do I?"

He stopped. He held my gaze for a few inscrutable seconds before dropping his eyes to the floor and resuming his hair ritual.

"Will you tell me about Ed?" I asked.

"Ed?"

"You know, your brother? I heard you say his name instead of Woody's." I tossed him a towel from the stack Dad had provided. "I'm not *that* fucking self-centered."

He padded across the freshly scrubbed tile, toweling off. "I know. It's just—" He ran the towel over his face and hair. He didn't seem nearly so tall with his hair down. "Ed has night terrors, too." He dried off. "From combat. PTSD."

"Like what Woody had?"

"Worse." He glanced around and held up the towel. "Where do we put these?"

I took it and folded it while he slipped into his sweats.

"You really want to hear about this?" he asked.

"Yeah."

He pointed at the towel in my hands. "What're you going to do with that?"

"I'll get a box or something tomorrow." I dropped the towel on the bench. "Wanna head outside? It's kinda sterile in here."

"Which is a good thing for a locker room."

I held the door for him. "Not so much for late night conversations."

We killed the lights and walked closer to the stream so we could watch a tiny slice of moon dance on the water.

"My room's across from his," K-pop said once we'd settled in. "So when he freaks out at night, I'm pretty much designated guy to talk him down."

Oh man. That's why we never had sleepovers at his house. In case Ed started screaming. Or? "Do we always hang at my place because you're embarrassed or because it's nice sometimes not being the designated guy?"

His tiny snort told me he was surprised I came up with that. "A little bit of both, I guess."

"You don't need to be embarrassed," I told him, "but any time you need a break, you're welcome to crash at my place. I hope you know that."

"Thanks."

The gurgling and rippling stream lulled me, drained the adrenaline out of my system.

"I've been a freak my whole life, Ethan," he said so quietly, I had to watch him so I could tell what he said. "I don't remember a time without someone teasing me or jumping me or pounding on me."

Why hadn't Ed helped out? Maybe some families weren't built that way.

His face was peaceful in the moonlight. "I didn't tell you because I figured you wouldn't care. No one ever has." He smiled. "Wow, that was pathetic." The smile slid off his face. "It's true, though."

"Not pathetic," I told him. "Just. . . kinda sad."

He looked up. "Grilled Cheezus, there's a lot of stars up there. We need to go midnight swimming before this is over." He pointed. "Satellite."

"Where?"

"In Orion, it's the star that's moving."

Still didn't see it. "How do you know it's a satellite?"

"Stars are stuck in place. Shooting stars burn out." He lowered his arm. "I want to be a satellite. They just. . . fly."

"K-pop." It was all I could say.

He chuckled. "Sorry, bro—"

"Don't." We stared at each other. "I should know more about you," I said. "I care. I really do. I'm just. . . not so good at it."

He smiled. "You do better than you think."

"After everything you did for me. . ."

He shrugged. "I told you once before, brother. It's not a contest."

"I want to do better. Tell me something I should already know."

Our eyes locked for a really long time.

"Before Kiki," he said at last, "I was convinced I would die a virgin. Now? Maybe I have a shot at someone seeing my dick before I'm eighty." He smiled. "Well, someone other than you and Corey."

He talked. I listened.

Corey was first to rise the next morning. "Come on, guys! First day of shooting! Let's get famous!" And all those exclamation points were warranted. Nearly everything any of us said could've used one.

"So the makeup guy said shower and shave but no gel or anything." Retro's reminder was pretty unnecessary as we hurried together into the bathroom. He poked K-pop with a finger. "That means you, too, Major Product."

"Yeah, yeah." K-pop turned to me. "Think they'll make me cut it?"

"Nah, they can always shove it under a hat." Inside the building, the tile floor chilled my feet, but the showers heated faster than expected.

"Stellar." K-pop shook his hair under the spray and splashed Ephraim.

"Because the Jew needs baptizing, right?"

"Your dad did a great job cleaning this place." Corey's shampoo smelled like coffee, of all things. "We need to do something nice for him."

"Did anyone else think that thing with the song yesterday was weird?" I asked. "Do you really think it was a coincidence?"

"It was a radio station." Woody banged his shampoo on his palm. "*Mierda*. Can I borrow someone's shampoo?"

K-pop tossed him a bottle. "That's just it. Why would he use a radio station to test the system? Especially out here. An MP3 makes more sense."

Woody tossed the bottle back. "Wow. Paranoid much?"

K-pop let it drop, but not before he and I scowled at one another to acknowledge our mutual paranoia society.

Corey nudged me, his brow furrowed.

I shook my head. Not the time or place.

"Ah, shit," Retro called out. He was already at a sink. "I forgot my razor."

Woody laughed. "*You* have to shave?"

Retro scoffed. "Coming from someone who completely shaves his junk, I am not insulted."

Woody snatched a towel and bound it around his waist. "Okay, everyone needs to stop staring at my nuts."

"Unless you pay him first," Ephraim tossed out, then abruptly covered his mouth.

Everyone froze.

Woody looked around. "Is there anyone in this room who *doesn't* know?"

"What, that you whack off online for cash?" Corey toweled off, unfazed as usual. "Ephraim told me, bro."

Woody turned very slowly to Ephraim. "Who else did you tell?"

"Wait," Retro interrupted. "You whack off online?"

Woody covered his face with his hands. "And I thought last night was embarrassing."

K-pop laughed. "Dude, last night was just another day ending in Y at my house. Don't sweat it."

Woody looked up. "Really?"

I rummaged through my bag and threw Retro a disposable razor.

"Always carry a spare?" No doubt grateful for a change in topic, Woody hurried into his clothes.

"Sorry. Habit." Still in my towel, I chose a sink and sprayed foam into a hand. "When I competed, I was on my own to remember stuff like that, so I'm just used to overpacking."

Corey took the sink next to mine. "His Dad totally packed it for him."

"*Totalmente.*"

"He's better than a Jewish mother that way."

"*Sin duda, ese.*"

"Hai."

You know, as much shit as Tango gave me about my bromances, sometimes I felt those guys actually *did* get me better than her.

How sad was that?

Twist's ghostly entourage kept him informed. A squirrel had an eye on Lizard. Since he was the youngest, Twist hoped he'd give up what exactly the band had planned.

"It just seems. . ." the kid said.

"It seems what?" His older brother pulled on a fresh t-shirt and sat beside Lizard on the cot. "Super great? Because that's what Sony's going to tell us when they see we have ten thousand followers on YouTube. Ten thousand, brother, and I guarantee we'll have twice that by the end of the day, maybe ten times that by the end of the weekend."

Lizard shook his head. "I know, Ben. But if they knew. . ."

Whiskey threw an arm around him. "But if they knew that we were capitalizing on their trauma, they'd tell us to go fuck ourselves and then no one would benefit." He gave his brother's shoulders a squeeze. "Once they realize we're all going to make a million freakin' dollars, they'll thank us, right?"

Lizard sighed. "I just hate lying to Ephraim."

"Seriously?" Whiskey nudged his brother. "He lives halfway across the state, anyway. What chance. . ."

"He's a nice guy. I *like* him."

The brothers sat in silence a moment, then Whiskey chuckled. "You got a crush, little brother?"

"Don't."

"Lizard and Ephraim. . ."

"Screw you." He punched Whiskey in the arm and pushed to his feet. "I'm not like you. I can't just bang whoever I want and pretend it doesn't matter."

Whiskey didn't speak, just stared at his brother.

Lizard sighed. "You are such a jerk sometimes. Okay, so I've never banged *anyone*, but. . ."

"What a gas!" Whiskey rose and moved closer. "You really like this guy. You'd let him. . ."

"*Let* isn't part of it, you asshole." Lizard gave Whiskey his back. "He's. . . I really like him, okay? I just don't want to. . ."

Whiskey spun Lizard and grabbed the front of his shirt. "We will all make millions on this. Your new boyfriend, too. After we're done, he'll thank you with the world's best blow job." He settled Lizard onto his feet. "You need to trust me, *Lagartija*. I love you. I wouldn't do anything to hurt you."

Lizard sucked in several deep breaths. "I know. I know that."

Twist drew away from the squirrel.

What the shit?

Chapter Nineteen

When Dad, the guys and I reached the cafeteria, tables along one wall held breakfast. Woo-hoo! Coffee! The girls already wore costumes and makeup and yowsa they looked hot nibbling to avoid ruining their lipstick.

Tango set down her java and ran over to me. "Oh my God, this is amazing!" Big hug. "Good morning, sexy. I'd kiss you but we're about to tape the girls' routine." She swirled a hand over her face. "Makeup."

"I would not have thought it possible for you to look hotter," I said, "but I stand before you corrected."

She blushed and hugged me again. "So we're okay?"

"Outstanding."

She gave me a little peck on the lips, then rubbed the lipstick off. "Not your color."

"Places, ladies," Sarah the director shouted. "Guys to makeup and wardrobe."

Tango made an oh-my-God face and fluttered her hands before running off. All the girls bounced and bounced. Ecstatic energy filled the space.

It seemed to infect the guys, too. They scarfed donuts and coffee and laughed and pointed as we filled plates to take with us to makeup.

Mom appeared, made up and costumed just like the girls. Yowsa!

"Holy MILF, Batman!" Woody called out.

"Dude!" Corey punched his arm hard enough he splashed coffee.

Mom beamed and turned a circle for us. "So, I look okay?"

"You look beautiful, Mom." Corey elbowed Woody again. "You're in the shoot, too?"

She folded her hands. "Well, they want me and Dad both." She beamed at Dad. "Can you believe it?" Her excitement stripped decades from her. It was something I'd seen at innumerable comps. Something about a fun costume and makeup turned all women into teenage girls. Way cute. "They want us to kind of stand there and sway to the music looking like teachers or principals or something." She clapped. No. Seriously. Clapped. "We're gonna be in a music video!"

Dad laughed and hugged her.

Lizard ran up. "Let's go, guys." He and Ephraim exchanged smiles that rated way past anything on the Disney sweetness meter. "You too, Mr. Fox. We forgot to fit you yesterday, so I need to make sure your suit works."

Dad laughed. "I doubt you'd happen to have anything on hand."

"No, no, no," Lizard insisted, taking Dad's arm and dragging him away. "We brought one for you." Dad let himself be led away, eyes pleading with me over a shoulder.

I laughed and waved. "See you in wardrobe, Dad."

Hm. They sure planned ahead.

Mom clapped again. "Isn't this exciting?" She ran off as the girls started moving through their choreography.

"Boys get to your damn dressing room!" Sarah managed to shout at us with her camera pointed at the girls.

"Come on, guys." I led the way.

Two dudes from the band changed in the middle of the room. They snickered. "Look at the wittle boys," one of them mocked, "wif dere wittle dressing room."

The other guy laughed.

Woody paused. "Dude, I make my money shooting porn," he

deadpanned. "You need to *pay* to see all this. Back off."

The guys lost their grins, not quite sure whether he was serious.

Without expression, Woody turned and led the way to the dressing room. "Eh, it's not such a big deal, anymore, I guess."

Ephraim scoffed. "I've seen your videos, and that's not true." He patted Woody's shoulder. "By the way, young Padawan, that was impressive."

"Huh, you think *that's* impressive—"

"Don't push your luck. I'm a Master."

"A master—"

Ephraim grabbed his arm and raised an eyebrow threateningly.

Woody's hands came up quickly. "I'm sorry, I'm sorry. You're the comedian. I'm the straight man."

Ephraim nodded. "And don't you forget it." He passed through the curtain.

Woody bumped my chest with a fist. "There are so many jokes I want to make about this guy named Lizard," he whispered, "but Effy would *shred* me. Help a brother out?"

I pushed him through the curtain. "I will give it my undivided attention."

"Fuckin' A."

Effy? Those two must be *really* tight.

Fully dressed, made-up and coiffed, I found a spot near the food to watch Tango perform with Whiskey. The director shot the ass grab move over and over again, like it was a new toy. Whiskey *so* put her up to that.

Jimmy Russo joined me. "Hey, Foxtrot." Fist bump. "So the director wants to do a series of shots here, then over at Corporate for the green screen."

Whiskey worked the mic stand like he was fucking it, and Tango danced around him. He sang directly to her the entire time, seduction and horniness blowing off him in waves. The pure, sultry hotness in Tango's face boiled my blood.

"Then we'll put on death makeup for more green screen."

He tossed the mic stand and grabbed Tango, spun her a few times, drew her close and they pivoted around the stage Velcroed at the hips, which is actually necessary for pivots, but Tango didn't need to act like she enjoyed it so much. Well, yes, she did need to act that way. Crap.

"We'll add full-on corpse prosthetics and distress the costumes." He waved a hand in front of my face. "Dude, the jealous boyfriend expression of pure hatred will entertain Whiskey to no end."

I started and gave Jimmy my full attention.

"Do you want to give him the satisfaction?"

Indeed, I did not.

Jimmy handed me a printout of the schedule.

"Thanks."

"You've been in this business how long?" he asked.

"I know, I know." And Monika had done a bunch of far sexier routines with other pros. That had never bothered me. "He came out and told me he wants to score with her."

"That does not surprise."

Tango finished her scene and gave Whiskey a big hug. The whole experience was like a dream come true for her, and he'd granted her wish. Not me. Him.

"I love to play with the man," Jimmy told me, "And the man can wail a tune. He's also good at the business, which is not a common thing."

I waited for the but.

"But I would not say we're anything like friends."

Tango spotted me and ran over. Big hug. "How did it look?" She opened her hands and scoffed. "I didn't extend the kick nearly as much as I could have." She hugged Jimmy, too. Adrenaline brought out the hugger in her. It was cute.

"You were phenomenal," I said.

"Really?"

"Really."

A petite redhead approached. I recognized her as the female lead singer. She extended a hand. "Hey folks, I'm Ginger." She shook my hand. "I know, I know, I hate my parents." She had to be mid-twenties and she had the film noir *femme fatale* casual attitude nailed. "I like your work." She shook Tango's hand. "Especially you and the Asian girl. I can tell pros when I see them."

Tango grew three inches.

Ginger smiled at me. "Ballroom, right? World stage?"

I nodded with a smile.

"Thought so. Your form is impeccable even when you're bouncing around with the other monkeys." She tossed her hair. "They have great energy. The extremely tall boy has promise. I hope you keep working with him."

Tango chuckled. "They're practically married."

Ginger raised an eyebrow and smirked. "Cute." It was exactly the kind of world-weary, blasé attitude Monika had always attempted. This woman was a champion with it.

She laid a hand on Tango's arm. "By the way, Whiskey and I dated before the band took off. I dumped him because he decided success meant he needed to live up to the rock star stereotype of shagging groupies. He considers it an obligation or something."

Tango smiled uncomfortably. "Why tell me this?

Ginger laid down the perfect expression of big sister compassion. "Sweetie, I see the way you look at him when you're dancing. I really don't care, but you deserve to know exactly what you're getting into." Wow. Feral and concerned all at once.

"I have a boyfriend." She took my arm.

Ginger's eyebrows rose as she appraised me. "Oh. And he's cute. Sorry." She regained her film noir composure. "You're a *really* good actress. I was completely convinced. My mistake." She turned to leave, then stopped to look at me. "I thought you and the very tall boy were almost married."

"Bromance, not romance," I said.

She sniffed and nodded. "I see. Also by the way, I've noticed your youngest dancer and Whiskey's brother flirting." She smiled. "Lizard is a darling and nothing like his brother when it comes to affairs of the heart. Please don't paint him with the same unfortunate brush."

And away she walked.

Awkward.

Tango released her hold on my arm. "Don't," she warned. "Just don't."

After a few moments of silence, Jimmy Russo spoke up. "Yeah, she has that effect on a lot of people. You can't decide if you should worship her or burn her at the stake."

Yeah. Nailed it.

We had a mix of run-throughs and really short one or two move shots scheduled. Right away, the imbalance in gender was obvious. With me, the crew had one extra guy, anyway, and since Tango was stationed on stage with the band, we were six boys to four girls.

"So the extra guys can dance together," Whiskey called from the stage. "Easy fix."

"And that's stellar," I said, aiming my comments to the director, "but it does reduce the number of bodies on the floor." I gestured. "It's a big space."

She shook her head and waved her hands. "Not a problem. We'll be adding couples with the green screen."

Oh, well, that was cool.

Whiskey jumped off the stage and settled way too close to me. "I was hoping you'd let Lizard sit in on the green screen." He leaned even closer. "I know he's not part of your crew, but I think it'd be a total gas to let him and Ephraim dance together."

Total gas? Really?

"That would be really cool," Ephraim said.

"It'd be freakin' stellar," I added. "Lizard follows, so Ephraim can lead him in the same sequences he already knows."

Whiskey grinned. "That's great." He turned to Ephraim. "Hell, we should do some group shots with just guys dancing with guys." His face grew concerned, and he turned to me. "Of course, you don't have to, if you don't want to."

"Why wouldn't I want to?"

He raised his hands defensively. "I don't know. You seemed a bit uncomfortable dancing with me. Hey, open minds, right? We're all entitled to our opinions."

Dumbfounded does not approach my shock.

Corey jumped in. "Ethan's not like that. We dance together all the time, boy-o." In his enthusiasm to defend me, he pointed at K-pop. "Him, too. We even worked on tricks and shit in the pool, naked." He threw an arm around my shoulders. "He's totally secure in his manhood."

A horrifically awkward silence tortured me and then transformed into even *more* awkward titters. No. Really. Titters. Actual behind the hand titters.

"Wow." Whiskey moved away with his arms wide open. "I stand corrected."

Okay, so this one time we were in our sweats practicing acro lifts in the backyard. We jumped in the pool to cool off, and suits are for suckers, right? Then we realized, hey, falling in the water would hurt a lot less than on the grass. So we practiced the tricks in the pool. Yeah. . . naked.

Why is it stuff that seems perfectly innocent at the time always sounds freakishly homoerotic when I tell it?

Juicy rescued me. "What about girl on girl action?"

Whiskey gave her two huge thumbs up. "I am completely in favor of girl on girl action." He shrugged in an exaggerated and humorous manner. "You can film it naked, if you like." Another shrug. "Just sayin'."

Ha, ha, ha.

Juicy and Cosita hugged.

Tango killed the buzz. "This isn't a scrap book for the happy couple, Juicy. These people are professionals. You don't see me and Ethan stealing screen time."

"But we will, right? That was part of the whole point, right? You said so."

"No, no," the director said definitively. "I want to keep Tango with Whiskey. People would notice her dancing with other guys in close-ups, and we've decided to create a storyline between the two of them across a couple of videos." She followed Whiskey onto the stage.

Tango grabbed my hand. "Isn't that exciting?"

"Yaaaaaay for you." Juicy's enthusiasm was decidedly fake. She and Cosita stormed off together.

Tango's face begged me to be happy for her. I tried. I sincerely tried, but we'd gone from the two of us dancing the features to the two of us dancing in some of the crowd shots to the two of us dancing not at all. The screen time didn't matter in the least, but I'd spend all my time dancing with everyone *but* her. And, okay, awesome, I loved dancing with all my friends, but, damn it, I wanted to dance with Tango.

You know, the girl I loved.

Who loved me. Right?

"I'm very proud of you." I squeezed her hand. "Congratulations."

I moved off to find Juicy. If I couldn't dance with my girlfriend, at the very least I wanted a shot at dancing with the best dancer there.

Because that would be fun, and for no other reason.

I found her at the water bottles. "Any chance you want to show the losers in this band what you can *really* do?"

Her eyebrows furrowed for a second, then she held out her hand with a sly, wicked grin. "I thought you'd never ask."

I led her to the floor and noticed that Woody and Ephraim had paired up for this run through. And that was fucking awesome: Ephraim, who'd just admitted to the crew he was gay, comfortable enough to shout it to the world. And Woody happy to help him do it.

Wasn't that the kind of thing this trip was for? What the whole team effort thing was for in the first place?

Adrenaline raced through my veins, and I bounced on the balls of my feet to channel it, to ride it hard so the moment the music started, I'd fly higher than a kite. Juicy noticed the difference and her eyes grew big. She'd never seen my full-on performance mode before.

"Get ready," I whispered. "I'm nailing this down from the first note."

She bounced with me. Found my rhythm. Nice.

I played the song in my head to match our pulse to the music before it even started. "You're a better dancer than me, so I'm holding nothing back."

She squeezed my hand. "You just try to keep up, Foxtrot."

The director called, "Action."

A click track ticked off the beats. Against all protocol, I counted softly with the tick. "Two, three, four—"

Juicy got the hint.

"5-6-7-8!" we screamed together.

The music filled the room. The band pretended to play along and bopped to the music. The singers sang along with the recording.

The crew danced.

Juicy and me?

We ran a runaway freight train into the side of a cliff.

We ticked and popped as hard as we could. The kicks were all more than head height and every spin was at least a triple. A couple of folks in the band whooped, so we nailed it even harder. When we launched into the side by side Charleston choreo, I added jazz spices to every move, the way the old school bluesmen really did it.

Juicy followed motion for motion and outdid me on every bop, which just pushed me harder.

When the entire crew stopped dancing and circled us, clapping and calling, I dropped the original choreo.

Juicy read my mind. "Do it!"

I launched into a sequence I knew from a world-class showcase I'd performed. I lifted her over my head and snaked her all the way down my body to the floor. I dragged her and slid her between my feet, yanked her back, using the momentum to haul her to her feet.

"Jump slide," I cued.

She jumped while I changed to a handshake hold, and she slid through my feet. I switched from my right to my left hand, allowing me to spin to face her as she popped to her feet on the other side. We circled each other, left-to-left handshake, waving crazy jazz hands with the right.

I pulled her in close. "Up for the *Dirty Dancing* press?"

Wicked, wicked grin.

We separated, clapping and kicking, working the circle, pushing the crowd back, creating space. We faced each other and synced our hitch-kick, kick, cross.

As the music hit its climax, she ran to me, arms down. They lifted to her sides as she reached me.

I lowered into my knees to let her know I was ready, and she hit my hands, lifting with her legs the moment I did so, too. Effortlessly, she soared over my head, arms spread, legs straight, face up and radiant.

Perfectly balanced and locked. Amazing.

Thunderous applause rose around us.

The song ended.

"Coming down," I muttered.

I lowered her a few inches and popped her up. She folded perfectly so I could catch her in my arms. Wow. Thank God for her cheer experience. We never should've done that without practicing together before. I let Juicy down to her feet, and our enthusiastic friends mobbed us.

She squeezed me hard enough I couldn't breathe. "Thank you so much for that. It actually makes up for outing me to all my friends and family."

Cosita drew her away.

"Well, now *that's* what I'm talking about." The director smacked me on the back. "You been holding out on me, Fox?" She smacked me some more. "I need to get more of *that* stuff."

I bent over, hands on knees, panting. "Juicy makes me look good, ma'am."

"Oh yeah?" She made a face. "That's all it is?" She seemed to notice the pandemonium around her. "All right, kids, costume change. Someone fix Trudy's makeup, and we go for the next song."

Hm. Trudy. Not a bad variation on Gertrude.

"Sarah?" Tango called down from the stage. "Don't we need to do a few takes for close-ups or anything?"

"Nah," the director waved it away. "We had three cameras rolling and they all loved those two. We try that again and someone could end up with a concussion."

Tango looked heartbroken. Damn it.

I took Sarah's arm. "Shouldn't we get cutaway shots of the other couples? And Whiskey and Tango?"

Sarah glanced pointedly at my hand. I yanked it away.

She threw her arm around me. "Frankly, Fox, now that I see what you and Trudy can do? I'm not sure we need anyone else to do much more than sway and swing in the background." She squeezed me. "You know, there's a couple of other projects I'd like to talk to you two about, too."

Shit! "Please, Sarah, I only did that to let you see what Juicy can do. She can dance just as well with the other guys."

She laughed and waved me off. "You keep telling yourself that if it helps you sleep better, Fox."

"I don't want to take their screen time. I'm not. . . I'm not in this the way they are."

She eyeballed me for a moment and her face softened. "I'm sorry, Fox, but this is business, and I need to shoot what's best for the finished product." She waved at the dressing room. "I'm sure your boyfriend will understand that." She walked away. "Not that I can actually tell which one he is. Could be any of 'em."

Tango no longer looked hurt. Now she was just pissed.

Because, the entire shoot was for *her* benefit, right?

Damn it.

I hurried into the dressing room. "Guys, I'm really sorry if that messes things up for y'all. I just—"

K-pop stopped me with both hands on my chest. "Bro, that was wicked. Juicy deserved that shot." He glanced around. Everyone nodded agreement. Dad was there, too. "We're *glad* you did that for her, especially since—"

Fabric snapped behind me, cutting him off. Every pair of eyes opened into tiny pools of panic, and the guys took their clothes with them as they dashed past me. Apparently, watching Tango eviscerate me was scarier than showing off their skivvies.

Dad wandered out with a wry smile and patted my shoulder.

I turned to face Tango—and jumped back a step. Yikes! No wonder the guys had all escaped without another word.

"What the hell was that?" Hands on hips, eyes blazing with fire and brimstone.

"That was me giving Juicy a chance to shine."

"What about everyone else?" The effort to keep her voice down was obvious. "Do you *not* realize you just killed every guy's shot at screen time?"

That cut it. I was done. "Because *that's* why you're pissed, right?" I kept my voice quiet, but allowed every ounce of venom I could muster. "Give me a break. You're up there playing grab ass with the rock star, they decided you're not going to dance with me at *all* and it didn't even occur to you to mention it to me?" Okay, keeping the volume down was hard. "It makes sense, though, since you don't seem to care in the least about any of that. You're just afraid that if they see Juicy's better than you, they'll give *her* the features instead."

Her face turned very ugly at the Juicy's better comment. "Whiskey already told me that's *not* going to happen. *My* part's solid. But you heard Sarah. Everyone else is back to hiding in the shadows bobbing and swaying."

I crossed my arms. "No, actually I *hadn't* thought about that." She opened her mouth, but I cut her off. "But I apologized to the guys, and they're fine. They *thanked* me for giving Juicy a chance to show off. That's what friends do for each other."

"What about me? Am I not a friend? I heard what Sarah said. She wants you and Juicy for other projects. I thought you were going to help *me* show off."

I tried to let it go, but how the hell could I show her off if we weren't dancing together? Somehow, logic seemed the wrong approach, though.

"Do we have to fight about this?" I moved closer. "I don't care about the fame. You know that. I'm already trying to figure out how to sprain an ankle so the other guys get the rest of the shoot. I won't do anything crazy again. Can't we just have fun together? That's all I've wanted from the beginning. I just want to have fun with you."

She backed away, arms crossed and face angry. "Oh my God, Ethan, do you *not* realize just how selfish that is when there are ten of us here who want to make it in this business? Who want more from dancing than the occasional Saturday social?"

She stormed off.

I couldn't move. My entire body shook with fury. *I* was the one being selfish? Me? I had never, *ever* in my life felt so angry, so completely and totally overloaded with rage.

Jimmy Russo poked his head into the room. "Um. Just wanted to let you know that Sarah called a break to fix a camera and there's a punching bag hanging from a tree outside."

Stellar.

Chapter Twenty

I bruised my hands within moments. I stripped off the shirt so I didn't stain it. Fuck it. I stripped off the shoes and pants as well.

Pounding the bag helped.

Anger consumed me. I couldn't think. Red tinged the world. I'd never, *ever* been so mad at Monika, and she was ten times worse than Tango. A hundred times.

Maybe that was it. Maybe I was mad because Tango was supposed to be better than this. She wasn't supposed to act like a selfish bitch.

The first week we met, she'd given me all her coaching money to help the team. That was selfless, right? That was something Monika would never do.

That was the girl I loved.

"Ethan." Dad. In his "cool-it" voice.

I still had a lot to work out, but he'd trained me well. I stopped hitting the bag, stood motionless, panting. "Dad."

"Look at me." He knew better than to touch a guy who was hitting the bag out of anger.

Please don't let him yell at me for acting like a little kid.

I turned to face him.

He held a pair of gloves toward me. "You're no good to these people if you break your hands."

"Thanks." Something about his thoughtfulness drained most of the rage out of me. He helped me into the gloves, then stood back while I hit the bag a few more times.

Yep. He knew how to work me. Punching the bag ceased to be necessary. I bent over with my hands on my knees while I breathed.

He held up a pair of sweats. "The girls in the band have all decided you have a better ass than Whiskey."

Nice. I rolled my eyes so he'd think I didn't care, then held the gloves out to him. "I don't know why I'm so mad."

He removed the gloves and handed me the sweats.

"Monika was way worse than any of this." I climbed into the sweats. "She was a selfish bitch through and through."

"So why are you pissed off, really?"

"Because Tango should be better than that." I spit it out before I had a chance to censor myself. "The last three months she's been generous and kind and selfless, and I really love her for that. She's everything Monika wasn't." I arghed and hit the bag. "And it pisses me off she's getting sucked into the same jealous, selfish bullshit that *everyone* gets sucked into in this business."

"Because she should be better than all that."

"Yes. She should." I arghed again. "Why does this suck so much more?"

"Ethan."

I looked at him.

He leaned calmly against a fence post, ankles crossed. "I'm going to ask you a question, and I want you to think about it before you answer me. Okay?"

I nodded.

"Did you really love Monika?"

Of course I did. What kind of stupid question was that? I didn't say that though. Again. Well trained. I wiped my hands over my face and through my hair.

I'd been mad at Monika tons of time. I mean, pissed, sure, but this? This hurt my heart. Literally. It felt like someone was squeezing my lungs in my chest.

"I think so," I said at last. "I don't know. Not like this." I leaned against the rail beside him.

"I'll leave the gloves if you need them." He pushed away from the post. "Take a few minutes. Pull yourself together. Dry off. We're heading over to Corporate for the green screen shoot." He moved away. "It would help your friends tremendously if y'all gave the roadies a hand moving the equipment. You know how that impresses them."

Oh, that's right. I was a professional.

I was supposed to set the example.

Good times.

Twist was bored. The dance crew was. . . well, they were what they'd always been. Meh.

The band and groupies were more fun. Lots of sex behind the scenes. And the band was very excited about the crew's past with Twist, the "psychopath."

He really hated that word. He wasn't psychotic. He was focused.

Whiskey had repurposed a shed out in the woods where Teddy, who didn't seem too worried about his missing girlfriend, uploaded video to the band's site. Whiskey had cameras everywhere, and the site ran 24/7, but it was all lame and boring.

Watch the band rehearse.

Watch the dance crew whine and argue.

The only vaguely interesting footage was from the camera in the girls' showers in the Corporate building. They didn't seem to sensor that. Although Twist could see more with his ghostly entourage, now.

When was something interesting going to happen?

Maybe it was time for him to make a move of his own.

Corporate was U-shaped with a grassy courtyard enclosed. The right-hand wing housed the band, roadies, video crew and whatever groupies they'd brought to stand around in costumes and fill out the shots.

We. were. not. allowed.

They'd trashed the left-hand wing for background ambiance, zombie chase scenes and stuff like that. All *that* was scheduled for the next day.

The central bar of the U had bathrooms, showers and conference rooms. It also had. . .

"Oh. my. God." K-pop stood open-mouthed and staring. "I no longer care if I die a virgin."

The green screen space was a central conference room that'd been painted over every square inch. Some kind of smooth, matte lacquer covered the floor.

K-pop dropped to his hands and knees. "Wow. This makes it easier to clean."

Someone tapped my shoulder. Ginger. "That cutie pie is a virgin?"

"Sweet seventeen and never been—" I stopped my joke. What the hell? I wasn't that guy. Not with K-pop.

Ginger passed me with a couple of girls. "*That* is a tragedy." Her friends seemed to agree.

See, that's why K-pop was a virgin. He was down on the floor jizzing over the expensive treatment while three hot babes checked him out and walked away.

I hauled him to his feet.

"Bro, this is so cool," he said.

I pointed. "See those ultimately hot girls?"

"I certainly do see them."

"Had you been on your feet, I suspect they would have helped you take care of that whole virginity thing, right here, right now."

Massive double take. "What?"

I repeated what Ginger had said.

"Whoa."

Yeah, now that they were gone he expressed interest.

He waved it off. "I have Kiki. We'll get there when it's time."

Woody poked his face around K-pop's shoulder and grabbed the watch on his wrist. "If it's not time for those girls, *ese*, your watch is slow." And off he strode after the trio of hotties.

"I have a girlfriend," K-pop reminded himself quietly.

So there was a central lobby where we congregated, where we'd hang, practice, feed and generally wait. It was also the makeup room. Segregated dressing rooms had been set up off of that. The furniture was late 1980s dentist office, but there were monitors so we could see the fun in the green screen and so we knew when it was our turn to film. Long tables along one wall held food and drink.

Interesting side note: film people expect to get fed. Theater types will rehearse for ten hours on nothing but cigarettes and a tuna sandwich. Dancers don't actually eat, anyway, apart from a leaf of lettuce and a can of tuna per week. But film crews? Yeah, build food into your budget if you ever want to shoot a video.

"Hey, fake Asian," Sarah called to K-pop. "You wanna play with a *real* camera? I could stand to watch the video monitor and check levels."

"Sure thing, boss," he shot back without missing a beat.

She turned away.

3-2-1. . . He dropped straight back. I caught him before his head hit the floor and stood him up on his feet again. He spun to face me, speechless.

I patted his chest. "Go get a camera before she changes her mind."

He grabbed my face, kissed my forehead and ran off after her.

Goofball.

So the green screen stuff was a total hoot. Lots of costume changes and makeup and facial hair, you know, for the guys. Corey freaking loved the mutton chops and moustache. We danced short bits to fill in the larger scenes, changing costumes so often even Retro lost his self-consciousness.

"*Chicos*, this gig is a total sausage fest," Woody joked.

"You say that like it's a bad thing," Ephraim shot back.

Lizard, who was nearly an honorary member of the crew as often as he'd buttoned our flies, slapped him a high five.

In the lobby/makeup room, Tango's stylist set the final touches on an amazing French braid. The woman saw me watching.

"You know. . ." She touched Tango's hair. "If y'all want to dance together, I could find a blonde wig and give you a total Marilyn Monroe makeover. I guarantee even Sarah won't know it's you."

Wow. That would be stellar!

Tango met my eyes in the mirror with absolutely nothing in her face, then she looked up at the stylist. "Thanks for the offer, but I wouldn't want to do anything to jeopardize Sarah's vision."

The woman grimaced at me and mouthed the word, "Sorry."

"I appreciate the offer." I touched my fedora in salute, turned and almost barreled into Ginger.

"If I had a guy as cute as you who also seemed to be a ridiculous gentleman, I wouldn't be such a bitch to him." She looked me up and down and whistled. "If only I was five years younger."

So. . .

The shoot itself was, to use Corey's favorite word, awesome.

We had moments with the usual pairings, making sure all the guys danced with all the girls, except for Tango, who watched conspicuously from the lobby after she and Whiskey filmed their scenes.

Once Sarah was satisfied that she had what she needed, we ran back to makeup while Tammy, Lizard and the costume crew "distressed" the clothes. That meant ripping them up and pouring fake blood all over them.

Before heading into the guys' dressing room, Lizard cornered his brother. "Okay, you realize after we're done, there's no going back, right? So you're one hundred percent certain we have what we need?"

Whiskey pointed at the guys' room. "Go. Destroy."

Lizard's eyes gleamed. "I am so ready for this." He dashed off.

Ephraim, two chairs down from me, sighed. "I could make a fool of myself for a guy like that."

"Oh my God, Sandra Dee, can I puke right now?" Woody sat on the other side of Ephraim, yanking off his shirt.

"Sandra Dee? Really?" Ephraim shook his head. "Who's the gay one here? Do you grant me these opportunities to mock you on purpose?"

When Ephraim turned his attention to the guy helping him with makeup, Woody caught my eye and winked. Yeah. He totally gave him those opportunities on purpose.

"Bro, bro, bro!" K-pop took a knee at my side. He was already in full on zombie makeup with a knife through his neck, his hair jacked all the way to Jesus and a shirt so far shredded he might as well be without.

When I raised my eyebrow at the skin he showed, he sort of pulled the shreds of fabric across his chest. "Yeah, yeah, yeah, Ginger told Lizard to make sure she saw nipplage." He blushed deep, deep red. I could see he was trying to die of embarrassment and puff up at the compliment all at the same time. "Come. with. me."

"Oh, hell no, fake Asian." The busty Black girl waiting to start on my makeup blocked his attempt to steal me. "I have to make this boy dead. You need to make out with him, I will watch."

He scowled at her. "Fine." He pulled out his tablet "I'll just hack the system." He worked for a moment, then hunkered down next to me. He made sound effect noises while he worked, then thrust the tablet in my face. "Check it out."

The screen showed me and Juicy dancing on a hellish desert plateau straight out of Borderlands, including full-on animation with post-apocalyptic lizards creeping around us while we danced.

"Holy shit." I grabbed the tablet and replayed the video. "Dude. Seriously? You just made this while getting turned into a zombie sex slave."

"Bro." He punched my shoulder and blushed.

"Damn, fake Asian," the makeup girl said. "All that wonderful hair and a pretty brain under it, too? Mmhm, that girl back home is a lucky one."

K-pop froze.

I nudged him. "Dude, Austin is a whole nother world. I keep telling you." I handed back the tablet. "I hope to shit you're getting copies of everything you make here."

"Tcha." He crouched closer. "And Saundra made it clear in the contract that I didn't give up creative rights to anything."

Fist bump.

"Okay, bright eyes," the makeup girl said to me. "Get rid of the sidekick so I can kill you."

Big grin and off he ran.

Once everyone was made up and in costume, Whiskey clapped to get our attention. We were an awesome death brigade. Seriously.

Although. . .

"Is it just me," Corey asked, "or are the guys' costumes more ripped up than the girls?"

Tammy brandished her glue gun. "Are you questioning my creative vision?" She moved forward. "I know you're not questioning my creative vision."

"No, ma'am," he submitted, ducking his chin.

In his defense, he actually had no shirt at all and his pants were so ripped up they pretty much highlighted his underwear more than covered it.

Whiskey took center stage. "Okay, folks. You've worked damn hard so far today, and we have some amazing footage. Way beyond what we could've expected."

He started to clap and all the techies and film crew applauded. Okay, that was nice of him.

"So for the rest of the green screen, we're going to pretty much fuck around. I want tons of footage of creepy weird shit. Have fun with it. I know this is important and a business and all that, but this is your chance to have a blast and make a few memories."

Juicy shot Tango a vicious glance. Oops.

A good time was had by all.

Juicy and Cosita danced together. Ephraim and Lizard.

Hell, I even danced with Dad, which was actually pretty stellar. I mean, he couldn't lead more than a few basic club moves, but having those moments with him were so total me and Dad before any of the bad stuff the year before. After about thirty seconds, he ran out of material, so he body-slammed me and went all WWE on my ass. Total hoot with me in Zombie makeup.

Ephraim and Woody danced together, and I had shots with both of my "boyfriends." Corey salsa-ed me 'til I nearly wept.

Oh, and his pants fell off. Lizard had "distressed" them too much. They had to rip a new pair. Ha.

The girls performed a zombie rendition of their routine, and, when

Whiskey asked if the guys would shoot a zombie version of the dude routine so he could be in it, I agreed without hesitating.

Damn it. He really seemed like a decent guy, if he could just keep his dick in his pants and out of Tango.

Although, when push came to shove, wasn't it Tango's job to tell him no? I mean, way back when Monika raped Corey, and before we knew she'd raped him, Tango wasn't mad at *her* because *she* wasn't the one in a committed relationship. Corey should have said no.

By that logic, Whiskey was just a horny dude. It was Tango's job to say no. Damn, there was that logic thing again.

When Jimmy Russo ran up and grabbed my arm, I needed a few seconds to process the really horrible expression on his face. Immediately, it transformed into a smile. "Can I steal you for a minute?"

"Is something wrong?"

"No, not really." He scoffed. "Not at all." His grin became huge and fake. "Can I talk to you alone, though?"

I let him pull me aside.

"Does anyone know anything about engines?" he asked.

"Oh, shit. Problem with the bus?"

His face and gestures dismissed it as an insignificant problem, then he seemed to give up, and his face changed. "Yes. Anyone?"

"Corey knows a lot," I said.

Big smile. "Great. We need to get him without a ton of people knowing." The fake smile continued.

"Why?" My heart dropped between my feet. I knew what he was about to say.

"Someone sabotaged the bus."

I knew it. "How?"

He shook his head and lost the fake positive attitude. "Man, you need to see it. If I just tell you, you won't believe me."

Corey was hanging with K-pop, so I tapped them both on the arm and snuck them out.

Four zombies made their way out to the bus in silence.

For the record, I would have believed it. The tires were slashed. Spray paint covered the entire bus. The windows had been shattered.

"Ah, man," Corey moaned. "That's a mortal sin, bro. A bus that awesome?"

What did the graffiti say? The entire lyrics to "Every Rose has its Thorn." Add in "Tears of a Rose."

Twist was back.

Corey ran over to the engine, where a couple of guys were shaking their heads and smoking joints.

"How did he find us?" K-pop asked. "*We* didn't even know where we were going."

Excellent question. "Has the band posted anything about where we are?"

"We've tweeted about the shoot, that it was out in the woods at an old camp," Jimmy Russo said. "We've never given the location. And we always refer to it as Kamp Lindy-Ho-Ho, not the real name."

"Creepy," K-pop muttered.

But Twist had been a deputy. He knew the entire county.

"You haven't seen the creepiest part," Jimmy assured us.

We made our way into the bus. Long-stem roses covered the seats and the aisle. Hundreds of them.

"I wonder what it means," I said.

"It's roses, right?" Jimmy said. "He did roses in Tango's car."

"He did rose *petals*. Pieces, not entire roses. Everything Twist does means something," I explained. "There are no accidents."

"Hai," K-pop confirmed.

"Saundra snuck me all the psych evals and reports," I explained. "He was smarter than he seemed. The whole Barney Fife image was kind of a put on." I picked up a rose. "The change means something."

"That sick fuck." Corey hovered in the doorway. "Major pieces of the engine are just gone, bro. The stoners have the right idea. There is nothing I can do."

"Don't panic," Jimmy said. "Whiskey's already called it in with the emergency land line."

And at exactly that moment, the song blasted over the PA.

Fuck.

"Tango," I shouted. "Where the hell is Tango?"

Chapter Twenty-One

Back in the lobby, I spotted Tango and ran to her. Dancers had their hands over their ears, but most of the band didn't bother. Used to loud music, I guess.

"What the hell is going on?" Tango asked as I wrapped her in my arms

"Twist is back," I told her. "He's here."

"What?"

"The bus was tagged," I shouted, "and there's roses all over the inside. Can anyone shut down the music?"

"We can't," Sarah shouted back. "It's not running through our system."

K-pop pulled out a tablet. "Let me see if I can find a signal."

"What can you detect?" I asked.

"Everything that floats through the air except smoke signals."

"What the hell is going on?" Whiskey demanded. "What do you mean, 'Twist is back'? Your stalker did that to our bus?"

"Him or the tooth fairy," I snapped.

Dad appeared at my side. "Calm down. Whiskey, round up all your folks and bring them in here so we can do a head count."

Tango huddled closer. "He's after me. He's always been after me."

"I'm not taking that chance." Dad followed Whiskey to start gathering the herd.

"We need to get control so we can make an announcement," I said. "K-pop?"

"I'm just getting the band's Bluetooth devices," he told me, "which means he's hardwired in."

"What?"

He looked up from the tablet. "He's physically jacked into the system somewhere. Could be just about anywhere with equipment this old. Let me try something." The music cut out.

"Thank God," Tango said.

K-pop breathed a sigh of relief, then held the tablet closer to his mouth. "Attention all campers." His voice broadcast over the PA system. "Report to the Corporate lobby immediately. I don't care if you're naked and five seconds from cumming. Get your asses to the main building *now*."

Within five minutes, everyone was present and accounted for, even if a few folks were somewhat underdressed and the entire dance crew was made up like zombies.

"What the fuck is going on?" Whiskey demanded.

Jimmy Russo told everyone about the bus.

Then I told them about Twist. All of it. The stalking, the kidnapping, the shooting me in the leg. I even gave a perfunctory gloss-over of how I'd been poisoned.

"So your psycho's come to pay y'all a visit?" Ginger snapped. "And we get caught in the crossfire? Thank you so very much."

"Because bringing everyone here in one vehicle was the height of responsibility," Dad threw in.

"Ah, damn it to hell!" Jimmy ripped off his shirt and threw it to the floor. "A black man *and* wearing a red shirt? I am so gonna die!"

"Oh, come on," Juicy said to the room at large. "It's not like it's a secret. It was all over the net."

"Because college students in a band are so prone to watching the evening news," Whiskey maintained.

Whatever.

"I'm sorry he came after us here," I said. "But how the hell were we supposed to know? I figured he bled out in the desert."

The mutters and cranky whining told me some of them were still pissed.

Jimmy Russo came to my side. "This ain't on you. I knew everything that'd happened. Everyone thought he was gone for good."

"You kept tabs on me?" I asked.

He shrugged. "Hey man, some of my best days were at your dad's gym. I kept up."

Deep breath. "Thanks."

Tango squeezed me. "Thanks, Jimmy."

Dad clapped to get our attention. "We're all staying in Corporate tonight." He gestured to gather the guys. "Come on. Let's go get our stuff. We'll get the girl's things, too."

A gun chambered loudly, startling everyone. Several musicians dropped to the floor.

"Oh, please." Mom collected the girls with a wave of her large, scary gun. "We're perfectly capable of getting our own stuff." She shouldered the weapon. "I shot him once. And this time I have the semi-auto."

Mom led us out of the building and across the lawn. Dad held the rear with a pistol borrowed from Mom. "That's my favorite pistol, Lucky," she said. "Be careful with it."

Whiskey and Jimmy Russo followed us. "Everything that happens here is my responsibility," Whiskey explained.

Whatever.

Danger lurked behind every tree and in every shadow. The dimly lit path and dark woods that had seemed peaceful and cosy the night before freaked me out now. In a movie, the scene would've been comical, Mom and Dad escorting a herd of zombies.

No one laughed.

Even the gurgle of the stream under the bridge struck me as sinister.

Schilling shrieked. She pointed off one side of the bridge!

Everyone shouted and clumped up against the opposite rail, Mom and Dad with arms up to bear.

"What? What?" Mom called.

A dark shape loomed in the middle of the stream, shreds of cloak fluttering in the breeze. The scarecrow.

"I am very sorry," Schilling said. "It looked alive."

Shadows played across it, shifting the fabric.

"Well, that was exciting," Jimmy Russo said.

Ephraim chuckled. "I can see from here your nipples are hard."

More chuckles. The scare actually seemed to defuse some of the tension.

"He didn't go after anyone who wasn't alone," I said, as much for myself as for my friends. "As long as we stick together, we'll be fine."

When we resumed our walk, Ephraim held his arms straight forward and made moaning sounds. "Bra-a-ains."

A few people chuckled. Woody punched him in the arm.

"It's my sworn duty," Ephraim pointed out, "to lighten the mood."

We stayed in one group as long as we could, but Mom insisted we'd all get back to safety faster if we split up. We separated between the cafeteria and the basketball courts.

I held Tango close and kissed her. "Mom's a better shot than any of us."

She buried her face in my chest. "Can our fight be over, now?"

I kissed her temple. "What fight?" All things considered, it didn't really matter, did it?

Jimmy Russo followed the girls. "Nothing sexist. Y'all just smell better."

So Dad led the guys past the courts. Leaves blew and rustled across the broken blacktop. A grackle called out and leapt into the sky.

We all jumped.

"I no longer need to wiz," K-pop muttered.

Woody took Ephraim by the arm. "No more jokes until we get back to Corporate."

Ephraim nodded.

We crossed the grass to the village of cabins, picking our way by the light of the one lamp standing in the center of all the clusters. Corey found a dead branch and picked it up. He cracked it over one knee into two three foot lengths and handed me the other piece.

I nodded my thanks and held it across my hips.

Dad walked directly past his cabin. "Nothing I can't replace. I don't want to take any extra time."

We reached the guy's cabin. Dad tromped up the wooden steps and posted himself beside the doorway.

I turned the knob.

It clicked.

It had never clicked before.

A pronounced ticking froze my blood.

Dad's arms surrounded me. "Get down!"

He lifted me from the porch and ran for it.

We were no more than a few feet from the cabin when he dragged me to the ground.

Boom!!

Fucking BOOM!!

I scrabbled away from the searing heat, utterly deaf. "Dad!" My own voice was muffled and drowned in a high-pitched whine.

Dad's hands dragged me farther away.

Flames lit the area bright as day.

Was anyone hurt?

The ground shook, and the concussion of a second explosion cut through my deafness. I spun. In the distance, over where the girl's cabin should be, flames leapt into the sky. "Tango!"

Dad held me fast.

"I have to go," I shouted, but he was likely deaf, too.

I glanced around.

Corey lay on the ground, unmoving, K-pop and Whiskey at his side. Oh, hell.

I shoved Whiskey out of the way. Blood poured from a gash on Corey's right temple, but he was moving by the time I grabbed his hand. He opened his eyes and blinked a lot. I tore off my shirt, wadded it up and held it to his head, then I took his hand and brought it up to the wound. He seemed groggy, but he nodded and pressed the shirt against his head.

Retro sat a few feet away staring into the fire. Woody and Ephraim sprinted toward the girls' cabin in spite of Dad's silent shouts. I glanced back at Corey. He was already waving me to go and shouting something I couldn't hear.

Away I sprinted. I grabbed a little stone and lobbed it at the other two as I ran, hitting Woody on the shoulder with a lucky shot. He spun. Ephraim barreled into him, and by the time they had themselves sorted, I'd caught up. We were safer together.

The deafening silence scared me even more than the dim light. He'd be able to sneak up on us without my ever hearing him. I hated that I had to slow down so Ephraim could keep up but having those two at my back mattered more than an extra two seconds.

There! Across the basketball courts, a group of girls ran toward us. Where was Tango?

Panic pushed me as fast as I could run.

Schilling led the way, with Jimmy Russo a step behind. Juicy and Cosita. Mono. Mom. Wait, there she was. Tango appeared from behind Mom as I met them in the middle of the basketball courts.

Tango and I crashed into each other and held on. "We're all alive," I said. "Corey got knocked out, but he's okay."

No one looked hurt, other than all the fake blood and torn flesh.

Tango's mouth moved but I couldn't hear a word.

"All the guys are okay," I shouted as loud as I could.

She winced, covered her ears and shook her head.

Oh, they weren't deaf, too.

The rest of the guys skidded to a halt with us, including Corey who had my shirt wrapped around his head.

I grabbed his arms. "You okay?" I spoke without shouting, but exaggerated my pronunciation.

He nodded. Mom found him and hugged him, then held onto him and checked his wound. Guess Dad wasn't the only parent who did that.

I looked everyone over. They all seemed fine, although the damn costumes and make-up made it a little hard to tell.

Holy shit. We'd almost died.

Tango tugged on my arm. She tapped an ear and waved a hand at a nearby post with a PA speaker at the top. "What? I can't hear anything."

K-pop thrust a tablet into my hands. Text wrote itself across the screen: *Don't worry kiddos. You've had a long day. Take the rest of the night off.*

Dad and Corey huddled close to read over my shoulder.

A second line of text appeared: *You're a paradigm of vulture you sick frock.*

What the hell? I looked up. K-pop was shouting at the speaker, hands in fists at his side. I turned my attention back to the tablet. He needed a better speech recognition app.

Now, now, K-pop. Such language. Had to be Twist.

Kenny. To you my name's Kenny.

That was K-pop? Wow. I hadn't known his actual name. How much did I suck?

Are we tired of the nicknames?

Only my friends get to call me K-pop.

Mom drew him away from the post.

Error. Please speak more clearly.

I could hear it though. Faintly. Laughter.

Another line of text wrote itself, and I noticed Whiskey talking. *Drawing his attention might not be the best idea. He didn't have anything against you until now.*

Are you kidding? I'm the one who got his internet activity off the computer for the cops.

Wait a minute, was that K-pop again? That wasn't possible. We'd killed Twist's hard drive. How'd he get anything at all?

Whiskey's mouth moved. *Wow. Didn't know that part.*

Wait another minute, hadn't Whiskey claimed he didn't know *anything*? K-pop caught my eye as he retrieved his tablet. But Whiskey had been right there with us. He could've been killed just as easily as the rest.

K-pop seemed to read those thoughts in my face. He shook his head and shrugged.

Sound started to return. If I stared at lips, I could understand what people said.

K-pop fiddled with his tablet. "I mouthed off to him so he'd talk longer while I recorded him for evidence." He made a frustrated noise. "Looks like he's smarter than Warren. He's using an app that actually swaps out the original voice. You talk into it, and it replays your words with a synthesizer. No way to run vocal recognition software on it." He dropped the tablet to his side. "And he's still linked in physically somewhere. No way to GPS him even if we had a signal."

"Wow," Whiskey said. "You know a lot."

"Yeah." He looked up, drawing my attention to a group of campers running our way. "Our first encounter with Twist was a learning experience for all of us."

Tango found her was back to my arms.

The cabin fires were already burning down, but faint, ghostly lights flickered around us.

Deep breath.

No, that's it. Just a deep breath.

Back at Corporate, we segregated again to shower off the makeup and soot. I hated leaving Tango's side, but Mom was insistent that an evening of terror was no excuse to relax our standards. Jesus. Seriously?

Dad checked all the guys for injuries, but Corey was the only one with more than a bump or scrape. His wound had bled a lot, but was pretty minor, too, all things considered. Whiskey stayed with us until he was convinced no one was seriously hurt.

Since we'd been in costume, our civvies had remained safe in the dressing room. Dad retrieved them for us and laid out jeans and t-shirts from the costume shop. Shit. Everything else I'd brought with me was ash.

Once we were clean and dry, the crew gathered in the lobby, where Mom handed out blankets and pillows.

"When does the damn cavalry get here?" Juicy demanded.

"In the morning," Whiskey said.

The room erupted in protest.

Why weren't they already almost there?

He held up his arms to restore order. "Look, when we called, all we had was a broken bus," he said. "I didn't know some psychopath was trying to kill us. It was dark, and I told them they might as well wait until tomorrow." His face dripped with guilt. "I figured we'd still have a chance to get some exterior shots in the morning before the bus got here."

"And you haven't called them back, *why?*" I asked.

He looked around at the expectant faces, and I read what he was going to say before he said it. "The line's been cut. It's an old land line. I didn't even know you could kill one of those."

More general protest.

"So we follow the line out and see where he cut it," K-pop suggested after the roar subsided.

Lots of folks agreed.

Whiskey held up a hand. "We tried that," he said. "Teddy followed it out to the road, and it's intact all the way. After that, he could have sliced it anywhere from here to the edge of the county."

Shitstix.

The crowd rumbled and complained.

"Okay, people," Dad shouted. "It's one night. The sooner we bed down, the sooner the morning comes. We'll arrange patrols in shifts. Dancers, we're all staying here in the lobby together. Don't go anywhere alone, not even to take a dump." He turned to Whiskey. "I recommend y'all stay here with us, but they're your responsibility, not mine."

Murmurs rippled across the musicians and roadies, who stood completely apart from the dancers.

"I'll put it out there," Whiskey said quietly. "But I'm afraid some of my folks. . . some of them think this is your fault." At least, he had enough humanity to look guilty about that, too.

Dad gave him his back. "Whatever. Like I said, your call." He gathered the dancers at the inside wall.

"I'm sorry, Foxtrot," Whiskey said. "They're just scared."

"I know. We are, too."

I joined the crew in our makeshift camp. Juicy and Cosita curled up together. I hugged Dad, then let Tango pull me under a cover with her. Because that was really how I'd hoped our first night sleeping together would go.

Ephraim's gazed down at us enviously.

"Must be nice," he muttered and threw down his pillow and blanket. Okay, I felt bad for him, but you know what? I was a human being, too, and if Tango wanted me to hold her while she slept, we deserved that much.

Woody was already curled up with blanket and pillow. "Dude. Come here. You're with me." He held a hand up to Ephraim.

Ephraim scoffed. "What? Because I'm gay so that almost makes me a girl."

"No." Woody extended his hand farther. "Because I don't want to wake up screaming in the middle of the night and scare the piss out of everyone and give those band assholes a reason to make fun of me."

All the sarcasm in Ephraim's face died a violent, guilty death. "Oh. Wow. I'm a jerk."

Lizard had wandered over, but pulled up short when he noticed Ephraim with Woody. "Oh, I'm sorry. I. . ."

Woody smiled and held his hand out a second time. "You're with us, but I'm not sleeping in the middle of all that potential wood."

K-pop curled up with his tablet.

"Dude?" I asked quietly. For him, I felt a little guilty after the way he'd looked after me while I was having nightmares.

He smiled. "I'm fine. There's no way I'm going to sleep, anyway."

Dad's shadow fell across me. "Sorry, son, but can I get you to take first watch with Corey?"

Damn.

Tango looked at me over one shoulder and patted my arm. "Go. But make sure you give me a watch, too, Mr. Fox."

He helped me to my feet. "Sorry, Tango. You're the focus of all this. I'm keeping you as far out of it as I can."

Before she could protest, Juicy patted her arm. "He's right, Tango." She tugged her sleeve. "Help keep us warm."

Cosita raised an arm to invite her as well. Tango jumped up to give me a squeeze and a kiss.

"I love you," she said.

"I love you," I told her.

This time it felt real on both sides.

Corey waited for me a few feet away with a pair of matching baseball bats.

Christ. How the hell had my life come to this?

Chapter Twenty-Two

"Bro, it was wicked how much you knew about that engine."

"Yeah. So wicked I couldn't get it to go."

"It would've taken a miracle to make that engine work."

"Yeah."

Corey and I sat in the dark at a glass door about halfway up the wing where the musicians and roadies camped. We sat in the dark so we could see outside. The light in the middle of the courtyard showed us the entire lawn.

Mom had placed us in that doorway because we could see anyone coming into the courtyard without exposing ourselves to someone trying to shoot us dead. Twist would need to be in the middle of the lawn before he had a direct line of sight on us.

Which was something we thought about now.

"So how many points did you score last week?" Yeah, I was totally obsessing on my conversation with Theresa while we sat there.

His brow furrowed. "Uh, which game?"

"Huh?"

"Well, we had a scrimmage on Tuesday and a varsity game on Friday."

"Oh, well, the varsity game." Because, you know, I understood the difference.

"Well, I scored one touchdown, but it was mostly a passing game."

"Oh yeah? That's cool." I had no idea what that meant. "How are the new first string guys working out?"

He stared at me in silence.

"What?"

"Why are you asking me about football?"

"What? Dude, it's your thing. I've seen you. . . captaining. Being captain? Anyway, you're really good at it. I figured I should, you know, take an interest." Wow. I sucked at taking an interest. "Can I ask you a dumb question?"

He laughed. "I thought all those were mine."

"What? No, geez, no. I was just wondering. . . Can I come to the. . . after. . . party with you after the game next week?" What the hell was a party after a game called?

Suspicion radiated off him in waves. "Bro, we're just going to drink beer and talk about the game. You'd hate it."

The baseball bat lay across my lap. I twirled it. "Okay, look, how many Twyla Tharp videos have I made you watch? I just. . . I was just thinking about how good you are with the guys on the team, and figured I wanted to, you know, hang out with you in your element."

"What did Theresa say to you?"

"What?" Just how guilty did I look? "Nothing." I made dismissive noises.

"I'm never telling her anything ever again."

"No, Corey, it's not like that—"

He actually rose to his feet. "You think I'm too dumb to watch your high-brow videos, so you might as well slum it with me on my retard turf, right?"

Oh Christ, I hated myself. I jumped to my feet. "We almost died tonight, Corey, blown off the map, and before Theresa talked to me, I had no idea how fucking smart you *are*, and I hate myself for that, okay?"

"Shut the fuck up. Smart? Now you're just—"

"How many points did the team score at the homecoming game?"

He scoffed. "Like, ten. We totally sucked."

"Okay, the game before that?"

"Forty-five. The old first string finally had their shit together."

"Finally? What changed?"

"What? I made up this pass drill that finally got them catching the stupid ball."

"Right, pass drill that *you* made up, right? And Gunner. . ." I didn't actually know the names of any of the other guys. "How many points did he score in that game?"

"What? Gunner's a linebacker, he doesn't score touchdowns. He's defense."

"See? I have no idea what any of those words you just said meant," I admitted. "Why do you think I've never been to any of those parties with you?"

"Because it's a bunch of lunkheads drinking beer and talking about a stupid game."

"No. That's what I've always wanted you to think, which makes me the biggest asshole on the planet." Deep breath. "I go to one of those parties with you, and I'm in a completely foreign world where they talk a language I don't speak. I won't understand a single word any of those guys says. It'll be all stats and second downs and flags on plays and shit. Dude, I go to a party like that, and everyone'll assume *I'm* stupid." Deep breath. "I don't like to do stuff I'm not good at because I'm too damn conceited."

I stared at the bat. I had no idea what he would say.

He didn't say anything. Finally, he sat down. I couldn't stop thinking about a night a few months ago when I'd called him a name he might've forgiven, but he'd likely never forgotten.

I finally looked at him.

He didn't look mad, anymore.

"No crying," I said. "We're on watch."

He managed a smirk. "Okay, Ethan. You can come to the 'after party' with me." Shit, they called it something else, then. "And any big words you don't understand, you just ask me. I'll explain 'em to you." That was a paraphrase of something I said to him from time to time.

"So what *do* they call a party after the big game on Friday?"

"We just call it a party, bro. You think way too much."

I sat and we stared at the lawn in case a psychopath tried to sneak past us and kill someone. 'Cause, you know, that was the new normal.

"For the record? I'm glad Theresa bitched me out. I needed it."

He laughed. "She bitched you out? Seriously?"

"Dude, my balls crawled into my pelvis and whined."

He nodded. "She totally works the dominatrix thing. This one time. . ."

Trust me. You do not want to hear the rest of that conversation. Corey had absolutely no filter. None. at. all.

"Okay, boys, middle-aged woman on deck, stop talking about sex."

"Mo-o-om!"

Wow. She was a lot like Dad. "See anything?"

"Grass." Corey rose to his feet and offered his chair.

"That's about what we've seen everywhere." She waved him back into his seat. Something about a petite, middle-aged woman with a semi-automatic weapon cocked on her hip was über cool. "Can I ask you a completely inappropriate question, Ethan?"

Uh-oh. "As cool as you seem to be, ma'am, I am not discussing my sex life with you because I am a virgin who has never even kissed a girl."

Corey broke out in hysterical laughter. "Dude, I so wish I'd recorded that. You will burn in Hell for lying."

Mom leaned against the door jamb and regarded me. "It's actually about K-pop."

Corey and I exchanged a confused glance.

"You know our family is ridiculously rich." She said it as if commenting on the fact that she was female. "Well, every year I give out a full scholarship to a talented senior who shows great promise."

She shouldered the weapon. "I pretty much pick the winner based on my personal judgment. It's my money; I'll spend it how I like." She was sooo cool. "I want to award it to Kenny this year but he didn't apply." Her mouth drew a straight line across her face. "That makes it awkward."

I gave her room to talk.

"The work I've seen him do here? He is genuinely the most talented person to come out of that school in years." She smiled. "Present company excepted, of course."

Yeah, I was still not saying a word.

"I'm afraid if I just award him the money, he'll think it's because of his friendship with Corey." She shrugged. "Frankly, I could justify giving it to him on that basis alone if I wanted to, but I think he'd. . . have a problem with what he might consider a handout, so I need to make sure he knows that he's earned it based on his merit." She sighed. "I'm hoping you can give me some insight on how to say that to him."

Wow. I thought about it. "I would just say, 'K-pop, you're the most freakishly talented student to come out of Dumass high in years, and I want to give you a big wad of cash.'"

She laughed. "Really? That simple?" She shrugged. "I overthink too much, sometimes."

Corey snorted. "My best friend and my mom are the same that way."

She kissed the top of his head. "There's one more thing." She regarded me directly. "I'm going to rent a house for Corey in Austin. I'd like you and K-pop to live with him there."

Holy. shit. She was sooooo cool. That would solve all my expense problems. And the three of us living together? Totally awesome.

"Why would you do that?" I had to ask.

"I'm rich. We do what we want." She kissed Corey's head again. "Since Corey started playing with you boys, his grades have gone way up. I'd like to keep you around him."

"What, like babysitters?" Corey lifted his chin petulantly.

She rolled her eyes at him. "*Mijo*, UT would've accepted you no matter what with the amount I donate, but the way your grades improved the past few months? Now they're actually glad to have you. I love you, *mijo*, you know that, but we all need help from time to time. Don't be too proud to accept it." She looked at me. "That goes for you, as well."

I had to tell them something even Dad didn't know. "I'm not going to UT, ma'am. I never thought to apply for financial aid because I wouldn't have needed it before. Now it's too late."

She shrugged. "So go to ACC for a year and apply next fall. K-pop will have to start there, too, since his application to UT was rejected."

Corey and I exchanged a confused glance.

"What? He wasn't accepted to UT?" I asked.

She shook her head.

I'd thought it was just a money thing.

She sighed and looked around. "His grades were fine for the most part, but there was an F for gym class because he stopped going last year. He had nothing else on the application, no academic clubs or sports. He's a bright young man, but he doesn't know *bubkus* about filling out forms. His essay needs work, as well. I'm hoping to help him with that, too."

The fact she knew about his application to UT was kinda surreal. The fact she wanted to help him rocked the world.

She moved toward the corridor. "So you think the direct approach? I'm glad. It's my *forte*." Away she walked. "I'll send relief shortly."

We sat in silence until she was gone.

"Dude? Your mom is just as stellar as my dad."

"Yeah, she is."

So why had I never met his dad? "When are you going to invite me over to your place for a beer-riddled sleepover?"

"The next time Theresa isn't sneaking into my room to jump my bones."

Oh, yeah, there was that.

Huh, terrifying guard duty could be fun.

"So. . . you wanna be roommates?" Corey asked.

"Sounds awesome."

Later that night, Twist crouched over Fox's sleeping body. The fact that his enemy slept with his mouth open made Twist's job easier. Magic kept everyone in the lobby asleep, and, with Fox's mouth open, all Twist had to do was drip a few drops of potion right down his waiting throat.

Fox smacked his lips and swallowed. Excellent. It was the same stuff he'd dosed him with before, the stuff that had connected their dreams.

Twist rose. All these little boys and girls pretending to be adults, pretending that fame and fortune were right around the corner. Band members thinking they could be the big bad big bad. Dancers hoping for their fifteen minutes in the spotlight.

Well, like the frat boys under the pontoon raft, in their own special way they were right. They likely *would* be famous after Twist was through with them.

Dead, but famous.

Let 'em cap on his gig all they wanted. When all was said and done, he was still the man in charge. Twist dripped a few more drops of potion into Fox's mouth. *Awaken into another dream*, he thought, wondering if he'd regained enough of his magic to make it work without an actual spell.

He stared down at Katy as she slept in Fox's arms. All the women he'd taken had pretty much worked her out of his system. He didn't want her anymore, but that didn't mean it was okay for anyone else to have her. Especially Fox. No. Even if he *didn't* want her anymore, she still should've been his.

He picked his way around the sleeping bodies. He wanted to start small, to keep it subtle while he waited a day or so for his power to build.

Twist wandered back to the shack in the woods to bed down and see if he could climb into Fox's dream.

Mr. Bunny joined him as he walked along the gurgling stream.

Damn it. Now, he had to wiz.

The house stood alone in a deep, grassy field. Moonlight rendered the scene in abstract blue-black and white, outlining the old boards of the ramshackle building. A million stars frosted the sky. Dad walked up to the cabin, then stopped, turned and regarded me with a nostalgic smile.

All sound pulled away, as if my ears were stuffed with cotton or water. Everything slowed. My heart pounded. Thump-pump. Thump-pump.

Thump. . . pump.

I tried to run to him, to stop him. My body moved like it was under water. I had to stop him, had to prevent him from touching that door.

He turned away. I tried to shout, but my words were swallowed by the night. Slowly, so painfully slowly, he tromped up the steps and across the wide wooden porch, past the wicker chairs. I had to push harder, I had to reach him in time, had to pull him away.

Then he stood at the door, reaching for the handle.

I shouted to him, but my words were once again swallowed in silence.

He touched it.

White-hot light destroyed the night. A fireball burst from the cabin in slow motion, every flame swarming my father like a hive of angry bees.

The fire consumed him, burned his skin away. It flaked black and dry, and the muscles peeled from his bones.

He turned, stretching one skeletal arm toward me, his face a smiling rictus of bone. Then he turned to ash and blew away as the fireball rolled toward me, hit me full in the chest and fried me to a cinder.

"No!" I sat up in bed, the comforter falling to my naked lap. I reached a hand forward pointlessly. My breath exploded from my body in harsh gasps.

Instantly, Katy's cool hands touched the bare flesh of my chest, my back. "It's all right, Ethan. You're awake."

I drew her to me. Drew her smooth, naked breasts to my side. She cast her arms around me and held me tight. "It's okay, Ethan," she assured me. "It was only a dream."

"Only a dream," I said, attempting to bring my breath under control. "How, Katy?" I asked in desperation, "How am I to know it was only a dream?"

She barked a laugh. "Listen to the way you're talking, you dipshit." Her hand drew back. It held a huge kitchen blade. "Of course it's a fucking dream."

The blade plunged into my chest. Hot, bitter pain tore my heart asunder.

Her eyes! They blazed with an unnatural fire! Her hair! It blew out from her face in a surreal wintery wind! The knife! It plunged into my chest again and again, more painful than anything I had ever experienced!

"Holy fuck!" I forced myself up, gasping.

Hands grabbed me.

I opened my eyes and hurried away from them until the back of my head smacked a solid wall.

"Fucking *ow*." I brought my arms up to guard.

My chest throbbed. Damn, that hurt.

"Ethan. You're awake." Dad knelt there, his hands up. "You're really awake." It's what he'd said when I was having those horrible dreams from Twist. Was it real? *Was* I awake?

My eyes flashed around the room. I was in the cafeteria. Light from the windows told me it was morning. Tango sat at one side, her face panicked. Lots of faces stared at me. I was wearing sweats and a t-shirt, which made sense. Curled up with Tango in public, I'd be fully clothed.

Ouch. I rubbed the back of my head where it'd smacked the cinder block wall.

Ah, shit. Lots of people stared down at me.

Woody strode forward. "Okay, folks, everyone needs to piss off, now." He physically pushed people away, giving me an understanding nod as he forced the crowd to disperse. Which earned him his place at the table, right?

"Can I check you?" Dad asked.

"Yeah. I'm chill."

He pounced on me, hands on my face, checking the bump on the back of my head, but I knew he was mostly touching me so we both knew I was safe. "Mike told you this might happen," he whispered. "With all that poison, there might be something hitting you weeks later."

"I know, I know. Flashbacks. Yay."

The crowd dispersed. Tango sat staring at me, her face still worried.

"Sorry," I said to her.

She shook her head. "This is what you went through back home?"

I nodded.

She shook her head again. "You screamed. . . I thought something was killing you."

"Ah shit, did I shriek like a little girl?"

Dad chuckled. "Actually, it was a deep, manly bellow, so I knew it was real." He sat back but kept one hand on my knee.

Good ol' Dad.

"I woke up, but I was still dreaming," I told him. "I had no idea I was still asleep. It was more real than anything I have ever had." I winced. "Although, I sound like a douchebag in my dreams."

"A-a-and you're back." Dad held out a hand to help me to my feet. "You okay?"

I nodded.

Him, too. "We can't find Jimmy or Ginger."

That woke me up completely. "What?"

"They were on watch together," he explained. "I was on my way to get you when you screamed."

"What do we know?" I asked. "Should we keep this quiet to avoid a panic?"

The video screens jumped to life with a literal gasp. Jimmy Russo and Ginger, tied to chairs, gagged, blindfolded, their eyes darting from one side to the other, their faces bruised.

My heart pounded. I couldn't breathe. Why them?

"I want you to hand over Tango," the heavily affected voice said. "Hand her over and all this ends."

Tango's arms around me tightened. We rushed closer to the monitors. K-pop appeared at my other side. Corey was there, too. . . and Dad.

Tango shook her head in tiny, tiny movements. "Oh God."

Murmurs filled the room.

"No way in hell," K-pop yelled.

"Okay, that's easy for you," Whiskey argued. "Those aren't your people up there."

Tango froze in my arms.

"Something's not right," K-pop whispered. He moved so close to the screen I swear his nose touched.

"Send her outside alone or these two die," the synthesized voice said.

The dance crew closed ranks.

We weren't going to let anyone near her.

"I can't," she whispered. "I can't."

"We wouldn't let you," I told her. "Okay, Twist, there has to be a compromise. You haven't killed anyone yet. You don't want to add that to your list, do you?" I turned to the crowd and lowered my voice. "He won't do it. He hasn't killed. It's not his thing."

Bang!

Screams filled the room.

Fuck! Blood poured out of Jimmy's chest.

Ginger screamed.

Bang!

She fell back.

They lay there, unmoving. So still.

The screens went black.

Holy fuck!

Sobbing. Hysterical sobbing broke out across the room. Tango buried her face in my chest.

Jimmy was dead. Jimmy Russo who'd knocked me out once. Dead.

Ginger, who was hot for K-pop. Dead.

Cold, cold water poured over me, freezing me.

"Oh my Lord," Tammy called out, "the black man died first. Why does the black man always die first?"

K-pop pointed at the screen. "That's it. I knew I saw something."

He pulled out his tablet and the screen flicked back to life.

"What are you doing?" Whiskey demanded.

"I hijacked the system on Bluetooth," he said. "I've taken over, and I'm operating it remotely."

"You can do that?" The panicked edge in Whiskey's voice had vanished.

"You'd be amazed at what I can do." His voice was freakin' calm, considering what we'd just witnessed.

"Wait," Whiskey said. "Maybe we shouldn't mess with the system."

"Why not?" His voice was laden with innuendo.

The screens flashed apps I didn't understand.

"Who the hell knows what he might do."

K-pop scoffed. "I think it's more likely *you* don't want me to show this."

What?

He tapped the screen. Jimmy Russo and Ginger reappeared.

"Jesus Christ," Whiskey shouted, "What kind of sick fuck are you? No one wants to see that."

"No one?" K-pop asked. "Or you?" He slowed the video. "There. That's it."

Blood spurted from Jimmy's chest. The sound of a gunshot, low and slow, rattled the speakers a second afterward.

"Look!" K-pop pointed at the screen. "The bullet hits Jimmy's chest first and *then* the sound happens." He played it again.

"So what, you sick fuck?" Whiskey shouted. "It's some kind of glitch in the system? So what?"

K-pop froze the image and stared Whiskey down. "So it's fake, *you sick fuck*. It's the exact same camera you're using for the dance videos, too, you idiot. They have identical issues with low light. They pixelate. You didn't even take the time to buy a different camera?"

He addressed the crowd. "They use a blank for the noise and a thing, it's called a squib, a tiny explosive in a bag of fake blood under the shirt makes it look like they got shot."

He focused on me. I could tell my opinion was the only one that mattered to him. "You can't have the gunshot *after* the bullet hits, unless the whole thing is a fake. You think people who can do zombie makeup that real can't fake a gunshot or bruises? No one is dead. It's all a fake."

Silence descended on the room.

Holy. shit. Every single suspicion I'd had suddenly made sense. K-pop just got there first.

Then one tiny voice spoke. "This all sounded cool when it was an idea." Lizard tugged Whiskey's sleeve. "But these are real people, Ben, and they're scared shitless. I can't let you do this to them. And even our own people?" He looked around at the musicians and techies, many of whom seemed just as freaked out as my friends.

Wait. What?

Lizard seemed to read my mind. "If everyone knew, it could slip out. It wouldn't look real for the hidden cameras."

"Hidden cameras?" K-pop asked.

Lizard pointed out a few places in the room. "There's cameras all over the building. I can't believe Mr. High-tech didn't notice any of them."

Utter silence filled the room.

One. Two. Three. . .

Tango flew out of my arms and slugged Whiskey. "You blew up our shit!"

"No!" Whiskey said, holding his jaw. "It's in the cottage next to where you were staying."

I shoved him into the wall. "And what if my dad hadn't thrown me down, you motherfucker? We'd be dead!"

"No, no, no!" He grabbed my shirt in desperation. "The bomb wasn't going to go off until everyone was clear. Why the hell do you think I was there? If your dad hadn't sussed it, I would've warned y'all like *two* seconds later. Nothing was going to blow until they saw we were clear." He held my shoulders. "I would not have let anyone get seriously hurt, that's why the girls' cabin went up before they even got there."

Wait. "Until *who* saw we were clear? You have cameras out there, too?"

Whiskey froze.

Lizard stepped up. "There are cameras hidden all over the campground. We've been streaming live the whole time. Like a reality show. We hoped it would land us the Sony contract."

Ho-ly shit.

"There's another bus waiting a few miles up the road," Whiskey insisted. "We can call, and it'll come get us. We have three hundred thousand followers, Ethan. Three hundred thousand."

"How do you know that?"

He stared at me, then looked at the crowd, one face at a time. "The land line's perfectly fine. We've been streaming and monitoring the site the whole time," he said. "We're famous."

I so wanted to hit him.

Really.

I looked around. The dancers all seemed equally pissed.

"How nice for you," I said.

We left.

Part 3
Walking on a Dream

Chapter Twenty-Three

We split up to grab our gear. No one spoke a word. We found our packs right where he'd said, shouldered them and headed to the cafeteria, where we'd agreed to meet the girls.

I started my speech before the door was closed. "We get online in their secret lair, contact the police, have them send a couple of buses and Dance Monkey goes to live at the zoo."

Nods and angry glares encouraged me.

"I say we beat him up a little." Of course, Corey had my back, but it was nice to hear.

K-pop and Juicy seemed to like his suggestion, too.

"Or. . ."

Silence.

Every head turned to stare at Tango so fast I finally understood where that whip crack sound effect came from.

What the hell?

"Or what?" I tried to smile, to pretend I didn't know exactly where she was heading. Please God, let me not know exactly where she was heading.

"Or we finish filming and have a chance at starring in a Sony video production or two."

More silence. Every person in that room had their own opinions, surely, but in that moment the only two people who mattered were Tango and me.

"After everything that happened with Twist. . ." I said as quietly as possible. I loved her and didn't want to take this argument somewhere with no reset button. "You can pretend that they aren't supervillains?"

She rolled her eyes and took a deep breath. "No one was hurt, Foxtrot." She glanced at Corey. "Not seriously hurt."

Was she keeping her calm for the sake of our relationship or because she was hoping to change my mind?

"Thousands of people are watching us here. *Hundreds* of thousands. There's no way we'd have this kind of attention on our own. Do they suck? Sure. But there's no way to say they haven't actually done us a huge favor, too."

"Favor?!" I lost my inside voice. "They lie to us, play on the most horrifying shit that's ever happened to us. Strand us here. And they've done us a *favor*?"

I looked around for agreement. And it was there in a few faces, but a few seemed to agree with Tango and a few sheepishly tried to avoid reacting at all. Standing in the corner, Mom and Dad were the only ones who managed to actually mask their opinions.

"They made us think Jimmy and Ginger were dead," I said. "Have you forgotten what that felt like?"

"No." It was her calm voice, which made it worse. "But they pull that kind of shit on reality TV all the time."

"People get punked way worse than this, *ese*." Well, Woody wacked off online. Of course, he'd play along.

Fuck it. It was too much. After reliving that nightmare, the last thing I needed was my girlfriend more interested in her fifteen minutes of fame than in. . . in what?

Then in not being treated like . . .

"Fuck it." I stalked out, letting the door slam behind me. Not nearly loud enough to satisfy.

It slammed again.

"Ethan."

I stopped and turned.

Juicy rushed toward me. "I know, I know. You wish I was Tango, but if it was her, you'd both say things you couldn't take back." She shrugged. "Deal."

"This is why I gave up the circuit, Juicy." To her I could say it exactly the way I felt it and not because she didn't matter, but because I knew she'd actually listen. "You have to put up with this kind of shit, with people using you, taking what they can and throwing you away."

She raised an eyebrow. "Issues much?"

"No shit I have issues. I gave up fame and fortune because a night out on the town at the Dumass Starbucks is so much more glamorous? Listen—"

"No," she interrupted. "You listen to me, you selfish prick." I would've chewed her out, except I flashed back to a certain dressing down outside the studio where our roles had been reversed. "You spout off all this smarmy bullshit about loving your friends and *that* being more important than anything, but when push comes to shove, you're still a selfish douchebag." She lowered her voice now that she had my attention. "Without this, how do you suppose K-pop gets into UT?" She didn't let me answer. "Something like this in his portfolio could change things for him at the film school there." She opened her arms. "Can you imagine what this would do for Retro's self-esteem? I could say something just as important about every person on this crew." She raised a finger. "And don't you dare make this about me. I don't give a shit. I don't need this the way they do."

Her hands went to her hips. "You want friends, Ethan? You get their shit, too, along with all the hugs and kisses your gay ass seems to need."

I couldn't speak for a second. Because she was right.

"Who's been bullying him?" I asked. "Kenny, I mean."

She took a deep breath and relaxed. "The usual assholes. Gunner to start." She shook her head. "Does it matter who? You won't know the names, anyway."

She was right, damn it.

"It might even be a way for Woody to get some modeling jobs where he can show his face."

Whoa. "You know about that?"

"I also knew that Ephraim's gay, that Mono had a miscarriage last year, that Schilling would almost rather die than go back to her parents in Russia." She shrugged. "I could go on."

"How do you know so much?"

"I listen. I ask." She smiled. "Back after the big reveal, I became everyone's go-to girl for secrets and pain. Go figure."

She moved closer and touched my arm. "Relative to a lot of the shit we've been through, is this really that big a deal? Really? When staying could mean so much for everyone?" She squeezed my arm. "Tell you what. Let's make it *not* about the fame. It's a chance for you and me to do another kickass duet and make Tango sick jealous. And you and your sidekicks can do your bromance thing for the camera again."

She smiled. "And me and Cosita, too. These folks are from Austin. They're eating up the gender fuck." The smile turned to a grin. "And if we promise not to press charges we can ask them for *anything*. Reckless endangerment alone would cost them a small fortune. I read the scary lawyer lady's contracts. They want to post *any* of the final videos, hand *any* of it over to Sony? They need *our* approval."

The anger bled out of me, leaving me tired. She was right. Everything she said was spot on. Saundra's contracts were binding.

"They're committed to the crew now," I admitted. "If this has gone viral, they can't cut us out of the project."

"We get whatever we demand. The folks who want it are pretty much guaranteed their fifteen minutes of fame."

"Why do *you* want to go through with this?"

She moved away with that sly grin. "You tell me."

"It's your chance to flip Dumasss the finger in the rearview mirror."

She clapped. "See? You're not hopeless."

Wow.

We walked back to the cafeteria. The gang was arguing, but their hearts didn't seem to be in it. The room fell silent as we entered.

"I'm still new guy here," I said, "and it sucks for me to try to make this decision for y'all. You're also my friends. I'm sorry." Deep breath. "Y'all want to stay, I'll stay."

K-pop tried really hard not to grin.

How much did I still owe him? "I'm staying for one reason. I promised K-pop we'd go swimming at midnight, and I don't break my promises."

Katy seemed to notice that was meant as a dig. Good.

"If we go through with this," I said, "we're being more professional than anyone has a right to expect. So from here on in, we do it for fun."

The agreement was unanimous. Katy wasn't as enthusiastic as the rest, though. I could tell she was just glad we were staying, and she wasn't going to push her luck on the whys and wherefores. At least, that's how I read her expression.

Dad drew me to one side. "Lisa and I chose to let y'all handle this for yourselves, and this *is* perhaps the most professional response. . . but I need to say I'm not all that thrilled about y'alls decision."

Neither was I, but why dwell on it? "Don't worry, Dad. You are officially invited for the midnight swim."

Ha, got him. His lips pressed into a thin line. Thankfully, he didn't call me out on the cryptic redirection this time. "Right, because the middle-aged gay man skinny-dipping with the teenage boys is *such* a good idea. Besides, I'll be guarding to make sure none of the girls sneaks over."

"Because that would be a horrible thing."

He just raised an eyebrow.

"Kidding. You know I'd never want beautiful, nubile girls swimming naked with us and ruining my bro time with K-pop."

He ruffled my hair and wandered off to talk it over with Mom.

Okay, so I knew that he'd decline, but since I'd invited him he wouldn't suspect that I planned on boozing it up, as well.

A short time later, I confronted Whiskey in the lobby of Corporate with K-pop filming at my side. He dismissed Sarah and glanced at K-pop.

"Tell me one thing," I said to him, "and if you're not honest about it I will sue you and have you arrested for reckless endangerment."

He nodded.

"Is there really a contract with Sony?"

He stared directly into my eyes. "No. We're hoping this gets us one. We know a guy who bought us a meeting."

Okay. That was the truth. "We're staying for the rest of the shoot."

"Wait, what?" His whole body radiated shock. "Half of my own people are done with me."

Good. They must've been pissed that he left them out of his evil plot. K-pop circled us.

"Do you still have enough techies to finish the shoot?"

"Yes. But why would you stay?"

I stepped close enough to breathe on him. "While I hope you rot in Hell for all eternity, my friends deserve a shot at the big time. How soon for wardrobe and makeup?"

He shook his head. "Well, we lost most of wardrobe and half of makeup."

"We can likely dress ourselves," I told him, "and Katy and Juicy can help with make-up. They'll be able to copy everything that was done yesterday."

"Ethan. . ." He touched my shoulder.

I shrugged away. "Don't thank me. This isn't for you. We're not friends. We will never be friends. I hate you, but it won't be the first time I've worked with someone for whom I had absolutely no respect." Oh wait. "One more thing. All the cameras outside the buildings get turned off. If you have any footage of anyone naked. . ."

He shook his head. "Nothing like that." He seemed to remember something. "One camera recorded you and Woody talking outside in your BVDs. But I'm the only one who saw it. It didn't get posted, and I deleted it."

Because either of us would have cared. Although. . . "Tell me there wasn't audio."

"No. The exteriors were just cameras. Nothing in the cabins and nothing in your showers. Ninety percent of the dancer footage was in the cafeteria and here in Corporate. The only butts we showed were my people who knew about the cameras and signed off on it."

I had to keep it professional. For the next part of the conversation, that would not be easy.

"You knew about Twist all along. You picked us on purpose because you knew that riffing on the fucked up tragedy that happened to us would make a great show. You deliberately took advantage of my friends and terrified them, all the while making them feel like it was their fault and that they were somehow wrong for being scared."

K-pop continued to circle, but kept the camera on Whiskey.

"If this has been streaming live, how the *hell* did you keep their parents from descending on you like a pack of wild dogs?"

He glanced nervously at K-pop. "Once y'all were out here, away from the cell phone towers, I called all the parents individually and told them you were in on the joke. Whenever one of them contacted us after the video started streaming, we told them to be proud of what amazing actors y'all were. I assured them none of you wanted to break character to come to the phone and it was only a couple of days. Everyone knows that reality shows are fake."

So they all bought it. Wow. He was a skilled liar.

"But after I exposed you," K-pop threw in, "not one of them raised a fit?"

He shifted uncomfortably. "As soon as you highjacked the system, my man Teddy cut the feed and put up a screen that made it look like it was part of the show. To build suspense. He called the families to reassure them it was all just part of the roleplaying."

And most of us were such closet geeks that the idea of us getting into the whole roleplay aspect was not too much of a stretch.

"Do you still have the footage? When K-pop figured it out?"

He nodded.

"My father will call all the parents to warn them using your land line," I told him, "then you will play that footage, uncensored, along with everything K-pop is filming right now. You will look like the world's biggest douchebag, and it may also make this whole project go viral worldwide."

His brow furrowed. "You do realize being the bad guy isn't a problem for me?"

"No shit. The only thing that matters to me is that your parents know what you did to Lizard, your own kid brother, that you forced him to play along with this and set him up with the most vulnerable guy on my crew. That you played that sick mind game on your own flesh and blood."

He tried to interrupt.

"You may be twenty-one years old, Whiskey. I know you're not a little kid. But you're still young enough to hate the disappointment in your parents' eyes the next time you see them."

He stared at me longer than I liked. Then he walked away.

K-pop and I headed back to the crew.

"Ethan!"

Jimmy Russo ran up to us.

"Ethan!" He panted. "Hit me."

"What?"

"Hit me," he insisted. "I'm serious." He glanced at K-pop, who was filming again. He shook it off. "I didn't know what was going on until this morning when he asked me to be in the video. I thought. . . I don't know. I thought. . . I swear I didn't know what we were doing. I thought it was publicity." He shook his head. "I guess it was, but I thought like a commercial, not something he'd lay on y'all. Fuck, it all made sense this morning. He's damn persuasive. Seriously. Hit me."

He closed his eyes and waited, totally wrecked.

Eh, what the hell.

I threw an arm around his neck. "Come on over to our camp so I can get some gloves and we'll spar for awhile. Those fake bruises look like shit. You need the real thing."

K-pop lowered the camera and fell in step with us.

Jimmy Russo punched my side. "Man, I hope your dad takes that job again."

"At the gym?" I scoffed. "Even if they offered, it's not bloody likely."

"What?" His face read utter shock. "Oh well, rumors, I guess."

"What rumors?"

He shrugged. "A few months ago, it was going around the gym that the owners were offering your dad his old job. Those assholes who took over gave up on it, and the place is a wreck. We thought they were going to close it down, but all of a sudden, there's been a lot of whispering again. What, you don't know anything about it?"

I thought about that meeting Corey and I had dressed Dad for. "About four months ago?"

"Yeah."

"Dad told me about investors," I said. "He said it was for a gym in Dumass."

"Oh, well, you know how rumors are."

Yeah. I also knew my dad.

Twist scattered blood across the road. "*Et usu corrumpit vulputate definiebas.*" He needed to make sure the barrier took hold the first time and that it would keep everyone out.

That poser thought he could steal Twist's show? He thought he could get famous stealing Twist's thunder? Well, now there wouldn't be any interruptions while Twist showed them how it was done.

It was bizarre that the dancers had decided to stay after the geek freak figured out the plot. Helpful, though. He'd have been hard-pressed to find a spell strong enough to compel eleven dancers. He didn't need them all, but knowing the way they rolled, if any of them had wanted to go, all of them would have.

With the barrier in place, he could take his time. Let them settle back into a routine. He could wait for the perfect moment to finish Fox and have his revenge on that poser, Whiskey.

Chapter Twenty-Four

I have to admit the video shoot that day was pretty stellar. We worked hard as hell. With the profound lack of sleep and general exhaustion, it reminded me of competition weekends. Back then, I'd push and push and push, and it always felt great at the end of it all.

It felt even better this time. Back then, when Monika and I fought, I was stuck in her face all weekend with no one else to talk to. Here, I had a crew full of friends to take my mind off the crap with Tango. Plus a few choice members of Whiskey's folks chose to hang in when they heard we were staying. They all wanted to hear our stories about Twist and Warren.

Plus. . . Tango wasn't Monika.

While a few of the guys shambled down a deserted hallway made up as zombies, Tango tapped my shoulder. "Can we talk?"

I followed her around the corner where we wouldn't distract Mono and Schilling who were getting ready to run screaming down the hall away from the guys.

Before Tango could even speak, I wrapped my arms around her and kissed her neck.

She hugged me back and found my lips with her own.

We leaned into one another, and, you know? Sometimes it's better to just make out and skip all that heartfelt emotional crap. When it came down to it, what would we think to say that half an hour of heavy petting couldn't fix? So we found an unused room and did just that. Since the door didn't lock, we kept our clothes on, but it still felt nice.

Once we rejoined the crew—and I had to do a serious amount of adjusting before I could leave the room—Sarah brought us outside. We danced around the scarecrows, all of which radiated zero on the spooky meter in the light of day.

K-pop assured us that the final product would look like the dead of night and would, indeed, spook.

We faked a couple of death by drowning scenes in the boathouse and rowed out to the pontoon raft to film dance sequences out there, as well.

K-pop nudged me, staring straight up. "No moon tonight, dude. Do you—"

"I know *exactly* how many stars there will be out here tonight," I said. "And you can help me find the satellites."

"Hai."

"Oh sweet Jesus on a tortilla," Juicy exclaimed, "you're not really going to come out here to play *Teen Wolf?*"

"I told you I don't break my promises," I said in all seriousness. "So dibs on the pontoon tonight. You'll have to find someplace else for your lesbian sex."

She opened her mouth to complain.

I leaned in close. "I know a love shack in the woods that's not on the map. Not even Mom knows about it."

She shut her mouth and held up a hand.

I gave her five.

As the sun set, Whiskey gathered everyone outside the cafeteria. "Today's shoot was fucking incredible." He threw up his hands. "Hell, the whole damn weekend has been ten times what I'd hoped for." He found my gaze. "And thanks to everyone for. . ."

"For not beating your ass into the ground?" Juicy called out.

Somehow, everyone laughed.

"Yeah," Whiskey laughed. "Thanks for that." He waved an arm vaguely. "We're going to build a huge bonfire for the final shoot. We want everyone in comfortable civvies because we're going directly into the wrap party from there."

Many hoots and hollers echoed across the campground.

"But before we do that. . ." He held my gaze. "I ask everyone's permission. . ." He dropped a hand on Sarah's shoulder. "Our director would like to perform a controlled explosion of one of the cabins with all cameras shooting."

Of course. They had footage from the hidden cameras, but filming a controlled explosion with the professional cameras made a lot of sense. It *was* asking a lot of the folks who'd thought they were nearly incinerated. You know. . . us.

Fine. Suck it up.

"Only if we get to watch," I said. "It might be fun to see you blow the shit out of something when we're not, you know, in fear for our lives."

Folks laughed. Good. In for a penny, in for a pound.

Fucking BOOM!!

The bonfire was epic. They stacked wood eight feet tall and the flames lit the entire playing fields bright as the noonday sun. I have to admit, I was really freaking anxious to see *that* footage once it'd been run through the effects software.

Once again, we mostly played around. I danced with Tango a lot, and with my buddies and my dad. I even danced with Lizard while Ephraim looked on in jealousy.

While other folks were shooting, I dragged Effy to one side and taught him how to dip someone all the way to the ground and still get back to his feet.

"That," I assured him, "will get you laid."

When he and Lizard had their chance in front of the cameras, Ephraim worked it in. The look on Lizard's face when Ephraim kissed him in the deepest dip ever created told me I had not overestimated the power of the move.

Whiskey nudged me. "So your problem dancing with me was just that you've hated me from day one, wasn't it?"

"My Dad's gay," I said. "And I love him more than anyone on this planet. So. . . yes."

"That's fair." But his smile told me he knew I'd coached Effy, and he appreciated it for his brother's sake.

Once the official shoot was done, the techies had us drag all the sound equipment from the cafeteria, and we set up for the wrap party.

Booyah! Time for fun.

I dragged Whiskey aside. "Favor?"

He did a complete, befuddled double take.

"Ask K-pop to DJ, stream it online and tell him to mix in his own videos."

His expression was confused.

"You do that, and we will almost, *almost* be even."

He shook his head. "You sure you're not bisexual?"

I laughed. "He's family, Ben. Family's more important than sex."

He wanted to make a joke. I saw it. But he couldn't. He nodded and walked off to make the arrangements.

"Whiskey!"

He turned.

"When you credit him, make sure you use his real name. It's Kenny."

"Kenny what?"

Holy shit. I didn't know.

He stared at me for a moment, waiting.

I couldn't speak. I mean, I'd just told him Kenny was family, and I didn't know his last name. How messed up was that?

He smirked, turned and walked away.

"Incoming!" Kenny leapt through the air at me, fully expecting me to catch him. He wrapped himself around me, and I eased him to his feet.

Somehow, I couldn't ask him his last name right then. I mean, how could I *not* already know it?

"Dude," I said, "Get your tablet ready."

He disengaged and gave me his question mark face.

"You're about to DJ your first party online, streamed to hundreds of thousands of fans, and you need to mix in your own videos."

He froze. His face went pale.

I grabbed his shirt. "And you need to lose the shirt." I tugged. "Be sexy as hell."

He didn't move.

"You can do this, brother. Just do it and don't think."

"How well do you know me? Can I ever *not* think?"

"I got you this. It brings me one step closer to not owing you my entire life." I squeezed his shoulders. "Don't think. Do." I forced the shirt over his head, then grabbed a shoulder and planted a hand on his chest, just like Dr. Mike had done to me in the school when he was Dr. Lopez. "It's a lock-in. Play it like it's a lock-in."

He didn't move.

I channeled Dad. "God damn it, Kenny. Go!"

He shook awake, grabbed his tablet and ran over to the rapidly growing sound system.

Dad barked a laugh beside me. "Do you have any idea how much you just sounded like your old man?"

"If only, Dad. If only."

He seemed surprised. Nice.

"Let's help haul stuff," I suggested.

He squeezed me with one arm.

We stared at each other for about three seconds.

Nothing needed to be said.

'Cause that's how we rolled.

Everyone danced around the bonfire until we were hot, sweaty and exulted. A flask of bourbon made the rounds surreptitiously.

Dad pretended not to notice.

Tango and I made out in the shadows. Nice.

Around midnight, I spotted Ginger and her friends chatting with Kenny at the DJ booth. So, you know, if the swim was a no-go, I'd understand. But he waved me over.

He wrapped an arm around my neck and pulled me close so the girls wouldn't hear. "If you don't drag me away, bro, I'm going to cheat on my girlfriend, and I don't want to be that guy."

I pulled away enough to raise my eyebrows at him.

He yanked me close and whispered into my ear. "Ginger has made it clear she wants to suck my dick before we leave."

I jumped in surprise.

"No, seriously, dude. She said so. Literally."

"Well, I told you girls were different outside Dumass."

"Can we go swim?"

Wow. He was that devoted?

"I don't want to buzz kill you and Tango, bro." But his face was desperate.

I swatted his cheek. "Dude, I have a privacy fence. I can have fun with Tango whenever I want."

He raised an eyebrow.

I waggled mine.

"Do we need to have a conversation?" he asked.

I laughed. "Later, maybe. Not right now." I glanced around. "Right now it's all about you. You have a playlist that can take over?"

He nodded and messed with the tablet.

We found Woody and Ephraim.

Woody had girls on either arm, but took a moment to chat with us. "*Ese*, you know I'm down for hanging with y'all, but I think I have a line on a techie chick interested in some naked action."

Ephraim hemmed and hawed until he finally admitted, "Lizard might be willing to let me see his lizard."

I bopped Ephraim's shoulder. "Pool party at my place over Holiday break. We can even invite girls. Or boys."

"What, because. . ." Ephraim began, but stalled out.

"Because what?" I asked

"Sorry. Long day." He shook his head. "I got nothing."

Woody gave me a hang loose sign and threw an arm around Ephraim. "Don't worry, if nothing happens with Lizard's lizard, I'll let you see my junk again. That always cheers you up."

They walked away.

"Wow," I said. "That man is secure in his masculinity."

K-pop nudged me. "Dude. He does porn. How was that even under question?"

"True dat."

And Retro was just gone. Not sure where he'd found to pass the time, but good for him!

So Kenny and I wandered back to the new guys' cabin for towels.

Corey was there refilling his flask. "Going swimming?"

"Not without you."

We lay on the pontoon raft, heads together, bodies splayed out casually across the ragged artificial turf. Me, K-pop, Corey.

"See there!" K-pop's arm stretched above us. "See that light moving? Satellite."

"Bro!" Corey said. "I see it. That's awesome." He pointed, too. "It's like a star some dude made." His hand dropped to flail at my shoulder. I handed him the bourbon. Glug, glug.

I spotted another satellite and pointed. Now that I knew what to look for, they were easy to see.

"Ethan?" a voice called from shore. "You there?"

"Come on out, Jimmy."

"Cool." Splash.

"We need to sit up and say hello?" Corey asked.

I made a dismissive sound. "Jimmy's chill. Gimme that bottle." I drank.

The sound of swimming. He hit the ladder, splashed his way up. "Hey guys, thanks for. . . oh. It's casual Friday."

"Hey, Jimmy Russo," I said. "This is K-pop and Corey." I held up the bottle. "And this is Johnny Walker."

He took the bottle, lay down between me and Corey, and we all shifted to give him some room.

"What are we looking at?" he asked.

"Satellites," I said.

"Yeah? You can see those?"

Twist hid in the trees, staring in disbelief at the four boys sprawled on the pontoon. Ugh. Just ugh. He'd been regularly disgusted by all the emotional displays and gay tomfoolery by, well, pretty much the entire dance crew. The boys paraded around half-naked and the girls barely took off their clothes to shower.

Twist missed the good old days when girls ran around topless in slasher films and boys kept on their God damned pants.

He called Mr. Bunny closer and looked around. With his magic, the area appeared brightly lit and a nearby owl was easy to spot. "Take the owl, Mr. Bunny."

The sight of the devil rabbit's eyes glowing hot red and his mouth opening to reveal enormous fangs never got old. Mr. Bunny leapt into the owl, who hooted once. His eyes glowed devil ghost red, and he swooped down to Twist's upraised arm.

"You're getting pretty good at the flying thing."

The owl hooted and nuzzled Twist. Awww.

He held up a medicine dropper. "You know who it's for?"

The owl hooted.

"I'm not getting suckered into *that* joke, Mr. Bunny." He held the dropper higher. "Can you manage it?"

The ghost was far more intelligent than an actual rabbit, but owls didn't have opposable thumbs after all. The owl hooted, leapt into the air and grabbed the dropper from Twist's fingers. As it flew across the water, Twist stretched a hand toward the raft.

The boys slept.

The dropper fell into the water with a quiet *plop*.

The owl hooted and dove, but missed it.

Damn.

Wait a minute. He had a ghost beaver, didn't he? Maybe it could find a live beaver to possess. Those things were great with their little agile hands. He closed his eyes and called out to his petting zoo.

What the hell *did* devil ghost animals do in their free time?

Chapter Twenty-Five

The sound of splashing woke me out of a sound sleep.

Huh, must've drifted off on the pontoon.

"Ethan? Ethan!"

I jumped up.

Kenny floundered twenty feet away. "Something has my leg!" He disappeared under the water.

"Kenny!" I shucked my sweatshirt and t-shirt together and toed off my shoes. No time to waste on the jeans or socks. I dove in. The water was cold. Cold and dark, but I could see Kenny, white in the moonlight that rippled about us.

He sank, arms stretched up to me, eyes wide in panic. "Help me, Ethan. Save me!" Even under water, his words were perfectly clear, his face pale, pale white.

I swam as fast as I could, but no matter how quickly I dove, the water pulled him down faster.

With a final quick movement, I snagged his hand and gripped it hard, my lungs protesting the lack of oxygen. But I was a dancer, damn it. I had breath control.

I pulled on Kenny's hand.

Whatever had him wouldn't let go.

I tugged harder but with no luck.

Terror filled his face.

Then it happened.

He lost all his breath in a flurry of bubbles

No! Fucking *no*!

He sucked in a huge lungful of water.

He choked on it.

His body jerked.

He gulped.

He squeezed my hand frantically and begged me with his eyes to rescue him.

I pulled and pulled and pulled, my own lungs on fire now.

He thrashed again. Wildly.

Then his face went slack. His hand released its grip.

His eyes lost focus. He stared right at me, and I saw the exact moment he died, the moment the light in his eyes went out.

I hung suspended in the water, watching the moonlight play across his pale skin.

Wait a minute. Why wasn't I drowning?

I sat up with a gasp. "Fuck!"

Where was he? Where was Kenny?

All three guys were there, still on the pontoon, sitting up with me.

Kenny was fine. He was breathing. His eyes tried to focus on me, but the booze must've made that difficult. I shivered.

Jesus, I'd seen him die. Fucking *die*.

I closed the distance and wrapped my arms around him, pulling him close so I could feel his heart beat. "I saw you die," I told him. "I saw you die, and it was so fucking real." I pressed my face against his for a second, then released him and pushed away before things could get awkward. Although, it was Kenny, and from the look on his face, hugging him would never be awkward.

"So, y'all are pretty close around here," Jimmy said quietly.

"Shut up, Jimmy," I muttered. "I have these dreams." I looked into

Kenny's face because he'd been there. He'd almost watched me die for real. "And now I can't even *tell* I'm dreaming. It's like it's real."

"That's two nights in a row," Corey said quietly.

I nodded. "Must be all the excitement."

A whistle pierced the silence, and we jumped.

"Okay, guys," Dad called from shore, "we want to get out of here before noon tomorrow. Bring it in."

I opened my eyes to bright morning light filtered through the windows of the cabin and the snores and breathing of the guys around me. I lay still for a few moments. Was I really awake? Was something bizarre about to happen?

Someone farted. Okay, most likely awake.

Once my morning wood died down, I slipped out of my sleeping bag and picked my way over the sleepers. Jimmy Russo had crashed with us. Everyone was there except K-pop.

The morning air had a hint of chill to it. Man, we'd lucked out with the weather. When I reached the shower building, I heard the water running. K-pop stood with his back to a shower post, eyes closed and really enjoying the water.

I shucked my shirt and had my thumbs at the elastic of my shorts when I realized K-pop was really, *really* enjoying the water, but his hands were up behind his head.

I stepped closer to the hip wall.

Holy shit!

Ginger knelt there. . . naked.

It wasn't the water giving him the pleasure I saw in his face.

I froze.

It had to be a dream. It had to. What I saw wasn't possible, not in the real world. I was still asleep in the cabin. The guys were all snoring around me.

Wake up. Wake up. Wake up.

I thought about trailer hitches.

When K-pop's mouth opened wide and his entire face pinched tight, I jumped back to myself.

Shit. I *was* awake!

He pressed his hands in fists to his face.

I tore myself away and hurried into the next room, sliding my shirt on. I'd already seen far more than I should've. Shit, I should've left as soon as I saw her there, but. . .

Holy shit. I wasn't dreaming. That was real!

The door squeaked open.

Woody and Ephraim stopped in the doorway, faces curious.

I must've looked freaked out. Well, duh.

"You have to come back later," I said quickly, moving to them and forcing them out. "Ginger's in there showering, and I'm standing guard."

"What the hell?" Woody's voice was indignant.

"Something about water," I improvised. "The main building doesn't have hot water, or something. Come back in half an hour." Although from the look I'd seen on K-pop's face, it wouldn't take that long.

They walked away, muttering.

I turned and let the door close behind me.

"Shit." K-pop stood there, still dripping, his eyes wide, his clothes and a towel clutched over his nakedness. Because that actually mattered, now. "How much did you see?"

"Enough to know you're a grower not a shower," I said. "Get dressed, dude. We should get out of here."

"Hai." He scrambled into jeans and we hurried out of the building, leaving Ginger to fend for herself. He bundled his clothes together and passed them to me, working on himself with the towel.

We stopped near the stream, blocked from the building by a screen of shrubbery.

"Holy shit, dude," I said.

"I know, right?" He shook out his hair and nabbed his t-shirt.

"How did that happen?"

He took a deep breath and shook his head. "I was just in there, rinsing the soap out of my hair. I heard a girl say my name. And there she was in nothing but a towel. I covered myself with my hands. She dropped the towel. Dude, she was naked."

"I saw."

His eyes opened wide for a second, the closed in embarrassment. "I guess you did."

"Dude, I thought I was dreaming."

He opened his eyes and spread his arms wide. "You and me both. I swear to God I wondered if your dreams were contagious." He wiped his hands over his face. "So I realize I'm, you know, rising to the occasion, and she takes my hands away and says, 'I want to watch. I've never seen one grow.'"

"No shit?"

"None at all. So she's standing there, holding my wrists, staring right at me, you know, *at* me?"

I nodded.

"Then she looked me in the eye and asked if she could go down on me."

"No way."

"Way. Just like that: 'Is it okay if I go down on you?'"

"Apparently you said okay."

"Dude, I didn't say a word. I just nodded and down she went."

"Holy crap, dude, you just had every guy's porn fantasy come true."

He grinned. From the look on his face, he was still in shock about the whole thing. "Dude."

The sound of the screen door drew our attention. Ginger walked very casually away from the building in Capri pants and a white blouse.

"She is so hot," K-pop whispered. "Why me?"

"Dude, she has had her eye on you since we got here."

He grinned. "That is so bizarre to me. I mean, *look* at her!"

"Number one porn fantasy right there."

He shook his head. "Identical twin Swedish nurses in a hot air balloon."

Okay, granted. "Top ten, then."

He nodded. He smiled. "Dude, that was the coolest thing that has *ever* happened to me."

I would've nudged him, but, frankly, after what I'd witnessed, touching him wasn't going to happen unless we were both fully dressed. "Check another one off the list."

He grinned and met my gaze.

Then his face fell flat. Panic covered it.

"Kiki!" His hands grabbed at his hair. "Holy shit, bro, I just cheated on Kiki." He moved away, farther into the shrubs. "I'm that guy, that guy who cheats on his girlfriend." He turned back to me. "I don't want to be that guy."

"Dude, even the Pope would give you special dispensation for this one."

No." He turned to me, his face bleeding guilt. "She asked. I said yes. I knew what I was doing. I'm an asshole."

"K-pop—" How to say it. "You've had a girlfriend for all of one percent of your life. For ninety-nine percent of it you thought there wasn't a single girl out there who wanted you. She can't blame you for this."

"That's crap, Ethan. I mean, I know that's what you need to say. That's cool. Thanks for having my back, but. . . I don't think Kiki's going see it that way."

Okay, I shut up to let him process.

He sat on a stump, all the joy from his porn star moment lost.

I gathered my thoughts and crouched down, facing him. "You take full responsibility and that's good. You should. It means you're not a douchebag. A douchebag would just do fist pumps and celebrate, hai?" I waited for the nod. "But, dude, you didn't even remember you had a girlfriend until a minute ago. It's a brand new thing for you. I'm not saying this doesn't suck for Kiki, because it does, and I know you well enough to know you'll take full responsibility for your actions, and that is going to suck, too."

"Can you stop using the word 'suck,' please?"

I had to work to avoid laughing. "Point taken. The thing is, you're going to take whatever. . . punishment or whatever. Don't ruin the memory, too. When we first started talking out here, the look on your face? I have never seen you that happy. For that moment, you went from an insecure guy who didn't think any girl would want him to a confident dude who knew he was hot enough for a smokin' babe like Ginger to throw herself at you. Don't lose that. So much shit has happened here. We almost died, like, a day ago. That look on your face is the only good thing to come out of this weekend. You're going to take your due, hai? You should get to keep the moment."

He stared into my eyes a long time, then almost sort of smiled. "You are the best bullshit artist I have ever met." He waved a hand before I could protest. "No. I get what you're saying. It's kind of whiny of me to curl into a heap of hideous guilt and pathetic angst when every guy in this camp wishes he was in my shoes right now."

"Yeah, you aren't wearing shoes." I raised an eyebrow.

He smiled, then his lips pressed tight and his entire face pinched shut. He opened one eye, and his thoughts might as well have been written in a comic book bubble over his head: *You just saw that, didn't you?*

I nodded with my best bemused smile: *Yes, I did see that, and it is something I can never unsee.*

He chuckled and rose.

I followed his example.

"I'm so *not* hugging it out with you right now," he said.

"No," I said quickly. "Not right now. Bad."

He nodded and hugged himself. "Maybe not at all today."

"Not a problem."

We stared awkwardly for a second, uttered a rousing chorus of, "Hai," and went our separate ways. I still needed a shower.

"Oh, Ethan?"

I stopped and turned.

"Ginger said the band wants to do a few filler shots before we go. Hands and feet and things. Apparently, some of the video didn't turn out right. I'm going to see if I can find out what's going on."

"Okay. I'll grab a shower and meet you at the cafeteria." Hm. "You think Ginger's going to say anything?"

He shrugged. "I hope not. I don't want Kiki to find out from anybody but me." He hemmed. "If that's what I decide to do." He turned away.

I made my way to the shower. Whiskey and Ephraim showed up while I was toweling off, and I told them about the extra shots.

Another thought. "Did y'all see Ginger?"

"Yeah." Woody passed the shampoo to Ephraim. "I thanked her for using up our hot water."

"What'd she say to that?"

Woody rinsed his hair. "*Nada.* She just ignored me and kept walking. *Puta.*"

Well, for the moment at least, she was keeping her mouth shut.

Unlike, you know, when she'd been kneeling in exactly the spot where Ephraim showered.

Yowsa.

I dressed in a clean shirt and jeans. Hopefully, Tango and I could find a few minutes to ourselves so we could continue kissing and making up. I really needed a long session of the kissing and making up. Emphasis on the kissing part.

As I reached the center of camp, music blared from the cafeteria. Ah, folks must've already heard about the extra shots. Knowing Tango, she'd thrown everyone into a hardcore practice to wake them up. Good for her.

I reached for the handle the exact moment the door flew open, forcing me back. K-pop hurtled into me, literally, and I had to hold onto him while we sorted out whose legs were whose.

"Sorry." He looked me in the face, then clutched me harder. "Foxtrot?" He glanced over a shoulder. "Just the guy I wanted to see." His clutch turned into an insistent arm around my shoulder. He moved us away from the door. "Everyone is over at the big kids' camp. We're supposed to meet them there."

I pulled away. "What the hell was that?"

He glanced at the door. "I... I just..."

The door banged open to eject Whiskey, in as much of a hurry as K-pop had been. "Okay, peeper, you need to—" He spotted me and drew his shoulders back and relaxed into one hip. "Oh well, too late."

Then he just walked away.

What the hell?

I gave my full attention to K-pop. "What. the. hell?"

"I just. . . he just. . ." His arms flopped up and down like wings. "I walked in on him and Tango making out."

My heart stopped. "Making out or 'making out'?"

He waved again. "Kissing. They were kissing. I figured it must be rehearsal? You know, for a new scene?" He scrunched his face as if even he knew how naive that sounded. "I didn't want to think. . . you know? But when Tango saw me?" He cringed. "I don't think they were practicing for a new scene."

My mind spun. "And you were going to drag me away, what, to cover for them?"

His mouth dropped open. "Bro, seriously? You think I'd do that to you? I was afraid you'd haul off and hit the dude. Assault charges you do not need."

I held up my hands. "Sorry. Sorry. Please." Deep breath. What the hell was I thinking? "I'm sorry."

K-pop needed this gig. I couldn't let my drama mess up his life. "Okay. I'm calm. I'm going to talk to Tango. Maybe, maybe it *was* a scene? Maybe he tricked her into *thinking* there was a scene? Maybe. . ."

Maybe unicorns farting glitter would suddenly drop out of the sky pulling angels on a sled.

"Maybe."

Yeah. I knew what his sheepish look meant.

Opening that door was one of the hardest things I'd ever done.

Tango fidgeted on the stage, as if she was waiting. She looked up, and the world dropped into slow motion.

Her face lit up. Normally, that would've been a great sign, but with the sun behind me, I couldn't be more than a silhouette.

The door closed and blocked out the sunlight.

Her whole face changed.

Remember the slow mo.

The smile faltered, and the light in her eyes died a little.

My feet wouldn't move.

My stomach fell down into them.

She caught herself and stretched the smile across her face again, but it was a different smile, just a little bit fake. And the light in her eyes wasn't as bright as it had been when she hadn't known it was me.

When she'd thought it was Whiskey.

She tossed her hair. It looked like a vain attempt to pretend I hadn't seen the look in her face, hadn't seen the disappointment in her eyes when she'd realized who was there.

For the record, that look was the absolute worst thing I could see in the eyes of the person I loved. And I did love her. So much.

She jumped off the stage and hurried to my arms. Her hug was enthusiastic, but it felt fake. Everything she did would seem fake to me. I didn't even care that she'd kissed Whiskey. The look I saw in her eyes was so much worse.

"Good morning, sexy." She kissed my cheek. "You sleep okay?"

"It was fine."

She pulled out of my arms, and the smile on her face seemed like such a mask. "Did you see anyone on your way in?" She stepped closer. "We need to get everyone together for some fill-in shots." Fake smile.

I glanced at the door. "Just K-pop." I looked around the room with fake question marks in my face. "He said you and Whiskey were working on the new love scene."

Her faced scrunched up. "There's no love scene. . ."

All emotion dropped off her face for a second, then her lips pressed into a long thin line.

Her eyes searched mine.

Could she play it off? Could she still make it work? Had K-pop really misunderstood?

I saw the calculations, had seen them in Monika's face a million times but only recognized them for what they were the very last time I'd ever seen her. Oh my God. Tango was trying to figure out the best way to work me. She sighed and shoved her hands into her pockets.

"It's exactly what you think."

I scoffed in disbelief. "Well, *that's* a novel approach."

She pretended to think it through a second or two. "I make him think he has a shot at me, and I get a contract for every video this band ever produces." Her face seemed sincere. "If it *had* been a scene for the camera, it wouldn't have mattered, right? It would've been acting for the job. So I kissed him to get a contract. Same thing. Fake."

Except it wasn't fake. Except I saw the light go out of her eyes when she'd recognized me. I'll give her credit, she didn't slink up to me and try to manipulate me through my dick the way Monika would have.

She looked at the floor and shook her head. "You live in this black and white world, Ethan. The rest of us have to figure out how to live with the gray."

And there it was.

It was a different play, but it was still a play.

She looked up at me. "I care about you, Ethan."

Oh Christ, not "I love you," but "I care about you."

"Really, I do." Had she seen my reaction? "And if you care about me, you'll trust me and try to be as professional as possible. This is a job, right? That's what you said to Juicy. I'm just doing my job."

What did I want to say? I wanted to mention there was a very specific word for the kind of job she was talking about, but I still loved her.

I wanted to give her the benefit of all my years as a professional.

I wanted to, but I couldn't.

Why not? Because the only thing I could see was the way the light had gone out of her eyes when she'd recognized me. The image replayed again and again in my mind's eye. Nothing she said would erase that image. It wasn't even about a kiss.

If I opened my mouth, really bad things would emerge.

Without a word, I turned and left the building.

To her credit, again, she didn't try to stop me.

But I really wished she had.

The fact that she didn't meant I was right to leave.

K-pop hurried to my side. "What happened?"

What had happened exactly? Who knew?

I knew what came next, though.

"I'm leaving."

"Leaving?"

"Leaving." No feelings. No thoughts. Just action.

We reached the cabin and thank God no one was there.

"Leaving where, bro? We're a hundred miles from anything."

"I don't care." I stuffed stuff into my bag. "I can't stay here."

"Ethan. Don't be crazy. Let's think about this."

I rounded on him. "No. I'm *not* thinking about this."

He recoiled, and I remembered other times I'd shouted at him.

"I'm sorry, Kenny. I'm not mad at you." I went back to stuffing stuff. "I can't stay. I can't do that."

He deserved more. I was certain I knew the questions he wanted to ask. "I'm seventeen years old, bro. Since I was ten, I've tried to be 'professional.' Broken wrist? Be professional. Heartbroken? Be professional. Your dog dies? Be professional." I pulled the pack across my back. "I'm only seventeen years old, Kenny, and for just this once, I don't want to be a fucking professional." We stared at each other. "Are you going to try and stop me?"

I saw in his face that he wanted to help me but had no idea what that meant in this situation.

Wait a minute.

"What's your real name?" I asked. "First and last."

He reeled at the non sequitur. "What?"

Deep breath. "I don't know your last name, Kenny. Until yesterday, all I knew was K-pop. How messed up is that? My God damned best friend, and I don't know your real name."

He needed a second to process. "Valentino. Kenny Valentino."

"Dude, that is a *stellar* name. I am so jealous."

He smiled.

Back to business. "I'm leaving."

He nodded. "Hai." He grabbed his backpack and shouldered it.

"What?"

He shrugged. "I don't have a dad what normally picks up after me, so my bag's already packed."

"You're coming with me?"

His whole body projected disdain. "No offense, city boy, but if you really try to hoof it to civilization on your own you're going to die. I've been camping hundreds of times. I even have a compass."

Compass? Oh. Yeah. One of those was a good idea. And beyond that? "Dude, if I ever find someone half as badass as you with a vagina, I will marry her."

He laughed. "Unfortunately, the only girl we know like that is a lesbian."

I laughed, too. "True dat."

We stared at each other.

"Are we really doing this?" he asked.

I couldn't even begin to process what it would take for me to stay.

He nodded. "Let's go."

Twist hated waiting. His ghostly eyes and ears kept him fairly entertained, especially in the musicians' camp. *Those* people knew how to party. Their wing was practically an orgy, with someone having sex nearly all the time. And the girls seemed to have forgotten how to wear clothes!

If only he could make recordings of his magical spies.

The dancers mostly just whined and complained. He only watched them to find the right moment to—

Wait.

Fox was heading out of camp with boyfriend number one. He looked pissed.

One of Twist's birds found Katy with Whiskey.

"All K-pop saw was a kiss," Katy insisted. "If you go find him, you can tell him—I don't know, you can tell him you tricked me into it or something."

"I tricked you?" He laughed. "Did I trick you last night, too?"

"Shut up," she looked around. "Someone might hear you."

Aha. So Fox knew about Katy and the rock star.

Twist swapped animals and rode the bird following Fox out of camp. He and his boyfriend both had their packs.

Wait. Was he trying to *walk* home?

Yeah. That wasn't going to happen.

He'd probably last a couple of hours, pissing and moaning the whole time, then they'd turn around—

Wait a minute. The path he was on made a loop. He'd follow it all the way around and end up pretty much where he started. Perfect. That gave Twist time to set the stage, then he'd pay Fox a personal visit in the woods. He could intercept him as he headed back.

He held out his arms and gathered his menagerie. They ran, hopped and flew to him in a matter of moments. He reconnected with them all and sent them out across the campground.

He started with Teddy, that loser who spent all his time in the command center. No one would suspect him, since he was in charge of everything out there, anyway. He took a baseball bat to the junction box that connected the land line to the outside world, then he dug out the crate with the leftover explosives. Where should he set up his surprise?

And who should he use? Ginger was too pretty. She'd been a nice diversion, and he'd enjoyed the show she'd put on with Valentino. No. Ginger should get to live, so who?

He glanced through the eyes of half a dozen different spirits before making the perfect choice.

Mono.

The quiet one. The nearly invisible one. The one Fox didn't know at all. He was so busy gushing his heart out over the boys in the crew, that he'd completely missed spending any time with the most vulnerable member.

He sent the fawn into her. Perfect.

He walked her over to the command center.

And there was only one way to make sure his real target got nailed.

Twist rode the hawk ghost directly into the ringleader of the entire gang. Whiskey struggled for control, more than most, but Twist's power was returning with every passing minute. He marched him out to the command center where Mono and Teddy waited.

Time for some fun.

He gave control of Teddy to Mr. Bunny. "Just hold him still," he told the rabbit through Whiskey's mouth.

Teddy's eyes flashed red for a moment.

Twist used Whiskey's fist to punch the asshole techie. Bam!

That was fun.

"Ease up a tiny bit," he told the rabbit. "Just enough to let him talk."

He punched the techie again, harder. He felt Whiskey struggling inside, trying to stop himself.

"What the fuck is going on?" Teddy asked.

Bam. Bam.

Twist's hand was starting to hurt, but in a good way.

"What did I do, Whiskey?"

Twist gave Whiskey a tiny bit of leash.

"It's not me, Teddy. I don't know what's happening, but I can't stop it."

Twist nailed Teddy in the kidneys a couple of times.

He doubled over, and when Mr. Bunny yanked him upright, he was crying. "What's happening?"

"I'm sorry, Teddy. I can't stop." Whiskey cried, too, as he punched his friend again and again, in the sides. . . in the face. He bawled like a little kid when he kicked his buddy between the legs.

Twist kicked him a second time, square in the nuts as hard as he could.

Teddy puked so hard, Mr. Bunny lost control for a second and his meat suit fell to all fours and spewed blood. So Twist kicked him. He kicked him again and heard a rib crack.

Yeah, that's the sound he liked. He kicked him a few more times. It felt good. It felt good to wail on someone, to let out all his anger, all his blood-boiling fury. He hauled Teddy to his feet, threw him against the wall and nailed him in the face until the pain in his hand registered. Son of a bitch, that hurt.

He had to be careful. If he broke the hand, it'd swell up and someone might notice.

"I'm sorry, Teddy." Whiskey sobbed like a little kid. "I'm sorry, brother."

Big, tough rock star.

Just like a little kid.

Twist took complete control and shoved the douchebag into a dark corner of his own mind.

"Sit Teddy in the chair, Mr. Bunny." He turned to Mono.

Her eyes were big and innocent and moist, although that might just be the deer controlling her.

His fist throbbed and he shook it out. Blood spattered the floor.

Damn it. He didn't want to mess up Whiskey's body any more.

Teddy kept whimpering and crying.

"Shut him up, Mr. Bunny. I'm sick of listening to his whining."

Teddy froze as if a switch had been flipped.

"Better."

Twist looked around. There had to be something he could use.

Oh yeah, there'd been a baseball bat.

Where had he left it?

"So, this is my room." A ghost squirrel watched Lizard wander into the tiny space. A cot stood in one corner. An open suitcase spilled its contents in another. "Pretty crappy, huh?"

"No, no. . ." Ephraim turned a circle. "It's cozy. You have an actual bed for. . . you know, sleeping. . . and stuff." He cringed. "Wow, that was the most self-conscious statement ever. I should die of embarrassment." He looked around.

Lizard chuckled. "No, I get it." He faced Ephraim. "So, yep. This is the room."

Ephraim sighed. "Is there any chance this is as weird for you as it is for me?"

"Oh my God, I'm so glad to hear you say that." He stepped closer. "My brother is this huge stud who gets any girl he wants, and. . . I don't know what I'm doing."

"That's just like Woody. He's all, 'Just go up to him and kiss him or something.' Like it's that easy." Ephraim shoved his hands in his pockets. "I'm used to being the suave one, but in Austin? I can't even imagine. . ."

Lizard waved him off. "Oh my God, don't think it's any easier. I mean, I dated this one guy for, like, a month? But. . . he was an asshat. I don't know what I was thinking."

"One more than me."

"So you've never. . .?" He moved a step closer.

Ephraim shook his head. "Not even remotely."

"Me neither."

"No?"

Lizard shook his head and stood almost nose to nose with Ephraim.

They kissed.

Which was about all Twist could stand. He threw the squirrel into Ephraim and took control. The kid convulsed just once.

"Ephraim?" Lizard held his arms. "You okay?"

Twist held the kid steady for a second to make sure he had control. "Ephraim?"

He walked him out of the room.

Lizard called after him a few times but didn't follow.

Twist looked down at Mono where she lay in a heap at his feet. He piled her into a chair and threw the bloody bat into a corner.

He glanced around. The scene was set. Two victims, bruised and battered. The cameras were ready to record. He parked Whiskey in the corner for a moment, leaving the hawk in charge.

He shifted his sight and checked on the gay Jew. He told the squirrel to walk him out to the shed where Fox had been too stupid to fuck Katy. Huh. If he'd sexed her up himself, maybe she wouldn't have turned to the rock star.

One key player was missing. Where was she?

Ah. There she was.

He sent another bird, then ran off to find Fox for a little face time.

Chapter Twenty-Six

How much of a chode was I? Well, there was this time when I was about sixteen that I'd decided to surprise Monika at her house. I had a bouquet of roses, candy and condoms. We'd had a fight about something or other, and I was hoping to fuck and make up.

Her mom let me in and told me she and Devon were in the rumpus room studying. I'd not heard of Devon before, but she knew a lot of guys in her home school group, so I didn't sweat it.

Read that last sentence again. Yep. Total chode.

I reached the rumpus room. She and Devon were on the couch making out.

"What the heck?" I'd shouted. That was pre-foul mouth.

Monika jumped to her feet and said, "Wilt thou be gone? It is not yet near day. It was the nightingale, and not the lark, that pierced— Foxxy?"

She passed it off as practice for a play. *Romeo and Juliet.*

I bought it.

There'd been a thousand signs. Once she'd let the cat out of the bag that she'd cheated on me, all the pieces fell into place. I was a chode. For anyone my dad's age, chode is the same thing as chump.

"Do you have any idea where you're going, bro?" K-pop's anxious call brought me back to the present.

I pointed. "It's a path. It's gotta go somewhere."

"It's a path at a campground." His effort to avoid condescension was there but not obvious. "It most likely goes in a great big circle back to where we started." For him, that was probably not a bad idea. He could've let it happen but didn't.

Shit. We'd been hiking for an hour.

I looked around. Trees. Rocks. "I'm going to get us hopelessly lost if I step off the path."

He cringed. "If I add, 'and most likely killed' will it make me a bad person?"

"No." I shrugged off my pack. "I'm sorry, dude. I should let you lead."

He dropped his own pack to the ground. "My GPS isn't hooked into a tower anywhere, but I still have the last map from before we went off the grid."

"Seriously?"

He pulled a face. "I camp a lot, dude. Ed was a frickin' SEAL."

Ed. His brother with the night terrors.

I looked all around. Trees. Rocks. "We can't walk out, can we?"

"No?" His face went back to supportive. "If we had more water and food, I would totally be on board and get you there, but. . . I'm utterly hoping you'll decide to return to camp at some point."

More looking around. More trees and rocks.

"At least I know you're honest with me, dude. Right now that means a heck of a lot."

Bang! A gunshot out of nowhere!

K-pop screamed and fell into me. "My leg!"

I latched onto him. Holy shit. Blood soaked his jeans around a ragged hole.

I brought us to the ground, holding him close.

I scanned the trees and bushes. Nothing. Not a damn thing.

"How sweet." A voice behind us.

What the hell? I'd just looked there.

Who?

Twist? With a gun pointed directly at us.

What the fuck? But—but it was *fake*. It'd been Whiskey the whole time. Right?

It was fake!

"Surprised to see me?" His face was dark and his hair long. He was beefier than he'd been last time. He looked so different. Grown up. Just like he'd been in the dreams.

"Are you working with that fucking band, you asshole?"

K-pop groaned. I eased him down and checked his leg. There were two holes in his thigh, front and back, so no bullet to remove.

Twist spat. "Those *asshats* need to die. Taking *my* story." He pounded a fist on his chest.

I pulled off my flannel shirt and wrapped it around K-pop's leg a few times. When he tried to talk I cupped my hand over his mouth just long enough to stop him. "Just breathe." I tied the shirt.

Since Twist hadn't fired any more shots, I felt safe for the moment. "What the hell's going on, then?"

He had to have a reason. He always did.

"When I saw those posers' webcast? And I saw that everyone was buying it?" He waved the gun. "I couldn't let them steal my thing." He waved the gun some more. "All this. It's my thing. *My* thing."

"So if you're pissed at *them*, why shoot K-pop?" I searched the ground for a big stick, anything that might make a weapon.

"To torture you." He said it like I was simple.

"Me? I didn't steal your thing."

"You came into town and stole Katy from me!" He shouted so loud he spit. Good, maybe if Twist kept up the noise, someone would hear us.

"When I came into town she was with Corey, not you!"

He advanced and pointed the gun right at my head.

I closed my eyes. Maybe antagonizing him was the wrong approach.

"Don't worry, Foxtrot. I'm not going to kill you." He laughed. "Not you."

Me, he wanted to torture.

"I do plan on killing people, though." He tapped the gun on his chin. *Please-go-off-please-go-off.* "Who should I kill? Maybe a couple of people. Your dad? Corey?" He dropped onto his haunches so we were eye to eye. "You can try to beat me there and warn someone, or you can stay here and keep K-pop from bleeding out. If I see you following me, I might just double back and finish him." He grinned. "No matter what you do, Fox. Somebody dies."

Jesus. Christ. "But if you were watching, you must have seen her kiss Whiskey. She's not even with me, anymore."

He rose and walked around. "Yeah, she's kind of a slut that one."

Seriously? Okay, don't try to get it to make sense. Just don't try.

"But if I don't have her anymore," I asked, "why try to hurt me?"

He rushed close to me, his eyes wild. "If I can't have her, no one can!"

"Oh hell, did you really just say that?" I forced my voice to stay quiet and steady. "That's, like, the worst psycho stalker cliché *ever.*" It was a risk, but if I could get him fuddled, I might have a second to grab that branch over there. "It doesn't even make sense in the situation."

He smiled. It grew into a grin and he chuckled. Yeah. He was channeling the ghost of every dead psycho movie villain ever. I kept waiting for him to quote Norman Bates.

"The race is on," he said instead. . . and dashed off.

I worked my arms completely around K-pop and lifted.

"You have to go warn them," he said.

"No." I got him to his feet. "I am *not* leaving you to die out here alone. At the camp, they have each other. They have my dad and Corey's mom and guns."

He couldn't stand on his own. "But they don't know he's coming."

I tightened my arms around his waist. "I'm not leaving you out here alone, Kenny. I'm not." I started moving so he'd have to walk.

"Wait, wait, wait."

"I'm not leaving you."

"Ethan, wait a second."

"I've decided."

"You're going the wrong way."

I stopped. I chuckled.

So did Kenny.

Our laughter threatened to turn into sobs of hysteria, so I propped him against a tree. "I need to look at that leg a second."

"What about—"

"Don't." I tightened the binding. The bleeding seemed slower, but it would likely amp up as soon as we started off. "We can't think about it. We can't worry about anything other than staying alive until we get there." I took my place at his side and squeezed him tight against me. "Let's go."

I wasn't exaggerating either. If we worried about what was happening at the camp, we'd drive ourselves crazy. Wow. I could feel K-pop's heart beating. Fast. Okay, that meant there was enough blood to pump. Keep walking.

He pointed. "This way's shorter. We were going in a circle."

Of course, we were.

Trees. Rocks. Walking. . . well, hobbling.

I needed to do something to distract him from the pain. "Why'd you never tell me about the bullies?"

"Dude, when you breezed into town, you had your dad to deal with. Then Twist. Then you got shot. There really wasn't time to talk about my drama."

"But after all that?"

"What? I'm just supposed to say, 'Hey bro, forget about your crap. I have emotional issues'?"

We trudged in silence.

"You can do that, you know," I said at last. "You can."

He waved at the path ahead. "Let's get back to camp."

We hobbled along, and I felt more and more of his weight. I refused to think about what that meant.

He stumbled.

"Come on, Kenny. This isn't fucking *South Park*."

Oh shit. Had I really said that?

He chuckled, stumbled and fell.

I slowed his decent as much as I could.

"Kenny, come on. We're almost there."

He smiled and tried to catch his breath on all fours. "You have no idea where we are."

True. "You're the navigator, man. Come on." I tugged up, but he didn't even try. "You can't give up. Please."

"I need to tell you something."

"Awesome. Road trip conversation."

He shook his head. His blood was warm against my leg, but I did everything I could to ignore it. If I could've carried him, I would have.

"I know you think this is your fault," he said.

Not think. Knew. I knew it was my fault.

"So you need to know. . . You've already saved my life once."

What the hell?

"Seriously. The day you moved here? If I hadn't met you I would've committed suicide."

Shit. What?

He forced himself up to his knees. "Yeah, I know that doesn't go with the whole happy-go-lucky persona I try to exude." He clutched my shoulders and stared me in the eyes. "I had the pills and a bottle of JD. Remember our first sleepover? I told you there'd been one time before that I'd been drunk? That was it. I was gonna kill myself, but then I met you and you liked my t-shirt and my hair and you danced to my favorite band."

I'd never seen tears in Kenny's eyes. Never thought I would.

"It was like a sign, bro. It probably seems totally lame, but you were the first person in my life to get me. At all. It gave me a reason to live, and then the team started to like me and your dad? Well, he practically adopted me." Tears ran down his face. "And if it wasn't for you, I'd never have met Kiki. So whatever happens?" He hugged me. "I still owe you."

His entire weight collapsed into my arms.

"No." I shook him.

He sagged like a rag doll.

No! Fucking NO!

I pushed to my feet with him in my arms, but his head lolled to one side.

"Kenny!"

He was dead weight.

"Help!" I had no idea where to go. I mean, there was a path right under my feet, but which way were we going?

"Help!!" All the fucking trees looked alike.

I actually felt his heart slow down.

"Help!"

"Ethan?" Dad's voice was the most amazing thing I'd ever heard.

"Dad!" I screamed hysterically "Over here!!"

He appeared on the path, and when he saw me and Kenny, covered in blood, he broke into a sprint. "What happened?"

"Twist," I said. "He shot Kenny."

He almost tripped. "Twist is really here?"

I gave Kenny into Dad's strong arms.

Dad would fix everything, right?

"He is. He's not in the camp?"

"Jesus, he's bleeding out." He lowered Kenny to the path and snatched my pack. "Run to the camp. Tell everyone." He rummaged through the pack.

"Kenny. Is he—?"

"Go!" He pointed and shouted.

He had me trained. I ran.

Please, God, let him be able to fix Kenny.

Chapter Twenty-Seven

Shooting the geek freak had been great fun for Twist, but not nearly enough. The anticipation of the mayhem about to ensue had him positively hard with excitement. He ran through the woods to the spot where he'd left the dream catcher and his tablet. He hunkered down with both and prepared to multitask like a motherfucker.

He touched the hawk feather and jumped into Whiskey, sending him to meet Fox as soon as he reached the camp. He thought back to how the egotistical douche spoke so he could fool them all.

At the same time, he worked the best spell he'd ever found. Combining magic and technology was ridiculously hard, but while searching for a way to record his ghost spycams, he'd found a starting point.

Magic was energy. Since it was energy, it could be harnessed and broadcast like a radio wave, so said aeschtvick.com.

The site even had a kickass app that would let him link his tablet into the PA and video systems without the geek freak noticing. He worked his way in and decided to play music the way Whiskey had. What would be appropriate?

He thought about the little gay Jew. Something by Harvey Fierstein? No. Too obvious.

Wait. He thought of the perfect song as the sun fell closer and closer to the horizon.

The camp was freakishly quiet. Woody, Schilling and a couple of roadies played hacky sack. I broke into the clearing, tripped and fell to my hands and knees.

Woody laughed. "While you're down there—holy shit!" He'd noticed the blood.

Whiskey ran up. "Ethan? Did you kill the command center? The land line's dead."

Well, then we were on our own. Woody helped me to my feet.

"Twist is here," I said. "Really here. We need to tell everyone."

Whiskey laughed. "Brother, if you're trying for payback, you need to work a lot. . ."

I punched him. Not hard, but enough to get the point across. "Twist saw your feed and now he's really here. He shot Kenny—*shot* him—and Kenny's bleeding out, you pathetic sack, so get everyone together to see who's missing."

No one moved. They must've been in shock.

Or they didn't believe me.

Music started on the PA. "Sunrise, Sunset" from *Fiddler on the Roof.*

Oh shit. "Ephraim."

Woody's eyes opened wide.

I shook it off. "Probably just a coincidence."

I grabbed two roadies and pointed out the path I'd taken. "Go find my dad. Help him with Kenny. Bring him to Corporate."

Woody, Retro and I ran around the camp gathering everyone. Most of the band folks wanted to think we were messing with them. Apparently my blood-soaked jeans and t-shirt weren't enough proof. Once I started screaming at the top of my lungs, though, they paid more attention.

When we had everyone together in the Corporate lobby, Lizard, Ephraim, Mono and Mom were missing, along with a few of Whiskey's people I didn't know.

Woody grabbed my arm. "Why'd you say Effy's name?"

"The song," I said. "It's from a musical about Jewish people. I just jumped to a conclusion."

Dad walked into the lobby with Kenny in his arms. The roadies trailed after, looking pale.

Oh-shit-oh-shit-oh-shit. "Dad!"

He glanced at me but made a beeline for the boys' dressing room.

I followed. "How is he?"

He lay Kenny on a couch and pulled out a knife. "Keep everyone out of here."

I directed the roadies, who seemed only too glad to work guard duty rather than nursing.

"Help me get him out of these," Dad said. "Damn skinny jeans."

When we had him cut out of his jeans, Dad wrapped the leg tightly. "Try to wake him up."

I patted his cheeks and called his name. His pulse was weak, but his breathing was regular. No reaction. "He won't wake up."

"That's weird," Dad muttered. "He must've lost more blood than I thought." He looked up at me. "Is everyone accounted for?"

"No." I draped a blanket over Kenny to cover his nakedness.

"What?"

Kenny was so damn pale.

Dad grabbed my arm. "Ethan." He shook my arm until I looked at him. "Ethan. We need to get everyone together. Where's Tango?"

"I don't. . . I don't know."

He took a deep breath. "You need to find someone to watch Kenny. Then you and I need to find Tango and everyone who's missing."

Kenny was so pale. If he died, it'd be—

"Go!"

A crowd had gathered outside the dressing room. The roadies must've been hard pressed to keep them out. Whiskey stood at the front of the pack.

"Is this everyone we have?" I jumped up onto the nearest chair I could find. "Where's Tango?"

"Here!" She huddled with Juicy and Cosita a few feet away. I wanted to take her in my arms and protect her, then I remembered why Kenny and I were in the woods in the first place and my stomach squirmed.

"What the hell—" Whiskey jarred me back to the real world.

"We're all in danger," I said. "I am not fucking with you. The guy who shot me four months ago, the one you were pretending to be? He saw your reality show and decided it wasn't real enough. He's here. He shot Kenny."

A riot of noise erupted from the crowd.

Woody whistled loud and piercing. He would be perfect.

"Woody, go to Dad. He needs you to watch Kenny so he can help us figure out what the hell to do."

"What about Effy?"

"One thing at a time, *ese.*"

He nodded and ran into the dressing room. Watching Kenny would distract him from Effy's absence.

That damn song kept playing on repeat.

The video monitors jumped to life with static. Everyone crowded around them. A familiar image faded in: two people strapped to chairs, blindfolded and bruised.

A guy and a girl. But who?

Was the guy Ephraim?

"Mono?" Schilling's voice was thin.

Oh crap, I hadn't even recognized her. How much did I suck?

"That's Teddy," one of the musicians said. "Oh my God, it's Teddy."

I had no idea who Teddy was, but he had to be one of Whiskey's people.

✔

Twist held the tablet to his face so it would record nothing of his surroundings. "Hello, 'kiddos." He laughed. "Kiddos? Really? Did you do absolutely no research on me to see how I talked?"

Everyone in the lobby huddled closer together. With his grackle ghosts monitoring the space, he could see and hear everything perfectly.

"It's really him," Tango said.

No shit. "So, I guess you see I have a couple of your friends. Just like the fake shit that band threw together. But *my* video is going to be better. The bruises are real for one thing. Originally, I wanted to get the same two victims, but then I decided it would make me racist if I killed a Black man first." He grinned. "Or *will* this be the first? Hey Fox, how's your boyfriend doing? Has he bled out yet?"

Everyone glanced at Fox, but he just shook his head. Pussy. Too afraid to talk, no doubt.

"They're in the command center," the Black Italian said. "It's the same place we filmed the fake kidnapping."

Twist grinned. "Wow, give that man a gold star. So the question is. . . can you get here to stop me before I shoot them dead? For real?"

He felt stretched a little thin, so he closed his video in order to work the Whiskey puppet. He ran the singer to the door, but that giant Fox bastard grabbed his arm.

"We have to stop him," Twist shouted through Whiskey's mouth.

"It's a trap, Whiskey," big Fox said. "He wants you to run over there blindly."

Twist yanked Whiskey's arm free. "Teddy's my friend. I have to try."

He ran out the door before anyone could stop him. He needed to get there first, but knowing Fox—

Yep. He followed the singer and dragged his ape boyfriend and the Black Italian along. Nice. A bigger audience for the show.

"Corey, Jimmy Russo, you're with me," I called out, heading for the door. "I'll stop him, Dad."

"He wants to separate us!" Dad was right, but even though

Whiskey was a dick, he didn't deserve to run headlong into Twist's trap.

"God damn it," Dad shouted as I followed Whiskey's distant form. "We need to get organized."

Jimmy Russo caught up to me. "It's off the path. Let me lead or you'll never find it."

I let him take point.

Would Twist shoot them? He hadn't killed anyone yet, so I sincerely believed he'd avoid taking that step. He'd been a cop. He knew that in Texas murder made the difference between going to jail and going to the chair. He would *not* kill anyone.

Jimmy left the path and I followed, with Corey just a few steps behind.

There was Whiskey. Farther ahead than I liked.

"Wait up!" I shouted. "You can't run in there alone!"

He ran on.

"Does he think this is just a game like before?" I asked.

"Dude wants to be a superstar, so he tries to play hero." Jimmy Russo panted. "He thinks he's invulnerable."

I lost sight of Whiskey, but caught a glimpse of a wall painted camouflage green and brown. "Damn it, Whiskey—"

Twist ignored all the lame shit they said. He had to pay attention to run his puppet fast enough that Fox wouldn't catch up. His ghost petting zoo could keep their victims immobilized on their own, but sprinting someone else's body through trees and over branches was really hard.

But, Jesus Christ was it fun!! It was like the world's coolest roller coaster, and the final corkscrew was going to blow Twist's mind.

He grabbed the door handle. Somewhere in a dark corner of his soul, he felt the singer, so full of himself and self-important, screaming and weeping like a baby. He prevented him from actually crying out.

He took a deep breath. And yanked open the door.

BOOM.

Major fucking BOOM!

Jimmy Russo slammed into me, and we flew ass over head as the world filled up with white hot light. I landed hard on my back with Jimmy on top of me and all the air forced out of my lungs.

I rolled onto my stomach, trying to breathe.

What was left of the building burned hot and wild, the brush that had hidden it reduced to kindling. Stuff fell from the sky.

He'd blown the building.

It had to be a trick. He wouldn't blow the building when he was in it. They all had to be somewhere else.

"Shit!" Jimmy rose to his hands and knees, puking.

Wait. Where was Corey?

Strong hands grabbed my shoulders and lifted me to my feet. Corey. Thank God.

"What is it, Jimmy?"

He pointed.

A hand lay in the grass a couple of feet from him.

A real fucking hand. With a silver ring and a black stone.

"That's Teddy's hand, man," Jimmy wailed, scrambling to his feet. "Daila gave him that ring."

I stared at the burning building. It wasn't a trick.

If Teddy was dead, then so was Mono.

And the rock star, had he reached it?

"Whiskey?" I hurried closer.

Had to know, to see.

I tripped and almost fell, but caught my balance at the last second, glancing down.

A body.

Blackened and charred.

The smell hit me.

I turned and puked my guts out.

The only way I knew it was Whiskey was his boots, his damn motorcycle rock star boots.

Corey stopped at my side. We stared at the corpse.

I'd hated the guy. Now, he was dead.

"Ah, Jesus." Jimmy Russo crossed himself.

What about Twist? Had he blown himself up?

The blast ripped his skin off and threw his body through the air.

His breath blew out of his lungs, seared in a volcano.

The universe flashed white and yellow and hot.

So amazingly hot.

Twist slammed back into his own body and fell over. He landed on his back and stared straight up. "Son of a bitch!" Once he had his limbs sorted out, he jumped up and did fist pumps. "What a ride!" That had been the most intense, coolest experience he'd *ever* had.

Wow.

Okay. The game wasn't over yet.

He pulled himself together and sent his feelers out across the campground.

Fox stared down at Whiskey's charred corpse with his ape and the Black Italian at his side.

Twist reopened the PA app.

"Uh-oh, hero. Too slow."

I looked around. Twist's voice came from a nearby speaker on a post.

"Did you hope I was dead, too? Just for a second? Any chance you'll figure out where I really am?"

"Sunrise, Sunset" played again, but there was another noise over the PA. Whimpering. The soft sound of crying and sputtering.

"And now you know I like to kill. Acquired quite the taste for it, actually. And just think, now that the rock star isn't in the way, anymore. It's just between you and me."

Wow. Of course, Whiskey had been his target. He'd stolen Twist's "thing." How could he have known he'd be the first to get to the building, though? That he'd go there at all?

"So who should I kill next? Someone right here with me?"

The whimpering grew louder. "Please don't," a guy's voice said.

"Ephraim." Corey and I said it at the same time.

"Jesus."

"And where do you think we are, Fox? Where would I be?"

The song played and my mind spun.

"Where will you find me that no one else knows?"

What the hell?

"Well, *almost* no one else knows about this place."

I sucked in a quick breath. The shack, the love shack where Katy and I had almost, but not quite, had sex.

That had to be it. I ran.

I didn't wait for the other two. I didn't call for help.

"Sunrise, Sunset" kept playing over the PA with Ephraim's gentle whimpering barely audible over the top. I ran harder, faster than I've ever run in my life.

Twist played with his victims, he wanted them to suffer. If I ran fast enough I could get there in time.

Except he'd just blown three people into pieces.

Did I understand him at all?

"I see you, Fox." Twist's voice echoed through the woods. "Run, rabbit, run."

He had cameras? Or was it more of the game?

Branches slashed at my face and arms. I didn't feel them.

"Run, run, rabbit."

He'd said that to me before. When?

I focused on my breathing. Had to be calm.

Had to be ready for anything.

"Will you make it in time, hero?" The sound of a gun clicking came over the PA. "Can you save the day, hero?"

I ran faster, pushed harder, splashed through the creek.

Ephraim had just told the world his secret. He'd had his first date. He didn't deserve to die.

"Can you. . . save. . . the day?"

Ephraim's voice grew louder. "No, no, no, no, please God, no, no."

"Sun-rise. Sun-set."

A gunshot and a scream, but not over the PA.

Just ahead.

Twist played with his victims.

It had to be a leg shot. I could still save him.

I broke into the clearing and stumbled to get my balance as the ground sloped down. I tore across the grass and slammed into the door. It wasn't locked.

I ripped it open.

And stopped.

I've actually watched someone die.

I'd just seen a blackened corpse.

This was worse.

This was someone I knew. Someone I cared about.

This was a dark red stain on dirty grey boards, blood dripping from eyes and ears and mouth. This was one of the kindest voices I knew silenced forever.

"Ethan?" Corey's shout reached me despite the cotton in my ears. "Where are you?"

I sucked in a breath.

"We can't let him see this." I tore my eyes away from the stain on the wall. "Ephraim, you have to help me stop him."

He didn't move.

"Ephraim."

He started and looked at me. "We can try." He rose from where he'd been kneeling, holding the lifeless hand of Corey's mother. Mom.

We met Corey just outside the shack, and the moment he saw Ephraim, his face lit up for two seconds. Then he saw my expression and all the color drained out of his skin and he rushed us. Ephraim and I each grabbed an arm.

"You don't want to see her, Corey," I told him. "Please don't go in there."

"Mom?!" It was a shout. Then a scream. "Mom!!"

We couldn't hold him back. He was too strong.

He stopped in the doorway, took two steps into the shack. "Mom?" His voice dropped to a whisper. "Mom?" All the fight drained out of him.

"What happened?" Dad's voice behind me was a punch to my gut. "I heard the gunshot."

I wanted to be a little boy, to let Daddy hold me while all the bad things went away. But Corey needed me more than I needed my dad.

"We need to keep everyone out of here." I stepped aside so he could look into the shack. *Please don't let him touch me.* If he touched me, that would make it real, and I'd lose it.

"What?" He stopped a few inches away and looked through the door. "Oh, fuck." He stared. He breathed in deep panting gasps. "You can handle Corey?"

I nodded.

"Have you seen Twist?"

I shook my head. "Not since—" I grabbed his shirt sleeve. "Kenny. How's Kenny?"

"He's better. He just woke up all of a sudden.

Of course, he did. How had Twist done that?

Didn't matter. Kenny was alive.

Corey just stood there. Silent. No tears. Nothing.

"Ephraim, you need to get out of here." Dad's voice faded a bit. "Jimmy? Take Ephraim back to my cabin and get him into a bed."

Dad was smart. Grief was a funny thing. Corey could decide to hate Ephraim for living. Who knew what he would do? I didn't.

Woody appeared. When he spotted Ephraim, he grabbed him and held on tight. That's when Ephraim lost it. They fell to their knees in the grass. Ephraim sobbed and sobbed.

"Just keep him out of the shack then," Dad said.

Corey dropped to his knees. "Mom?"

That was the second punch to my gut.

Everything blurred out. I wiped my face and knelt beside Corey, staring at his eyes.

What was he seeing? I mean, I knew what was there, but what did he see?

I reached out one hand and turned his face away from the stain on the wall.

He blinked a few times and seemed to focus on me.

There was nothing in his eyes. Nothing.

Denial is a calm and beautiful mistress.

He blinked again.

His brow furrowed. "Why are you crying?"

Then he looked at his mom.

That's when he lost it.

He folded in on himself until his forehead touched the ground.

One fist pounded the dirt.

His whole body convulsed, but my ears were filled with cotton, so I only barely heard the noises he made. They were far away.

In another world.

I wrapped my arms around him and pressed my cheek into his broad, shaking back.

Because that was my world now.

Something hit Twist. It felt like getting nailed with a baseball bat on every square inch of his body at once. It yanked him out of every ghost and puppet in the campground.

He came back to himself and opened his eyes to a very frightening and familiar silhouette.

"Hello, David. Miss me?" Mary stood a few feet away in a felt skirt and blue sweater, her hair and makeup done the same as the girls in the video shoot. Very 1940's.

Fuck. Would she at least sex him up one last time before killing him? He could only hope.

She moved closer, swaying coquettishly. "That was not very nice what you did to me." She pouted. "Keeping all that power away from me." She waved a finger at him. "And you lied to me about the redhead." She "tsked" three times.

"Okay, so you're going to suck the life out of me and send my soul to the ninth circle of Hell, I get it, but is there any chance you can let me finish this game before that? I really, really, *really* hate this guy."

Her mouth pressed into a thin line. "Ordinarily, I'd say no as a matter of principle, but I have to admit it's been fun watching you torture them." She smiled approvingly. "These kids are going to need years of therapy after you're done with them. Especially the little one, Ephraim? Stroke of evil genius."

Twist smiled in spite of himself. It was always nice to be appreciated.

"The ones who live, anyway." She stepped up to him and placed a finger on his nose. "Okay. Keep me entertained and you get another day or two." She patted his cheek. "But, lest you forget, this is me shortly after you put three slugs in my brain and blew me up. . ." She grabbed his face and kissed him. Then the kiss turned into a powerful suction.

Which was always nicer on a different part of his anatomy.

His power siphoned up from his soul and out through his mouth.

Weaker again. So much weaker.

Worse than before. Well, she knew his game, now.

It felt like his lungs were ripped up through his throat.

And his heart.

It really, *really* hurt.

When she released him, he fell to his hands and knees.

"That'll hold me for a day or two," she said. "Bore me and I finish you. Enjoy the game."

In a rush of wind, she was gone.

Twist yakked. Apparently, his stomach was the only thing left to his insides and it missed the rest of his major organs.

Christ, that hurt, too.

He crawled away from his own vomit.

Think, think, think!

As the darkness deepened, his silvery petting zoo slipped through the trees and dropped out of the sky, lighting the trees around him. They crowded around as if trying to cheer him up. That was highly unlikely. He had at most two days until he not only died but was blown off to the worst eternal punishment imaginable.

Twist wasn't sure he really believed in Hell, but if someone had asked him a couple of years ago if he believed in magic, he'd have laughed.

He pushed to his feet. The squirrels crawled to his shoulders. The birds fluttered about his head. Mr. Bunny nudged his knee as if he could feel it. It was nice to be loved, even if was only by devil ghost animals he'd blown to guts to create.

He wondered if the band had any explosives left. Riding Whiskey into oblivion had been the most fun he'd had in a long time. He might as well try it again before. . .

Mr. Bunny hopped around to his other leg and nudged that knee. He gazed up at Twist with intelligent eyes. He twitched his nose.

The devil rabbit controlled bodies extremely well.

All the animals did.

And they were all *far* more intelligent than they'd been as living creatures. They were far more *powerful* than they'd been as well.

Death hadn't been such a bad thing for them, had it?

Wow. He closed his eyes and sucked in a deep, deep breath.

It was an insane idea. Absolutely insane.

But it just might work. It might be the only way to keep from getting dragged into whatever hell actually existed. He could take the night to research.

He crouched down to look Mr. Bunny in the eye.

"She tried to snuff you out, Mr. Bunny." He held a hand for the devil rabbit to sniff with its cute twitchy nose. "It didn't work, did it?"

My universe devolved into a circle of pain with Corey at the center. Someone else would have to worry about Twist. Not sure how long I sat there with Corey curled up in my lap. Hours. Dad brought in a lantern. Maybe I slept.

"Ethan?" Woody had to repeat my name a few times before I thought to look up. His eyes were bloodshot, his dark skin blotchy. "Please. I need to talk to you. It's. . . please?"

Corey was sound asleep. I stroked his hair and rose to my feet. "Any word on Kenny?"

"He's alive. That's all I know. . . Sorry."

It was enough.

We passed two big guys who stood on either side of the doorway with tire irons in their hands. Roadies had lots of uses, apparently. They nodded.

The sun was rising.

Huh. We'd lived through the night.

I led Woody away from the shack. "Any more action from Twist?"

He shook his head.

"How's Ephraim?"

His face screwed up like he was about to start bawling. "Those dreams you had, where you almost killed yourself?

"What about them?"

"Twist *made* you do those things, right? He made you do it and you couldn't stop yourself, right?"

"I was poisoned, Woody. It was a drug. It was like sleepwalking." I shook my head. "What does that have to do—"

"Effy shot Mom."

I stopped breathing. No way.

He nodded. He had to suck in a couple of breaths before he could talk again. "It was like a dream. He was making out with Lizard, and he just left, just walked away. He couldn't stop himself, like he was riding bitch in his own body. And he walked right out here to this shack, and he'd *never* been here before. He didn't know it was here, but his body just walked him right here." He hugged himself tight. "And Mom was already here tied up. And he just took the gun out of her lap and pointed it at her. He tried to stop. He begged for that sick bastard to stop, but then he just. . ."

His face screwed up in so much pain.

I held his shoulders. "He didn't do it, Woody. Ephraim didn't do it. Twist *drugged* me, remember? Made me see things that seemed so real I almost killed myself. But it was just the drug. He must have drugged Effy and made him *think* it was him who did it. Ephraim was just trapped there while Twist shot Mom, and he made Ephraim think *he* was the one."

The hope in Woody's face broke my heart. What had Ephraim called him once? Sam?

"Ephraim *didn't* do it, Sam." I squeezed his shoulders.

Was I that certain? No, but what was the alternative? That Twist had somehow possessed Ephraim's body and forced him to kill Mom against his will? No. I'd tricked myself into thinking my dreams were supernatural. I was done with all that magic bullshit.

But he'd been standing there when I found them. The gun had been in her lap and Ephraim hadn't been tied up. Something horrible had happened, but I wasn't prepared to even consider the possibility that Ephraim had killed her of his own free will. No.

Sam grabbed my arms. "You have to go tell him that. What you just said, you need to go tell Effy. He's just this innocent kid, *mijo*. He can't. . . he can't handle it if he thinks he—"

"I'll go." I wanted to check on Kenny anyway. "Stay with Corey."

He seemed conflicted for a second then nodded. "*Si*. I can do that. I'll try to get him to come back to the main building. We should all be together." He squeezed my arms. "Go tell Effy he didn't do it."

I ran. It was something to do. It was simple and clean.

The sky glowed pink and yellow through the bare branches.

Where was that bus Whiskey had promised us?

Ah, hell. Whiskey was dead, too.

If his plan was going to work, Twist had to push Fox hard and fast. The loser was a total pussy, and he had to be the one. It had to be Fox.

Twist had studied page after page of the old witch's book. She had an entire section on containment. He'd misunderstood when he'd first made Mr. Bunny. The spell wasn't meant to hold the victim in the circle. It was designed to bind the soul to this plane.

There had to be a difference between him and the animals, though. The animals were tied to him by the containment spell. If he was going to avoid having a master controlling his actions, the spell needed to work differently.

He'd still go through the rage phase, and he wanted Fox to be the focus of that rage.

He had one chance to make it work.

One in a million.

He gathered his tools and sent the flock out to investigate the camp. The night had passed since he'd killed the Van Zeeland bitch, and he'd been preoccupied.

And he was weak. He actually needed the book again. He needed the spells.

He needed a heavy stick.

Fox ran out of the shack, heading for the main building. Perfect.

"*Vel ludus postea.*" Twist's hands faded from view in front of him. Running when he couldn't see himself took a few tries to sort out, but he met Fox halfway to the building. "Hey, pretty boy."

Fox slid to a halt. He looked one way, then another.

Twist slammed the branch across the back of his head.

He dropped like a sack.

"Just like old times."

He crouched and laid Fox's body flat out. He pulled the vial of potion from a pocket and opened Fox's mouth to drip it inside. It was a special potion. It had to work more than once and had to be more than real. "*Ne modo commodo.*"

He closed Fox's mouth and hid off the path behind a tree. He leaned back against the smooth trunk and closed his eyes.

Chapter Twenty-Eight

I opened my eyes. The ceiling of the Corporate lobby and someone warm at my side. Tango? What the hell? I jumped to my feet.

"Ethan?" Tango sat up and rose beside me.

The crew lay huddled around us in blankets.

"What the hell?" Okay, that was loud.

Had it all been a nightmare?

All of it?

Faces across the room turned to me. Dad. Mom.

Mom?

I looked down. Mono sat there beside Schilling. She rubbed sleep from her eyes.

Jesus Christ, had it all been a horrible nightmare? I dropped to my knees and threw my arms around Mono.

She eeped.

"Oh my God, you're alive." I squeezed her one more time. "Mono, what's your real name? Please, I need to know."

"Jane. My name's Jane."

I kissed her forehead, released her and jumped to my feet.

Her name was Jane.

Dad seemed puzzled. I didn't care. Mom and Mono were alive! That's all that mattered. I grabbed Mom in both arms, lifted her from her feet and swung her around. She felt so light.

She was alive!

Holy shit, all that horrible stuff had been another nightmare.

No one had died!

"What the hell is going on, Fox?" Whiskey padded over, shirtless and barefoot.

I threw my arms around him, too and held him close. I felt like Scrooge on Christmas morning. I even kissed his cheek.

They were alive. They were all alive.

Of course, Whiskey needed to go a little easier on the cologne.

Wow strong. And smoky. I coughed.

Smoke filled my lungs and choked me.

I held Whiskey out to get some breathing room.

His face blackened and melted, but his eyes, his eyes were still alive. "What's wrong, Fox? You don't like your friends extra crispy?"

I tried to pull away, but his hands snatched at me, held me tight. "I'm dead, Fox. We all are. Because of you."

I tried to pull away.

"All because of *you*!"

Everyone around me morphed into bleeding, rotting corpses. Not like the makeup we'd used, this was real. The smell turned my stomach.

Tango reached toward me with charred, bloody stumps, her hair matted in clumps, the skin on her face hanging by threads. "Dead."

Dad grabbed my arm with a bleeding, sore-ridden hand. His entire naked body was covered with oozing pustules. "Dead."

"Dead," they all chanted. "Dead. Dead. Dead."

They reached for me. Closed in and trapped me.

"Dead. Dead. Dead."

I closed my eyes and covered my head.

"All except for you."

Twist!

I spun. He stood a few feet away, exactly as he'd looked in the forest when he'd shot Kenny. "Hello, Fox."

"It's a dream. It's just a dream. You can't hurt me."

He laughed. "Well, no. I'm not Freddy-fucking-Krueger." He raised a hand. "I can make you hurt yourself, though. I made you fall into the pool. I almost made you fall down the stairs." He shook his head. "That suicidal wannabe is *way* too helpful." He smiled. "I could even make you kill someone for me. Hey, how about Kenny?"

"Ephraim," I said. "You *did* make him do it."

"Of course, I did. Stroke of genius that."

The zombies of my dead friends and father gathered around me muttering, "Dead. Dead. Dead."

"Absolutely no way to connect me to the murders." He opened his hands in a ta-daa pose. "Ephraim's prints are all over the gun."

"What about the command center? What about Whiskey? And Mono?"

He laughed. "What about them? Teddy? He rigged that place up with the leftover explosives the band brought with them. He set the charges himself." More laughter. "The cops are going to go batshit crazy with this one, and nothing will lead them to me."

"How?" I demanded. "How the fuck do you do it?"

Cold hands caressed my arms.

Twist smiled. "Now, Ethan. That would be telling."

I opened my eyes.

I lay on my back on the ground in the woods.

The trees above me were pretty. The sky glowed pink and orange and yellow. People were dead.

People I cared about were dead. And people I loved had to deal with that. *That* was reality. What had just happened was fake. I'd been drugged again. That had to be it.

Who knew where he was or how he'd done it, but he'd drugged me again. I'd created an avatar of Twist to tell me exactly what I'd wanted to hear after Woody's. . . Sam's heartfelt plea.

My entire body shook. It vibrated.

I wanted to lay there and cry and cry and cry.

But there'd been this time. Years ago, when I was ten.

I'd had one pet. A dog. Josh. Don't know why I called him that, but after about a year, Josh got out and a passing car hit him.

I was devastated.

I also had a performance that night. A benefit for homeless kids.

Dad held me while I cried and cried. That'd been his gig for as long as I could remember. "You don't have to do this, Ethan. You can stay home and no one, *no one* will think less of you."

"Monika will kill me slowly."

Dad had laughed. "Don't you worry about Monika. It's up to you. You can stay home, but if we go to the show, people will rely on you. You'll need to do it for real. You'll need to smile and dance your little ass off for them." He'd kissed my forehead. "I will support you if you want to blow this off tonight, but if you go, you need to do it for real."

I lay on the path at Camp Lindy-Ho-Ho and took another deep breath.

My head hurt. How many times could I get hit in the head without permanent brain damage?

I made the same choice I'd made years ago and a thousand times since then. Big or small, the choice was mine, but if I was going to go out there, I needed to dance my ass off.

I sat up. I pushed to my feet.

I headed for the Corporate building, and I broke into a run.

The day after the benefit, we'd buried Josh in the backyard, and I'd balled my eyes out.

There'd always be time for that sort of thing tomorrow.

When I reached Corporate, a couple of roadies came out to meet me. One held a shotgun. The other held a baseball bat. Good. They got a good look at me and waved me inside the building.

The first thing I noticed was Kenny in the middle of the room cussing at his tablet. He was awake and sitting up. Jesus Christ, I almost lost it right there, but he was surrounded: Dad, Jimmy, Ginger and lots of folks I didn't know.

"Twist is the king of the airwaves," he said. "I don't know how the hell he's controlling things."

He looked up at me.

Fuck it. I didn't care what anyone thought. I grabbed his face in both hands and kissed his forehead. "I thought you were dead, brother." I gulped. Almost really lost it right there, but people needed to be kept alive.

He grabbed my wrists. "Glad you're among the walking, too."

Dad touched my arm. I gave him my competition face. He nodded and drew back. We'd deal with all that later.

Tango. She was in a pile with the rest of the girls. All of them but Mono. She looked up at me. Her eyes begged me to comfort her.

I couldn't. If I stopped to hold her, to console her, I'd never get moving again.

Way too many people were depending on me.

She saw it and looked away.

That made me want to die.

No. Seriously. Die.

"Ethan." Kenny's hands shook me. "The land line's dead, and we don't know why the cavalry is absent. That bus Whiskey ordered should've been here long ago."

His mention of Whiskey made me think of Lizard and then Ephraim. "Don't hate me, bro, but where's Ephraim?"

His face changed, softened. "In the dressing room." He met my eyes. "He thinks. . ."

"I know."

I dashed into the dressing room.

Yeah. 'Cause that's where things were better.

Twist followed Fox to the main building and sent his ghostly petting zoo ahead to spy for him. Fox wandered into that stupid little boys' dressing room. The gay Jew and his boyfriend were all cuddled up and weeping.

Ha. Wow. Mary'd been right. Those two were going to be in therapy for decades. Hey, if the movies had it right, they were perfectly set up to be the psycho killers in the sequel. Ha!

"You didn't do it," Fox said to the little gay Jew.

Wait. What? Jesus Christ, he thought the whole thing was just the drugs? He thought it was a hallucination? All that work at perfecting his power and they weren't even quaking in fear at the magnitude of his ability?

Wait again. That look in Fox's eye. He doubted his own words. The gay boys ate it up because it was what they wanted to believe, but Fox? He wasn't so sure.

Although, keeping him in doubt might help. Might make it less likely he'd figure out Twist's true plan. Okay. He could play with that. It could be fun.

He tapped his tablet. What should he play? Oh. Yeah. Perfect. He broadcast "Dream a Little Dream of Me" over the PA. Nice.

That did it. Fox ran into the main lobby, leaving the gay boys to cry it out.

"So, Foxtrot," Twist said into the tablet, "who should I kill next? Your Dad?" He let the song play for awhile. "Tango?"

Fox looked shocked.

Ha. "You thought you knew me, thought I wouldn't kill. Maybe I'm just tired of even thinking about that slut. She fucked him, you know. The rock star? He rode her long and hard."

Fox looked right at Katy across the room.

The slut shook her head.

Fox nodded. Holy shit, he believed her! What a gullible idiot. They'd done it right on the stage while Fox and his gay boyfriends were "bonding" on the pontoon. He'd watched the whole thing through the eyes of the beaver until he'd needed it to drug Fox.

Fox grabbed his dad's shirt. "Let me do this, Dad."

Do what?

"You have to let me do this," Fox cried melodramatically, "or so many more people will die."

The old man stared at him, then shook his head. "I can't, Ethan. I'm your dad."

He couldn't what? What the hell were they talking about?

"Twist?" Fox looked up at the PA speaker. "Put him out."

Kill him? No, that couldn't be right.

Oh! Fox was playing hero!

Perfect! It was exactly what he'd hoped would happen.

"*Ne nam graecis deterruisset.*"

Inside the lobby, the gay giant folded slowly in half and slid to the floor. Everyone who saw it screamed and wept. See, *that* was how they were supposed to react to magic. Fear. Panic. Awesomeness.

Perfect timing, too. Twist reached the building. He repeated the spell. Just ahead, the two goons at the lobby doors slumped and fell together in a pile.

"All of them, Twist," Fox said quietly. "Put them all out. This is between you and me. It always has been."

Perfect. "*Ne nam graecis deterruisset probatus.*"

Inside, everyone drifted to the floor.

Twist entered the building quietly and watched the scene with his own eyes. Mr. Bunny remained at his side.

The birds flew around the room leaving silvery vapor trails.

The other animals stationed themselves nearby.

I stood in the middle of a roomful of sleeping friends.

'Cause, you know, that was the new normal.

How. the fuck. did he. do *that*?

I knelt beside Dad. I kissed him and closed my eyes.

Was there any chance I knew what I was doing?

"How Sweet."

I opened my eyes.

Twist crouched in the doorway, drizzling something onto the floor. He drew a complete circle.

Everyone was gone. We were alone.

I pushed to my feet and backed away. "This isn't real. I'm dreaming." Moonlight filtered through the windows, casting erratic shadows.

Twist smiled up at me and kept at his work. "Haven't you been dreaming all along?"

"What are you doing?" I demanded.

"Casting a spell."

I scoffed. "Is that from one of those Wal-mart witchcraft books they found in your apartment?"

"No." He rose to his feet, brushing his hands, and stepped forward into the circle he'd drawn. "This is from a witch I killed out in the desert. She was my first. After the first, it's always so much easier. Less awkward. Less embarrassing. Am I right?"

"You poisoned me again," I said, certain I was right. "You got that shit into my water bottle or something. That's why I'm having these dreams again. You poisoned me."

He chuckled. "If that's what you need to believe to help you sleep at night." He made a circular motion with one hand. "Close your eyes."

My eyes closed without my permission.

I forced them open.

Dad lay beside me. Everyone else was there, too, asleep.

The morning sun was bright outside.

I was awake, now. Right?

Twist blinked a few times to complete the transition.

Yep. Sleeping bodies. Devil ghost petting zoo.

"How sweet." Twist repeated what he'd said in the dream to make Fox doubt himself.

"How'd you put them to sleep?"

Twist pulled a plastic gun from the back of his pants. "Dart gun." It was a toy he'd found in the band's junk.

What would Fox do with that?

"Everyone in the camp is asleep," Twist said, trying for creepy. "So no one's going to interrupt our fun."

The pretty boy moved to stand over his father, as if that would stop Twist. "So loyal." He dropped the plastic gun to see if he'd go for it. "In the movies, the hero always asks, 'Why, Twist? Why did you do such a horrible thing?'"

Fox's eyes glanced to the toy gun. Ha! Made him look!

He followed my eyes to the dart gun. Crap. He'd dropped it there so I'd go for it.

"No questions?" he asked.

I had one chance: Dad was packing heat. "No, Pal. No questions." He'd taken Mom's favorite gun. Deep breath. I channeled Frank Sinatra dancing Twyla Tharp to let my whole body droop as if I was giving up.

He pulled a face. "Pal? What happened to Twist? I like Twist." He grinned. "Much better supervillain name."

I slid to the floor beside Dad. "I can't play games any more. People are dead." I curled an arm protectively around my father, praying that all the manipulation I'd once considered my forte would actually work for a change. "You want to be called Twist? Stellar. Twist it is."

He crossed his arms and scowled. "You're no fun, hero. You were a lot more fun in the woods with K-pop. I liked the way you ranted at me out there."

"Kenny," I said, losing my inside voice. "His name's Kenny."

Twist moved closer. "Kenny Valentino. Should be a heartbreaker that one." He raised his eyebrows. "Oops. Maybe he is."

I fought for my smooth persona. "Cameras in the *boys* showers? Really?"

He chuckled. "No, no, just the girls'. But ears everywhere."

"So are you going to kill me or what?" Adrenaline made me lightheaded. I curled over Dad. Is there any way that just looked exhausted?

He smiled and held out both hands. "No gun."

Yeah. Didn't buy that. "Then what? You kill me with your sharp wit?"

He laughed.

Twist lifted his face when he laughed and closed his eyes to give Fox his chance. Would he take it? Yes! He jumped up to one knee and pointed the gun straight at Twist's chest.

Of course, he left the safety on.

He flicked it with his thumb and tried to play it off. Idiot.

Slowly, he rose to his feet.

This was it. Twist raised his hands away from his sides.

How would he get him to pull the trigger? If he tried to antagonize him, he'd just start blabbing his anger out. No, better to just let him stew. Let it build on its own.

He tried to mock the little prick with his smile, one of those "you are such a little prick, I'm not afraid of you" smiles. But subtle. Not too obvious.

"Why didn't you just come after me in the first place?" Oh Jesus, was Fox going to try to talk him to death? "Why everyone else?"

Nope. No words. Let him stew. Let the tension build.

Wait. One thing might do it. He thought there was no such thing as magic, that the dreams were just a drug. Well, maybe he'd go a little crazy if Twist changed his mind.

"I told you way back in the wheat field, Fox. I don't want you dead. I just want to drive you insane."

Fear flashed across his face, panic. Yes! It would work.

Fox would do it.

The sound of a gunshot is the loudest sound in the world.

A blossom of dark red sprayed across the wall behind Twist and his head jerked back. A circle of fire ignited the floor around his feet. A brief flash of light and a column of smoke rose up to meet Twist's body as it fell to the ground like so much dead meat.

I hadn't fired.

Who had?

I spun. Smoke rose from a steel barrel a few feet away.

My unknown savior lowered his gun and held it out to one side. "You weren't going to do it."

The smile registered. It was a smile from my nightmares.

My *other* nightmares.

"Gunner? What the fuck are *you* doing here?"

Was I dreaming *again*?

He moved toward me quickly, and the snarky comment suddenly seemed like a poor choice, but he made a point of swerving around me. "Looks like I just saved your ass, hero."

He hurried to Twist's side and knelt beside the body. "What the hell was that flash? Ha! I bet he was counting on it to distract you while he got a gun out of his sleeve or something." He punched the body in the kidneys. "Didn't work, did it, douchebag?"

"Aha!" He held up a gun and waggled it. "In his waistband." He forced it into a lifeless hand. "Look out."

He raised Twist's arm with the gun in hand and pointed it right at me, but when I dropped to the floor, the gun kept its aim at the wall.

Bang!

He fired it directly behind the spot where I'd stood.

"What the fuck is going on?" I asked.

"Has to look like self-defense." He said it as calmly as if he were explaining a ham sandwich. "He needs to have powder burns." He dropped Twist's gun, then held out a hand. "Give me that gun." He wore rubber gloves.

Well, if he planned on hurting me, why save me from Twist? I passed him the gun.

He held out the pistol that'd killed Twist.

I didn't move to take it.

"Go ahead, hero. You saved the day, right?" He rose and shook the gun at me. "You need powder burns." He pointed over his shoulder with it. "Just shoot it into the wall, and it'll look like one shot hit and one missed." He grinned and held out the gun. "No one'll believe you nailed him with one shot anyway, hero."

"Stop calling me that." I backed up a step. "And I'm not touching that gun until you tell me what you're doing here."

"I thought you were the smart one." He shoved the killing gun under an arm and wiped Mom's weapon with a cloth before he slipped it back into Dad's belt. "We need to make it look like you killed Twist in self defense. I wasn't here." He rose and held out that damn gun again.

"What do you mean you weren't here? Why don't we just tell the truth?"

"God damn it!" He grabbed my wrist and forced the gun into my hand. "Because I don't want people asking why I skipped juvy and hauled ass across the state to save Corey." He gestured at the wall. "Shoot the fucking gun, you pussy."

I didn't.

"It has to be you, hero. No one is going to believe I figured out those posers were full of shit. No one is going to believe *any* of it."

"I'm not sure I do."

"Just fire the damn gun."

"I don't—"

He jumped at me and screamed. "Fire the fucking gun!"

I fired the fucking gun and hit the wall where Twist's blood ran.

"Thank you." He stripped the gloves from his hands.

No one stirred.

"How did he do this?" I turned in a circle.

"I don't know how he put them all out at once." He crossed his arms. "He wanted you all to himself. Didn't want someone else to interrupt and actually kill him." He smiled. "Guess he didn't know I was here."

"You can't mean Twist was counting on the fact that I couldn't shoot him." It was too much to believe.

"Pfft." He moved back to the door he'd used to make his entrance. "He counted on you not checking to make sure there were bullets in the stupid gun."

Wow. Hadn't even thought of that.

Fuck me. My gun would've just gone "click"?

He turned to leave.

"Wait a God damned minute, Gunner."

He stopped.

I didn't even know what to ask.

He seemed to understand. "Look, I followed the live feed, just like everyone else from Dumass. Soon as the bus got trashed, I knew it couldn't be Twist. He wouldn't have done that. The paint and the roses, sure, but not the windows and the tires."

"Why not?"

"Not his gig. Twist didn't trash Katy's car."

What the hell? "Yes, he did. I saw it with my own eyes."

"You saw it after it was trashed. You didn't see him do it." He crossed his arms. "And you *couldn't* see him do it."

"Because he didn't do it, right?"

Gunner shrugged with a you-tell-me-if-you're-so-smart face.

"What the fuck makes you think *that*?"

"Because I did it." He smiled. "I trashed her car."

Okay, what episode of *Twilight Zone* had I just walked into?

"Why would you do that?"

"Because I knew the bitch was gonna break his heart." He shoved his hands in his pockets. "Turns out I was right." He shrugged. "All that pussy did was throw petals in her car and spray it with homecoming paint that would've come off in a car wash. Without what I did, it's almost cute."

He walked over to Tango's sleeping form. "When the live feed went out for real, without a stupid 'technical difficulties' sign copied from some stupid black and white TV show. . ." He scoffed. "Doesn't *anyone* watch real TV?"

His face grew serious. "I knew Twist for years. He was *always* a jealous little prick. If he thought someone was stealing his gig, and doing it *wrong*? Pfft. He'd find a way to get here no matter what. I knew I had to protect Corey." He looked up at me. "I couldn't trust *you* to do it."

For Corey. He'd skipped out of juvy, made his way to the woods. . .

"That's a lot of love for—"

"No!" He pointed at me. "Don't say it like that, you fag. I love Corey like a *brother*. Don't you dare make it something sick. If I ever, for one fucking *second* thought you were right, that my parents were right, that I was a fucking deviant, if I thought that for one second—" He pointed at the gun on the floor. "I'd put that gun to my own head and pull the trigger."

He glanced at Tango one last time and headed for the door.

He stopped.

He didn't look at me.

"I'm going back to juvy, and I'm going to tell them I just needed out for the weekend. Took a joyride. They'll never know I was here." He took a breath. "Don't ever tell anyone I was here."

Because they'd figure out the real reason Corey was so important to him. And then he'd kill himself.

Jesus Christ.

"I'll do my best."

"You suck at lying, hero. Do *my* best." He looked at me. I could see that in *his* eyes, this was a gift. I'd be the hero who saved Corey's life and avenged his mother. Corey would always love me now.

Yeah. Not a single thing I could say to that.

He left.

I dropped to my knees.

After he was gone, the people around me started to move.

Yeah. You explain it.

Somehow, against all odds, I knew I wasn't dreaming.

Chapter Twenty-Nine

Most of the next twenty-four hours dropped into the same dark pit as the assault last September. Moments remained. Bits and pieces.

When Katy woke up, she threw her arms around me, squeezing me tight. "Oh my God, Foxtrot. I thought we were all dead."

I hugged her back, forgetting where we stood for a moment. For that one second, she was warm and pure and good and I felt at peace. Then I remembered.

I remembered why Kenny and I had been in the woods, and I asked myself if it still mattered. After everything that had happened, did it matter? If I gave out Gunner's story, I'd be a hero. Heroes got laid. Heroes got their buddies laid.

Then I noticed Kenny and Dad waking up. They were heroes, too. So were we all.

Shortly after my grip loosened, hers did, too. She searched my face, and her eyes were full of love and desire. In her eyes, I saw that I was the most important person in the world. She was happier to see me than she'd have been to see anyone else.

Because Whiskey was dead. Because she felt guilty.

She searched my face, and I doubt she liked what she saw, because all I could see was what her face had looked like when she'd wished I was someone else.

I didn't know what to say.

Dad saved me. His arms surrounded me, and he did his survey top to bottom thing, then he held me tight.

"I'm fine, Dad." I buried my face in his chest and closed my eyes so I wouldn't look at Katy. I didn't want to see the pain in her face. In spite of everything, it would still kill me that I'd caused it.

"Are *you* okay?" I asked him. "You got tranked." One sharp laugh escaped my mouth. "Holy shit, did you ever in your life think that was a thing someone would say in the real world?"

He didn't relinquish his hold on me.

In my peripheral vision, Katy hung her head and walked away.

Yeah. It killed me a little.

"Is she gone?" Dad asked.

"So that was on purpose?"

"Bad call? I can go get her."

"No. Good call. I didn't know you knew."

"Bits and pieces." He squeezed me. "Although the look on your face when she hugged you would've told me pretty much everything I needed to know."

That's when we heard the helicopter. We wandered outside. It hovered over the courtyard in the warm, morning light.

"Helicopter," I said. "Cool."

He took my face in his hands and checked me for shock.

Well, duh.

"Before the police get here, tell me what happened."

So I told him. The truth, not Gunner's made up bullshit. Give me a break, this was my dad and Gunner was a sociopathic asshole. I had sympathy for how messed up he was, but why the hell do people in stories actually go along with the stupid lies some random asshole tells them to spew? I hate when writers do that.

So, yeah, I spilled the truth to Dad, and he absolutely checked my head for bumps because it was so completely unbelievable.

When the first cops jumped out of the helicopter, Dad informed them I knew my rights better than they did and that I wasn't saying a word to anyone until they made a call to find out if Gunner was in lockup.

He wasn't. Heh. I'm pretty sure the call was as much for Dad's benefit as the cops. "Go ahead and tell them everything, son. You're just a victim in this, and they need to know that there's a juvy out there with a gun."

"He left it here."

"And you strip-searched him to check for another one?"

Oh.

"And the fact is, he escaped custody and showed up here with a gun from *somewhere*."

Well, yeah. Except. . . I pulled him aside. "Except they need to be careful because. . ." How the heck to say the rest, even to Dad? "He did all this because he's in love with Corey and he's afraid that if anyone knows he was here, they'll guess what his true feelings are and if it comes out that he's gay, I think he'll try to kill himself again and Corey has enough shit to deal with this week."

He stared at me for a long time, then told me to stay where I was while he found a way to contact Dr. Mike. "And I think it's time to move back to the big city where things are simple and safer." He walked away.

"I keep saying." Sam walked up to me. "It's all the alien abductions and cow mutilations. *Nos hacen loco.*"

"Make sure you feed that line to the press," I told him. "It'll go viral."

In spite of everything, he smiled.

Corey came up behind Sam.

We stared at each other.

If we hugged it out, we'd both lose it forever.

So I got to ride in a helicopter.

Ephraim was strapped in and sedated. I couldn't even imagine what he was going through.

Corey curled up in a corner before we even lifted off.

The ground raced past below. Somewhere close to home, we flew low enough to the ground to see cows freaking out and running away.

I chuckled.

Kenny leaned over me. "Heh, heh. Cows." He rested his chin on my shoulder.

I spent a lot of time at Corey's that next week. He wouldn't talk to anyone but me, and he mostly taught me about football and Bessie. He'd talk quietly, on and on about how parts of the engine worked. Once in a while, he'd ask a question, and I always got it wrong. He'd smile for a second, as if he'd forgotten how much his life sucked. Then he'd remember and lose the smile.

I answered wrong on purpose most of the time.

His dad spent the week in bed.

People brought food.

Theresa tried. She really did, but Corey couldn't see her.

"What did I do wrong?" she asked one night on that enormous front porch.

"Nothing," I said. "You didn't do anything wrong."

"Then why won't he see me?"

It was so hard to say. "His mom really loved you. A lot. And. . ."

"And?"

"And now she'll never see the two of you married, and every time he sees you he thinks about that and he won't be able to stop crying"

She covered her mouth with both hands. I think *she* really had to work hard to keep from crying. After a while, she nodded and crossed her arms. "Take care of him for me. Let him know I love him, and. . . let him know he can call me any time, whenever he's ready."

"I'll tell him."

She touched my arm. "I'm so sorry about those awful things I said to you before you went away to camp."

"Don't be." I covered her hand with mine. "I'm truly glad you did. You were right."

She kissed my cheek and headed off.

"Theresa?"

She turned.

"I know how to change the oil in my car, now."

She smiled, then looked over at the window to Corey's room.

We both knew he was in there crying.

Dr. Mike and Kenny pretty much lived at my house the entire week. I mostly gave up on sleep while I did my best to be two places at once.

As the one and only shrink in town, Dr. Mike stayed insanely busy. "One reason I never left Dumass was I liked helping simple people with simple problems."

I poured him a drink. "Austin seems more and more attractive, doesn't it?"

"It'd sure be more peaceful than *this* small town."

I handed a drink to Dad. "You could even get your own bathroom so I wouldn't walk in on the two of you in the shower."

Dad ruffled my hair and kissed my forehead. Yeah, there was even more of that than usual.

I brought sodas upstairs and handed one to Kenny, who was laid out in my bed while his leg tried to heal. It'd seemed like the same place I'd been hit, but his wound was a lot worse. Nerve damage. Splintered bone.

I'd had to beg his mom to let him stay with us. After about the fourth go around, I'd finally told her the truth. "If Ed wakes up screaming in the middle of the night, Kenny will freak out, Mrs. Valentino. He loves his brother, but he has his own post traumatic stress issues right now. Just for a little while. Please."

Kenny had the bed, and I stayed on the air mattress.

"We've shared this bed before," he protested for the tenth time.

"I won't sleep for one second, dude. Way too paranoid that I'll kick your leg or something." I had to help him out of his sweats so we could change the bandage on his thigh. "I still owe you, anyway."

His eyes flashed with the uncomfortable memory of the suicide attempt he'd told me about in the woods. "No, you don't."

One day soon, I'd ask him the rest of that story. It's not like he could escape.

The holes in his leg seemed to be healing well. No infection, anyway. I helped him back into his sweatpants.

He lay back and closed his eyes. "Tell me a million people didn't get to stare at my junk when you cut my jeans off after that asshole shot me." Because, you know, that actually mattered.

"No, only Dad and I had that privilege."

"Your dad?" For a second, I thought that was going to be weird for him, then he shrugged it off. "Dude, I don't think *my* dad's seen me naked since I was ten."

Huh.

"Ethan?" Corey stood in the doorway. Wow. First time he'd left his house.

I rose from Kenny's bed, er, my bed that Kenny was confined to for the moment.

"Your dad said I could come up." He gestured down the hall. "I can go."

"It's a party," I insisted. "Stay."

He glanced from me to Kenny. "Can we watch movies and drink beer here? I can't be around my dad, right now." He looked down at Kenny. "Hey, Kenny."

"Hi, Corey." He threw the blanket off. "You'll need to help me downstairs."

Apparently, nicknames felt pretty lame when everything sucked so badly, especially when Katy had given them to us.

She kept leaving me messages and texts.

I didn't return one of them.

A week later, I stood in the cemetery of my dad's home town. Corey stood beside me, staring down at a chunk of rock. I still hated the word tombstone. Made me think of pizza. The sun warmed the air enough I didn't need a coat, but only barely.

How did grackles make that freaky noise? It sounded like an electrical discharge.

I'd found Corey there and stopped beside him for a while. We'd had all the hugs, weeping and maudlin stuff we could stand, so we just stood there for a long time.

I glanced down at the rock. "Any particular reason we're standing at my parents' grave?"

He shrugged. "You're going to think I'm mental."

"Not likely."

"Your mom's been there longer, you know, wherever there is? My mom believed in Heaven so she's probably there, and I figure your mom's been there longer, so maybe she could, I don't know, show her the ropes and stuff? So I was asking her to look after my mom up there in Heaven."

All moms go to Heaven.

"See? Mental."

"Not at all. Furthest thing from it." I nudged him. "That's what you did for me when I first came to Dumass, right? Showed me the Mall and stuff. She'll repay the favor."

He managed the first full smile I'd seen on his face in days. "Awesome."

A little while later, Kenny hobbled up on his crutches and stood on Corey's other side. Then Trudy arrived with Cosita, whose real name I didn't know. They stood beside me.

One by one, the entire team showed up. Ephraim and Sam, Schilling, Retro. Katy was the last one there. I was a bit surprised to see her, but I shouldn't have been.

Mono didn't make an appearance. She was in the ground on the other side of the cemetery. Her stone called her "Jane." Her name was still the only thing I knew about her. At her funeral, her boyfriend had sobbed and sobbed. I didn't even know *his* name, which made me hate myself a little.

Ephraim was there because absolutely no one believed he could have killed Mom. Dr. Lopez was working hard to make sure Ephraim knew it, too.

"Soooooo. . ." Sam said after a while. "Am I the only one who notices that we're at the wrong grave? Who's Megan Adams?"

Corey looked up at me and smiled, and for the second time that week, the smile didn't die right away. Nice.

"Excuse me?"

We all turned to face a guy in a trench coat who'd kinda appeared out of nowhere. Hispanic. Smallish frame. About my age.

"Is one of you Ethan Fox?"

I exchanged a glance with Corey. "I am."

The guy extended a gloved hand. "My name's Morrison and I'm an investigator. Can I have five minutes of your time?"

Kenny and Corey each took a shoulder to bookend me.

"For?"

"My client would prefer you be the only one to hear what I have to say." He withdrew his hand and looked at my bookends. "Just out of earshot, but close enough your bodyguards can be there in ten seconds."

"And your client is?"

He folded his hands over his crotch. Wow. For a teenager, this guy really had the mannerisms of a cop down pat.

"Fine." I glanced over my shoulder at my friends. "I'll be right back."

Corey and Kenny nodded.

Morrison gestured for me to lead the way, then fell in beside me oblivious to whether he was stepping on graves. "I'm sorry for your loss."

"She was Corey's mom."

"It's still a loss for you, isn't it?"

A flock of grackles cursed us in grackle-speak and flew off as we passed. I stopped and turned to him. "Four and a half minutes."

"Bad things happen around you, Ethan Fox." He stared at me very directly. I refused to look away. "Going all the way back to your parents' tragic deaths. Your father's accident in Austin. Everything since you moved back to Dumass."

Moved back? "I came here for the first time four months ago."

He tilted his head briefly. "Technically, not true. You lived here the first six months of your life. You were born here."

So what? "Three minutes."

"Gunner's parents died in a fire last night."

Ice drizzled through my veins. "What?"

"Gunner's my client. The cops think he killed them. I think not."

Gunner's parents? Dead? "Well, he has every reason to do it."

"He does." Morrison shoved his gloves in a pocket. "He's the obvious suspect. Too obvious."

Meeting his gaze was like having a staring contest with a cat. "What the hell does this have to do with me?"

"May I have more than the two minutes remaining?"

My friends huddled together watching. I could tell Corey was poised to run my way if I needed him.

Shit. I wanted to hear what this guy had to say.

"It's fine," I called. "I need a few more minutes."

Several of them nodded and turned to one another. Kenny and Corey didn't take their eyes off me. That felt good.

I turned back to Morrison. "So talk."

The way he just stood there without fidgeting kinda freaked me out. "I originally came to town to investigate you."

"Me, why?"

"My team has a pretty sophisticated search algorithm that finds when bad things cluster together. Single black female dancers go missing in three states over the course of a few weeks, a flag goes up and we check it out, stuff like that. Stuff the cops might miss."

Was he a Fed? And why the hell was I thinking words like "Fed"?

"Our system flagged you because a number of unusual tragedies have dogged your path, going all the way back to your parents' death."

"Wait. You think it's all connected?"

He shook his head. "I don't. I've checked into a few things, and I'm convinced it's a series of unfortunate coincidences. Some people just have sucky lives. But it brought me out here a few days ago. When I heard about the latest fire, it made me wonder again."

I turned away from him and rubbed my face.

His eyes made my skin itch.

"So do you think this has something to do with me or not? And you said your client wanted you to talk to me. What's that about?"

"Gunner's afraid that. . . the one we suspect killed his parents might be after you or someone close to you."

I spun back to him. "What? Dude, okay, I get that you must be the cub scout version of a PI, or whatever, but can you put this in some kind of order like an actual cop?"

He smiled. "Sorry. I came to Dumass to check you out, to see if someone was messing with you long term. Angry ex of one of your parents, whatever. I came up empty, and then Gunner's evil parents got torched. Raised another red flag. Just the fact that it happened while I was here seemed a bit farfetched, so I talked to Gunner. I'm convinced he didn't kill his parents."

"Why?"

"It's really difficult for people to lie to me."

I scoffed. "And this certainty comes from your years of experience as an investigator?"

He stared at the grackles. "Hey, the actors on *Glee* are all in their thirties. I'm older than I look." His eyes darted to catch mine. "The fact is, I know I'm right."

His eyes were so deep and dark.

I shivered. "What do the cops think about what he has to say?"

"They don't have him."

"Then how did you talk to him?"

"My years of experience as an investigator helped me find him."

"And you didn't tell the cops?"

He held up an arm and a grackle flew up to it, tapping at crumbs of whatever in the guy's hand. "If I'm right about who killed Gunner's parents, he isn't safe in custody. He'd be dead within a day."

"So who *do* you think killed them?"

He stroked the bird's head with one finger. Fucking creepy.

When he didn't answer right away, I clapped my hands.

The bird flew off.

"Who do you think might want to kill me?"

He brushed the rest of the crumbs from his hands and glanced up at my friends, who were on their way over.

"I'm going to tell you," he said. "You'll scoff and insult me. Then, in less than a week, after someone else dies, you'll call me." He held out a card.

The card read: *Morrison "Spook" James, paranormal investigations.*

A phone number.

I scoffed. "Paranormal? Seriously?"

One side of his mouth quirked.

"So which Winchester brother are you?" I asked. "Or are you the plucky sidekick for the new season?"

He smiled.

My friends closed ranks around me.

Morrison regarded them with all seriousness. "Watch out for your friend here. And each other." He pulled on his gloves. "Gunner may have killed Twist, but that doesn't mean he got rid of him."

He walked away without another word.

As he passed through the flock of grackles, they leapt into the air around him. Squawking and obscuring him from view. When the birds were gone, so was Morrison James.

To be continued. . .

acknowledgements

As always, love and gratitude to Ryan, Hope and the B-boys, Blake and Byron. I know this sabbatical is taking a lot longer than originally intended. I hope you're not sick of Uncle Jack, yet! Many thanks to my editor, Lauran Strait, for your faith in me. Hugs to Austin Tedder: it was the photo of him, which was intended to be the cover of Step One, that inspired the entire second novel. No, really. We need to wander around a graveyard sometime soon. Thanks to Jennifer Neidfeldt, Jacqui Pomeranski, Candance Moore and Stephanie Brannick for beta testing. Without y'all, the novel would suck. Gratitude to Michael Khandelwal of the Muse writing center in Norfolk. Thanks for helping me into your workshops and for all the good advice. Now you know what I've been doing during the break! *Muchas gracias* to Healing Spirit for checking all my Spanish. A special nod goes to Caren Bevill (C.L. Bevil) for her sage advice regarding mysteries. A firm handshake to Jeff Andrews and Dawn Dowdle for time and advice. Kudos to the Hampton Roads Writers, a wonderful and welcoming organization. Go to their annual conference. It rocks. Fist bumps forever to Kevin Maurer for doing me a solid. And thanks to Sarah, Dan and Andrew for being awesome.

about the author

John Robert Mack grew up in Kaukauna, Wisconsin, fled the snow to Texas and has moved to Virginia on a writing sabbatical. He taught dance full time for twenty years, published the short story "Jonny Hates Jazz" and self-published the inspirational book *KEEP BREATHING: Zen and the Art of Social Dance*. For two years, he wrote the column "Dancing the Rainbow" in the Texas periodical *Dancer's Guide*. He has written twelve novel manuscripts as well as six full length plays (one on commission) and ten screenplays. He hopes to see them all published/produced. By the time you read this, John could be living and teaching just about anywhere.

For more info, visit: johnrobertmack.com.
Stalk him at: facebook.com/johnrobertmack.

www.ingramcontent.com/pod-product-compliance
Lightning Source LLC
Chambersburg PA
CBHW072124250626
47159CB00007B/2555